MY NAME IS NOT ROSLYN JAMES

Book Two Of The Search For Hope Trilogy

KERRI McLOONE

Cover design and original artwork by Kerri McLoone
Author photograph courtesy of Kerri McLoone

Contact:
KerriMcLooneBooks@gmail.com

Follow Kerri McLoone on social media:
facebook.com/KerriMcLooneBooks
instagram.com/_kmbooks_
twitter.com/_kmbooks_

DISCLAIMER: This is a work of fiction. Any names, dates, likenesses or events described herein matching actual persons or instances is entirely coincidental.

*For my mother, who is in the strongest of terms,
my hero*

PROLOGUE

The burns on his arm sting with heat, causing him excruciating pain. In his agony-induced stupor, he has vivid dreams of his battle with the girl. He'd foolishly thought she would run scared, be unprepared to face him.

He imagined a child with no knowledge of his abilities or her own. What he faced was a woman determined to make it out of that basement alive or take him down with her. Novice as she was, she held her ground and gave as good as she got. Worse, in some cases.

Foolish.

He let his arrogance cloud his judgment. He was so sure that the witch wouldn't engage him, that she'd flee, allowing him to chase her down and easily rip her to pieces.

There was no reason to bring more than two Victus with him; why should he need to? Now they're both dead. One a pile of ash, the other skewered through the neck.

And to only have three Victus after all these years. In all the time he'd spent waiting since the girl turned eighteen, why hadn't he amassed a larger army? He could have overpowered her with the sheer number of Victus alone.

Cocky. *Stupid.*

Laying bare-chested on the stained mattress in a bedroom above the bar near Atlanta, his black hair is dripping with sweat. His body spasms as it tries to repair all of the damage the girl inflicted. He feels a sudden spike in pain radiating from the burns on his left arm.

He lashes out weakly through his haze to ward off what he interprets to be an attack. The sensation is merely his sole remaining Victus wrapping another ice-cold towel around his body. He hears a deep voice that he knows must be Viribus but is unsure who he's talking to.

Images flash through his mind as the girl uses her powers again and again. He can see how vulnerable she is now, her group exposed and injured. He lets out an audible growl at his inability to seize the opportunity that mocks him only inches out of his grasp.

There is nothing he can do in his current state. His near-comatose mind and highly weakened body can only lay prone on a soiled mattress as the girl heals herself and her comrades. He can only remain static instead of pursuing her as she escapes.

He growls again loudly as she disappears from his radar, shutting her powers down. He had been close. She was in his crosshairs, in his literal sights. Now she's escaped once more, and he has to start his search for her all over again.

Foolish.

Matt and Cali stare at me blankly. Even my dog Milo tilts his head to the side, his lack of understanding clear.

We're standing near the entrance to Mount Tabor Park in Portland, Oregon. I can't hear the dozens of sirens, nor see the flashing lights of the emergency response vehicles I know are currently swarming in on what used to be the Central Library some miles away.

The three of us seem to be no worse for the wear now. Matt had a severe injury to his leg, and Cali an apparent concussion, but I used my projection power to heal them. All that's left now are some scars.

"The Eternal City. The place where all roads lead," I say again. "You know, all roads lead to…"

Neither their expressions, nor Milo's, changes.

"Really? Nothing?"

My best friend looks to her best friend for a clue, and Matt offers a shrug. Cali turns back to me and shakes her head with a baffled frown. She lifts one hand and sails it quickly backward above her head. Then she does the same to Matt and Milo as well.

"Your history teachers would be appalled."

"How do you know Ms. Paul?" Cali asks.

"Who's Ms. Paul?"

"Our history teacher."

"What?"

"*What?*"

I look at them and sigh. "Rome," I say flatly.

"Oh," Cali draws out. Her face then brightens with excitement. "Rome! Like Italy? I've always wanted to go there!"

"Awesome," Matt adds. "So, we just hold onto each other and pop on over there?"

"No."

"No?" Cali pouts, disappointed.

"If we transport right to Rome," I explain, "Darius is going to know exactly where we are and send someone for us, or come himself."

"You mean he didn't get blown up with the library?" Matt asks.

"No," I kneel on the ground to rummage through my laundry bag for my phone. "I saw him drink something, yell out, and then he disappeared."

"Ah, nuts," Cali says, plopping down next to me.

Matt sits down on my other side, our thighs touching. He puts his hand on my knee and asks, "So, where do we go, babe?"

Cali makes a face and asks, "Babe?"

"I don't know, I'm looking now," I say, choosing to ignore her look of mock disgust at Matt and me.

I open the maps app on my phone and drag my finger across the screen until the image centers on Rome, Italy. I don't want to transport directly to Italy, nor the immediately surrounding countries. I don't want to leave Darius any clue that gets him to me before I've had enough time to find the twin of *The Book*.

"We should go to a place that we can get lost in crowds of tourists," I tell my friend and boyfriend. *Still can't quite get over how excited I get at that word,* I think. "Somewhere that we can still easily travel place to place and somewhere that will confuse Darius as to what the hell we'd go there for."

I turn my phone around with Egypt centered on the screen.

"How do we get from there to Rome, though?' Matt asks.

"I don't know yet. Maybe we charter a boat or find a cruise or something?"

"We could fly," Cali says, holding up her passport.

It's not a bad idea, and I think it's perfect until Matt points out the obvious flaw.

"If we fly, and show American passports with no stamps saying when or how we entered Egypt, that's going to send up red flags and alerts all over the place."

"No, I mean like literally fly from here to Egypt, or Spain, or Norway, or Germany, and then make our way to Rome from there. We can buy tickets and take the next flight out."

"How could we do that? Our names would show up on a flight manifest," Matt says, directing his question to either me or Cali. "I mean, Darius knows who we are now, right?"

"Actually, no, he shouldn't," I say, realizing that what Cali's saying is true. Right now, we could go anywhere.

"But I am going to have to change my name again. Start over again fresh so that he can't trace *me*."

I rummage through my bag again and pull out the mahogany wooden box that is intricately carved and has five words etched across the top: *Hope will heal the world*. The contents include a letter from my mother, almost five-thousand dollars cash, and a picture of my family with my real license hidden in a false bottom. Plus, the old identities I'd used before I got to Portland, and the last unused one—the only one out of all of them that includes a passport.

It's a shame I have to change my identity again. A lot has happened while I was Alexa Pearce. I got used to being her.

"So, who are you this time?" Cali asks me.

I squint in the low light to read the name printed in block letters on the laminated identification card. "Straight from Torrance, California, meet Roslyn James."

PART
ONE

• 1 •

"ROSLYN"

Cali scans multiple websites, trying to find a landing spot. I'm hesitant to fly right to Rome and would prefer to start somewhere else and make the next decision from there.

"Amsterdam," she says, showing us her phone screen. "It's the next flight out of Portland, is in the general area, and just so happens to be the least expensive."

She buys four tickets, with Milo getting his own seat. Our 7 A.M. direct flight with one stop in New York leaves in three hours and gets into The Netherlands just before 6 A.M. tomorrow.

We walk out of the park and a few blocks over to wait for the cab we called to take us to the airport. We all agree it would be a little odd, and considerably too memorable, for a taxi to pick up three people and a dog from a closed park so early in the morning. I don't know what kind of issue our duffle bag of supplies could cause at the security gate, so I want to get to the airport with more than enough time to deal with it.

I bite my lip, unsure of how to broach the next thing I need to tell them. Cali and Matt are happily playing with Milo, tossing one of his tennis balls between them, causing my dog to jump back and forth excitedly.

I wouldn't have made it through anything the past five years without Milo, my six-year-old Chow/Labrador mix. He always wears a lime green collar that has a red crystal hanging from it. The crystal cloaks him from being sensed by other magical beings, so Milo can use his training and his own power to scan for evil or threats without detection. He has short, floppy, expressive ears, a sweet face, and a stocky body. Right now, his thick, normally black fur is more of a dark gray, coated with ash and dirt from the library caving in on us.

I start to think about all that's happened to us in the last twelve days.

Cali Jacobs started as my roommate and has become the greatest friend anyone could ask for. I've lived with her for the past eleven months in Portland, Oregon. She was the first person I told who I really am, why I was in Portland, and what led me here. I told her almost everything, short of what my real name is.

Even though it meant leaving behind her girlfriend, Mickey Westin, she told me there was no way she was letting me go up against Darius without her, and she signed up to be one of my Extensios with zero hesitation, to be bound to me and take on the power of telekinesis.

Mathias Moorely—Cali's best friend since they were "yea high" in kindergarten—and I worked at the library together for over a year. He originally introduced me to Cali when she was looking for a roommate. We were friends instantly, but he and I have gotten very close these last couple of weeks. I've been attracted to him since the moment I laid my eyes on him, and we've only gone on one official date, but right before Darius showed up at the library, he did tell me he's in love with me and called me his girlfriend.

We haven't really had a chance to discuss those words or their meaning, what with a demon and his Victus launching fireballs at us over and over and the eventual explosion of the entire building.

Darius is my magical antithesis. When he showed up in this world, *our* world, over twelve hundred years ago, he wasted no time in causing problems. No one was powerful enough to stop him, but they were able to curse him. My magical ancestors pooled their powers together and damned him to roam the earth until his powerful match was born.

That turned out to be me.

I am the descendant of dozens of generations of magical creatures. My family tree can be traced back to the original seven tribe leaders who came together to curse the demon. If Darius can defeat me, he'll take my powers and use them to open the portal to his home permanently. His demon brethren will be released, and it will be the end of this world as we all know it.

When I was born, my family knew I was the one Darius had been waiting for. My birth fulfilled a prophecy that had been passed down through generations, along with the story of the demon. They hid me from him by binding my magical abilities with a potion and spell until noon on the day that I turned eighteen.

Within minutes of my powers reawakening, Darius attacked my home to try and to get to me. My family did everything they could to hold him off as my grandfather whisked Milo and me away to safety. He had me read a spell that cloaked them all from Darius and gave me a wooden box. *Inside*, he said, *are instructions and an explanation of everything.*

I spent almost four years traveling across the country, plus over a year in Portland, searching for the one thing that would help me win this war. From the letter my mother left in the box, I knew that I was searching for something within a library, and that turned out to be a book actually called *The Book*.

Every day of the five years I spent looking for *The Book*, I battled constant internal battles. I had to keep my guard up and suppress the desire to see my family, always careful to remember the role I was born to play. At the same time, I desperately wanted nothing more than to be normal and deal with the things most everyone else my age was—a regular girl, working a regular job, navigating my early twenties, and new relationships.

Plenty of moments were hard, but I have never wavered from this simple truth: I know who I am, and I accept the responsibilities that rest on my shoulders.

Shortly after I held *The Book* for the first time, Darius sent two of his Victus after me. When they caught up to me in Portland, they accidentally bumped into Cali on the street a block away from where I was working at the library. One of them grabbed her so tight he left bruises.

Four days after that, I gathered up the courage to tell Cali the truth. And then, only a day later, the demon himself came to Portland. He tore his way through the building to where we were hiding in the basement, trying to protect *The Book*. In the first major fight between us that ended only hours ago, Darius not only destroyed *The Book* and where it had been hidden for years, but the entire library was obliterated, which left us—

I'm brought out of my head and brought back to the moment by Cali's loud laugh at something Milo's done.

"Um, guys?" I start. Matt catches the tennis ball, and they both look at me. "We need to talk about your Extensios power."

"What about it?" Cali asks.

"We know Darius can track me whenever I use any of my powers, right?" They nod. "Well, what I don't know is if that's the same for you guys, too. But regardless, we can't take that risk. Plus, if anyone sees you moving things with your mind, that would be *really* difficult to explain."

"So, until we need them, we'll all keep our powers under wraps, okay?"

"Yeah, of course," Matt says.

"No problem," Cali says.

"There's one more thing..." I let the words hang in the air for a minute before I gather the courage to keep talking. "Do you have your letters?"

"I didn't get the chance to write it before that demon showed up," Matt sighs.

Cali unzips her backpack as she speaks. "I was able to salvage it, but I don't think the post office will deliver this."

She holds up an envelope that's severely singed with at least a third of it burnt entirely off. The sight of it makes what I'm about to say even harder now.

"We have to be as careful as possible. It's too easy for calls or texts to be tracked, and we can't give any clue of where we are or where we're going. So we have to keep contact to a really tight minimum. Only what's absolutely necessary, and even then it has to be an emergency."

They both look at me with expressions I can't quite read. I jump to explain myself. Rambling more than anything, hating that I've caused more problems.

"I know how much that is to ask of you both, how unfair it is. But I wouldn't ask it unless it was life or death. I couldn't handle it if your families got pulled into this, and if they got hurt, I'd never forgive myself, and—"

"Lex, take a breath," Matt says.

"Roslyn," I immediately correct him.

He repeats my name and keeps talking. "After everything that's happened the last few hours, I think we both understand that if you ask us to do something, there's going to be a really good reason for it. Knowing what we know now, I don't want my mom or brother anywhere near me until this is finished, and that thing is dead."

"Yeah," Cali agrees. "After this is all over and done with, our family will understand why we kept them in the dark. We're with you, and if you say this is the number one ground rule, then that's what we're gonna do. When Darius is dead, and this is all finished, Mom, Josh, and Mickey will be there waiting for us safe and sound."

"Okay," I say, nodding. "Thank you for understanding. I know how hard it is to have to get up and go, leaving everything behind."

I feel Milo press himself against my thigh. He rubs his head a little on my leg before sticking it into the space between my knees. I bend over slightly to scratch his floppy ears.

Cali looks at Matt. They stare at each other briefly before they both nod in sync.

"We're with you," my best friend says.

"No matter what," my boyfriend adds.

I close my eyes and let out a long breath. I bob my head slightly, accepting the fact that they are putting their lives in my hands and the additional responsibility that comes with it.

"All right," I say.

Bright headlights flash on us as a car slowly pulls around the corner. A white minivan stops right next to us, and the front passenger window rolls down. A faceless voice calls out from the dark interior, "You guys call for a cab?"

● 2 ●

Matt loads all of our bags into the trunk of the van. I get in the back, sitting on the bench seat, and call Milo to sit in front of me in between the bucket seats that Matt and Cali settle in. Once the doors are closed, the driver gets onto Interstate 205 North from SE Washington Street. The early time of day and lack of traffic allows us to get to the airport in less than fifteen minutes. The cabbie pulls over to the curb at international departures.

Matt hands the guy some cash and gets out to unload the bags. While Cali and I are making sure we have everything, he walks over to the one attendant working and begins talking. I see him gesture a few times, spreading his arms to about the size of the duffle bag holding our supplies. The attendant replies to him, and I see Matt nod and thank the guy.

"Okay, I asked about customs and stuff," he motions with his thumb over his shoulder at the attendant. "He said that each country has its own customs restrictions, and The Netherlands' is pretty lenient. But based on what's in the bag, the only thing that may be confiscated or thrown out on arrival is the protein bars, trail mix, and maybe the vitamins. So I think we should be okay."

When I got home from work, what seems like weeks ago but was somehow only yesterday, Cali greeted me in the living room with a gray duffle bag that was practically the same size as her. Knowing that we would have to leave Portland and unsure of where we'd wind up or how we'd possibly get there, Cali had gone out and purchased anything we might need.

She got everything from bandages and dry shampoo to glow sticks and chapstick. Plus, a Swiss army knife, matches, soap, water bottles with filters built into the straws, bug repellent, and more. It seemed like she went up and down the aisles of the closest drug store and put at least one of everything into her cart.

Each of us has a bag of our own packed with extra clothes and some necessities. I've become pretty adept at grabbing just the essentials, and the biggest bag I had was my canvas laundry bag. So I threw everything in there, plus some things for Milo, and have been lugging that around since.

With Matt hoisting the larger duffle over one shoulder and his smaller one on the other and Cali and I each holding our respective bags, the four of us enter the airport. We go to the automated kiosk to check-in for our flight and print our tickets. We get into the checked baggage line deciding rather than lugging it through the airport, that it's easier to check the duffle. It also contains things that definitely are not allowed on planes, like a Swiss Army knife.

Milo has a special ticket because Cali checked the service animal option when booking online. I explain to her, again, that Milo is not a service animal. Cali likes to tell people that he is, especially to allow Milo into places that dogs usually aren't, like restaurants and the zoo. Cali frowns at me and retorts that he absolutely is.

"He protects us from evil because he's able to sense it. He can understand literally everything we say, like getting the remote when we're too lazy. And, he can always tell when someone needs some extra love."

I let the squabble go for the moment as we get on the security line that is surprisingly long, given what time it is. Getting through security, thankfully, isn't much of an issue. My passport and ID are flawless, but I hold my breath as the TSA agent scrutinizes both. There isn't even a second glance or consideration they could be fakes, and I'm waved through with no problem—a minor perk of the things being magically created by my grandfather.

Milo has to be scanned by hand with a wand, which agitated him for a moment. He starts to whine and backpedal but with some scratches under his chin and soothing sounds, I'm able to calm him. I kneel in front of him and quietly explain, so no one else can hear, that it is just a metal detector.

The TSA agent who steps up to Milo has a tight frown making her look like she's sucking on something sour. He lets her wand him and even offers the woman two friendly wags of his curled, Chow-like tail. I see her cold exterior briefly crack as she gives my dog a quick smile. But it's gone as swiftly as it appeared.

Cali goes through the full-body scanner first, so she's able to take Milo's leash and bring him through while Matt and I wait to get through security.

The three of us walk with Milo through the relatively quiet airport and easily find our gate. We plop down into the faux leather chairs that have been softened by the thousands of people who've used them before us.

Right as I'm thinking it, Cali says, "How many hundreds of butts do you think have sat in these chairs?" I can't help but chuckle at my friend's ability to provide levity no matter the situation.

My body is slumped, but my mind churns as my eyes dart all around to assess for any threat. Milo sniffs the area surrounding our chairs before curling up at my feet. When he tucks his head in by his tail, my brain finally accepts that we are safe where we are.

Matt takes our orders and goes to get us breakfast at the small coffee shop near our gate. He comes back soon with a cappuccino, an espresso, a hot chocolate, six water bottles, some muffins, four breakfast sandwiches—Milo gets his own—and three bear claw pastries. He even stopped at one of the stands and bought a couple of puzzle books. Cali had gotten some, but they're secured in the duffle bag that is zooming on some conveyor belt through the bowels of the airport.

Anyone passing by us would assume we're just three regular people about to take an early morning flight. No one could possibly be able to tell the literal life and death battle we've just come from.

The four of us are so worn out from the night before that within minutes, the food is reduced to crumbs, the water bottles are empty, and we're each holding our hot cups, letting the liquid cool. Now that there's nothing left to do but wait for the flight, the reality of what's happened to us all in the last ten hours is setting in.

The picking up and moving to a new location is old-hat for Milo and me. And I've known my whole life that demons like Darius are real and not part of some fictional story told to scare people. But knowing about something and literally fighting it to save your own life are two completely different things.

Cali's had about a day and a half to wrap her head around magic and witches and demons being real, but Matt has only had a third of that time. So I completely empathize with however lost or scared they are feeling right now. The two of them look shellshocked, staring vacantly at the blue, geometrically patterned industrial carpet that covers the floor of our terminal.

Milo instantly picks up on the shift in both of their moods. He gets up from his place at my feet and moves around to sit in front of the two of them. His black, floppy ears are pricked up, and his fluffy curled tail is swishing across the floor in a happy wag. He starts panting, displaying the bluish-purple spots that dot his tongue. It makes his puppy-like face appear as if he's smiling.

I watch the impact Milo's presence has on the two of them. Matt blinks a few times, coming back to reality. As he looks at Milo, I see his eyes soften with a smile. Cali reacts similarly, but slower. I can only imagine what she's thinking, but I'd put good money on it being how long until she can see Mickey again.

Milo scoots in closer to her and puts his head on her knee, and looks up at her with sweet eyes. Cali can't help but ruffle the long fur on top of his neck and chuckle.

My mind changes, and I think that Cali may be right about Milo being a service animal. *That's my boy.*

• 3 •

I'm just starting to doze off, my chin dipping to my chest when over the loudspeaker, I hear the announcement that Flight 404 direct to Amsterdam with one stop at John F. Kennedy airport in New York will begin boarding shortly. I yawn and rub my hand up and down my face a few times to wake up.

My muscles are starting to seize from being thrown around by the explosions earlier, so I stand up and stretch my arms up, arching my back. I sigh in relief as a few of my joints crack and loosen. Matt and Cali follow my lead before the three of us pick up our assorted bags.

Because of Milo, we luckily get priority boarding. The plane is large, an Airbus A330. Entering the plane, we go to the left toward the first-class section. We aren't in the super suites section with the lay-flat beds, but we are still riding in some ser ous comfort. Our seats are in the third row, so we're in the middle of this part of the cabin. There are four seats in each row separated into pairs by the aisle. Matt and Cali's seats are 3A and 3B on the right, Milo and I are 3C and 3D on the left.

Milo hops up onto the oversized leather seat by the window. He's never been on a plane before, so I'm not entirely sure how he's going to react. Our primary modes of travel over the last five years have been buses and trains.

I quickly pull the shade down, figuring the less he sees out the window, the better. I stash my canvas laundry bag and my purse, which has the ever-important wooden box, a notebook, my wallet, and my phone inside of it in the footwell of Milo's seat rather than the overhead compartment.

I sigh as I sit down next to my dog. I loosely loop his leash around the armrest between us. Milo is sitting up in the seat, looking at me and panting. I take a sip of my hot chocolate and swing my head to the left to see how Matt and Cali are doing.

The two of them are bickering like brother and sister as usual. From what I can hear, it's something about the armrest—which is plenty wide enough for them both. They do a quick rock-paper-scissors, and by Matt's reaction, I assume Cali has won control of that coveted piece of real estate.

She's in the window seat bent over her bag, rummaging for something; he's sitting next to me across the aisle. His small duffle is in the compartment above him, he has his espresso in one hand, and the other is gripping the aisle armrest almost possessively. His eyes are closed for the moment.

I take the chance to really look at him. The scratches that covered his face and hands in the library from exploding glass and chunks of concrete are gone. They disappeared when I healed him after transporting us all to Mount Tabor Park. He's clearly exhausted, both mentally and physically, but he's not asleep. I shamelessly look at this gorgeous man and can't help but get a flutter in my chest.

He can have anyone he wants, I think. *And he wants me.*

He must feel my eyes on him because he opens one of his to look at me. The smile that spreads across his face is one of familiar comfort like he's looking at something that's always given him joy.

But even through that, I can see he's uncomfortable. His shoulders are practically touching his ears.

"You okay?" I ask, then immediately feel like an idiot considering everything we went through last night.

"I'm not a good flyer," he says.

"That's a blatant lie," Cali instantly chimes in. "He's not a flyer, period. This is his first time on a plane."

"That's okay," I say, trying to keep things light. "It's Milo's first time, too."

My dog has settled down into a tight ball on the seat next to me but hearing his name, he lifts his head and lets out a very tiny bark. It sounded like he was punctuating my sentence, and it makes Matt relax. I see his shoulders start to lower a bit as he laughs.

The flight attendants come around and ask us if we would like anything to drink before take-off. I ask for a bottle of water for Milo but say I'm okay with my hot chocolate. Matt and Cali don't ask for drinks, but Cali asks for two blankets.

Cali takes one royal blue blanket out of its plastic bag when the attendant returns and drapes it across her legs. She tosses the other across to me. I don't even have to ask to know that the blanket is for Milo only.

I stand up, take it out of its plastic packaging, and shake it out. For Cali's benefit, I drape it over my arm, making a big show of offering it to Milo. He sniffs it before snorting in satisfaction. I gently place it over him and tuck him in, so just his head is showing. Cali nods in approval and readjusts her own blanket.

Before I sit back down in my seat, I look around and realize that we are the only passengers in the five rows of first-class. The curtain for coach is still open, so I peek to check out the rest of the plane. The cabin behind us is only about half full.

I'm hoping the plane fills up in New York so that it's a full flight to offer us more camouflage. I will take all the blending in I can get right now.

I sit down in my seat and check on my friends again. Cali is teetering on the edge of sleep, but Matt still looks nervous. I reach across the aisle and squeeze his hand. When he turns to look at me, he lets out a short sigh as he smiles.

For a moment, everything around us stops, and it's just him and me. He pulls my hand up to his mouth and places a kiss on the inside of my wrist. His eyes are droopy; I can see how hard he's fighting his exhaustion. I squeeze his hand one more time before pulling mine back across the aisle.

Milo shifts in his seat as if he's trying to get closer to me. I remove his leash from around the armrest and push on it lightly to see if it'll move. It does, so I fold it up into the space between the backs of the chairs. As soon as the obstruction is removed, Milo shimmies over to me.

He puts his head on my thigh and lets out a long, content sigh. I lightly run my fingers through his long fur. I watch his eyes slowly close as he gets closer to sleep. When he sighs again, I take in a deep breath of my own as well. If Milo is relaxed, that means I can be too.

Only seconds later, the flight attendant begins the safety procedures demonstration. It's more like a one-on-one show since I am the only one still awake of the four of us. The captain comes over the speaker system greeting everyone on board. She gives us a rundown of how long the flight will be, our estimated time of arrival, and what the weather should be like when we're wheels down in New York.

I see the first rays of sunlight starting to come through the open shade of Cali's window just as the female pilot's confident voice comes over the speakers again.

"In-flight crew prepare for take-off."

● 4 ●

Almost the entirety of the flight from Portland to New York, I have my red leather notebook in front of me on the tray table. I look across the aisle and check on my friends periodically. Both Matt and Milo did well with take-off. Shortly after the plane leveled out, Matt and Cali reclined their seats and have been asleep since. Milo has been in the same position since I lifted the armrest.

Once the fasten seatbelt sign turned off, I gently got up mindful of Milo's head on my lap, used the bathroom, and when I came back, I started writing.

I don't remember ever being this tired, but I don't want to give in to my fatigue. And I have to admit a large part of me feels like I can't just yet.

I write down everything I can remember about the day I first found *The Book* listing in the library database twelve days ago and everything that's come since.

I write down how the hair stood up on the back of my neck in reaction to when I first saw the listing on the computer screen. I write how my boss offered me a chance to work on a project in the library's climate-controlled storage and how I *knew* I was in the right place as soon as I walked into CCR3.

I write everything I can remember, from holding *The Book* for the first time to Victus arriving in Portland, then telling Cali the truth to where we are now. With it all written out in front of me, it's hard to believe all of what's happened in less than two weeks.

When my hand cramps, I take a break and flip back through the pages and reread what I wrote at the laundromat with Cali. I have a list of what powers both the magical princess from the story and Darius have. Based on what I remember seeing last night, I add notes:

1. Darius drank something to transport himself... *could that have been a potion?* I ask myself.
2. He was grazed by a fireball and took one in the arm—both wounded, but neither killed him. Would that be the same for me? *Best not to find out, "Roslyn."*
3. He couldn't sense me when I eavesdropped, but I couldn't read his thoughts when right in front of me.
4. Enlarged the fireball by pulling his hands apart. I mimicked that action, but I'm not sure exactly how I did it... *Maybe with projection I could use that to my advantage.*

I skim through my favorite childhood story, one I must've heard thousands of times. The story about my past and my destiny, and suddenly I can hear my grandfather's familiar voice narrating in my head as I read the snippets.

I close my eyes and let memories from my childhood wash over me for a minute: times my brothers and I turned the couch into a fort so we could plot our strategy, us taking down the imaginary Victus one by one, cornering my grandfather playing the role of Darius, me ending the battle in victory.

Tiny little barks next to me bring me back from my memories. I open my eyes to look at Milo, who's curled up under his blanket. His ears are twitching, and he snorts a few times at whatever dream he's having.

My hot chocolate has long since gone cold, so I hit the call button above me. The same flight attendant who brought Cali the two blankets earlier comes by. I ask her for some orange juice and the time.

"It's right before ten o'clock now in Portland,' she says. "Just about two hours remaining until we land in New York. That'll be around 3 P.M. eastern time."

"Thank you."

She comes back moments later with a sealed, small plastic carafe of juice. She asks me if I'm finished with my coffee, pointing at my paper cup, and I say yes.

"Thank you, again," I say as she picks it up to throw it away.

I turn to the next page in my notebook, and the words staring back at me are in Latin. This is what I copied out of *The Book* about Extensios. Cali's name is written and circled multiple times. Written next to it is Mickey's name with a question mark. My chest tightens as I think about her, about everything Cali and Matt left behind.

I look across the aisle at the two of them fast asleep. Matt looks relaxed, his mouth hanging slightly open. Cali has her legs tucked underneath her and is resting her head on Matt's shoulder. With her brow furrowed, she looks like she's in pain, and I can't help but wonder, again, if she's thinking—or in this case, dreaming—about Mickey.

I shake my head to clear the thoughts and look back to my notebook. I turn the page and am met with more Latin. I look at all of the pages copied from *The Book* over and over until my eyes cross. I wish I understood Latin and could read these pages easily. I took Italian in high school, most likely by design considering where I'm heading, but unfortunately, I remember very little of it.

I open my orange juice and drink the whole thing at once. I decide to close my eyes for five minutes to reset and then go over everything again. I want to figure out as much as I can about what Darius's next move could be, and a lot of that will depend on whether or not he knows there is a second copy.

What feels like only five minutes ended up being the rest of the flight. I'm woken by a big tongue licking my cheek and a wet nose sniffing my ear. I can see out of Cali's open shade that the plane is lower in the sky, probably starting its approach into JFK airport. As the plane banks, I can see the Tri-State area's hazy form and the unmistakable shape of Long Island jutting out into the Atlantic.

I can't stop the sharp stab that suddenly tears through my heart. We're still thousands of feet in the air, but this is the closest I've been to home in five years.

I know it's dangerous to dwell on it for too long, it's cruel to even put myself through it, and I run the chance of possibly removing the cloaking spell that is protecting my family. But it's challenging to be so close and not miss it, miss *them*, more than ever.

You never realize how hard it is to leave something until you don't know how long it'll be before you get to see it again.

I miss the smell of it. My mother's cooking, woodworking projects my grandpa and brothers made in the garage, the scent of trees in the backyard, and the herbs in my father's garden. Every once in a while since my eighteenth birthday, I would randomly get a whiff of my mother's perfume that speared me through the chest every time.

I miss the sound of the creaky wooden staircase when my brothers and I would chase each other down them. I miss the chill of the winter and the way the cold wind would whistle through the drafty back porch. I miss the heat of the summers and the sound of the brush crunching under my boots on long hikes in the nearby woods.

I pinch myself hard on the thigh to break the stream of memories, shaking my head and wiping my eyes roughly. I put my notebook away, making sure none of the loose pages have fallen out. I take my glasses off and pinch the bridge of my nose before putting them back on. I angle myself toward Milo so that I'm facing away from Cali's open window. I start scratching his ears to anchor myself to reality. He loves the touch, and his little grunts of satisfaction make me smile.

The plane makes an easy landing on a mostly cloudy Tuesday afternoon in New York. The pitstop is less than an hour, just enough time to load the additional passengers before we are up in the air again. Cali was able to get Milo off the plane to stretch his legs and relieve himself in the specific service dog area, so after giving him some water, he curls up in his seat and easily falls back to sleep.

As the plane again reaches cruising altitude, I'm finally able to relax. No one was waiting to storm the aircraft or intercept us when we landed at JFK, which means that right now, no one is searching for us on orders from Darius. Or from the police—that little destruction of property technicality regarding the mound of rubble that used to be the Central Library. For the next seven and a half hours, we are as safe as we are possibly going to get.

Once my shoulders fall from their spot up at my ears and I roll out my neck, it's easy to finally give in to the exhaustion that has been pulling at me since we sat down in the terminal at Portland PDX. I recline my seat as flat as possible, place my right hand on Milo's warm back, and quickly fall into a deep, mostly dreamless sleep.

• 5 •

VIRIBUS

The sole remaining Victus has rarely left the demon's side since he returned from his fight against the witch. He watched Darius shiver and lash out, trying to protect himself from the towels Viribus periodically laid across his brow. He's heard the demon mumbling incoherently under his breath and groan as his ancient body slowly heals itself.

Darius has been silent for a while now. The only indication he's not dead, other than the presence of his body rather than a pile of ash, is the erratic up and down motion of his chest as he breathes.

The giant man is leaning against a stained plaster wall across the room from where the demon is resting. At almost seven feet tall, Viribus has to hunch forward to avoid smacking his head on the ceiling. His Titan-like muscles and incredible strength only bolster his size.

The quiet in the room is interrupted by the muffled ring of a cell phone. To get more comfortable, Viribus sits on the floor before he reaches a broad, frying-pan sized hand into the inner pocket of his black blazer to retrieve his phone. He's been waiting for this call the past ten hours, ever since Darius returned bloody and burnt. He checks the caller ID before swiping his sizable thumb across the screen. The smartphone disappears in his mammoth hand as he lifts it to his ear.

"Yeah, Blue. What've you got?" Viribus asks. On his knee, he positions the pad of paper he grabbed from one of the waitresses downstairs. His size makes the paper look like a pack of sticky notes.

"Viribus, hey," says the echoey voice of Rodger "Blue" Blusseau, a New Orleans parole officer. He's a former co league of Julius. They had known each other for decades before the latter met his end by the girl in Portland. Now that he's gone, all of his former contacts have transferred to Viribus.

"I did the search you asked for," Blue continues. "And I've got six guys I think could fit your, uh, specific parameters. Possibles on another ten. I'll email you all their files.'

"Good, that's good," the Victus replies in a deep baritone.

"But there's a slight problem," Blue continues hesitantly.

"What?"

"These guys are all local. Right now, if they break parole and come to you, they're going to be flagged, hunted down, and thrown back in jail. That's a lot of heat that I'm sure the boss doesn't want coming down on him. So, if you really need these guys, your best bet is to come here."

Viribus grunts a begrudging concession. "The boss is a little, resting at the moment. Send me the files, and when he's more like himself, he'll decide what to do."

"I already sent them."

"Alright, thanks, man."

Viribus hangs up the phone and tucks it back into his pocket. He stands and checks over Darius before exiting the small bedroom that sits above the bar.

He heads down the stairs and enters the large, dimly lit bar. The room is practically empty, customary for this time of day. The usual bartender is behind the long, solid wood counter, wiping it down with an old soiled towel. He's a middle-aged white man whose wrinkles and gray hair have increased exponentially since the demon first set up shop here. When he sees the tremendous Victus enter the bar, he immediately reaches for a quart-sized glass mug and begins filling it from the tap.

He places it down in front of Viribus, who wastes no time polishing it off. The bartender reaches to refill but is stopped by Viribus placing his hand on top of the mug.

"You got a printer around here somewhere?"

"Office," the bartender says flatly. "Back of the kitchen, behind the flattop."

Viribus nods and removes himself from the bar to make his way through the kitchen. Immediately upon opening the door, the perpetual stink of rancid oil fills his nostrils. He easily finds the office, goes in, and closes the door behind him.

The small rectangular room must have been a pantry at some point in time and was repurposed into an office. Against a wall are two sawhorses with a piece of plywood across them functioning as a desk with a folding metal chair. On top is a relatively new all-in-one desktop computer and a printer off to one side. There are no shelves, nothing hanging on the walls, and no window. A short filing cabinet is pushed back underneath the desk. The room smells just as bad as the grimy kitchen it sits in.

Viribus pulls the chair out and sits down. The metal shrieks in objection to his considerable size. He sweeps away the office supplies scattered across the wood and double clicks the mouse to wake up the computer.

He opens a browser window and logs into his email account. The second item from the top is a message from Blue with an attachment. He clicks on the subject line to open it. It has a short body and sixteen attachments.

Viribus opens and prints each attachment before logging out, clearing the browser history, and putting the computer back to sleep. He makes sixteen bundles, stapling each file securely.

Leaving the office, if it could even be called that, he catches the cook's eye. He tucks the papers under his arm and pulls out a wad of cash from his pants pocket. He makes sure he has the man's attention as he peels off three fifty-dollar bills. He hands it to the guy with strict instructions. He tells him to go to the grocery store, get a twelve ounce filet mignon, a twenty ounce T-bone—both prime—asparagus, and some fingerling potatoes. Viribus gives specific instructions on how he wants the food prepared.

"You do that, and as long as it's exactly how I asked for, I'll give you another two-hundred on top of whatever change is left. You give me anything that comes out of that walk-in over there, or it's not cooked right, I'll tenderizer you myself. Got it?"

The cook gulps and nods his head in understanding. Viribus hands him the cash, and the smaller man scurries away. The Victus heads back up the cramped stairs to the small bedroom that houses the demon. Darius is as he left him, except he is sweating more.

Viribus checks his temperature to make sure the demon isn't getting too hot. Even a slight fever could be extremely dangerous to the cold-blooded fiend, and before he even touches the pale face, he knows the demon is burning up. The large man goes down the narrow hall to a tiny bathroom. He runs the cold water in the sink and soaks a fresh towel in the cold water. After loosely ringing it out, he brings it back to the bedroom and lays it on the demon's exposed chest. He takes the small towel from his head and does the same, soaking it in cold water again.

The soldier resumes his spot on the floor across from Darius's bed and rests his back against the wall. He separates the stapled papers into two stacks—the six that are ready to go and the ten that might be.

The first file he picks up is for Terrence Hunter. Blue is right; this guy will definitely work. His resume runs the gamut, everything from breaking-and-entering to grand larceny, to a felony assault that earned him a ten-year sentence. He's been on parole for three months and is working as a mechanic at a body shop suspected of actually being a high-end chop shop. His build matches that of Damon—one of the Victus that the rotten little witch killed in Portland. Tall, muscular, and athletic.

Viribus has gone through another two files when there's a soft knock at the door. The cook from downstairs pokes his head in.

"Your food is ready, sir," he says in a small voice. "Would you like me to bring it up here for you?"

"No," Viribus answers, getting to his feet. "I'll come down and eat at the bar."

He stops the cook by hooking a finger in his collar. "And don't ever come into this room without explicit permission to do so again."

The cook nods and hurries back down the steps. The enormous man follows and sets himself down in Darius's usual perch at the bar's back corner. The covered tray in front of him smells delicious, and the bartender sets down a frosted mug of beer to the side of it.

As Viribus eats his impeccably cooked meal, he scans the top news headlines on his phone. The top story on many of the 24-hour news websites is the Central Library explosion in Portland, Oregon. The reporters all have the same thing to say: the blast killed one employee who was working late, but no name has been released to the press yet.

Viribus smiles around a large bite of steak. As soon as they release a name, he can start digging around who she was in contact with and use it to his and the demon's advantage. The boss said she wasn't dead, so it must've been one of the Extensios she had with her.

He reads every story about the blast to make sure he doesn't miss anything. He swallows the last gulp of his beer and leaves the empty mug and tray where it is. The only thing left on the plate is the sucked clean T-bone, with every trace of meat gone. As he passes through the kitchen to go back upstairs to where the demon lays, he hands the cook the $200 he promised earlier.

The cook takes the money with wide eyes. Viribus claps the man on the back of the neck in approval, nearly knocking him down, before heading up the narrow staircase to continue scanning through the men who will soon become the demon's newest recruits.

• 6 •

Cali

Early Wednesday morning, seven hours after Viribus enjoyed his steaks, Flight 404, which became Flight 46 once it left JFK, lands safely at Amsterdam Schiphol Airport. Cali, Matt, Milo, and Roslyn groggily follow the rest of the passengers filing off of the plane. The group slept for the majority of the second flight but are still groggy and spent.

Cali puts her hand in her pocket and powers on her phone without removing it. It buzzes to life and continues pulsing as it receives notifications.

The group waits for the duffle bag to come around the belt with all the other checked bags. When it finally comes around, Matt reaches in through the rest of the waiting passengers and easily plucks it off the line.

Cali's ticket is the one that notates a checked bag, so she brings it through customs. As they were warned in Portland, Cali is asked to throw away the protein bars, the trail mix, and the gummy vitamins. After complying, she's waved through. Matt has nothing to declare and is waved through as well with little issue.

When Roslyn steps up with Milo, she is asked to produce his medical history to prove that he has been vaccinated and properly cared for, in addition to his service cog certification. Cali sees her friend pale and mouth "shit" as she reaches into the canvas laundry bag she uses as luggage.

"Miss, if you do not have the proper paperwork, the animal must be placed in mandatory quarantine."

"I understand. I'm just looking for the right things," Roslyn says, sifting through her bag. "Okay, here you go."

Cali sees her hand reappear, holding a stack of papers. She can't read what any of them say but can see an official-looking seal on the top of one.

The customs agent flips through the papers making sure everything is in order. Every other page, she raises her eyes to study the face of the young woman in front of her. As she hands the papers back, she stares Roslyn down with no emotion showing on her face for an extended amount of time.

"Welcome to The Netherlands," she finally says in accented English as she stamps Roslyn's passport. As Roslyn thanks her and gathers her things, the customs agent adds, "He's quite a beautiful dog."

"Thank you," Cali hears her friend say. Roslyn steps up to Matt and Cali, who are waiting just beyond the customs line.

"Shit, that was close," she says to them in a quiet voice. "I had to use my projection power to produce the papers she needed, which is definitely something I was hoping to avoid. *Fuck.*"

"Don't worry about it," Matt quickly says. "It was something small, so maybe Darius won't even notice.'

"Yeah, Moose is right," Cali says. "All we have to do is figure out how we're getting from here to Rome."

The three of them move over to a wall of the airport with Milo to stay out of the way of the other travelers. Her phone buzzes again, but she ignores it. Cali reaches into her bag and pulls out her wallet. She instructs the other two to do the same.

"We need to convert our cash to Euros. All of it," she says, looking at Roslyn.

"That's a lot of money, Cali. I'm not going to just whip it out in the middle of the airport."

"Fine," Cali says, trying to think of an option. "Okay, how about this? Moose and I will give you the cash we have, and you can take it to the currency exchange counter, then you won't have to take out your money until you're there. Moose, you can take Dog Man for a little stroll to stretch his stubby legs."

"And what are you going to do, Squirrel?" Matt asks. "Hmm?"

"I'm going to sit here and call my credit card company to tell them I'm traveling through Europe, so we'll have a high-limit card in case we need it."

"Oh," Matt says quietly. Cali gives him a look that puts him in his place.

"That works for me," Roslyn says.

Matt stacks his bag on of the duffle, and Cali sits down on top of them. He takes Milo's leash from Roslyn and hands her all the cash he has in his wallet before replacing it in his back pocket. Cali hands over her money and takes out her phone and credit card.

She watches the couple walk away with the dog and pretends she's dialing the number printed on the back of the card until they are out of sight. She has six voicemails and more than fifteen text messages from Mickey.

Deciding to listen to the voicemails later, Cali clicks the home button on her phone and reads the torrent of messages that have been sent from her girlfriend over the last fifteen hours and only arrived once she turned her phone on as soon as the plane landed.

MICK: good morning baby! i'm heading into the studio soon. do you want to come by for lunch later? love you

After reading the first message, she can't help the smile that crosses her face at the thought of Mickey. She keeps scrolling past texts that are mostly schedule updates and inside jokes. It's the last six that really stick out.

MICK: holy shit have you watched the news yet today???? something exploded at the library and the whole building is completely gone!
MICK: cali, call me back. i've tried to reach you a bunch of times and left a tor of voicemails. do you know if lex was there last night? i know she's been working late a lot recently
MICK: baby please call me. it's been hours and i can't reach you OR matt OR lex. what is going on?????
MICK: i don't know what to do. i don't want to call matt's mom and worry her if everything is okay, but I'M getting REALLY WORRIED. call me. wherever you are. i love you
MICK: i went to your place and milo is gone too???? i called the police but it's too soon for them to do anything. and the explosion is taking priority. WHERE ARE YOU????? please please PLEASE call me back

The last message breaks Cali's heart at how hopeless it sounds.

MICK: i don't understand what's going on or where you are or why you aren't answering your phone but i hope you're safe. the news just said that lex was killed in the blast. i can't believe any of this. i don't know what else to do. i love you so much and i'm going to keep calling you until you answer

Reading the escalation of Mickey's worry and desperation devastates Cali. She quickly writes a text message back to her, typing as fast as she can.

CAL: can't explain everything right now but i'm safe
CAL: I LOVE YOU SO MUCH

The phone rings almost immediately, but Cali forwards it to voice-mail.

>   **CAL:** can't talk on the phone
>
>   **MICK:** i've been trying to call you for hours cali!!! are you ok??? where the hell are you?!? and did you see what happened to the library?! it's all over the news! they're saying that lex is dead but it can't be true can it?
>
>   **CAL:** i did see. i was there with rob and moose
>
>   **MICK:** who's rob?
>
>   **CAL:** i meant roz
>
>   **MICK:** roz? who the fuck is roz??? WHAT is going on?
>   **MICK:** i'm calling you again
>
>   **CAL:** NO
>   **CAL:** don't call me. i can't talk right now babe. just trust me. i'm ok. we're all ok. and we have milo with us. i'll try and call you later. I LOVE YOU

Lifting her head to make sure Matt and Roslyn aren't on their way back to her yet, she quickly looks down at her phone again and sees that Mickey is typing a response. The bubble with three dots vanishes and reappears at least a dozen times before her phone softly vibrates as it gets two messages one after the other.

>   **MICK:** ok. i'm so confused but if you're all safe that's all that matters
>   **MICK:** i don't like this but i trust you baby. call me whenever you can. i swear i'll answer. and PLEASE be careful wherever you are. i basically lost my mind not knowing what was going on and i know i couldn't handle anything happening to you. so just be careful. ok?
>
>   **CAL:** i will

As much as she wants to hear Mickey's voice right now, she knows she can't take that risk yet. Cali exits her text messages and finally dials the credit card company to alert them to her travels. She's just finishing up the call when Matt and Roslyn come back to her with Milo, holding hands.

The sight causes a surprising flash of anger to stab through her chest, but she smothers it instantly. By the time the couple reaches her, she's successfully quieted her roiling emotions.

Milo comes right up to her and starts licking her face. His dark brown eyes look concerned as if he can tell how sour her mood really is. She reaches out and hugs the dog; he always makes her feel better.

"Everything go okay at the currency exchange?" she asks.

"Yeah," Roslyn answers. "Between the three of us, we had $9,120 American, and that translated to seven-thousand-seven-hundred-and-five point seven-zero Euros."

"That works for me," Cali says, repeating Roslyn's earlier words. "I called the number on the back of my card and told them I would be traveling throughout Europe for about two months. Linda was quite nice and said there was usually a fee, but because I'm a long time customer, and in *such* good standing, she's waiving it."

Cali smiles triumphantly at her uncanny ability to save a buck.

"You gotta teach me how you do that Squirrel," Matt says.

"Do what?"

"Talk people into giving you exactly what you want. You're like a world champion at saving money."

"It's a talent, Moose. What can I say?"

"You could say you figured out how we're gonna get to Rome from here," Roslyn says. "We can fly, take a train, or rent a car and drive. Thoughts?"

"Honestly, I'm still pretty tired. Could we find a hotel nearby and rest? Like really rest," Matt says. "We can decide from there what the best option is."

"I second that, Moose," Cali chimes in. "I'm beat, Lex—I mean, Roz. Man, that's gonna take a bit to get used to. Let's spend one day here and decide what to do later."

Roslyn looks back and forth between her boyfriend and best friend. When she looks down at Milo and sees just how much the travel has taken out of him, Cali can see that the decision's been made.

"There's one more thing," Cali says hesitantly, looking down at her phone that's still in her hand.

"What is it?" Roslyn asks nervously.

"Well, um, my condolences and everything. But, you're dead."

● 7 ●

"ROSLYN"

Cali quickly explained that she was browsing on her phone while waiting for me and Matt to return and got a breaking news bulletin. It was an article about the library explosion, which listed my previous identity as the only casualty. I told her we shouldn't talk about it at the airport, that we should get to a hotel and then figure it out.

As soon as we walk into the double room in the hotel nearest to the Amsterdam airport, Milo wastes no time jumping onto one of the two beds and making himself comfortable. I used our recently converted Euros to pay for the room with cash and booked it under a fake name. Cali takes out her tablet and signs on to the hotel WiFi. I watch her type furiously to find the article attached to the bulletin she got at the airport. She looks up at me, her mouth moving but no sound coming out.

"What is it?" I asked.

She turns her tablet around so that I can see the screen. It shows the homepage of The Portland Tribune, a bold headline across the top reads: One Confirmed Dead In Central Library Explosion. Next to the picture of the remains of the library is the photo from my employee ID badge. I take the tablet from her and start reading the article out loud.

" 'Authorities released the name of the employee who was in the library at the time of the explosion earlier this morning. Alexa Pearce, 22, had been an employee of the Multnomah County Central Library here in Portland for just over a year. She was working on a project in the building's sub-basement that would update the library's database and online presence. Investigators determined that the origin of the fire was in the large underground storage that Pearce had been working in.' "

I start pacing as I realize how much detail the story has. This is not just a blurb for a local paper; this is a news bulletin to be sent to media across the country.

" 'Her boss, Jeff Daley, called Pearce a "warm person, who worked hard and always had a smile on her face." At a press conference with Fire Chief Chip Emerson, Mayor Tess Morales, and other library personnel, Daley said he left with Pearce and a few other employees when the library closed at 8 P.M. As of right now, it is unclear as to why Miss Pearce returned to the library later that night, but a digital log lists only her key card as being used to unlock and enter the building after hours.' "

I glance back and forth between Matt and Cali. Both sets of eyes looking back at me are as wide as saucers, filled with dread. I close my eyes and exhale heavily before reading the rest of the article.

" 'Investigators have released a preliminary report on what the suspected cause of the blast was. A mainline ruptured, which caused the sub-basement Pearce was working in to fill with gas. It is unclear what caused the initial spark that ignited the gas, but the resulting explosion caused the ceiling of the sub-basement to cave in, which then created a domino effect with the main floor, two upper floors, and roof collapsing as well.'

" 'With the inner stability of the building compromised, the external walls and structure fell in on themselves. The blaze that consumed the ruble took firefighters over six hours to put out. Once it was clear the building was lost, their focus transferred to the surrounding block's integrity. "If there's any consolation," Chief Emerson said at the press conference, "it's that Miss Pearce was killed instantly. This is a tragic loss of a remarkable and kind young woman, but we must all be thankful that this accident happened after hours, and not when the library was full of additional employees, patrons, and children." The chief ended his press conference by saying the investigation is ongoing at this time.' "

The tablet practically drops out of my hands as my legs give out from underneath me. Even though it was fake, having my identity released is possibly one of the worst and most dangerous things to happen since my eighteenth birthday. I half sit on the bed behind me. The backs of my thighs slide from the quilt, and I slowly land in a small heap on the floor. Matt and Cali stare at me, unsure of what to do.

Milo whines and immediately comes and sits in the space between my legs. I cover my face with my hands and focus on my breathing to stave off the panic attack looming inside, ready to crash through my chest.

I count to four as I breathe in, hold it for seven, and count to eight as I slowly exhale. I breathe like that until the black dots in my vision clear, and my heart rate calms.

"This can't be happening," I mumble through my hands that are still trembling.

"What can't be happening?" I hear Matt ask with a worried voice.

"I've been identified," I say, dropping my hands to my lap. My eyes shine with unshed tears.

"But that's okay, babe," Matt says, coming to sit next to me.

"Yeah, it was a fake name," Cali says, moving to my other side, sandwiching me between them. "So, that's okay, right?"

"No, it's not," I say, shaking my head. "If it's been reported in the news that Alexa Pearce was the employee who was there when the library exploded, that means that Darius will find out the identity I was using. He already knew I was working there, that's why he sent those two Victus last week. But now he knows what my name is, or was. Shit. Shit, *shit*."

They look at me, neither of them understanding just how bad the situation is.

"If Darius knows what name I was using, he's going to go backward from there and track every detail he can, as big or as small as it may be, to find out everything about my life in Portland. He's going to find out who I knew, where I lived, and who I lived with."

I look Cali dead in the eye.

"And he's going to find everything he can about who I lived with. Including—" I drift off.

"Including what your roommate did and who she knew," Cali finishes for me, the horrific realization making her alabaster skin turn nearly translucent.

"It's just barely 1 A.M. in Portland; this article has only been up for a few hours, so there's a chance that Darius hasn't seen it yet."

"Are you willing to take that chance?" Cali stands up and asks in a shrill voice. "Because I'm not!"

"No, of course not!" I answer, surprised by how quickly her anger rises. "I was about to say that we need to contact Mickey and warn her. She has to avoid our apartment like the plague. *And* she needs to be extremely careful going and coming from work."

Cali starts to pace the room, frantically mumbling to herself. I want to say that I warned her something like this could happen, but that would be severely tactless and not helpful right now.

"Cali." Compartmentalizing my own anxiety for the moment, I stand to stop her in her tracks. I put my hands on her shoulders and wait for her to look me straight in the eye. "We are going to do everything we can to make sure Mickey is safe and stays that way. If I have to transport back there and get her myself, I will."

"But that'll give Darius—"

"I don't care," I cut her off. "If Mickey is in trouble, we'll fix it. I promise."

I can see her warring with herself that she doesn't believe me.

"Cal, I swear, I'll do everything—*we*," I point at her, myself, Matt, and even Milo to make my point, "will do everything we can to keep her safe."

"She's right, Squirrel," Matt says from his spot next to Milo. "We're in this together, and we're going to make sure nothing happens to her."

Cali's features turn from scared to desperate, then surprisingly to anger, and back to scared. She shakes her head quickly and then hugs me fiercely. She goes up on her toes so that her five-foot-five frame matches my five-nine one. I feel her body tremble as the rush of her emotions peaks.

"She's my entire world," Cali says through her tears. "I would never be the same if something happened to her. I don't know if I could even get through something like that."

I hug her tightly and whisper, "I'm sorry, Cali. I'm so sorry this happened, but please trust me. I swear I'll do everything I can to keep her out of the line of fire."

Cali sniffles and pulls away. I put my hands on either side of her face and use my thumbs to wipe her cheeks. There's little privacy in the room, so I tell her to go to the bathroom to call Mickey.

"What do I even say to her?"

I open my mouth to give her an answer, but nothing comes to me.

"It doesn't matter what you tell her, Squirrel," Matt says. "Mickey trusts you, and if you tell her to stay away from your apartment, she'll listen. You may need to reassure her that we're all okay, but Mickey knows you would never just leave without there being a very good explanation. And she also knows that you will tell her everything when you can."

He stands up and wraps his long arms around the person who has been his best friend for the last seventeen years. Because of their nine-inch height difference, Cali disappears into his embrace.

"Everything will be okay, and if something happens, we'll figure it out together."

"Okay, you're right, okay," Cali says, taking a couple of deep breaths to regain her composure. She takes her phone and goes into the bathroom. I watch her as she closes the door. I hear the shower turn on to create white noise for privacy, and then to my surprise again, the sharp click of the lock engaging on the door.

● 8 ●

I sigh wearily and pinch the bridge of my nose under my glasses. I run both hands through my thick hair. *I can't believe this,* I think.

I'm turning back around to ask Matt what he thinks when I'm met with his lips crashing into my own. I don't hesitate to kiss him back with the same intensity. I've wanted to jump him since he came out of the bathroom in Mount Tabor Park.

I feel his tongue swipe across my bottom lip, and I open my mouth to his. I wrap my arms around his neck at the same moment his encircle my waist. His tongue massages mine, and I take in a deep breath. Even after two long flights, his scent fills all of my senses; Old Spice, laundry detergent, and peppermint.

He pulls his mouth away from mine just long enough to say, "I've wanted to do that since we got out of the libr—"

I pull him back into me, cutting off the last syllable. I feel my arousal building quite rapidly. A thought goes through my mind that we happen to be standing in a room with beds.

If only Cali wasn't in the bathroom, I think.

It stops me cold. My best friend is on the phone with her girlfriend to tell her to stay away from our apartment because of the demon who is chasing *me*. And here I am, just a door away, ready to rip off the clothes of *her* best friend and wishing she wasn't here.

I put my hands on Matt's shoulders, and with my eyes still closed, I gently push him back. I need to put physical space between us before I go too far.

"Stop," I say.

Matt freezes immediately. I feel him let go of me, and I take a step backward. I slowly open my eyes. He's looking at me with a confused expression. "What? What's wrong?"

"We can't do this right now."

"What do you mean, Lex?"

"That's not my name," I say softly, looking away from him, realizing yet another of the many complications and obstacles to this relationship. One that hasn't even had the chance to fully start yet.

"Roslyn," he corrects himself. "I don't understand what you mean."

"I mean that I can't stand here kissing you and wanting you when Cali is right there," I point at the bathroom door. "She's calling Mickey to warn her to be careful from half a world away. But you and I, we're right here together. It's not fair. I can't do that to her right now."

Matt swallows hard and clenches his jaw. He steps back, creating more space between us.

"What do you mean you can't do this to her? What about me? I've given up everything to come with you, too."

"I know you have. That's not what I'm saying."

"Well then, what *do* you mean? I joined you, I told you I'm in love with you, you won't even tell me your real name, and now you're breaking up with me?"

"What? No! That's not what I'm saying at all!"

"Then what?!"

I'm shocked at the way Matt is reacting. He's staring at me with his arms crossed—hurt, confusion, and anger written on his face. I immediately go into defense mode. I cross my arms, too, staring right back.

"First, please keep your voice down,' I hiss. "And second, you cannot speak to me like that. In this relationship, you will treat me with the same respect I show you. That is the bare minimum I will accept, and there is no relationship without it."

We stare at each other, and once my words register with Matt, his gaze drops to the ground. I bite down on my tongue hard. If I talk now in anger, I will berate him, which would cause a fight, and I want us to have open communication with each other as much as I can.

"Matt," I say softly. "What I am saying is that if Cali were to walk out of the bathroom and see us… like that, she'd feel betrayed and angry. I know that's how I would feel if the situation was reversed."

I gingerly step forward and uncross his arms, intertwining the fingers of my right hand with his left.

"I've never wanted to be with someone as much as I want to be with you. And I know how you feel about me; my heart pounds every time I think about it. And every moment, I can feel myself falling for you further and harder."

I squeeze his hand, causing him to look from the floor to our fingers. He pulls me into him and holds me loosely.

"Matt, at this point in time, you and Cali are the most important things to me."

I hear a yip come from across the room. Someone is voicing his offense at my statement.

"And Milo, of course," I add with an eyeroll. "You're all that's keeping me sane, calm, alive even. I don't want to break up with you. That's not what I'm doing; that's not remotely close to what's in my mind or heart. I just think we need to be considerate that you and I each got to run with our partner, and Cali had to leave hers behind."

Matt's shoulders slump now that I've been able to explain everything.

"You're completely right. I jumped to the exact opposite conclusion. I was wrong. I'm sorry. And I'm sorry I got so upset at you. That wasn't right, either."

"Thank you," I say, giving him one last kiss and stepping out of his embrace and over to the large sliding door that leads to the room's balcony. As I'm pulling the large, thick curtains closed, Cali comes out of the bathroom.

She plops down on the bed closest to her, patting a place on the plush blanket next to her. Milo jumps up and, after licking her face a few times, lays down next to her. She wraps her arms around his neck and buries her face in his fur.

"Did you speak to Mickey?" Matt asks. He moves around the bed and sits behind her with one leg tucked underneath him.

"Yes," she says. Milo's thick coat muffles her voice. "She was at her place."

I can't help the sigh of relief that floods out of my lungs. I expect a similar reaction from my friend, but Cali's mood isn't relieved; it's hurt. "Are you okay, Cali?"

"It's just hard," she says without looking up. "Harder than I expected it to be, I guess. We haven't been apart for more than a day or two since we got together, so it's weird her not being here. It's like a piece of me is missing."

My heart breaks for Cali right now. I catch Matt's eye and mouth, *"See?"* He nods solemnly back.

I kneel on the floor beside the bed and rub her back. I nudge her a bit to make her look at me.

"I know how you feel," I tell her. She rolls her eyes back at me and puts her head back into Milo's silky hair.

"No, really," I say, getting her to look at me again. One eye peeks out from behind a curtain of black fur. "You feel heavy, but like you are hollow and incomplete at the same time. Like you're lost, and you know the one thing that would make you feel like you can make it is the one thing you can't have. You ache in places you didn't know you had in your heart. It breaks you to be apart, but you know it's what you have to do to keep them safe."

I prop myself up on an elbow and angle my hand toward her. My fist is closed except for my extended pinky finger.

"I swear to you she'll be okay. We'll check in with Mickey every few days, especially now that my name was released. And if she says something that gets us worried, or she doesn't answer you, or something just feels off, then we will all go back and get her. Okay?"

Cali stares at me. She studies my face as I stare right back. I want her to know I'm serious, that at this moment, I believe myself and mean what I'm saying. Finally, she props herself on an elbow and hooks her pinky finger in mine. "Okay," she says with a small smile before sitting up entirely and reaching for the leather folder on the small table between the beds.

"Now, how about some food?" she asks. "I'm fucking starving."

• 9 •

Cali

After turning on the shower in the bathroom, Cali thinks twice and locks the bathroom door. She needs to be able to talk to Mickey as long as she wants without the risk of anyone else walking in. She sits on the closed toilet and presses the video icon next to the top name listed under her phone contacts' favorites. She has no idea if the call will connect since it is international, but she crosses her fingers to give it a little extra help.

The line rings in her hand. Three rings, four rings. Her heart starts to race, thinking the screen would display "unavailable" under Mickey's name, and all the scenarios that could be the cause of that begin playing through her head. The main one that plays on a loop is Darius has somehow found Mickey already.

At the end of the fifth ring, the call connects. The video shakes in her hand as she hears the out of breath voice of her girlfriend say, "Cali? Is that you?"

"Yeah, it's me, baby," she says.

"Oh my god! I'm so happy you called," Mickey's usually calm and soft voice is frantic. Cali can see the worry written all over her face. "I've been waiting for you, and I must've fallen asleep. The phone woke me up, and then I couldn't find it. I practically ripped my couch apart, and I was so worried I would miss the call."

Cali can't help but smile whenever she talks to Mickey, now especially. The smile vanishes quickly as she remembers the warning she must give her girlfriend before anything else is said.

"Baby, listen to me," she says to the older woman. "You have to stay away from my apartment for a while, okay?"

"Why? What are you talking about?" Mickey asks. "Where are you? Are you okay?"

"I'm okay, I promise. And Moose, Milo, and Lex are okay too. But I need you to promise me that you'll steer clear of my place. At least for a while."

"I don't understand."

Cali hesitates, unsure of how much to tell Mickey. She rubs her freckled forehead before deciding to go for it, and she'll answer as many questions as she can.

"I'm going to tell you something, and I need you to really listen and believe me. I don't know how long I can talk, so please let me tell you everything, and then you can ask me whatever you want, and I'll try to answer it."

"Okay, okay, I'm here," Mickey says. On the screen, Cali can see Mickey stand up and move within her apartment. She hears a rustling and then something thunk onto the coffee table.

"Okay, so," Cali starts then stops. "Okay... Alexa is a witch. Lex isn't even her real name, right now it's Roslyn, but that's fake too. She's been traveling across the country for the last five years searching for something that's literally just called *The Book*, which will tell her how to defeat a demon called Darius, who's been searching for *her* and wants to kill her to end the world.

"Darius was at the library, and he's the reason it blew up. He and Lex—uhh, I mean Roslyn, have actual powers. Like, they can both throw fire and move things with their minds. It was nuts to see it up close, although I missed some of it because I got knocked out for a little when an explosion blew Roz into me, but—"

"Wait, what?! You got knocked out?"

"Babe, questions."

"Sorry, continue." Mickey holds a finger to her lips, silencing herself.

"Right, so before Darius even got there, Moose and I became Extensios. Which, well, Jesus, how do I explain that? We're basically, um, like soldiers for Roz, and now he and I have a power too. But Darius brought some of his own soldiers too, called Victus, though, but I'm probably not pronouncing that right.

"Anyway, we made it out of the library before it collapsed, but so did Darius. And unfortunately, *The Book* blew up with the building, but that's why we're here now in Europe. There's another one here, somewhere in Rome. And we have to make our way there and find it before Darius does.

"But the reason you have to stay away is that now that the name Alexa Pearce has been released through the media, Darius is going to use that to find out where she lived, who she knew, and who they knew. So you have to be extremely careful, even when leaving your place and going to work.

"Okay, I think that's everything. You can ask questions now."

The image of Mickey is frozen. The line is silent for so long that Cali checks the phone to make sure she hasn't lost service.

"Mick? Baby? You there?"

She hears Mickey exhale. The image bounces as her girlfriend moves through the apartment. It's quiet again before the distinct *bunk* of a cork being pulled out of an open bottle of wine sounds. Cali smirks as she remembers her own reaction when she first learned all of this and the amount of vodka she drank to help her process it.

Her girlfriend drinks half of what's left in the bottle. She puts it down, then picks it up for two more gulps before she speaks, "Okay, first question: you're serious? You're not fucking with me, and this wasn't just a prank that got way out of hand or something?"

"No, baby. I'm completely serious."

"Okay." She watches Mickey finish the wine. "Next question, are you fucking serious?!"

Cali rubs her forehead with her free hand. She anticipated a reaction like this and lets Mickey just talk it out.

"The library exploded—like, it's literally gone Cali, and you're telling me that not only were you there but Lex *didn't* die like the news said, that she and Matt are with you, and so is Milo! And you're in Europe about to go to Rome?! Plus, if that wasn't crazy enough—which trust me, it is—you're telling me that Alexa is a witch and that she's been running from a demon for five years."

"Baby, I'm telling you the truth."

There is a long stretch of silence before Mickey speaks again.

After a drawn-out exhale, she says, "I know you are; you wouldn't lie to me like this. I just can't believe it. I have a million questions, but the one that I have to ask first is how will this guy know where your apartment is, or who you are, or who *I* am?"

"Remember those guys from last week? The ones who bumped into me and then grabbed me?"

"Yes, of course, I remember those assholes. If I ever see them again, I'll kick their asses."

"You definitely don't need to worry about seeing them again. Darius brought them with him to the library. They were Victus and didn't make it out. Milo went so nuts because he can sense evil."

"Of course he can," Mickey replies sarcastically.

"No, I'm serious. Milo has a crystal on his collar that protects him but allows him to sense evil in others. It's like he's got his own stealth mode."

"Ya know, I've seen that on his collar," Mickey says absently. She takes in a deep breath and holds it with her cheeks puffed out. Cali waits, giving Mickey time to work her way through all the information.

"So I have to stay away from your place because we don't know what kind of reach this... demon has.

"I can't believe that's a sentence I actually just said."

Cali chuckles, "I know, baby. But it's the truth. Darius was pretty beat up when he got away from the library, but if he was able to put people in Portland before he knew for sure it was where he needed to be, I can only imagine who he'll have out there now that he has an actual name to go off of.

"So I need you to swear you won't go to my apartment for any reason. Seriously. If you think you left something there, buy a new one. Please, baby."

The brunette holds up her right hands as she says, "I promise I won't. But how will I know that you're safe?"

"I'll try and call you every couple of days. But you still have to be careful, even when you go to work and when you leave. And you know people are gonna ask about Lex, how you're doing, or how I'm doing—just play along or come up with something."

"You sure you're okay, though?"

"I am, baby. I just wish I brought my sketchbook or something with me to keep my hands busy and my mind calm."

"You better be careful too, Cali. You come back to me, okay? If you die, I'll find you and kill you myself."

Cali thinks about correcting the redundancy of that statement but laughs instead.

"I mean it!" Mickey continues. "I can't imagine my life without you in it. I need you to be okay, and I need you to stay that way."

"I know. I love you, Mickey. I'll call you soon."

"I love you so much. Please be safe. Bye."

Cali sadly blows a kiss to the screen then reluctantly taps the red icon to end the call. Now that Mickey's sweet voice isn't in her ear and her beautiful face is gone, she feels somewhat guilty about telling her all of those things. She knows Mickey will worry and stay glued to her phone until the next time they talk, but she also knows that she was meant to keep a lot of this a secret.

Her internal monologue suddenly switches sides, and she thinks that if she had to leave Mickey back home, then the least she could do is tell her the truth, and too bad if Roslyn doesn't like it. The argument flips again, and she reminds herself that it's not just about saving her partner—that they are on a trajectory to save everyone's partners.

All of it makes Cali feel like a heavy weight is pressing down on her. When she unlocks the bathroom door and reenters the hotel room, she flops onto the first bed she sees and pats it for Milo to come and snuggle.

She hugs him close and feels only slightly better. It's not until Roslyn puts into words exactly how she feels and makes her a pinky promise that they'll keep tabs on Mickey, she becomes something of herself again.

Although it is only 10 A.M. in Amsterdam, it's 2 A.M. Portland time to the group. They have traveled for over half a day; they are tired, dirty, and hungry, and decide to tackle those things in reverse order. They place their room service order and ask for it to be brought up in an hour. Matt takes the first shower, then Cali, then Roslyn.

Even Milo gets a bath to wash out any remaining debris from his thick fur. He's so amped after his bath that Matt volunteers to take him for a walk.

Once the boys leave the room, Roslyn and Cali lay in the same bed and turn on the TV, flipping through the channels until they find a syndicated American sitcom overdubbed in Dutch. A few minutes later, there is a knock on the door, and a voice says "room service" in accented English. Cali and Roslyn look at each other before springing off the bed and checking the peephole in the door.

"Do you think it's a trap?" Cali asks in a panicked voice.

"No, I think it's just room-service," Roslyn says. "But, be ready just in case."

Roslyn goes to open the door but instead darts away and calls over her shoulder, "Just a minute!"

Her quick movements startle Cali, who instantly dives into the open bathroom expecting a ball of fire to blow the hotel door off of its hinges. She covers her head and waits. Cali realizes her mistakes as she hears the door open and the room service cart rattling in.

"Thanks a lot; here you go," Roslyn says, paying the bill and handing the waiter a tip in cash. The door to the room closes, and Roz pokes her head into the bathroom. "You okay?"

"What?" Cali asks, popping up from the floor quickly and brushing her clothes off, her face red with embarrassment. "I was, uh, just checking something on the floor, like, in the back, uh, back behind the toilet."

"Right, of course."

Roslyn moves out of the way so Cali can get by, her face red with embarrassment.

"Shut up," Cali mumbles as she walks back into the hotel room.

• 1 0 •

VIRIBUS

Right around 4 A.M. on Wednesday in Atlanta, Viribus is getting ready to turn in for the night. He checks on Darius, who is resting comfortably since his fever has broken, and his cold-blooded body is finally cooling, then wedges himself into a corner of the room. He's propped against a pillow stuffed into the right angle of the walls, and he has the last of the "sure thing" files in his lap.

He reads through the file for Marcus St. Vincent, whose rap sheet mirrors closely each of the other five files that Blue has marked as the best Victus candidates. Viribus writes down notes on St. Vincent until his eyes droop. He sets the files aside and lets his head fall back until it rests against a wall. He hears his smartphone chime with an alert before he falls asleep, but he ignores it and drifts off.

Only three hours later, he's awoken by the demon groaning in agony on the bed across from him. Viribus gets up as quickly as his sizeable frame allows and goes to Darius's side. He checks for fever but finds none. Darius continues groaning, getting louder and louder until he's yelling. Right at that point, Viribus smells burning flesh.

He looks down and sees the skin of the damaged left arm smoking as it regenerates itself further. With no idea what to do, Viribus runs from the room, pounding down the stairs to the closed bar.

The demon only ever informed him of what to expect after a Victus transformation. He's never seen Darius injured and is only guessing on what will help.

He gets an empty pitcher from behind the bar and fills it with water. He's about to run back out when a mostly full bottle of whiskey catches his eye. He grabs that too and pounds back up the stairs.

When he enters the small bedroom, Darius is delirious, saying things that Viribus can't understand.

The demon is saying random syllables that don't add up to any words. He groans through every other word.

"I'm here, boss," Viribus says, kneeling next to the mattress and putting the water and bottle of whiskey on the floor.

The demon keeps his eyes screwed shut as he speaks. His voice almost sounds pleading, like he's willing the Victus to understand.

"I'm here, boss. Just rest, you need your rest now."

Viribus tips some whiskey in the black-haired man's mouth. The demon suctions his lips to the bottle and swallows greedily. With the quart finished, the Victus refills it from the pitcher with water. The demon finally settles down after emptying it two more times.

He seems to be in less pain but is still mumbling the sounds over and over.

The words come out slower as Darius relaxes, his current pain soothed. When he's completely quiet, Viribus reclines against the corner he occupied minutes before and picks up one of the "maybe" files Blue sent. He goes through another four names and picks only one out to explore further: Collin Kings—the same man who put Blue and Julius on to the library in New Orleans that ulti-mately led them to Portland.

Still too wired to fall back to sleep, he goes down into the kitchen and puts on a fresh pot of coffee, deciding to just stay awake. He pops into the bar and takes a new bottle of whiskey out from under the bartop. When the coffee finishes brewing, he pours half a cup and tops it off with the alcohol.

It's too early for any of the cooks to be here, so he braves the walk-in fridge looking for something to make some breakfast with. The stench that hits his face as soon as he opens the heavy door decides it for him. It smells like the rank combination of moldy bread, putrid ground beef, and spoiled milk.

He slams the fridge closed, walking away from it, mumbling obscenities. He exits the kitchen through the alleyway; the wall at the end of it displays scorch marks from his boss's last release of tension.

He walks out of the alley and makes a left onto the street. Viribus heads down the block to a small deli and takes place in the long line of the morning rush.

"Good morning, friend," the man behind the counter greets Viribus when he gets to the counter. "What can I get you?"

Viribus grumbles a greeting and orders two double sausage breakfast sandwiches and one triple bacon sandwich. When his order is done, he takes the white paper bag and throws a fifty dollar bill down on the counter. He walks out, not bothering to take his change.

On the walk back to the bar, he's already half done with the second sandwich. The Victus hears his phone ding from the inner pocket of his blazer. He hasn't checked it since the last time he ate, so he sticks the half-eaten sandwich back inside the bag and slides his hand inside his jacket. He has multiple notifications from news apps about things happening around the country, but one, in particular, catches his eye.

It's a news bulletin about the destruction of the library. His vast thumb taps to open the article. He stops dead in his tracks in the middle of the sidewalk. His eyes scan the screen. They widen before turning into slits as he sneers wickedly.

He closes the window and goes through his recent calls tapping on Blue's contact. The call goes to voicemail, but based on the hour, the Victus knew it would.

"You've reached Officer Rodger Blusseau," the recorded voice says in Viribus's ear. He waits impatiently for the message to finish.

"Blue. It's me. I need you to run a name for me. Get me address, associates, bank statements, everything. Call me when you have literally anything, no matter what time it is. Location is Portland, Oregon. Name, Alexa Pearce."

• 1 1 •

"ROSLYN"

Loud bangs sound as part of the ceiling falls to the floor. Matt is screaming. I hear Darius taunting me, see Milo running through clouds of smoke and dust.

I can feel the heat from the fires filling the room. I see Darius running toward me, and I turn to flee. He's suddenly behind me and catches me by the throat. I see Matt's body bloody and motionless on the floor. I hear Milo whining in pain and Cali screaming.

I feel the demon run his hand through my hair and pull a clump to his nose. I hear him inhale deeply. I feel his nose press against my cheek, and a rumble comes from his chest.

"Gotcha, girl."

My eyes bolt open, rushing blood thunders in my ears. My heart is pounding like a hammer.

I'm in bed facing Cali. For a moment, I think the last few days are actually just a disturbing, recurring nightmare; that we're back in our apartment and have just fallen asleep after being up late talking. I roll over onto my back and close my eyes to go back to sleep when I hear a snore coming from somewhere in the room. My eyes snap open again. Milo snores every once in a while, but that definitely wasn't him.

I gingerly lift my head to see who the noise is coming from. As my brain fully wakes up and my eyes take in the hotel room we're staying in, I remember that the last few days weren't a dream. I push the covers off of myself and pile them onto Cali's form next to me.

My muscles scream at me to stay still as I sit up. I don't remember my body ever being this sore—not even after one of Mickey's advanced classes. I get out of bed as quietly as I can. Putting on my glasses, the room comes into full focus. The room-service cart is pushed into a corner, the plates on it completely barren. I hear Cali shift under the covers, wrapping herself tighter within them.

The boys are in the opposite bed. Matt is on his back with an arm thrown over his face, and Milo is on his side, all four legs straight out as if he fell asleep standing and then fell onto his side.

The room is dark; we had closed the long blackout drapes just before we all got washed up. I can't tell what time it is, but I don't see any outline of sunlight surrounding the curtains. I'm actually more concerned with how sore I am rather than what time it is. I need to loosen up and decide taking another shower is the only way to soothe my aching muscles. I maneuver quietly through the meager light to where I know the bathroom is.

I go in and close the door softly behind me. After turning on the shower as hot as it will go, I check my reflection in the mirror and can't ignore the circles under my eyes noticeable even against my brown skin and my overall haggard look.

I pause to really stare at myself in the mirror. I can see a little of each of my magical ancestors in my reflection. In my almond-shaped eyes, I can see the elves from generations ago. The spark of green in the irises comes from leprechauns, highlighted now by the artificial light. The blonde that streaks my curly dark hair can be traced to fairies, the curls themselves coming from the Romani side. My skin color and height come from the African shamans on my father's side. My jawline, nose, and mouth are all my mother, though.

As I start to undress, I turn in slow circles, checking my body. The only physical reminders of my fight with Darius are a long, jagged scar on my right shoulder and a line that bisects my upper left arm. The burns that covered my arms and legs thankfully left no trace when they healed. The scars are a stark white against my mocha skin. It's as if they've been there for years instead of barely a day.

Even though I used my powers to heal myself, I can still feel the pounding that my body took. My ribs are sore from multiple impacts, my shoulder with the gash is very stiff, and I just overall feel as I assume anyone would after getting thrown around like a rag doll. It's just that none of it is visible now.

Maybe I didn't do it right, I think. *Or maybe it only works on the really big injuries.*

As steam starts to fill the room, my glasses fog up. I take them off and remove the rest of my clothes before stepping into the glass stall. The hot water stings at first, but I force myself to stay under the spray, and gradually I not only get used to it but can feel my body start to relax.

Whether it's real or imagined, I can still feel the residue of dirt and dust from the destroyed library on my skin and in my hair. I lather myself head to toe, rinse off, and repeat. I stand under the spray and count to one hundred, then finally turn the water off.

I stand motionless in the stall. As droplets fall from my thick hair and fingertips, I can feel the full weight of my current predicament. When I had to leave home five years ago, my grandfather gave me a spell to say that would cloak my family from Darius. But Cali and Matt, and Mickey, are my family now too. And this time, I don't have a spell to keep them hidden. All they have is me. And all I have is very limited knowledge of who I'm up against and what either of us is capable of.

If I think about the entirety of what has to be done, I'm afraid I'll go insane. So I'll have to do what I've always done—tackle things one at a time. The most pressing thing that needs to get done right now is figuring out how we are going to get from Amsterdam to Rome.

I get out of the shower and realize I didn't bring any clothes in with me. I curse under my breath and wrap a towel around my body. I peek my head out, but I shouldn't have been worried. All three of my companions are still out cold. I run on my toes into the room and grab the canvas laundry bag that's full of my clothes. My skin breaks out in goosebumps as it hits the cool air, which makes the steam from the shower all the more welcoming when I dash back into the bathroom.

I reemerge with a towel wrapped around my head, and the first things I pulled out of the bag—an oversized sweatshirt and stretch skinny jeans. Without disrupting Cali, I sit on the bed and recline against the headboard. I pick up her tablet to start looking up flights from here to Rome, train schedules, and car rentals. We're all still twenty-two and twenty-three, so we can't rent a car in America, but I check to see what the laws are in Europe.

Price-wise, the best option seems to be a plane. Flights aren't that expensive, and we could be there in less than five hours from start to finish. It also leaves us with the most cash left in hand for when we get to Rome.

The train is the next viable option—it would take us almost an entire day, and we'd have to transfer more than once. But we could book a small cabin for the whole trip and stay mostly out of sight. However, Milo's needs could only be addressed at transfers.

While driving would potentially be the safest because we could move throughout the continent on our terms, it is the least cost-effective and the longest option. It would take us at least two days to get there, and we'd have to pay for gas and hotels along the way. Plus, at least four border crossings between Amsterdam and Rome means a check at each one, which means our names would be repeatedly put into a system.

None of that takes care of where we are going to stay when we get to Rome, or how we're going to even begin searching for *The Book's* twin, for that matter.

I know Cali is a wiz when it comes to saving money wherever she can, so I leave all the sites open and will lay everything out for her and Matt when they wake up. I put the tablet down on the table between the beds and check the time on the digital clock.

It's 9 P.M. local time. To me, it's one o'clock Portland time, and although I slept for roughly eleven hours, I'm still mentally, emotionally, and physically exhausted. Leaving the towel on my head, I slink down into the bed and gently pull the covers back from Cali. She has them clenched tight, so she ends up sliding across the bed with them.

It's either try to fall back to sleep without covers or be her big spoon. I guess I could dump out my entire bag to find the blanket I brought, but I'd rather not if I can help it. So the choice is really already made for me.

****

The next time I wake up, there is more activity going on in the room. Milo is awake and is doing something to make Cali laugh. My head is bare, the towel having unraveled at some point. I hear a backpack unzip, and someone, who I assume is Cali, pokes through it before the bathroom door closes. The shower turns on, and I realize she must have the same idea I did a little while ago.

Once his source of entertainment is gone, Milo jumps into bed with me. He lays down on his side, facing me with his head on the pillow that still has a fresh indention from Cali. I rub under his chin a little, and he scoots over toward me. I pull my head back just in time to avoid getting a wet lick on my face. I love my dog, and I'll give him a bunch of kisses on his head, but I've seen the kind of things he puts in his mouth and want no part of that.

I play with Milo while the two of us lay there. I make his floppy ear stand up straight. He puts his paw on my arm, and I tell him he needs his nails cut. Milo instantly snatches his arm back and tucks it underneath him. He makes me laugh when Cali hits an off-key high note of whatever song she's badly singing in the shower, and he covers his face with both paws.

He rolls on his back and twists a few times to rub his back against the blankets. He lets out a big sigh before stretching his legs and slumping back onto his side to face me.

"Milo, you trying to steal my girl?" I hear Matt's voice above us say. I look up at him out of the side of my eye and smile.

"Actually, Milo came first, so technically, you stole *his* girl," I say in a playful voice.

"Oh, is that so?"

"Yes, it is." Milo licks my cheek to emphasize my point. I scrunch my nose and use a handful of the sheet on top of me to wipe it away. When Matt leans down to kiss my forehead, though, I leave his there.

Cali comes out of the bathroom in sweats, steam billowing out of the door behind her, face flushed red from the heat of the water.

She sighs, "That feels better."

"I think I'm going to have to do that next," Matt says. "I feel like a giant ball of knots."

"All yours, Moose," Cali says. "And when you're done, it's time to figure out just what in the hell the four of us are going to do next."

• 1 2 •

It's early Thursday morning in Amsterdam. I'm still beyond exhausted, but I can't sleep at the moment. I keep replaying the last few hours, trying to make sure that we didn't miss something.

After I transported away from my family on my eighteenth birthday and first started my search in Florida, this was a frequent problem. I was scared and alone and continually replaying my actions to make sure I didn't leave any tracks. Now, I'm basically starting all over again, but this time I'm not alone. This time instead of feeling protected, the pressure has grown.

Once Cali got her hands on the sites I had left up for her to check out, she made the travel decision for us. She booked us a flight for mid-morning later today. Once she was done with transportation, she moved on to where we would stay.

She asked me what the inscription said if it gave any clue as to where the twin book would be. I told her it was exactly what the front cover inscription said, except it had another line:

"The holder of this book possesses the history of and key to defeat the greatest darkness to walk this world. The twin of this book is housed in the Eternal City. The place where all roads lead."

"And all roads lead to Rome," Matt said. "That's like world history 101."

I smirked and decided not to remind him that both he and Cali stared at me blankly when I first said that in Mount Tabor Park.

"Right, but Rome is huge," I countered. "We need to find a map of what the city looked like twelve-hundred years ago and circle the libraries."

"It's really unlikely that the libraries from that many years ago haven't been torn down, or their collections moved to another building at some point along the way, though," Cali said, making a very valid point. "I think we should find either an Airbnb, a small apartment, or a cheap hotel in the dead center of the city."

"So we get a place and just start knocking out the libraries one at a time, right?" Matt asks. "Because now you know what you're looking for."

I nod before adding, "But what happens if the twin is in, like, the library at the Vatican. How are we even going to get in there to get it?"

"There's no need to worry about that yet, Roz. Let's just figure out where we're going to stay right now."

Cali started searching through sites on her tablet while Matt called the front desk about the room service cart before he moved it into the hallway. I occupied Milo for a bit with his tennis ball. I don't know how he always does it, but in all of the times I've just played with or focused my attention solely on him, everything else just fades away. And it's like for just that brief amount of time, I'm living the ordinary life that I wish, sometimes desperately, was mine.

Matt decided to take Milo out for another walk around the block. I unpacked and repacked my bag, separating out the clothes that need to be washed once we get to Rome. Before Matt left, we all agreed we would rather stay at the hotel than go out to get something to eat, so when I finished packing, I called to place another room service order.

"So," I heard Cali prompt me so I would pay attention to her. "If we're living in a hotel for however long we're going to be in Rome, we'd need a suite with a small kitchen because room-service would cost too much after like, two days. Plus, we need a pet-friendly hotel. Or, we could do this Airbnb."

She handed me the tablet and started to narrate what I was looking at.

"It's in the center of the city, near tourist sites, so it'll be easy to blend in should anyone be looking for us. It has a kitchen, so we'll be able to cook there and save money. It says pets are allowed, so that takes care of Milo. And it's less expensive than a hotel."

"You're okay with the price?" I asked.

"I am."

"Well then, sold. Thanks, kid," I said, handing her back her tablet. I didn't let go when she grabbed it, holding tight until she looked at me. "You know I'm going to pay you back for all of this."

She waved me off, but I stopped her keeping my grip on the tablet.

"No, Cal, I'm serious. Everything you've done for me since the moment I met you 'til now. From giving me a home to letting me trust you on my own terms, to dropping everything to come with me. I swear I'll pay you back somehow."

"I know," Cali said simply. No expectations of when or how just a promise between friends. She tapped her screen a few more times and reserved the AirBnB starting around 3 P.M. on Thursday.

After eating again, Milo, Cali, and Matt were all luckily able to fall back to sleep for another few hours. After running through everything another three times, I finally closed my eyes, forcing myself to relax until we have to be at the airport in six hours.

****

We're all up, packed, and back at the airport mid-morning with plenty of time to spare. Repeating like on our trip to Amsterdam, we check the large duffle bag of supplies, and Milo's ticket is marked as a service animal.

The flight is one hundred and thirty minutes, just enough time to watch the in-flight movie. We land safely and go through customs without any issues this time. Because of his service dog status and paperwork, Milo is again allowed into the country rather than placed in quarantine.

We walk out of the airport unimpeded, and I make a mental note that right now, that means one of two things: Darius hasn't had time to investigate the Alexa Pearce identity, or his reach doesn't make it this far. Either way, it's good for me.

Cali emails the Airbnb host to let him know we've arrived. He responds back quickly with the code for the lockbox that the keys are housed in. The four of us take a bus to the center of the city and walk to our new place from there. I give Milo his "casual" command, so to everyone else—including my Extensios—Milo looks like he's just out for a walk, but I know he's actively scanning everyone around us for potential threats.

It's getting toward late afternoon by the time we find the building. It has a stone and plaster outer facade and a marble lobby with columns and a wood-faced elevator. The apartment itself is a perfect size. With a living room and an eat-in kitchen, plus two bedrooms and two full bathrooms, I think we'll all be very comfortable here.

When it came to sleeping arrangements, there was a narrowly missed awkward moment. Matt and I are still so early on in our relationship that sharing a room and a bed is a huge step after only one official date. But Cali being Cali, eased any tension before it started.

"Milo and I get the big bed!" she yelled, running into the room and throwing her stuff on the king-sized bed.

That left the queen bed in the other room for him and me. He nervously scratched the back of his neck and asked me if I was okay with this. I said I was fine with it, as long as we were both still on the same page about us taking things slow.

The apartment also has an in-unit washing machine, so I do a load of all our dirty laundry since we all packed a limited amount of clothing. While I'm waiting for it to finish, I flip through my notebook that has hand-copied parts of *The Book* in it. I wasn't very focused on much of anything other than the fact that I knew Darius was on his way, so I don't fully trust that I copied everything accurately.

When the washer buzzes that the load is done, we hang everything on a clothesline strung up in one bathroom since there is no dryer in the apartment.

The weather is nice, and we don't know exactly how long we'll be here, so we decide to walk the neighborhood. It's reminiscent of something Milo and I did when we first moved in with Cali. We walked every block in the neighborhood so that we'd both know how to either get home easily or out quickly no matter where we were.

We take in the warm spring air as we walk. A crisp breeze blows by, bringing with it the smells of fresh flowers and fruit. We round the corner and come upon a small market with a stand out front. On the stand are bundles of asparagus, artichokes, leeks, lemons, kiwis, and strawberries. We are relatively close to where the apartment we're staying in is located, so Cali and Matt head inside the market to see what else they have.

Milo and I wait out on the street scanning the area. My dog is standing watchfully at my knee, wagging his tail, so I take a deep breath and relax for the moment. *I'm actually in Rome,* I think. *A place some people dream of visiting.*

Matt comes out of the small market empty-handed, but his shorter best friend has an almond biscotti in her mouth and a white paper parcel filled with more cookies. Cali smiles at me as she takes another bite.

"What?" I ask.

"She has an idea," Matt replies, the smile never leaving Cali's mouth as she chews.

• 1 3 •

Cali

She started to explain her idea as the group walked back, but Roslyn asked her to wait until they were inside. When they enter the building, Roslyn puts her arm out, stopping Matt and Cali in their tracks. She gives Milo a command under her breath and lets him off of his leash. The black dog walks the lobby with his nose to the ground and his ears at attention.

When he comes back to Roslyn and sits at her side, wagging his tail, she clips his leash on again and tells the other two, "All clear."

They step into the narrow elevator, its walls and floor paneled with stone tiles, and ride it up to their fourth-floor accommodations. The cables creak, and the motor whines, but the box raises them up the forty-odd feet without issue.

Cali has been put in charge of the keys and opens the door. She's about to walk in when Roslyn places a hand on her shoulder to stop her again. She unclips Milo and lets him in first. When he comes back to the three waiting outside the door happy and calm, Cali and Matt step into the apartment. Roslyn follows, giving Milo praise for a job well done.

Matt and Roslyn plop onto the couch very close to each other while Milo laps up some water from his bowl. Cali goes into her bedroom, picks up her tablet right away, and opens the browser to do a search. She comes out of the room and purposely wedges herself into the small space between her friends on the couch, still tapping away at the screen.

"Tell me again, Squirrel, how you're going to find the libraries we should check out," Matt says to his smaller best friend.

"Easy, *mio amico*," she says without looking up from the screen. "We know that Darius showed up about twelve-hundred years ago, right? So we need to find a map of what Rome looked like at about that time, say 750 to 800 AD."

"CE," Roslyn says.

"What?"

"It's not AD anymore, it's CE. Instead of it being Before Christ and *anno domini,* it's Before Common Era and Common Era now." Matt and Cali look at her with skeptical faces. "What? You can't work in a library the majority of your life without learning *something.*"

"Anyway," Cali says after staring at Roslyn an extra beat. "It's hard to know what it looked like exactly because that time was almost constant upheaval. But right around Darius's arrival is about when the Holy Roman Empire was formed.

"So what we do is, find a map of what Rome looked like in 750. But instead of what you said at the hotel about finding what libraries were there then, we use that as a guide and scale what Rome looks like now to match. And one thing that pretty much hasn't changed is the Tiber River."

She holds out the tablet so that Matt and Roslyn can easily see the screen. Going back and forth between the browser windows and using two fingers to zoom out or zoom in. Once she has the scale about right, Cali puts the tablet back on her lap.

"Now we search for libraries in Rome today, and *voila*! These are the ones we should start with."

The scaled map on the tablet screen now has many red pins on it, each with the name of a library attached. Roslyn gets up to retrieve her red notebook.

"Read them off to me," she instructs Cali as her hand hovers above a new page, uncapped pen in her grip.

"*Biblioteca Angelica*," Cali says with a very American inflection. "The State Archives in Rome, *Biblioteca di Archeologia e Storia dell'Arte*. There's *Biblioteca Casanatense* and *Biblioteca di Storia Moderna e Contemporanea*."

She moves her hand around the screen tapping on each pin. "Uhh, *Biblioteca Hertziana*, the National Central Library Vittorio Emanuele II, *Biblioteca Universitaria Alessandrina*—"

"Wait," Roslyn says. "Say that last one again.'

"*Universitaria Alessandrina*."

"No, the one before that."

"National Central Library Vittorio Emanuele II."

"Click on it for more information," Roslyn says, standing up and entering the bedroom again.

"Why?" Cali calls after her.

"What was the name of the library in Portland?" Roslyn asks before reappearing with her hands behind her back.

"Multnomah County Central Library," Matt says.

"Exactly," Roslyn says. She brings her hands around to her front and is holding the wooden box that her grandfather gave to her five years ago. She opens it to find the letter from her mother. She keeps it folded, clasping it in her hands.

"I always wondered how something so important, and obviously so old, could wind up in Portland of all places. I mean, if all the good magic in the world had to come together to curse Darius, then how did it get to a building that wasn't even built for another thousand years on a continent that wouldn't be discovered by Europe for another six hundred?

"My mother may or may not have known there was a twin to *The Book,* but let's assume she did. The likelihood of me getting to Rome before now was slim to none, so she made sure to secure the copy in a place I could get to, like Portland. There'd have to be some link between there and here to give me a clue on where to look next once I found the inscription."

"And you think that both of them having the word "central" in the title is that connection?" It's clear by Matt's tone that he's not buying this completely.

Roslyn gestures with her hands and says, "Why not? My family has played everything up to now infuriatingly close to the chest, so we shouldn't overlook any commonality or link."

"Does your mom's letter say anything about the one here in Rome?" Cali asks.

"No, and I think it's for the same reason that the library in Portland was so vaguely described. In case it fell into the wrong hands, she didn't want anyone else to know about it or the twin."

"I'm still not sure," Matt says skeptically.

"Well, how about to start, we check the libraries closest to here? If nothing turns up there, then we widen the search area to include the National Central Library."

The couple looks at Cali and considers her suggestion. They both nod in agreement. They spend the next few minutes writing down the addresses of the libraries. Once their list is complete, they decide that figuring out whether to take public transit or if the libraries could be within walking distance would have to wait until tomorrow morning.

The group is still plenty jet-lagged, so after closing Roslyn's note-book and putting it on top of her wooden box they turn on the TV to watch something to wind down. But, before they reach the first commercial break of the trivia show they settled on, all four of them are out cold.

Matt has slumped down, and his head is on the armrest while Cali and Roslyn are leaning against each other. Only Milo is in a bed, stretched out on the empty king-size one that he has entirely to himself.

• 14 •

VIRIBUS

It's taking Blue longer to get back to Viribus than expected. From his spot in the small room watching over Darius, he checks his phone every couple of minutes for either a response from the parole officer or a news update. The demon is resting comfortably, no murmuring or groaning, and his face looks almost tranquil. Viribus hopes he will wake soon so he can go back to following instructions instead of making decisions.

His left arm has mostly healed itself, but the white skin that had large, swooping black markings is now an angry red. It makes the designs even more prominent and chilling. All of the demon's major injuries have scarred red. But his pale face, for the sake of his copious vanity, was spared of any wounds.

To fill the time waiting, Viribus has finished reading through all of the files for possible Victus recruits. He has ten names out of the sixteen Blue sent he thinks will be a good fit. Of course, only the demon gets the final say in who he chooses to be his soldiers.

The phone in his massive paw starts buzzing, and the screen displays "Blue" on the caller ID. Viribus answers the call and puts it to his ear.

"What have you got, Blue?" he says, not bothering to waste time with pleasantries.

"Not as much as I'd hoped for," Blue's distorted voice answers. The parole officer is a fan of speakerphone and starts every call with it. Viribus tells him to pick up the phone and shut up until he does. The next time Blue speaks, his voice is as clear as if he was in the same room as the Victus and demon.

"This is still a hot topic, and apparently, the blast at the library is being called "suspicious." I was able to get an address before I got kicked out of the system for unauthorized access. My boss came in soon after and started asking why I was even running the Portland victim's name in the first place.

"I'm not sure what's being flagged, but it's still early in the investigation. So whatever the big guy decides to do, make sure it's entirely one hundred percent under the radar.'

"Understood. I'll take it from here. What's the address?"

****

The giant has just started to doze off in the corner of the room after ending his call with Blue when he hears a weak voice call out, "Viribus?"

Having not slept much the last two days, it takes the Victus a few moments to register the sound and open his eyes. When he does, he sees Darius's gaunt face slightly raised up and looking back at him.

"Boss," he says, shifting himself closer to the mattress. "What do you need?"

The demon lays his head back down. The pitcher from earlier is still next to the bed, and Darius moves his newly repaired arm to lift it. He grits his teeth and grunts, but the pitcher stays put.

"Rotten bitch," he hisses. "Give me a drink, Viribus."

The Victus obeys instantly, lifting the clear plastic to Darius's mouth. The demon leans forward and swallows the tepid water slowly. When he's had enough, he lets his head fall back, and Viribus sets the water down.

The warrior watches as the demon takes inventory of his body. He moves his arm up to his face, inspecting the scarred red skin. He bends the fingers of his left hand and rolls his wrist. He raises his other unscathed arm to compare the two limbs. His arms drop to his sides, the minor movements exhausting his meager strength.

"Food, Viribus. I need food," he says in a fatigued voice.

The giant is momentarily taken aback. He's been loyal to the demon for many, many years, and in all his time as the demon's number two, he has never seen the black-haired man eat—not a single morsel. He's seen him put away a case of whiskey without the slightest impairment, but not once has he seen him take in any food.

"I need meat," the demon says. "Red, raw, fresh, cold."

When Viribus doesn't move, Darius's eyes flash with anger.

"Now!" he yells, enraged that his Victus is staring at him instead of following his order.

"Yes, boss," Viribus says, scrambling to his feet.

He goes downstairs and finds the same cook that made his steak yesterday. He considers making up a story that he wants to stretch his legs but decides he doesn't have to explain himself to these people and brusquely asks where he got his food from. The short man furrows his brow in confusion but answers Viribus none the less. He offers to go for him again, but the Victus shuts him down and exits the kitchen through the alleyway yet again.

Walking into the small organic market, which is severely out of place in this part of town, Viribus heads directly to the butcher counter. He does not know how much to get the boss, so he asks the man for the freshest and best steak he's got. The butcher goes through the swinging white door behind him and comes back with a four-pound cut of beef tenderloin. The meat is bright in color, and even raw makes the his mouth water.

"I'll take two and cut the second one in half," he tells the butcher. Viribus then goes through the store to pay, grabbing himself some fixings as he goes. When he gets back to the bar, he hands one of two plastic grocery bags he's carrying to the same cook, offering the same deal as the day before.

He makes his way through the kitchen and grabs a clean knife as he passes the stainless steel sink. He brings it and the other bag upstairs with him. When he enters the bedroom, Darius is quiet and motionless on the bed. For a moment, Viribus fears the worst, forgetting again that if that was the case, the body would be replaced by sulfuric ash. He stands frozen in place until, relieved, he sees the demon's chest rise and fall slowly as he breathes.

"Boss," he says quietly. "I got you something."

"I know, Viribus. I can smell it," the demon says without opening his eyes. "Well done."

"You asked for it raw, boss. It's not cooked."

The demon growls in frustration, "Just give it to me."

Viribus realizes Darius was actually praising him, and his ego inflates with delayed pride as he sits down and unwraps the raw tenderloin. He's about to cut off a piece when a red hand steals it off the brown butcher paper. He watches as Darius lifts it to his mouth and takes a large bite. The demon barely chews before swallowing and taking another bite.

Blood from the steak drips out the side of his mouth, carving a path across his cheek toward his ear. He ignores it and continues eating. He bites and chews wetly, letting out little animalistic snarls as he consumes the steak until there is not an ounce of it left.

The savage sight makes Viribus slightly sick to his stomach. He watches Darius lick each of his fingers, sucking them hard until they each come out clean. His mouth is red; blood colors his top lip and the underside of his nose.

"Away, Viribus," the demon says, waving his hand dismissively toward his Victus.

"Boss, I have news."

"It can wait. I said away, Viribus."

"But, boss I—"

"Out! I must rest."

"Of course," the enormous man says, backing out of the room. He watches the ancient fiend settle back into the mattress, lying flat on his back. The restless twitching and trembling that jerked his body while healing is replaced by the still meditation that allows him to fully recharge.

As Viribus turns away and shuts the door behind him, he's simultaneously both relieved and rebuffed at being ordered from the demon's presence.

• 1 5 •

"ROSLYN"

I wake up on the couch Friday morning with a crick in my neck and a rumbling stomach. Without opening my eyes, I can feel the warmth of the sunlight coming through the windows on my face. I smell coffee brewing, so someone else is awake also. There's the faint sound of a broom swishing across the wood floor.

The first thought my cloudy brain forms is, *Who the hell is sweeping?*

I open my eyes to look around, ready to snap at whoever is making noise this early in the morning. But instead of Cali or Matt with a broom in their hand, I see Milo sitting in front of me, wagging his tail slowly from side to side across the floor. My irritation evaporates, and I smile at my dog. As always, he's looking at me with a calm, happy expression on his face.

"Hey, buddy," I say to him. He scoots closer to me and puts his head on the couch cushion. "We've been moving around a lot the last few days, huh?"

Milo licks my hand in agreement. I drop my voice so only he can hear me.

"We're almost there, pup. All we have to do now is find the twin to *The Book,* figure out how to get it out of the library without getting caught, and draw Darius here to us so we can kill him. Then we can go home. Should be easy peasy, right?"

Milo looks at me with a blank face and one ear pricked up at attention, so I scratch him on his head and say at a conspirator volume, "Okay, maybe not peasy, but we're closer than we were."

I get up off the couch and stretch out my body. With Milo trotting after me, I walk into the small kitchen, rubbing my neck, and sit on one of the stools at the extended peninsula counter. The kitchen is bright; white tiled counters with bright blue accents, warm oak cabinets, a mosaic backsplash, and large windows let in the morning sunlight.

Matt is leaning against the counter next to the stove, holding a coffee mug with both hands. His hair is sticking out in multiple directions, and he's staring vacantly at the floor. I'm not sure he sees me, so I wave my hand across his vision; he doesn't move or even blink.

I use the moment to really look at him. His beard is growing in a bit; it's not unkempt or anything, just slightly fuller than his usual scruff. His body seems relaxed, his shoulders aren't tense, and he has one ankle crossed over the other. His eyes look troubled, though. I'm sure he's still finding it hard to believe this is his reality right now.

The toilet flushes sin Cali's bathroom, but it's loud enough to snap Matt out of whatever thoughts he was encased in. He startles a bit when he sees me sitting at the counter smiling at him, but recovers quickly and offers me a genuine smile that churns up that hurricane of butterflies in my stomach again.

"Hey," he says, his smile crowding over to one side of his mouth. His light brown eyes focus solely on me, the sunlight making them look more like gold than brown.

"Hi," I reply back quietly, suddenly bashful. I hear the bedroom door open and turn my head toward the sound. I grimace as the movement causes sharp pain in my neck.

"You okay?" Matt asks, putting his coffee cup down and moving around the counter to stand next to me.

"Yeah, my neck is just sore. I slept wrong."

"Being a pillow for Squirrel can do that. You probably need a massage. Can I?" He holds out his hands, palms up.

"Sure."

I turn around slightly on the stool and feel Matt's hands glide across my back. His fingers start to knead the tight muscles in my neck and work down my shoulders. My eyes droop, and my head lolls forward as Matt applies just the right amount of pressure.

Cali comes into the kitchen, holding her own neck, and says, "I got next."

She takes the glass pot out of the coffee maker base and pours herself a cup. She yawns a few times before taking a sip.

"Holy shit, that's good," she says.

"Italian roast," Matt replies from behind me. He massages another minute, picks his cup up off the counter, then takes a few steps away to sit at the table.

"Are you sure you don't want some, L—" I raise my eyebrows to prevent Cali from the name slip. She draws out the L and continues, "—Lllet me tell you, *Roz,* it's really good."

"Nice save," I say. "And no, thank you. Smells good, but I can't stand the taste of coffee."

"But this is Italian roast," Cali counters. "From where we are currently standing."

I shake my head, no. Cali takes another long sip and sighs. She bends, gazing into the barren fridge, and says, "I kinda wish now I didn't eat all of my biscotti yesterday."

"We should stop at that market again later today," I say. "But before that, we have decisions to make—which library we're going to today, how we're going to get there, and what we're going to do with him."

I point at Milo, who's sprawled out on his side in a patch of sunlight. He thumps his tail twice on the floor to acknowledge he heard me but likes his spot too much to move.

I know he'll be okay here by himself for a little while, but in every new place he and I have traveled to, I've been hesitant at first to leave him. At least until we're settled in, I prefer him to be with me. But everything about this time is different.

"I think he'll be okay for a few hours," Cali says, closing the fridge. "I mean, we'll know pretty quickly whether or not the library has *The Book*, right?"

"Can't we just hang out today, though? Relax and get familiar with the area?" Matt asks. "We can go to the library tomorrow. Or even the next day."

I'm surprised by Matt's response. I glance at Cali by the fridge; her eyebrows raise but quickly settle as she forces her face back to neutral. I've sensed the beginning of something brewing between them since right after she talked to Mickey at the hotel in Amsterdam.

"No, we shouldn't wait," I say, making sure to keep my voice level even though I'm slightly irked at his lax attitude. "We don't have the luxury of taking our time here. I don't know how badly Darius was injured or how long it'll take him to recover. And now that my old alias has been released, we have to be doubly sure we get to everything before he does.

"Laying low and not attracting any attention would, of course, be nice, but we have to hit the ground running. Literally.

"If Darius beats us to the twin or catches wind of where we are, that's it. It's all over."

I look at Cali, who's taken the seat across the table from Matt. I get off the stool at the counter and sit down in the empty chair between them at the head of the table, physically putting myself in the middle.

"You should call Mickey later, Cal. Check-in," I tell her.

She keeps her eyes on Matt for a long, extended beat before she acknowledges me and nods her head. Cali gets up from the table, having not said a word to her best friend, and leaves the kitchen. I hear the whip of clothing being taken down from where it was hung to dry. I turn my head, and I can see Cali toss the pile onto the couch. She shakes each item out vigorously before folding it neatly and picking up the next.

Matt sighs and gets up from the kitchen table too. He goes over to Cali and starts copying her. I hear him talk to her.

"I'm sorry," he says. "I know this isn't a vacation and that out of the two of us, you got the shit end of the deal. But I'm still trying to understand all of this. Even with everything we've seen and done, it still doesn't feel real, you know?"

Cali stops mid-fold. "I know," she says softly.

They finish folding the small load of laundry and stand there quietly for a moment. Cali picks up the clothes and moves to walk away from Matt when I see him reach out to stop her. They look into each other's eyes and have a silent conversation. They both nod and then hug, holding onto each other.

They've been friends practically all their lives, so their squabble is quieted for now. But I can't help the nagging feeling in my gut that this fragile peace between all of us isn't going to last for long.

• 1 6 •

After folding the meager amount of laundry we had, Cali returns to the kitchen table. Matt offers to take Milo for a walk. I think he wants some fresh air after the tense moments between him and Cali earlier.

I get up from the kitchen table and retrieve my red leather notebook and Cali's tablet from the living room. After powering it on, I use the Airbnb's location on maps to figure out what the closest library is. *Biblioteca Hertziana*'s pin is the closest, so I map out a route that's only a short walk. I write down the address on a new page and the streets we'll need to take to get there.

I still have a strong gut feeling that the National Central Library is the most probable location. But there is a chance I could be wrong. Plus, it's on the farther side from where we are right now.

It's too late in Oregon now for Cali to try to call Mickey; she'll have to wait until this afternoon, and there's nothing left for us to do right now but wait for Matt to come back, so Cali and I end up unpacking our bags. We put our clothes away but decide to leave the duffle bag with our supplies full. I make a mental note to replace the protein bars that we had to throw out in the Amsterdam airport. Cali shoves the bag into a corner in her bedroom.

When Matt comes back with Milo, I tell him what the plan is for to-day. He nods, adopting a more agreeable stance compared to this morning. I grab my shoulder bag and take out my wallet that's bursting with Euros. I split the money evenly between us, so in case one of us loses anything, we'll still have cash.

Into my bag, I put my now much smaller wallet with my fake California license, my notebook, and my phone even though I've turned it off for now. I have no plans to turn t back on, seeing as the person it's registered to is technically dead. I put my Roslyn James passport and some money into a buttoned pocket on my favorite rust-colored, mock-necked, ugly-but-really-comfortable jacket.

I'm dressed in jeans and a clean white t-shirt. I put my jacket on and throw my bag across my body. Cali has on bright red jeans with a navy sweater that has thin vertical white pinstripes. Matt has on dark wash jeans, a teal polo short sleeve shirt, and a gray hoodie.

I tell Milo we'll be back as soon as we can and that we'll have food when we do. I make sure his water bowl is full before closing the door. Cali locks it then hands me the keys, which go into a different buttoned pocket. We make a left out of the lobby and a quick left onto the first block, Via Nazionale. After two blocks, we make a right onto Via delle Quattro Fontane. We follow that until it becomes Via Sistina, which leads us straight to the library. It takes us less than twenty minutes on foot.

I slow down as we approach the library, thinking of how to go about this when Cali walks ahead of me and strides right into the stone building. I follow her inside and see she's at an information desk. She's taking a brochure from the hand of a very attractive young woman sitting at the desk. When Cali turns back around to return to us, her cheeks are the same color as her jeans. The woman watches her the whole way, blatantly checking my friend out.

I raise my eyebrows and look at Cali, delightfully amused at her embarrassment. She hands me the brochure and mumbles, "Shut up." The paper has a brief history of the building as well as a timetable for guided tours.

"The next tour starts in ten minutes," I say, handing the paper to Matt so he can look at it.

"Carmela said that the line for the tour starts over there," Cali says. She points to a small group of people waiting within a roped-off area.

"Carmela?" Matt and I ask simultaneously.

"Shut uuupp," Cali drawls.

I look over my friend's shoulder and say, "She's still looking at you."

"Well, she can look all she wants. She's not getting any of this."

Cali crosses her arms and turns slightly, so just her back is toward the information desk.

"Really, Squirrel? Nothing? Your cheeks are still red, and she's really hot."

I position myself in Matt's way and stare at him with a look on my face that says, *You wanna try that again?* He sees my expression and immediately tries to save himself.

"What I meant was, uh, I-I-I umm. Well, I mean, she's here..." he puts his hand at chest level. "But you, you're like here." He raises his arm as high as it will go.

"She's not in your league, babe. She's not even in the ballpark. She's little league, and you're a total pro."

"Did you just call her a hooker?" Cali asks, egging on Matt's fumbling. I realize what she's doing and play along.

"Wow, Matt. I can't believe you just said that."

"What? No! No, that's not what I meant at all!"

Matt gets more and more flustered. He can barely get two words out. Cali and I snort and burst into laughter at the same time.

"It's okay," I say, chuckling. "I know what you meant."

I go up on my toes to kiss his cheek before I make my way over to the group of people waiting for the tour. I can hear Cali snorting as she tries to stifle her continued laughter at her best friend's expense.

"Shut up," Matt says, parroting Cali's response back to her.

"I didn't say anything," Cali defends herself, struggling to rein in her laughter as they come over to join me.

****

The tour of the library is not very long, but it is certainly beautiful. There are five floors in the long, relatively narrow building. The inside has recently been updated to a more modern design with blonde wood tones and a glass atrium that runs from the ground floor to the roof.

One room has a high, curved ceiling painted with scenes of angels and statues. Thick and sturdy shelves line the room, the borders carved to look like ropes. It's exactly the kind of room you would picture when you think of a very old library in Italy.

When the tour concluded, all of the group but the three of us exited the building. Matt and Cali look at me expectantly, as if I'm supposed to answer a question I didn't know they've asked.

"What?"

"Is it here?" Cali inquires.

"I didn't sense anything. When I first walked into CCR3 in Portland, I knew immediately that it was there. And when I found the listing in the computer's database, the hair on the back of my neck stood up. Nothing like that has happened here."

"Well, maybe it's the same thing as that," Cali says.

"What do you mean?"

"Maybe it's in storage because it's so old, that's why you can't sense it. So maybe you have to do the same thing and search the library's database."

"How are we going to search, though?" Matt asks. "None of us speak Italian on even a basic enough level to even use the computer, let alone get access to staff computers for the building's archives."

My face brightens as an idea comes to me. One I know that neither Cali—nor Mickey—is going to like.

"Maybe Carmela can help us," I suggest.

"Ha, yeah, okay," Cali says. When I don't say anything, she looks at me incredulously. "You're serious? No way!" Cali shakes her head repeatedly to emphasize her point, no sound coming out of her tightly closed mouth.

"Come on, Squirrel," Matt pleads. "Help us out. Take one for the team."

"Oh, sure! 'Take one for the team,' yeah!" Cali retorts sarcastically. "And I'm sure my girlfriend will be nothing but understanding about that, so of course!"

"I think if Mickey's been able to understand everything else that's happened in the last few days, then this should be like a drop in the bucket. Right?" She remains quiet for a long time as I clasp my hands and silently plead with her.

"Fine, but later tonight, when I talk to her, *you* are going to explain this."

"Thank you, and yes, of course," I say quickly.

Matt and I watch Cali stroll back over to the desk. The young woman, Carmela, instantly engages my friend. They talk for a bit, and before I know it, Cali has her laughing and has gone around to sit on the desk next to Carmela.

"Damn, she's smooth," I say quietly. I liked Cali from the moment we met. Her personality is infectious to everyone. She's bubbly, funny, and wickedly intelligent. But I've never watched from afar as she actively charms someone.

"Always has been," Matt replies. "You should have seen her when we were in college. At frat parties, some of the guys would try to copy her moves. They'd match her mannerisms, even use the same lines, but with a far lower success rate. There's just something about that little Squirrel."

"You sound impressed, almost jealous."

"I was jealous. Until I met you. And I was more impressed with her when she met Mickey. Women still fawn at her, but Squirrel's only got eyes for her girl and no one else.'

"I know," I say. "I love that."

"I've only got eyes for my girl, too," Matt says, lacing his fingers through mine and holding tight.

I roll my eyes only to hide how much I love hearing that. I duck my head to hide my obvious delight and turn my attention back to Cali and the young woman.

I see Carmela take a piece of paper cut from underneath her desk. She writes something across the bottom before handing it to Cali. I watch my friend slowly fold the paper and pocket it without breaking eye contact with the woman. She gets up from the desk and backs away, offering a shy smile and wave as she does.

Cali turns around and walks straight to the exit of the library with an easy gait. The only betrayal of her discomfort shows itself in how wide her eyes are. Matt and I openly snicker at her expression, so as she passes us, she doesn't stop moving but frantically says under her breath, "Let's go, let's go, shut up, let's go."

• 17 •

The paper that Carmela gave Cali had six libraries on it, each with a listing on file for something called *The Book*. Two have authors attached, so we cross those off right away. The other four are listed as "author unknown" or "N/A," so those are the libraries we choose to focus on. Of course, The National Central Library of Rome is on the list, which reaffirms my gut feeling that that's where it is. But for the sake of being thorough, we decide to check each one.

Cali was able to get in touch with Mickey later that day. She'd reported that the library had been the top story the last two nights on the news, usually about how the investigation is going as they clean up the rubble and still mention Alexa Pearce as the sole person killed.

I took the phone for a minute to talk to Mickey quickly. First, I thanked her for being so understanding about everything that's happened, and then I apologized for keeping her on the outs. Next, I made sure she's safe and okay. Cali was tapping her foot, silently telling me to get on with it so she could get back on the phone.

"One more thing before I give you back to Cali," I said. "I forced her to flirt with a girl at an information desk so we could get a list that will help us find the twin.' K, bye!"

Cali's mouth was hanging open as I quickly handed the phone back to her. "What? You said I had to tell her. So I did." I winked and walked out of her bedroom.

It was mean, but it was funny too. I popped back in seconds later to fully explain everything to Mickey, making sure to place the blame squarely on my shoulders and not Cali's. Mickey didn't give either of us too hard of a time about it. *Another thing you owe Cali for "Roslyn,"* I reminded myself at the time.

For the next two days, we visited a library a day. They were all similar to Hertziana—a relatively quick walk and enjoyable, to say the least, but a complete bust.

Biblioteca Casanatense has an unassuming exterior with a stone door frame around a double, heavy wooden door. The inside is bright with windows set in an arched ceiling and dynamic tiled floors.

Biblioteca di Archeologia e Storia Dell'Arte, or the Library of Archeology and History of Art, is an impressive structure. Very castle-like in appearance. Inside, every inch of shelf space filled. There must be at least three-hundred-thousand books within its walls.

In both libraries, we needed assistance in finding what they had listed as *The Book*. In *Casanatense*, their book is encased in one of their glass displays. Right away, all three of us knew it wasn't right. Aside from the fact that I had no physical reaction that would indicate it as being *my* book, the pages are parchment, not the leather-like vellum of *The Book,* and it isn't nearly old enough.

In the Archeology library, it was in a quiet room that holds many old volumes. Normally not open to anyone but members or scholars. Cali saved the day again, charming yet another librarian into allowing us access. It was very similar to what we saw at the Casanatense, and again clearly not what we're looking for.

Today, our first Monday in Rome, we plan to go to *Biblioteca Angelica*. The only other library on the list after this is the Central Library, so we'll hopefully have found something either today or tomorrow. The Angelica Library is honestly breathtaking. From the peach-colored plaster outside it to the large open room with an arched ceiling, triple-decker shelves, and double wooden tables, to the statues, globe, and old books in glass cases inside, the place is wonderful.

We ask a librarian for help showing him the print out from Carmela. He looks a little confused at our request but walks us over to a small, round table and hands me a fifty-page tourist booklet. The English translation of the title is *The Book: A History of the Angelica Library*. It is definitely not what we're looking for, but since they are free for the public to take, I thank him and tuck it into my bag.

Walking back to the apartment we're staying in; we're all dissatisfied and quiet. I'm lost in my thoughts and am just following the bright red of Cali's pants that she's wearing again, so I don't lose them.

The only other location on the list from Carmela is the National Central Library. If *The Book* isn't there, we don't have many other options. But I'm making a mental list of all the next steps from conning a professor at a college into finding it for us, all the way down to just using my powers and projecting it to us.

I'm so lost in my thoughts that I bump right into Matt. He and Cali have stopped walking and are both looking at something. I follow their gaze, and I see them looking into a touristy store like a couple of, well, tourists.

After five years, I'm very used to the all-business mindset that comes with searching for what I need to defeat Darius, so I easily forget that Matt and Cali aren't. The two of them are very close to burning out.

The last nine days have completely overloaded them both. Between learning magic, witches, and demons are real to becoming my Extensios and fighting for their lives, international travel, and multiple disappointing days of not finding the twin, we could all use an afternoon of normalcy.

As eager as Cali is to get home to Mickey, it's hard to be in a city like Rome and not get to enjoy any of its gorgeous offerings.

"Hey guys," I say. I wait for them to turn to me before I speak again. "I need a little break from all these libraries. Why don't we go back to the apartment, grab Milo, and spend the rest of the day together?"

They both give me wide smiles and nod enthusiastically. As we start walking again, Cali's step is noticeably lighter; she's practically skipping the last few blocks. Matt wraps his arm around my shoulders, holding me close. It's our first real contact since Amsterdam, and it fills my body with warmth. We've spent the last few nights in the same room, in the same bed even, but there's still been a sort of distance between us.

The rest of the day sees us taking in the city of Rome in all its glory. We take Milo around so he can stretch his legs after his sleepy morning at home. His easy trot and curled tail provoke multiple people to say, *"Che dolce cane!"* as they pass us. They say it with smiles, so I reply with, *"Grazie!"*

The three of us take turns holding Milo's leash outside of a boutique so we can buy some more clothes. We all packed light, and having to do laundry every couple of days honestly sucks, so we buy some basics to supplement what we brought.

I try on a long-sleeved, deep blue, lacy dress that is completely impractical but makes me look and feel like a million bucks. Its price tag is only a couple of Euros short of that. Cali talks me into buying it, saying I would regret it if I didn't. We end up leaving with two bags each, all of them stuffed to the brim. *When in Rome*, I justify to myself.

We stroll the streets and find a small touristy shop with trinkets and keepsakes. The shop owner takes an instant shine to Milo, and she not only lets him into the store but pours some water into a cup for him. Her English is very good, and she forgives us of the halting, translator-app Italian we're trying to communicate with. She says she'll keep Milo company while we shop.

After thanking her, I wander around the small store. I see a shelf of carved jade reliefs and jewelry. My eyes land on a beautiful jade brooch that looks exactly like the one my grandmother had when I was little. She left it to me after she died, but it was one of the many things from my childhood I couldn't take with me when I left.

I feel a familiar, welling up inside of me, and before I have a moment to even brace myself, the thought cascades into other memories of my childhood. Almost instantly, I'm aching for my home so badly I fear I might break in half. I squeeze my eyes shut and close both of my hands tightly into fists, forcing my nails to cut into my palms. The pain as they puncture my skin anchors me to what's real and what my current situation is.

When it passes, I unfurl my stiff fingers. There are four crescent moon indentions in each of my palms. I blink a few times and reset myself. Internally my emotions are slowly settling from the churning whirlpool that whipped them up, but externally I appear completely fine and normal.

I carefully move away from the shelves of jade and over to where Cali is standing, hoping she'll keep me distracted. She's looking at handwritten poems on thick card stock in smooth, swooping calligraphy. Each one is in a plastic sleeve that has a sticker with the English translation on the back. She's staring intently at the one she's holding. She hands it to me to read.

"I've been thinking a lot lately," Cali says in a calm and steady voice. "Even before you told me... everything that you've told me and since then. And I realized that it's part of the reason why I chose to help you. I want nothing more in this world than to spend the rest of my days on it with Mickey. So when this fight is done, when we win and the world gets to keep on spinning, I'm going to do just that.

"I'm going to give this to Mickey. And then I'm going to ask her to marry me."

"Oh my god, Cal! That's wonderful!" I exclaim. I pull her into a tight hug.

I have met a lot of people in my life—both magical and human. I've been to all parts of America and seen love in all of its shapes and forms. And I have yet to see two people on this planet more suited for each other than Cali and Mickey. Their love is real and spirited and strong.

Cali takes the poem up to the proprietress and pays. We leave the shop blissfully, albeit momentarily, distracted as to our reason for being in Rome, and spend the rest of the day enjoying the happiness of that expertly crafted illusion.

• 1 8 •

Cali

On their way back to the apartment, the group passes one last shop that immediately catches Cali's eye. In the front glass window is a display of handmade jewelry and blown-glass figurines. All three of their hands are full, and they still have to go to the grocery store, so Matt volunteers to quickly bring Milo home with some of the bags and come back to meet Roslyn and Cali at this shop.

After handing Matt as many bags as he could handle, Cali quickly enters the store. In a glass case close to the back, she sees row after row of rings, necklaces, and bracelets. One ring, in particular, catches her eyes. It is made of platinum, and rather than being smooth and unblemished, it still sports the marks of the hammer that shaped it. It also has an overlay of two twisting threads of platinum that intersect multiple times as they coil around the ring.

"Salve, come posso aiutarla?"

Cali looks up and sees a matronly woman standing behind the glass case. She has long dark hair that lays across one shoulder in a braid frosted with gray. She smiles warmly at Cali as she waits for a response.

"Ciao, lei parla inglese?" Cali asks. The woman frowns in regret and shakes her head no.

"Okay," Cali says. She pulls out her phone and opens the translator app that has been getting quite a lot of use in the last few days. She types in "can I see this ring please" into the app and hits the speaker icon.

An automated voice states, *"Posso vedere questo anello per favore?"*

The woman smiles as she removes the ring Cali is pointing to from the glass case. She hands it to Cali, who looks it over and rotates it gently to see the whole thing.

"Do you like it?" the woman asks in Italian

"Very much," Cali responds.

Roslyn, who had been looking through the rest of the cases, comes over now and looks at the ring over Cali's shoulder.

"Wow," she says. "That's gorgeous. Is there a matching one? Um, pair, *incontro?"*

"Ah, sì!" the woman says. She ducks below the counter, and when she reappears, she holds an identical ring in her palm. She hands it to Roslyn, mistaking the two of them as being the ones the rings are for.

Roslyn nudges Cali with her elbow and whispers to her, "Are these the ones, you think?"

Without answering Roslyn, Cali starts typing away again in the translator app. When she presses the speaker icon, the automated voice says, *"Sei l'artista? Li hai fatti tu?"*

Roslyn looks at the phone to read what Cali asked. "Are you the artist? Did you make these yourself?"

"Sì!" the woman answers proudly.

"Perfetto," Cali says before typing again. "I'll take both. Do you have necklace chains that match?"

The woman puts a finger to her lips and thinks. Her face brightens, and she turns toward a doorway behind, calling over her shoulder, *"Un minuto!"*

"Mickey is going to love this," Roslyn says to her friend. "But what are the necklaces for?"

"You're gonna tell me it's cheesy," Cali says, suddenly bashful.

"No, I won't! I promise."

"It's so until I can see her again, I can have this reminder of her and the future I want for us right next to my heart."

Roslyn tilts her head slightly, empathizing with her friend. "I think that's sweet, kid."

The woman returns from the back room with two twenty-four inch chains. They are both also made of platinum and have a twisting rope design that complements both rings quite well. She hands one to Cali, who immediately opens the clasp and slides the ring onto the chain. She hands it to Roslyn and turns around. Her friend dutifully secures the clasp at the back of Cali's neck.

Cali does the same to the other ring but asks the woman if it could be put in a box. The artist nods and pulls out a long thin jewelry box. Cali secures her purchase inside of it, gently closing the box. Cali uses her app again to request one more thing of the kind woman.

"I'd like to ship this to America," she says before having the app translate for her.

She holds up a finger again and goes into the back one more time. She comes back with a glossy white cardboard box slightly bigger than the one holding the necklace and ring. She hands Cali a square piece of bright white card stock, a mailing label, and a pen.

"Since my letter burned up in the fire," Cali starts. "'I'm going to send an anonymous gift to Mickey. A reminder of why I'm doing this and what I'm doing it for."

She writes the address of Mickey's studio rather than sending the package to her home. She leaves the return address blank for the moment. As Cali writes a note on the card stock, the woman is taping together a red and white postal box. She lines the bottom with crumpled paper then gently puts the necklace box on top, slightly pressing down to make sure it is nestled safely within.

Cali hands her the card, and the woman puts it on top before taping the box closed and affixing the mailing label over the taped seam. She picks up the package and moves behind the glass counters to the cash register. She takes an ink stamp from the side and presses it to the mailing label's top corner. Then three more times across the box for good measure.

The woman is about to ring up Cali's purchase but then she asks, *"Qualcos'altro di cui hai bisogno?"*

Cali thinks for a minute, correctly assuming the woman is asking if Cali needs anything else. She looks around at the other jewelry and the glass figurines when her eyes land on a pile of sketchbooks and colored pencils. Her face lights up, and she dashes over to them.

"Oh, thank god!" she cries. She picks up three tins of the pencils, each a different palate selection, and two different sized sketchbooks. She triumphantly places all five items down at the register.

"We've been here for days, Roz, and I was just about to go crazy, not having anything to draw with." Cali animatedly wipes the imagined sweat from her brow and lets out a, "Whew!"

The woman calculates the total for Cali's purchases, and the auburn-haired American takes out her wallet to pay with cash. She puts the money on the small plate next to the register, and the woman picks it up from there with a grateful smile to Cali in recognition of this Italian custom.

Cali is handed a paper bag with the store's name on it. Inside are her books and pencils and an empty box for her necklace. Before leaving the store with Roslyn, she tucks the chain into her shirt. Both young women thank the older artist profusely and wave at her, still standing behind her glass counter as they leave the store.

"Where to now?" Matt asks, having made it back from dropping off Milo.

"We have to go to a market and get some things for dinner," Roslyn answers.

"Right. That fridge is bleak at best. And I want some more biscotti."

He shrugs and says, "Okay."

The three set off toward the market and only get lost twice. Cali had been thinking about sending Mickey a text telling her to expect something in the mail but had decided not to. When they are finally on track, they pass a small gym on their way to the small market.

"You should text or call Mickey, let her know something special is coming."

"It's like you read my mind," Cali says. Roslyn just winks at the shorter woman facetiously. "Wait, did you!?"

When Roslyn rolls her eyes instead of voicing a response, Cali pulls out her phone to text her girlfriend.

> **CAL:** hello you gorgeous, wonderful, wickedly hot woman you! i have it on good authority that a secret admirer of yours may have sent you a little something . your secret admirer also told me to tell you that she loves you an astronomically large amount and is doing everything she can to be with you again as soon as possible

Cali sends the message and adds another text of a dozen heart emojis. She tucks her phone away and links her arm through Roslyn's for the rest of their walk to the market, grateful for the compassion and understanding of her friend.

• 1 9 •

"ROSLYN"

Tuesday morning in Rome, I wake up with Matt's arms wrapped around me, his chest pressed against my back. I take a deep breath and think about where I was a week ago versus where I am now. And where I could be in a week's time.

I feel Matt stir behind me, and he pulls me tighter against him. He uses one finger to lightly trace up my arm over my shoulder and down across my collar bone. It trails up my neck, under my jaw to my chin.

"Good morning," he says as he turns my face toward his and gently presses our lips together.

"Mmm, morning," I say back. We kiss again. It's a light kiss but immediately has me wanting more.

I roll onto my back and pull him on top of me. I lift my head from the pillow and capture his lips again. I can feel the want building within me as I run one hand through his hair and grip his back with the other. He cups my face with his hand then runs it down my side. For a brief second, I think about morning breath, but it disappears when he drags his hand up my stomach and stops just below my chest.

I take his hand with my own, pull it up the last few centimeters, and press it down onto my breast. I start moving his hand a little, and he takes the hint. While he massages my breast, he slides his other hand down my body to the back of my knee. He pulls up, and I bend my leg, opening my hips to him.

This whole time our mouths haven't parted, and the kiss is getting deeper and deeper. I can feel how aroused he is, my own rising quickly to meet it. I move my hand from his back to his firm ass and pull him into me so I can grind against him.

He moans softly into my mouth at the new contact. The movement creates enough pressure to rile me up further but does nothing to abate my growing hunger for the man on top of me.

I push him back a little so that I can pull his shirt off. He does the same to mine. We take a second to admire each other. I openly gawk at his hard abs and defined chest. He gulps at the sight of my exposed breasts.

I pull him back down to me, and instead of my lips, Matt wraps his warm, wet mouth around my nipple and swirls his tongue around the pert bud. I gasp as my hips thrust up of their own volition. He kisses across to my other breast and shows it the same attention.

I want his mouth again and forcefully pull him back to mine. As soon as our lips touch, I dip one finger underneath the band of his boxers. The rest of my hand slowly follows. When I close my hand around his erection, Matt lets out a long moan.

"Oh my god," he rasps as I start moving my hand to stroke him. I slightly tighten my grip and slowly increase the speed of my movements. Matt responds instantly. His hands are all over me, setting my skin on fire, and I no longer have control over the movement of my hips.

He puts one hand on my stomach to stop my pulsing hips. He pulls his mouth away from mine and painfully slowly begins to move the hand from my hip to where I'm aching for him to touch me the most.

"Is this okay?"

"Yes," I pant.

My whole body is tingling in anticipation of his touch. Matt is inches away, almost where I *need* him to be, when there is a scratch and whine at the door from Milo and a knock from Cali.

"Come on, guys, time to get up," she says through the door. Milo barks a couple of times to help make Cali's point.

Matt groans and drops his head to my shoulder. I let go of him and remove my hand from his boxers. He removes his own hand, having never reached its destination, and kisses my collarbone before moving back over to his side of the bed.

I put on my shirt and hand him his. I don't let go when he reaches for it and pull him in for one last kiss.

"To be continued," I say. His eyes are still hooded with want as he stares at me.

"Definitely."

I leave Matt to have a minute to situate himself and go into the kitchen to help Cali with breakfast. She gestures to a carton of eggs and an empty green bowl. She's whisking pancake batter in a white one.

We work seamlessly side by side, flipping pancakes and scrambling eggs. Milo is again sprawled out in the perfect patch of sunlight on the kitchen floor. When Cali accidentally drops a piece of eggshell next to his head, he doesn't even shift to investigate it.

The two of us set the table and bring our breakfast over before we sit down. Matt comes and sits next to me at the table. He's dressed in some of the clothes that he bought yesterday, and his hair is wet from a shower.

"So, what's the plan for today?" Cali asks with her mouth full.

"We go to the only place left. The National Central," I say.

"What do we do if it isn't there?" Matt asks.

I think for a moment as I chew. "Cross that bridge when we get to it."

Cali and I get ready for the day while Matt washes the dishes. I take Milo on a walk around the neighborhood. On a mostly empty street, I start talking to him quietly so that only he can hear me.

"This should be the last stop, Milo, and we'll finally know where it is. It's going to be a good day, pup."

We make our way back to the apartment, and while we wait for the elevator, I start talking to Milo again.

"You're being real good about being in a new place and moving around so much, but I think we'll be able to go home soon. And I'm sure Grandpa can't wait to see you again."

He wags his tail frantically when I mention home and my grandfather.

Cali and Matt meet us at the door. After telling Milo to behave and pausing in the door long enough to see him jump onto the couch and curl up to fall back to sleep, the three of us set off for the library. We go right out of our building heading toward the Termini, or Metro Station, to catch the Metro Linea B bus. It drops us off right in front of the National Central Library.

The property is enormous, with a large sprawling building and perfectly manicured lawns. Across from a small, stone amphitheater is the main entrance with a bank of sliding glass doors.

Inside everything feels exceedingly familiar, and I'm struck by how much it reminds me of the Central Library in Portland. As soon as we walk in, I have a noticeable reaction. My body breaks out in goosebumps, and every hair stands on end.

"Holy fuck, it's actually here," I say, repeating the same thought I had in CCR3 more than fifty-eight-hundred miles away.

"How do you know?" Cali asks from behind my right shoulder.

"I have this tingly feeling. Look," I hold out my arm and pull my sleeve up to show her my prickly skin.

"That's incredible," Matt says off of my left shoulder. "It's like it's calling to you. Can you tell where it is?"

"Not exactly," I say, taking a few steps to the side. "It's like something is pulling me, but it's hard to pinpoint exactly where it's coming from."

We walk throughout the library, Matt and Cali tailing me as I follow the intensity of what I feel. It's as if there is a rope around my waist, directing me where to go. It is a much stronger sensation than when I first entered the sub-basement of the Portland library. So much so that I wonder if this one is actually the original and the other was the twin.

I stop stone-cold in front of a gallery filled with some of the oldest books in the library's collection. Glass display cases with plaques dot the room. There are canvases hung on the wall and statues of both marble and clay placed throughout the space.

Beyond that, I can't say what else is in the room because everything around me fades away as I figure out exactly where *The Book* is.

Next to a large, intricate globe that is three times bigger than the one at the Angelica is a glass case. There is a plaque attached to the lid of the frame with a name and the date of when pieces of the collection inside were donated.

I run my eyes over the items in the box from left to right. Inside it are over a dozen books—some are open to pages covered in vivid, hand-drawn images, others are closed and stacked, and there off to the side on its own, is something I've never been happier to see.

The Book is sitting there in this glass case for all the world to see. I glance up at the other visitors, and some of them gloss over the cases, not looking at the contents twice as if they don't see anything of true importance inside them, just some old books.

It looks exactly the same as the twin version in Portland except for one distinct difference. The cover and spine are the same dark maroon, but instead of being completely blank of markings, designs, or words, there is something written across the front.

"Hope will heal the world," I say to myself with a soft smile.

• 2 0 •

DARIUS

The demon was recovering quicker than he anticipated. Although he's quick to tire and parts of him still ache, he's back at his usual perch in the far right corner of the bar. It's almost two in the afternoon on Tuesday in Atlanta, and he's been set up here for the last few hours waiting for Viribus to come back with the transport potions. The bartender certainly didn't look happy to see him but served him quickly and quietly none the less.

The demon sips his whiskey, the alcohol momentarily warming his cold blood. Undoubtedly he isn't back to fighting form yet but is getting closer by the minute.

Darius has spent the last four days in what could be called a meditative coma. Demons do not technically sleep, but they go into a deep vegetative state that allows them to recover. Before Darius could get any of this rest, his body spent the two full days prior to doing nothing but healing to reach a strong enough point where the coma would not kill him.

He depleted the entirety of his body's energy to heal himself. Once the demon was far enough along out of immediate danger, he needed to replenish that energy simply to enter his restful state. Viribus providing him with the raw beef tenderloin did just that.

Once Darius had woken up, Viribus caught him up on what he's found out. First, the Victus told him he was moaning some sounds repeatedly, but he couldn't figure out what they meant. Darius tried desperately to remember but had no recollection of saying anything or what it could mean.

Then he told the demon the name that the girl was using in Portland: Alexa Pearce. Viribus reported that he had Blue look into it, but because of some suspicions the fire investigators have, all he could get was a name and an address. The hired hand in New Orleans was unable to access any of the other now secured information on the girl.

Viribus still has the two transport potions he had made when the plan was to meet the demon at the portal after the girl was dead, but for the two of them, it's only enough to get there. Once they investigate all they can in Portland, they will be traveling to New Orleans to meet the men whose files Blue sent to the lieutenant. The Victus set about cooking another batch while Darius was recovering, and now the potion is hours away from being ready.

Until it is, Darius will sit on his stool at his bar, warming his body with whiskey and shaking his head at once again being sentenced to wait.

****

The demon has lost track of how many bottles he's drained and the time that's gone by, but by the large grin on Viribus's face and his oafish eagerness to get across the bar, Darius knows the potions are ready.

"Good to go, boss," the Victus says, confirming the demon's suspicions.

"Perfect," Darius says as he stiffly stands. "We'll go upstairs and leave from the bedroom. You have the exact address?"

In his substantial hand, Viribus holds up a piece of paper. The black-haired man swipes at it with his permanently scarred left hand and tucks it into a pocket in his blazer. He stumbles slightly from fatigue but angrily shakes off the help his warrior offers. Once in the room, he instructs Viribus to grab the files Blue sent over.

Each man puts an additional small glass vial of the black potion into their pocket. They'll use that for their next stop after they find what they need in Portland. Darius puts his red hand onto Viribus's shoulder after taking out the paper scrap with the witch's Portland address. Closing their eyes, the two men drink the black potion, and Darius says their destination.

They suddenly feel an aggressive pull on their bodies. Similar to having a thick rope coiled around them from head to toe and being dragged by a semi. The pull increases in strength until both men feel as though they will be severed across their middles. All of this happens instantaneously but feels like minutes to the two. When they open their eyes, they are standing inside the building of Alexa Pearce's apartment directly in front of her door.

Darius uses his powers to unlock the door with a wave of his hand, and the demon, with his Victus following close behind, enters it cautiously and quietly. They stand still, listening for any movement. When he is sure they are alone, Darius steps away from Viribus and slowly sweeps his gaze across the living room in front of him.

A folded blanket is draped across the back of the couch, a pillow angled in each corner. A bike leans up against its back. The coffee table is clear, except for three remotes neatly lined up. The power strip for the TV, cable box and BluRay player has been unplugged and pulled away from the outlet. The shades are down, and a lamp next to the window is attached to a timer.

He turns his head toward the small kitchen on his right and sniffs. No odors from garbage or spoiled food reach his nose. He strides over, sees a sink void of dishes and an empty garbage pail. He runs his fingertips along the counter through a week's worth of gathered dust.

"She didn't come back here," he says to Viribus from his place at the sink rubbing his finger against his thumb. The demon looks around, trying to find anything that could explain where the girl went and with whom. The counters are clear of mail and clutter, so Darius turns back toward the living room. He sees a short hallway and makes his way to it.

As he gets nearer, his sensitive nose catches something. He goes into the bedroom on the left, and the scent gets stronger. It's not the scent of a human but of an animal. It must be from that bothersome mutt that protects her. Darius starts tearing the room apart, searching for anything the girl might have left behind, any clue where she was headed.

Viribus stands at the door and watches, keeping one ear tuned at attention. Darius waves his arm, and the mattress flips through the air. Even in a still weakened state, his telekinesis power easily smashes it into the wall. He pulls his arm back to do the same with the box spring but freezes. The top corner of the fabric is folded back, revealing a hidden compartment. The demon sticks his hand in, hoping to find something, but it's empty.

He steps back now and whips his arm out, making the boxspring pop up. With a roar of frustration, he slams it into the mattress up against the wall hard enough that it breaks apart. Some pieces of the wooden frame puncture the mattress, others clatter to the floor. He steps into the empty bed frame and kicks over the nightstand. Darius's hand heats up, ready to burn the clothes left in the closet when he freezes again.

A bright white rectangle on the floor catches his eye like a homing beacon. It's lined, the top half covered in messy writing. He picks it up carefully. His eyes squint as they dart back and forth, trying to read the words that were clearly written in great haste.

"What is it, boss?"

In a monotone, Darius reads out loud, "*Et factum est cum terminus non est alter ex parte.*"

The Victus has a blank look on his face, no comprehension of what the demon just said.

"It means 'it will end only when one is dead by the hand of the other.' It means she actually fucking found *The Book*. But this has been copied from it, so she must have written it down when she found it and left it where it was." The demon sneers as he remembers seeing the girl dive into rubble after one of those giant glass boxes blew apart. "Pity it isn't still around."

He crumples the paper and lets it turn to ash in his hand, suddenly frustrated. "I don't understand," he grumbles to himself, thinking out loud. "It was in the library, and it was certainly destroyed, which means she has nothing left to guide her. But she didn't fight like someone who was cornered.

"I'm missing something," he growls. The demon's temper flares, and he storms out of the bedroom. He overturns the TV in the living room, the sound of the heavy plastic falling to the floor spurring him on. His hand sparks to life, and a ball of fire is hurled at the couch, causing it to explode into two burnt pieces. The bike is flung into the kitchen. It lands in the sink; the metal frame bent backward on itself at a sharp angle. Singed stuffing and down feathers float through the air, coating the room.

He turns on his heel and goes back down the hallway but enters the room on the right instead. Darius roars as he throws his arm across his body again, flipping both the bed and boxspring simultaneously. He picks up a lamp and throws it at the wall.

"What am I fucking missing!?" he screams, his temper raging at full force. The same way he did in the library days ago, he claps his hands together above his head and slowly pulls them apart. In the space between his red and white hands, a swirling orb of fire starts to grow. Darius's anger has taken over, and he's ready to burn the entire building to the ground.

"Hey! What the hell are you doing?!"

The voice comes from the hallway outside of the room. Startled, Viribus whips his hand out and uses his own power to pin the person to the wall. The breath is thrust out of the person's lungs as their back connects with the drywall. The Vctus exits the bedroom keeping the person in place; Darius follows and looks over the intruder.

"So much for keeping watch," he snarls at Viribus as he walks by.

Darius sees the goliath holding a scrawny man against the wall. He has greasy hair and is wearing a dingy white tank with jeans. He's doused himself in cologne rather than bathe today, or the last two days prior, it seems. The demon tilts his head, sizing the man up. Based on his first impression, he'll either be an asset or a roadblock that will need to be torn down.

"And who might you be?" Darius asks quietly, getting as close as his nose can handle.

"T-Tyler," he says in a frightened voice. "I live downstairs. Who the hell are you?"

"Gold star for you," the demon purrs. "Hell indeed."

"Wh-what?" Tyler's face grows more profoundly terrified.

"Oh, how rude of us. My name is Darius, and this is Viribus; he's my guard, as you humans might say."

"Hu-humans? What are you doi—"

"Tell me, Tyler," the demon cuts him off. "Who lives here?"

Tyler squints at the men. Viribus starts to close his fingers into a fist, and Tyler's eyes snap open. His breath quickens and becomes shallow; pain ripples throughout his body as his ribs contract under the crushing strength of Viribus's powerful magical grasp.

"I'm sure you're feeling a quite unpleasant sensation right now, Tyler," Darius says. His voice is smooth, like a used car salesman trying to unload a lemon. "That'll stop when you talk to me, of course. So, who lives here with Alexa Pearce?"

"Cali... Jacobs." Tyler gasps as the giant's grip tightens even more.

"Very good. Now, when was the last time you saw this Cali Jacobs?"

"Not for at least a week. But she could be staying at her girlfriend's place."

"And where is that?"

"I don't know." Viribus closes his hand tighter, and Tyler yelps in pain. "I really don't know! Stop! Please! I don't know where she lives, but I know where she works! I'll tell you where it is; I'll take you myself, just let me go. Please."

The demon sneers as the man dissolves into a sobbing mess pleading for Viribus to release him from his powerful grip.

"Excellent."

• 2 1 •

Cali

Cali watches Roslyn as she stands frozen in front of the wood and glass display case. She notices her best friend's face brighten into an amused smile, and her head shake slightly. The overhead lights reflect off of her glasses, whiting out her eyes. Cali moves to the case and looks into it. At first, her eyes are drawn to the open pages that show the highly detailed hand-drawn illustrations before she sees exactly what Roslyn is staring at.

"'Hope will heal the world,'" she says quietly reading from the top cover. She bends her head toward the taller woman and adds conspiratorially, "I'm sensing a theme here."

"Hmm, what gave it away?" Roslyn deadpans back.

"Okay, so, like, what do we do now?"

"I'm not sure, but whatever it is, we have to do it right. No mistakes."

"Do you still have the pages that you copied?" Matt asks. Cali notices his hand graze Roslyn's hip. She tears her eyes away to stave off the quickly aroused jealousy.

She reminds herself that she is happy that her friends have found and finally admitted how they feel about each other. But seeing them together and their ability to just reach out and touch each other only serves to remind her of the fact that the person she loves more than anything else in the world is back home on the other side of it.

"I do," Roslyn answers as she pats her hand on her bag twice.

"Well, why don't we use this library's obviously vast resources and translate it?"

Matt glances around at the people near them before he drops his voice and says, "There has to be more in it than Extensios and Victus. I think we can all agree on that. So now that we have *this*, we can start translating that."

"What do you think?" Roslyn asks after she turns to face her friend.

"I think Moose has a point. After twelve-hundred years, Darius probably has, at the very least, a working knowledge of Latin. Between the three of us, we've got squat. So I say we level the playing field as much as we can."

"Exactly," Matt says as he knocks on the glass lightly. "No one else knows what this is. And if Darius knew it was here, none of us would be, right? So it must be safe here."

Cali hooks her arm through Roslyn's elbow. 'Let's spend the rest of our time here preparing ourselves the best we can. The next time we face Darius, I don't want to have to hide behind glass cubes in a cinderblock room. I want to actually beat him."

After standing in front of the case for another ten minutes, ample time for Roslyn to be secure enough in its safety to pry herself away, the three of them head back through the library to set themselves up in the bright and open space of the computer lab. The trio picks out three open computers and sit down. Roslyn takes out her notebook from her bag and opens it to the folded pages she handcopied in Portland.

She divides the pages between herself and Cali while Matt tells them he's going to focus his search on what the world was like when Darius first showed up, looking throughout history for anything that might clue them in to where the portal is.

Navigating the computers is more difficult than any of them anticipated. First, they have to traverse through the Italian labeled application symbols to open a new browser window. Thankfully software icons act as a universal language. Once they are able to get to a translation website and set the languages "from Latin" and "to English," Cali and Roslyn get to work.

Matt has more trouble doing general searches. He ends up having to switch to the one computer designated for English on the other side of the lab. Matt goes over and sits right down to get to work.

Translating is tougher than they think. Roslyn's handwriting is hard to read, and there is some guessing involved in getting the translations to make sense. Plus, all three of them are fighting off the crash from the peak of adrenaline after finding *The Book.*

After a few hours of work, the three go somewhat cross-eyed from staring at the bright screens so intently. Cali sees Roslyn take off her glasses and pinch the bridge of her nose. She looks at her best friend across the room and sees him rub his face a few times and blink rapidly.

"Roz, this screen is making my head split. Maybe we call today a win and come back tomorrow?"

Roslyn opens her mouth as if to protest, but a yawn catches her off guard. She shrugs and nods in agreement. Cali gets up and goes over to Matt to let him know they're getting ready to go.

Before logging off the computer, Matt prints out pages with some information he thinks will help them in their search for the portal. As they're leaving to head back to the apartment, Matt inquires about a membership.

Somewhat satisfied with the bit of work they got done today and very happy that they finally found *The Book*, the three get set to leave the library. Before they leave, Roslyn tells Cali and Matt to wait.

"I have to go look at it one more time. It feels like there is a lasso around me, dragging me back to it."

They walk back and inspect the box containing *The Book* again. Roslyn stands stock still in front of it, gazing through the glass at the volume that was written over a thousand years ago just for her to one day find. Cali knows they're looking at the key to getting their homes, their families, every part of their lives back.

And it's hiding in plain sight.

After another few minutes of just quietly staring at the tome, Roslyn finally steps back and turns away from the case. Matt and Cali follow her out of the library. They stop just outside the glass doors and all turn their faces up toward the brilliant azure sky. Rather than take the bus, they decide to walk the entire way back to their Airbnb apartment.

They've found what they've spent the last five days desperately looking for, so they grant themselves another well deserved half day to relax. The three of them take a long walk through the neighborhood with Milo. They visit Parco del Colle Oppio and the ruins of the Colosseum. They blend in seamlessly with the crowd, camouflaged by the excess of other tourists at the site.

Matt and Roslyn hold hands periodically as they walk around. Whenever Cali catches a glimpse of it, she can't help the rumbling of jealously that fills her chest. She repeatedly extinguishes it and keeps reminding herself that it's only a little while longer until she sees Mickey again.

But when Matt puts his arm around Roslyn and whispers something into her ear, making her cackle loudly with laughter, Cali's jaw clenches, and she steers Milo a ways away from the couple to cool off. Rationally she knows they aren't flaunting their relationship in front of her, it actually seems like they are trying to keep it on the down-low, but it doesn't change how she feels.

Cali sits down on a bench and calls Milo to her. He sits down in be-tween her feet, panting faintly from the warm sun. She mindlessly pets him while she daydreams about her girlfriend. This is the long-est they have ever been apart since they started dating around a year ago.

She's so wrapped up in her thoughts that she doesn't realize Matt and Roslyn have sat down on either side of her. She doesn't snap out of her own head until Roslyn taps her on the shoulder, making her jump slightly. She gives her friends a half-hearted smile before looking back down at her hands running through Milo's fur.

"Whatcha doing?" Roslyn asks playfully.

"Thinking."

"Penny for your thoughts, then?"

"You're overpaying," Matt says with a straight face.

"I take offense to that! I have very advanced thinking going on in here. I've always been smarter than you, Moose. You know that."

"No, you've always *thought* that you are smarter than me."

"That's 'cause I am."

"Oh yeah? Prove it, Squirrel."

"I will!"

"Staring States?"

"You bet your ass!"

"Ready? Go!"

The two of them face each other and stare into the other's eyes as they alternately say state's names without blinking, looking away, or hesitating. When Matt gets stuck and can't remember another state, Cali points at him and says, "Ha! Loser!"

She jumps off the bench and hops back and forth on her toes with her hands in the air. She mimics a sports announcer's voice, complete with an echo, and declares her victory.

Matt groans loudly in defeat and crosses his arms. He ignores Cali's outstretched hand and offers of "Good game." He stands up and takes Milo's leash in his hand.

"Come on, Milo," he says with a huff. He gives a gentle tug to get the dog to follow him.

Roslyn gets up off the bench too and high fives Cali. They link arms and follow Matt and Milo. He turns around to say something to the girls, but when Cali sticks her tongue out at him, he scrunches his nose and turns back around without a word. Cali doesn't notice the wink and smile Roslyn gives her boyfriend, but she's definitely in a better mood than when she sat down.

****

When they return to the apartment, they are all physically and mentally exhausted. They plop down on the couch to rest a little before making something to eat. They turn on the TV, and just like their first night in Rome, all four of them, including Milo, quickly fall into a deep sleep.

When they wake up, it's dark both in the apartment and outside, just before 9 P.M. Cali does the time change math in her head and realizes it's almost one o'clock in Portland.

While Matt and Roslyn start making something for a late dinner by American standards but normal for Italy, Cali goes into her bedroom to call Mickey. The phone rings twice before Mickey's soft, silky voice comes over the line.

"Hey, baby," she coos.

"Hey, you," Cali responds.

"I was just thinking about you."

"Oh yeah?"

"Yeah. I got this incredible gift in the mail at work this morning postmarked from Rome signed by a secret admirer. I'm wearing it right now, and I can't wait to thank her."

Cali hums into the phone, briefly picturing what that might entail. "I expedited it to make sure it arrived in time for our anniversary next week."

The phone is quiet for a moment as the brunette realizes Cali won't be home before then.

"Do you know when you'll be back?" Mickey asks timidly. Then quickly adds, "I really miss you."

"I miss you, too. So much. And actually, we've had some progress on that."

Cali describes to Mickey the libraries they've gone to and how they finally found *The Book* today. She's about to ask Mickey what she's been doing when Mickey cuts her off.

"Babe, I got to go. Our least favorite person just walked into the studio, and he's waving at me to get my attention. He's got some guy with him, looks like as much of a creep as Tyler. Probably told him he could get the guy a discount or something. But I'll call you right back, okay? I love you."

"Wait! Don't hang up!"

Cali puts the phone on speaker and jumps off her bed. She throws the door open so hard it bangs into the wall leaving a small depression in the plaster. She runs into the kitchen, sliding in her socks to stop in front of Matt and Roslyn.

"Say that again, Mick." She holds out the phone, but no sound comes from it. The call was dropped.

"What is it? Is everything okay?" Roslyn asks, alarmed.

Cali looks at the phone in her hand then back at her friends. "I don't know."

PART TWO

• 2 2 •

DARIUS

He watches the tall, olive-skinned, and frankly, gorgeous woman walk toward him and Tyler. She's wearing tight legging capri pants and an oversized t-shirt cut into a tank top. And other than a necklace with a ring on it, she's not wearing any jewelry. One hand holds her cell phone. The brunette doesn't look remotely pleased to see the scrawny man standing next to him, but she attempts to mask it as she reaches the pair.

"Mickey, hey," Tyler says. He looks her up and down, practically drooling at the sight of her.

"Tyler," she says in an even tone.

Tyler licks his lips, making no attempt to hide his obvious attraction to the woman. She crosses her arms in front of her chest at his open stare. Darius can see that she's getting ready to kick his ass if he doesn't stop. And he has no doubt she could easily do it, and then some.

He clears his throat and gets the thin, angular man to snap out of whatever wet dream that has momentarily taken over his synapses.

"Right," he says. "This is Da—"

"David," the demon says, extending his right hand for a shake. He keeps his left hand out of sight in his pants pocket. "David Sanger. I'm an investigator with the Portland Fire Department."

"Oh, of course," Mickey says as she shakes his hand. The demon sees the moment she notices the tattoo-like markings on his hand. Her eyes follow the swirling black until it disappears under the cuff of his shirt.

"I understand you were friends with Alexa Pearce?" he continues without letting go.

"Uh, yes, I was."

"I'm very sorry for your loss, miss."

"Thank you, I appreciate that." She looks down at her hand, still gripped in his, "Is there something I can do for you?"

"Oh, I'm sorry," the demon says, releasing her. He's playing the bumbling nice guy quite convincingly. He even rubs the back of his neck as if he's uncomfortable with his next question. "I believe you know her roommate, Cali Jacobs? That the two of you are, um, that is, you and Ms. Jacobs are involved?"

The woman's eyes narrow slightly when Darius mentions the roommate. She straightens her posture to extend to her full height and puts her hands on her hips. The demon recognizes this as a subconscious protective reaction. *Typical human,* he thinks.

"Involved?" she asks with a raised eyebrow.

"Uh, yes." The demon glances at Tyler before continuing, "That you two are in a romantic relationship."

Mickey stares at Tyler with barely contained contempt for a long time. Her jaw clenches as she returns her piercing blue eyes to the demon and clears her throat.

"Were," she says.

"I'm sorry?"

"Were, not are. Cali and I were in a relationship. However, it ran its course, and we ended things over two weeks ago. Though I don't see how that is relevant to your investigation, Mr. Sanger."

Tyler can't hide his surprise as well as the demon can. He feels his anger spike at being misled by the imbecile standing beside him but keeps a level face.

"My apologies," he says, unable to stop the quick glare at Tyler.

"You see, I'm trying to reach Ms. Jacobs to discuss some things with her. I'm afraid I was knocking on her door for quite a long time before this young man came out to assist me.'

"What do you need to talk to Cali about?" the woman asks, crossing her arms again and locking her laser-like gaze onto the demon. She doesn't flinch or avert her eyes as the black-haired man looks back. Darius can see at that moment that he's lost whatever small trust his cover story had granted him.

"Well, if she knows why Ms. Pearce was in the library that night, the names of any of her family members, things of that nature. Tyler here thought you might be able to assist with that."

Mickey doesn't answer right away. She takes a long, slow look at Tyler with that same intense stare. The man visibly wilts under her scrutiny.

"Well, like I said, we broke up," her soft voice hardens with a distinct edge. "I haven't spoken to her since then. If you want to leave a card, I'll give it to her if she stops by. Not that it's any of your business, but we didn't leave things on the best of terms, so I doubt she will."

"That won't be necessary," Darius says too quickly. "If you do see her, though, please tell Ms. Jacobs to get back to me. I've left a card with my contact information under her door."

"Of course you have. Well, if that's it, then I must get back to work. I do have clients waiting. Mr. Sanger, Tyler." She smiles falsely at the men and lets her face return to an annoyed frown before she turns and walks away.

"Thank you for your time," Darius says to Mickey's back. He grits his teeth at the dead end and exits back onto the street where Viribus is waiting. He grumbles under his breath and starts walking down the street.

He snaps his fingers, and Viribus grabs Tyler by the arm, dragging him along. The demon makes his way back to the witch's apartment building, but this time kicks in the door of Tyler's place on the second floor.

The shades are drawn, making the place as dim as dusk. It has the same footprint as the apartment above it, but this one smells like body odor, weed, and sour milk. Viribus stoops his head to enter behind the demon and easily tosses Tyler onto his ripped dingy couch that's mostly held together by duct tape.

"My, my, my," he says, pacing back and forth in front of the man. "If that wasn't a complete waste of my time."

He reaches into his jacket and pulls out a pack of cigarettes. He puts the unfiltered, black papered stick in his mouth and lights it with the tip of his hot and glowing finger. The same tactic he used when first showing Damon his powers just weeks ago.

He takes a deep drag and exhales the smoke through his nose. The cigarette dangles from his lips as he drops his right hand to his side. It continues to glow instead of returning to flesh color.

"I'm disappointed and, frankly, no longer have any use for you."

His hand continues to brighten until it's glowing white-hot. A ball of fire suddenly appears in his palm. The color drains from Tyler's face as his body is encompassed by fear.

Darius raises his arm as if to throw, and Tyler bolts from the couch. Viribus slams him back down with his power and holds him in place. Darius takes a step closer to the couch. All he has to do is toss the flaming orb, and Tyler, along with the sofa, will be instantly incinerated. The bony man's breathing is fast and shallow. Sweat is pouring off of him; he looks on the verge of passing out.

Darius takes another step closer. Instead of launching the fireball, his red scarred hand whips up from his side and backhands Tyler across the face. The man is so shocked and terrified that he begins to sob.

"Please don't hurt me. Please," he cries. "I'll do anything you want! Just please don't kill me!"

Darius slaps him again to stop the crying. He bends over and brings the hand holding fire right next to Tyler's face. The man tries to shy away from the flame as he feels it singe his cheek. Darius claps his hands together quickly and loudly, making the fire disappear.

"Listen closely, you soiled, piece of shit. I have business to take care of somewhere else, so if you want to keep breathing and living this pathetic, worthless excuse of a life, you will listen closely.

"You are to follow that woman. I want to know everything she does every minute of every day. If she sees you, confronts you, or files a complaint with the police about you, I'll know, and I will be very disappointed and will be back here like *that*."

The demon snaps his fingers, and another blazing sphere appears in his hand with a small pop. Tyler cries out and tries to push himself away from the heat of the flame. Darius tosses the ball to his red hand and grabs Tyler by the throat. He squeezes the flesh slightly. The man is so terrified he doesn't even realize that Viribus has lowered his arm and is no longer telekinetically holding him in place.

"You will write down any person she talks to or any phone call she makes. From this moment on, your life is only about keeping me from killing you."

Darius tosses the ball of fire up and down in his hand a few times. Tyler's eyes follow along with every inch it moves.

"And the way you keep me from killing you is to do exactly as you are told. Do you understand?"

"Y-y-yes."

"Yes, what?" the demon growls.

"I understand."

"Do well, Tyler, and I will reward you with more power and wealth than you have ever known. Understand?"

"Yes."

"Yes, what? Speak up now, Tyler."

"Yes, I understand."

"Good. We'll reach out to you and let you know when we'll be back here."

"H-h-how?" he stutters out.

"Don't worry about it. Now, Viribus, I believe it's time to go, isn't it?"

The large oaf silently nods as he steps closer to his boss. He takes his phone out of his pocket to type a text and hits send. Within seconds he gets a return notification. He reads it and nods again at the demon.

"Right. Well then. Tyler, it's been tolerable, to say the absolute very least. Be a good boy now."

Darius pats Tyler on his raw cheek a few times and steps back from the couch. He and Viribus take out the small glass vials filled with the rest of the transport potion. They both swallow the liquid in one gulp and close their eyes. The demon says an address in New Orleans, and in less than an instant, both he and his Victus have vanished, leaving a shell-shocked Tyler frozen to his couch.

He stays completely still reliving everything that happened today. The more he thinks about it, the more ridiculous it becomes, and the less Tyler believes any of it was real. He relaxes into the cushions chalking the day up to a bad batch from his dealer laced with something extra.

He leans forward and picks up the remote to turn on the television, ready to forget the day. His arm freezes in midair, and his hand starts to tremble as his eyes land on the still smoldering black cigarette in the ashtray on his coffee table—a physical reminder that nothing about today was imagined.

• 2 3 •

"ROSLYN"

I watch Cali call Mickey back repeatedly as she paces the kitchen, but her girlfriend never answers. I'm beginning a mental checklist of what we'll need to take and what we can leave here if we have to transport back to Portland right now. Thankfully Cali's phone rings and the display lights up with Mickey's picture.

I close my eyes and sigh. I stand from the table and put my hands on my best friend's shoulders.

"Be calm," I tell Cali. "Let her talk and listen carefully if she's trying to give you any clues."

We stay standing across from each other, leaning on the table. Cali answers the call and puts the phone on speaker. "Hello?"

"Hey, baby," Mickey says. Her voice is tranquil and gives no indication that she's in trouble. Cali's body sags with relief at hearing her girlfriend's voice. She collapses into a chair as Mickey continues talking.

"Sorry about that. I just wanted to make sure Tyler and that guy were completely gone before I called you back."

"Mick, it's me," I say. "You're on speaker. Do you know who was with Tyler?"

"Oh, hey, Lex." I let the name go for the moment. I'm more concerned with who Tyler brought to her studio.

"He introduced himself as David Sanger and said he was an investigator. He asked me about both you and Cali, then tried to dodge when I asked him to elaborate."

"What did he want to know?" Cali asks. Her voice is a little squeaky; she's obviously worried about someone finding and questioning Mickey but failing to hide it.

"He asked if you and I were friends, and I said yes. He said he was sorry for my loss and then quickly started asking about you, Cal. Said he's been trying to reach you to inquire about if you knew why Lex was at the library that night or how to contact any of her family members."

Cali and I look at each other with raised eyebrows.

"I told him you and I broke up over two weeks ago and that I hadn't heard from you," Mickey continues. "He looked surprised, and for a split second, he looked angry with Tyler. If I had blinked, I would've missed it."

"Did he mention anything about me?" Matt has stayed quiet up until now, but I can see he's becoming concerned, probably wondering about his mom and brother.

"No, he only mentioned Cali," Mickey answers. Her tone becomes reassuring, almost motherly, and I can see Matt sigh in moderate relief.

"What did this guy look like? Anything, like, unique or different about him?"

"He was a pale, white guy, kind of lanky. Taller than both me and Tyler, but not by much. His eyes were dark, and his hair was jet black. He kept one hand in his pocket and held onto mine with the other when I shook it. He had big black tattoos on his hand, kind of swirly and tribal, and they went up under the cuff of his shirt."

I try to keep my face as impassive as possible, but my mind is thousands of miles away, back in the sub-basement of the Central Library in Portland. I see Darius in front of me, the reflection of the multiple scattered fires making his dark eyes glow as he taunts me. I see his marked hands as they launch balls of fire at my Extensios and me.

The more I replay images from the library in my mind, the more certain I am that the man with Tyler was definitely Darius.

Fuck. The demon who is searching for me and wants to kill me showed up in person at my friend's business. How can I tell Cali or Mickey without both of them panicking?

I know I can't, so I don't.

It's selfish of me, but I'm not ready to face him again just yet. *You're a coward,* I immediately think. *I know I am. But I need more time to translate* The Book *and get it in my possession, so I can learn how to completely beat him.*

"Right now, I think it's okay," I say, making sure my voice stays level and doesn't betray my true feelings. "If you notice that Tyler is hanging around more, or you see that guy again, let us know, and we can go from there."

Cali nods her head at every word I say, soaking up my reassurances and running with them. And a part of me instantly hates myself for deceiving my friends in this way.

"Yeah, yeah, baby. It's okay."

She squeezes my arm and takes the phone off of speaker. She walks back into her bedroom to finish her conversation. I sit down heavily on one of the chairs, thankful that Mickey is okay but already weighed down by another secret added to the vault in my chest.

Matt sits in the chair opposite me and places a steaming plate of chicken parmesan topped with fresh mozzarella on a pile of linguini in front of me. I had completely lost my appetite, even forgotten that we had started cooking, but my stomach comes to life when I smell the food. I thank him for finishing it and dig right in. I don't come up for air until the entire plate is finished. I lean back in my chair and sigh.

"That was really good, babe. Thanks," I say with a satisfied smile.

"You're welcome," he responds softly. With a clear of his throat, Matt continues, "What would you say to the two of us going out for a real meal? Not one cooked by someone trying to remember what he saw on an episode of Lidia Bastianich."

I pretend to think for a minute, if only to keep my pounding heart from making my voice shake. *How does this guy keep making me feel this way?* I ask myself.

"What did you have in mind?" I ask quietly.

"I thought that we could go to a nice dinner at a restaurant I saw nearby on one of my walks with Milo." He gets up and comes around the table behind me to massage my shoulders. I let my head fall forward, enjoying his touch again.

"Maybe afterward, we could walk through the neighborhood, then end the night with some nice wine."

"Honestly, that sounds wonderful," I admit. I hear the rattle of the knob on Cali's bedroom door, and Matt removes his hands. I miss them the instant they're gone. He goes over to the stove and makes a plate of food for her.

Cali sits down in the chair next to me. She doesn't look as worried as when she was waiting for Mickey to call her back, but she certainly doesn't look carefree. In fact, she looks sad. Matt puts the food in front of her. She picks up a fork but just pushes it around, not taking a bite.

KERRI MCLOONE

I know Cali well enough to know that she's rehashing every second of her conversation with Mickey in her head. I also know that she'll talk to us when she wants to, but right now, she doesn't.

Knowing it'll get her to take at least one bite, I reach over with my own fork for a bite of linguini, but Cali quickly swats my hand away, becoming possessive of her food. She squints at me as menacingly as she can manage and takes a large bite of the chicken, keeping her scowl in place as she chews.

I imagine she has a similar reaction to the one I had before because once she tastes it, the plate is finished in minutes.

• 2 4 •

After Cali finished eating, the three of us cleaned up and played a few games of cards to wind down from the day. Matt went to bed first, but Cali and I stayed up a little while longer. Milo must have sensed that Cali was still anxious about Mickey because he never left her side.

When her eyes started to get droopy, I called it a night and told her to go to bed. Milo came to me for some kisses and a good scratch before sleepily following Cali into their bedroom.

Three hours later, I'm still wide awake in bed, just like in Amsterdam. I keep thinking about how I didn't tell Cali that the demon we're hiding from and the man who visited Mickey today are one and the same.

I replay the questions she asked me and the answers I gave her. Each time the words echo through my head, my answers sound ever more hollow.

As she dealt out another hand of cards, she had asked, "How do you think Tyler got involved? Do you think the guy with him was a Victus?"

"I don't know. But maybe it's like the guy said, he's been trying to reach you and came across Tyler while waiting for you."

"But, reach me about what? What is there even to investigate? The building was completely destroyed."

"Well, Alexa Pearce technically doesn't exist, so it could be that they're trying to find a family member for a death notification and can't."

She looked at me over her cards, still not entirely at ease. We played a couple of turns in silence before she started asking more questions.

"Do you think he was a Victus, though?"

I thought about it before answering. I decided to go as close to the truth as possible if nothing else than to convince myself of what I was saying.

"Honestly, he could be. We knew that once my alias was released that it was a possibility. But Mickey sounded okay, normal. She didn't seem worried or upset."

"I guess." Cali picked up a card from the deck and tapped it on her chin. She tucked it dead center of her hand before she discarded one. Then she said something that still has my stomach knots.

"God, I miss her, though. I mean, we've spent nights apart, but I knew she was only a neighborhood away. If I really wanted to see her, I could just catch a cab and go. But this is just way harder than I thought it would be."

I took my turn silently, letting her talk.

"But I miss things I didn't think I would. Like, her feet are always cold, you know? And she'll tuck them into my pant leg sometimes when we're watching TV. I say it's because she's old. She says she has poor circulation. And she is so stealth about it that there's no warning either. Just, boom, all of a sudden, freezing cold toes tucked up into my pants." She chuckled then, so I smiled with her.

"Earlier today, when we were sitting at the computers in the library, I felt something cold on my leg, and I looked down, expecting her legs to be tangled with mine. But it was just the metal leg of the table."

She stopped then and just kind of stared at her cards until her eyes glazed over. She shook her head and blinked a few times.

"Sorry," she said as she picked up a card to take her turn.

"Don't apologize. I know you miss her. I do too. But you'll see her soon." I threw my last card down and put my hand on the table face up. "Gin."

"I thought we were playing Rummy."

"Gin Rummy."

"And those aren't the same thing?"

"Not technically, no."

"Then, I want a do-over because we were playing two different games."

"No way, don't be such a sore loser."

She scoffed, "I take offense to that."

****

I close my eyes and roll from my back to my side in bed and try to get in a comfortable enough position that my brain quiets down. The sound of a soft snore next to me makes me open my eyes again. I look at Matt, fast asleep on his back with his mouth slightly open. I smile, thinking about our upcoming date and where he's possibly going to take me.

And just like that, my self-reproach triples.

At the hotel in Amsterdam, I told the man lying next to me that we have to be considerate of Cali and the fact that Mickey was back in

• 145 •

Portland. That we're not on vacation, and we can't just relax and make out or steal time to be alone together.

And here I am, between what almost happened this morning and our planned dinner, doing the exact opposite of that.

Plus, you're lying to Cali, "Roslyn." Again.

It's useless to try and fall asleep; my brain won't allow it. I sigh as I get out of bed. I grab a blanket before I open and close my bedroom door as quietly as I can, pad across the apartment in my socks, and lightly knock on Cali's door. Not loud enough to wake her if she's sleeping, but enough that it'll get Milo's attention.

I pause to make sure Cali hasn't woken up, then slowly open the door. My dog is lying across the foot of the bed. His tail starts to sway back and forth, but I put my finger across my lips to shush him, and the motion ceases.

"Come on, pup," I whisper. He gets up quickly, jostling the bed in the process. Cali stirs, so I hold up both hands to stop him. Milo freezes in his tracks, holding one paw up in the air.

"Nice and easy, bud."

Milo gradually starts moving off the bed. I snicker to myself as I watch my dog slink down to the floor. He looks over his shoulder at Cali as he slowly comes out of the room. I hold my fist out, and Milo bumps it with his nose as he walks by. I close the door to the bedroom as softly as I can.

We plop onto the couch, and my dog tucks into my side. I scratch the top of his head, grateful for the comfort he always seems to bring me. I don't turn the TV on, choosing to sit in silence and create a plan.

After a stretch of time just sitting there, I'm not any closer to figuring out what to do about Mickey's safety than I was when she described Darius over the phone earlier. I need to talk to someone— someone who can guide me. Or just tell me what to do.

I need to talk to my mom.

With a blanket tucked under my arm, I throw my jacket and my sneakers on and grab the keys. I leave a note on the coffee table if Matt or Cali get up and sees that Milo and I are gone. I don't bother putting his leash on but give him the "side" command. Milo dutifully takes his place at my left knee. In my pajamas, I climb the two flights with Milo up to the roof access door.

I carefully open the door, unsure of what will greet me on the other side. I let Milo out ahead of me to check, and when he comes back without indicating there is something to be wary of, I step out of the doorway.

The roof has been set up like a patio. Two lounge chairs and a bench surround a circular glass table. There is a stone off to the side of the door-jam, so I move it over to prop the door open and prevent us from getting stranded up here.

I started doing this about two years into my search for *The Book*. My mom and I are very close and always have been. She's my sounding board, my role model, my rock.

Being so cut off from my family was extremely tough when I first set out on my search. But I knew that if I dwelled too long on what I was missing, there was a chance it could fracture the protection spell that's keeping my entire family off of Darius's radar.

This is the solution I came up with as a way to talk to my mom without actually talking to her: I speak out loud as if she's right in front of me; I don't imagine she's there or ask anything that I need a direct answer for; I only do it when I'm alone and usually outside on a roof or balcony; and, if I start to wish for her in any way, I cut myself off and go back inside. Doing it this way grants me permission to talk out whatever problem I'm dealing with without jeopardizing her safety.

I sit on the bench and pat it for Milo to jump up next to me. I close my eyes and start the same way every time, "Mom, I know you can't hear me, but I just need to talk to you for a minute."

• 2 5 •

I must've fallen asleep after talking things out because the next thing I know, I'm gently awoken by someone rubbing my arm. I open my eyes and see green ones staring back at me. It must still be very early because the sun is just starting to poke above the horizon. The beginning of the day's light brightens my friend's face with an amber glow.

"What time is it?" I ask.

"A little after six," Cali tells me. "What are you doing up here?"

Talking to my mom, I almost answer but catch myself. "I couldn't sleep, so I thought I'd come up here for some fresh air. Must've done the trick."

My body is tight from my time in the cold night air. I stand up stiffly and stretch myself out as much as I can. I expect to hear Milo's tags jingle as he stretches then shakes himself out. When I don't hear anything, my eyes dart all over the roof, looking for him. My dog isn't here.

"Where's Milo?" I say in a panic.

"Relax, Roz. He's inside," Cali tells me, putting her hands on my shoulders to calm me. "You were dead to the world, so I brought him inside and came back up to wake you."

Dead to the world? Way to keep your guard up, "Roslyn." What if it wasn't Cali that woke you? I shake my head to clear my thoughts.

"Oh, okay. Thanks."

"Of course. Now, do you want to tell me what you're really doing up here?"

Busted.

I look at my roommate and bite my lip. But after my "talk" last night, I came to realize that everything I am doing is to keep everyone as safe—and as calm—as possible.

Darius may have paid a visit to Mickey, but he didn't do anything to her. Yet. And telling Cali that it was him would only cause her to panic. She'd have every reason to say that Mickey is in danger and cash in on my promise to go back for her if that was the case.

But we can't go back right now because if we did, two things would definitely happen: Darius would be alerted not only to where we went but where we came from. And then he'd come after us hard and fast.

Laying low and monitoring the situation from here is the smart way to do it for now. I think it's the only way. It gives us a chance to work more on *The Book,* it keeps Darius in the dark as to where we are, and it keeps Mickey's story about her breakup with Cali plausible.

"Just needed to think is all," I tell her.

"What about?"

I knew she would ask that, so I have an answer all queued up, ready to go, "*The Book.*

"I mean, there has to be something more to it than just how to defeat Darius. I haven't had any training in my powers, but I could still face him without losing anyone. And he's, had what, over a thousand years here? Plus, who knows how many back where he came from. He still lost both of his Victus and was injured himself. We must be missing something, and I think that whatever it is, it's in *The Book*."

"I totally agree."

I'm caught off guard. I'm expecting Cali to call bullshit rather than agree with me right away. "You do?"

"Yeah. Based on the little we've both translated so far, it's all about who Darius is and what will happen if he wins the battle between good and evil. And being a demon that's older than dirt, he knows all of that already. He's counting on it. I think there's something more in *The Book* itself that we're missing."

"Well, the one in Portland got blown up, and the one here is in a protective case, so we can't exactly get our hands on it."

"Yes, we can," Cali says as if it's obvious. "We just have to steal it."

I stare at her for a moment, then start to laugh. Obviously, she's joking with such a ridiculous statement, but Cali doesn't laugh with me. "Wait, what?!" I shout. "Absolutely not. We cannot steal *The Book*!"

I move across the roof and go back through the door into the stairs. I quickly trot down to our apartment on the fourth floor. Cali follows me, calling my name the whole way.

"Roz! Roz, wait. Just listen to me."

I push through the apartment door that's propped open by the deadbolt and go right into the kitchen at the back of the apartment for a drink. I whiz by Milo, who is curled up on the couch, without stopping to pet him. That is highly unusual behavior from me, so he immediately hops off the couch and follows right on my heels.

I rip open the fridge and pull out the large glass bottle of sparkling mineral water. I'm drinking right from it when I hear Cali come into the kitchen, still trying to plead her case.

"Roz, please just listen," she says. "I have an idea, and it could be the key to figuring out what we're missing."

"What's going on?" Matt mumbles as he comes into the kitchen, rubbing the sleep from his eyes. If I wasn't so wired thinking about Cali's plan, I would note how he's able to be both sexy and adorable simultaneously.

You don't have the time for that right now! I yell at myself.

Cali turns away from me to talk to him. "I'm trying to tell Roslyn that I have a plan." She crosses her arms and turns back to me before continuing, "And she's getting all bent out of shape before I even explain it to her."

"What's the plan?" Matt asks. He moves to position himself exactly between us, much like I did when he and Cali got into it a few days ago.

"Grand theft in a foreign country," I say drily. I return the bottle to the fridge and cross my arms.

Matt's eyebrows shoot up to his hairline, and he turns just his head to look at Cali. The two of them have a silent conversation, the kind that is only possible between friends who have spent almost every day together for the past seventeen years. Their eyes search each other's faces, and their expressions morph in place of words. Finally, Matt looks up to the ceiling, and his jaw juts forward, turning his mouth down, but his face looks more contemplative than irked.

Right then, I know it's just become two against one. Without moving an inch, Matt has taken sides.

"Look," Cali begins. "I really do have a plan, okay? Can we all just take a breath, and I'll explain while Moose cooks breakfast."

"It's your turn!" Matt protests.

"True. But, if I make breakfast, then I'm probably going to make a mess and drop stuff, and you know you'd just have to come in behind me and clean it all up."

"You're right. It's easier if I do it myself," Matt sighs as he takes out a pan for eggs.

I can't help but smirk at how easily she just played his own need for everything to be clean and organized against him. Cali winks at me devilishly as the two of us sit at the table, the tension from before defused. I relax into the chair while Cali lays out her plan.

"Okay, here's the deal," she begins. "I'm pretty sure that if we can get special permission or access to it from someone who works in the library, then we could literally walk out the front door with it."

"Oh, really. And who exactly is going to let us do that?"

"I'm not proud of this, but Carmela."

"Squirrel!" Matt says scandalously from his spot at the stove.

"I know. And before we do anything, I need explicit permission on this from Mickey. But I'm pretty sure that I could at least talk Carmela into talking to someone for us. I think that if we can just get our hands on *The Book*, then we could go from there."

"What does that mean?" I ask.

"Well, you forget dear friend, that I am very good with my hands."

"I lived across a narrow hall from you for a year. I don't think I will ever forget that you are good with your hands."

Cali can't help the impish smile that appears on her face. It grows as we both hear Matt groan at being reminded of his pseudo-sister's sexual prowess.

"What I mean," Cali continues. "Is that when you have my level of skill, it's relatively easy to duplicate something with clay and paint."

"Wait a minute," Matt says, turning from the stove, silicone spatula in hand. "Tell me if I understand this right. You're saying that you think you can sculpt a replica of *The Book* that is good enough to sit on display inside the biggest library in Rome undetected as a fake?"

"Yep. And something is burning."

"Shit!" Matt whirls around and wraps a dishtowel around his hand. He bends and pulls a pan of bread out of the oven. The bread is black and smoking. He tosses the whole thing in the sink and runs some water over it.

When it's clear the apartment isn't about to catch on fire, Cali turns back to me and asks, "So what do you think, Roz?"

• 2 6 •

"I need to know why you are so sure this will work, that we'll even get the *chance* to do this."

"I had a dream last night," Cali says. "And it felt so real that I would've sworn it actually happened."

Cali explains her dream to me. She was in the library at night with everything dark. Candles were arranged in lines on the floor, directing her from the front entrance to the room where *The Book* is on display. Just the glow from the candles was enough to guide her.

She could smell incense, melted candle wax, and herbal tea. She heard bells softly ringing, the sound closer to wind chimes. She also heard a woman's voice with a distinct accent, telling her what to do.

My friend explains how she was instructed to open the case and take out *The Book*. She took one of the candles from the floor and brought it closer to illuminate the pages. What she saw was the Latin text within *The Book* disappear, and hidden English text written in gold materialize in its place.

Cali says that there was also a woman in the room. She was dressed in colored robes of emerald green, ruby red, and sapphire blue. She had frizzy, blonde-streaked hair that was held in place by a gold chain with diamond-shaped charms across her forehead. She wore four gold bangles on each wrist, and her wide-set lime-green eyes seemed to glow even in the dim light.

The woman didn't say anything to Cali. Even when she asked who the woman was, her voice just echoed through the large room, and she was given no response. She just stayed where she was standing, but even without words, Cali said she knew what the woman was telling her to do.

A bag suddenly appeared on the table, and inside of it was a duplicate, a replica of *The Book.* Cali took the copy out, put it in the case, and put the real one into the bag.

Cali finishes telling me about her dream, but at this point, I'm only half listening. I know who the woman was in her dream, and it's the last person I ever expected to show up and offer guidance, which is definitely what this was.

For her to reach out in this way is both good and bad. She is someone who has notoriously stayed away from any conflict or clashes within the magical community. So if she's taking an interest now, it means I'm on the right track, and her suggestion disguised as Cali's dream can only help me.

The disadvantage of her making contact is that she knows where I am and used magic to create a link to me. If that connection had been intercepted while it was live, then that could have been game over immediately.

It was an enormous risk she took in reaching out, so I can't ignore the obvious direction she wants me to go in. I have no choice but to admit that we have to steal *The Book* from the National Central Library of Rome.

"That wasn't a dream Cali."

"What do you mean it wasn't a dream?" she asks. She glances at Matt, who's turned from the stove with a matching confused look on his face. I suck in a deep breath and blow it out all once.

"I mean just that. It wasn't a dream. It was a magical projection sent to you by someone I haven't seen or spoken to in a very, very long time. Emel, a distant cousin of Romani descent."

Cali's eyes expand in fear. She glances quickly around the kitchen, looking to see if there is anyone else here.

"Someone was in my head?!" she asks in an anxious voice. "Are they friend or foe? Do we need to leave? Moose, get the bags!"

Matt whirls around from the stove again, ready to spring into action. I stand up with hands held up and loudly say, "Everybody stop. She may not be the warmest of people, but she would never directly wish anyone harm.

"Trust me. If she's taking the risk to get in touch with us now, we need to pay attention to it. And she could have reached out to me but didn't. It takes a lot of magic to do what she did. And she kept all of us off Darius's radar by contacting you instead of me.

"At the very least, we should explore the suggestion Emel is offering. Do you remember anything else from the dream?"

"Nothing other than what I told you. She wants us to create a replacement *Book* and swap them for each other."

"Hidden text," Matt says quietly as he scoops eggs from the pan onto plates. "I would've never even thought of that."

"Me neither," I say honestly.

"So assuming I can get Carmela on board, and I'm sure I can," Cali winks, underlining her flirting skills when it comes to the fairer sex. "Then what?"

I sigh and momentarily take off my glasses to rub my eyes. "I don't know. We need to go back to the National Central Library and work out the details from there before deciding on anything for sure."

"Yes, but first, breakfast," Matt says, putting a plate in front of each of us piled high with eggs and some freshly toasted bread. The ruined first batch that was burnt to a blackened crisp is still sitting in the sink.

"*Mangia, mangia!*" he says.

I take a bite and instantly feel the crunch of a piece of eggshell between my teeth. Based on Cali's sour expression, I think she's gotten a piece too.

"Uh, babe?" I say carefully. "I think you might've gotten some shell in the eggs."

"Either that or chunks of the pan broke off while you were cooking," Cali adds with less tact.

"Oh no, really?" he asks innocently. He takes a bite and says, "Huh, mine are okay."

He stands up from the table and picks up his plate. He scoops up another bite onto his fork and holds it next to his mouth. "Interesting. Maybe someone should've just made breakfast today like they were supposed to."

He shrugs and puts the fork in his mouth. He winks as he backs out of the kitchen. In the living room, he spins around in his socks with the fork still in his mouth, eases onto the couch, and lifts his feet to cross them on the coffee table.

Cali gets up and pulls the garbage over to the table. She scrapes both of our booby-trapped eggs into the pail leaving only the toasted bread on the plates. Shaking her head, she opens the fridge and takes out two yogurts.

"What's it called when the player is actually the one who gets played?" Cali asks me in a stage whisper as she sits back down with a pair of spoons.

"Karma!" Matt calls out from the couch.

• 2 7 •

DARIUS

After spending an afternoon with Blue going over the files of the parolees he had picked out, rather than stay in the cramped, one-bedroom apartment, Darius spends the night walking the streets of the Bayou. He stops at a liquor store to get a bottle of whiskey to warm his blood as he wanders.

He sips his drink as he silently watches three drunk men come to blows after being thrown out of a bar. He bumps into someone as he passes a food truck causing the person to choke on their food. The demon looks over his shoulder, and dead, black eyes connect with wide, frantic ones for a brief moment before Darius turns and walks on.

Having satisfied his thirst with the entire bottle of whiskey, he then satisfies his hunger for flesh with multiple bodies in the Red Light District. When he returns to Blue's place at sunrise, he sports a smear of lipstick on his neck, and his clothes smell of another man's cologne.

Darius sits in Blue's living room, chain-smoking cigarettes until the parole officer and the Victus get up. He doesn't move from his spot on the sagging, yellowed couch as they make breakfast and get dressed. The demon only gets up once the two men are ready to head to the parole office over an hour later.

Yesterday, Blue had called each of the sixteen men that have been selected. He gave them explicit instructions to be at the Probation and Parole Office at 10 A.M. So when the three men arrive just before nine, none of them are surprised to see the lobby seats completely empty.

As they pass the front desk, Blue tells the same young man who was there when Julius arrived weeks ago to put everyone in the conference room and buzz him only after all sixteen are there.

"Of course, Officer Blusseau," the young man replies. Shortly after ten o'clock, the phone on Blue's desk beeps with the youthful voice informing them that all of the parolees have arrived.

Walking into the conference room, the majority of the men stand out immediately. Darius can just smell it on them. Career criminals, an assortment of individuals who won't resist evil running through their veins. He turns his attention to the others that don't fit the bill.

He doesn't say anything while quietly circling the table, sniffing every so often. He points five men out as he loops the group, and Blue tells them they can wait for him in his office. Darius moves into the back corner of the room while the men leave. Three doughy white men of medium height and age, a tall but wiry black man, and a slightly older, balding Latino man silently get up and leave the room.

One of them opens his mouth, ready to question what's going on, but Darius's black, unblinking eyes silence the man's voice in his throat. Blue stands in the hallway to make sure the men don't leave the building but actually go into his office as instructed. He steps back into the conference room, and Viribus moves into place, blocking the door with his considerable size.

The parolees left around the table range in age from twenty-two to forty-seven. While their skin tones vary greatly, they predominantly resemble Damon in build and height. Their skill sets range from laundering to larceny, long cons to quick conflict. Each man possesses an ability that could aid Darius not just in battle but in other areas of business.

"Gentlemen," Darius says from his corner. He clears his throat and begins circling the table again. "You are here because you possess certain characteristics selected due to their... beneficial nature. In return, I have chosen to give you the opportunity of your lifetime—to be endowed with great power, and if you perform competently with that power, vast wealth as well."

When he circles around to a recently vacated chair, Darius sits. He reclines slightly and gazes slowly at each man, every pair of eyes in the room locked on him.

"This is your one chance to withdraw. If you are not interested, or I do not seem like a man who can deliver on his word, then you are free to leave right now." Darius stands and leans on the table. "But, if you stay, you do what I say the *moment* I say it. Without question.

"If you don't," Darius says, lifting his red scared hand and allowing a ball of fire to appear. "You will suffer the consequences."

The demon is not worried about this revelation of his powers. He, his Victus, and the parole officer know that anyone who chooses to leave at this point will be incinerated before they have the chance to tell someone.

He nods to Viribus, who slides over and opens the door to the conference room. Darius scans the men's faces in front of him, and of the eleven, only one stands to leave. From the files Blue sent over, the demon recognizes the man as Collin Kings. Blue catches him by the shoulder and whispers something in his ear. The man shakes his head as he exhales a large breath. He looks down at his shoes for a moment and nods. Blue claps him on the back hard. He turns and sits back down in his seat. Viribus closes the door.

"Excellent," he says. "Now, regarding your parole and its inherent restrictions, Blue will be arranging it so that those conditions do not interfere with the tasks I assign you."

He stands to his full height, radiating complete control as he says, "My name is Darius, and from this point forward, gentlemen, you belong *to me*."

****

The three men are sitting around Blue's desk after he talked with the parolees Darius dismissed earlier. The others are still sitting in the conference room. They've been told to wait there until otherwise instructed.

"Boss, if I may," Viribus begins but waits for a nod from Darius to continue. "I think it would be wise for us to get a private hotel room. Somewhere you will be able to recover from each transition without being bothered."

The demon is in agreement with his Victus yet still pauses. Giving Viribus credit too quickly would start to cultivate the idea that he can start making his own decisions. He's done enough of that lately. And if Darius has learned anything in his centuries on this earth, it's that men convinced they are right, more often than not, are the same ones who are devastatingly wrong.

Darius nods his head just barely. His red hand comes up to scratch an itch on his forehead. He stares at the angry scarring for a moment before addressing both Viribus and Blue.

"Find a decent location," he instructs gruffly. "While I am coming back from each transition, Blue, you are in charge of the men who have not yet been switched. Viribus, you'll be making more transport potions and keeping the new boys in line.

"I want to get this done as quickly as possible, which means two transitions at a time. I'll rest at least a full day after each one to recover but more likely closer to two. If it's longer than half the third day, you must rouse me to force food in. Viribus, you know what to get."

Blue's eyes widen in surprise. Much like Viribus thought up until a few days ago, he believed that demons don't eat. The parole officer looks at the Victus, who is nodding in understanding, and decides if the giant knows what Darius means, it's good enough for him.

"I'm going out for a cigarette. When I get back, I want the hotel booked and the men ready to leave. The first two will be turned as soon as we check-in."

"Sure thing, boss," Viribus says, taking his phone from his inside jacket pocket.

As Darius stands to leave, Blue gets up with him and opens the door. As the pair step out into the hallway, they can hear Viribus making arrangements on the phone. Before going down the hall to the conference room that the parolees are waiting in, Blue clears his throat to speak to the demon.

"Uh, sir?" Darius pauses and waits for the man to say something. Blue fumbles over his words, having never had the demon's full attention land directly on him before. He freezes under the intimidating gaze. Not knowing exactly how to start, the man blurts, "Do you need a light?"

The demon just looks at him blankly without responding.

"Oh, right, 'cause you've got the..." he holds up his hand and wiggles his fingers. "I guess you don't then." As Darius turns away, Blue hops his compact body around to get in front of the demon again. "Um, sir?"

"What is it?" Darius growls, annoyed at being blocked by the tiny man.

"I'd like to ask you something, sir, and no matter your response, it will not affect my, uh, association with you." Blue swallows hard and musters up all of his courage to say, "I would like to become a Victus. Sir."

The demon waits to see if the man will plead his case, but Blue stands quietly with his chin up. Darius admits to himself that adding someone with Blue's networking connections could prove beneficial to finding and killing that dastardly witch. Especially now with Julius gone.

"I'll consider it," he says.

Blue smiles and lets out a quick breath in relief. When he stays standing in front of the demon with the conversation now over, Darius frowns.

"Move."

"Right, yes, of course. Sorry, sir. Thank you." Blue scurries down the hallway and opens the door rejoining the group of convicts.

Darius ducks into the enclosed stairwell to light up. He takes long, deep drags and exhales upward toward the next set of concrete steps. He finishes the cigarette and tosses the butt into a corner without bothering to smother it.

Tendrils of smoke continue to curl upward as the demon opens the door to the hallway and goes back into Blue's office, ready for the creation of his new brood of Victus.

• 2 8 •

"ROSLYN"

After Matt's karmic breakfast prank, I take Milo for a nice stroll to try and loosen my body up. It's been years since the last time he and I spent the night on a bench, and the last person to wake us certainly wasn't as friendly or as welcome as Cali. I chase the memory away with a glance down at my dog. He is happy and relaxed, the two most important things when it comes to Milo.

He's easily settled into the new apartment. Even though it's been a while since he's been left alone all day, Milo's taking it in stride. I know that Milo's been given special training, but he's still a dog, and it's hard sometimes for his people to adjust to new places.

He's looking around as he trots happily in front of me. He hasn't shown any signs of alarm at our surroundings or anyone we've come across. All of that helps me relax just enough to let my mind really consider Cali's idea.

She is an incredible artist, I tell myself. *And if anyone can make a replica that could pass as the real thing, it's her.*

I've seen her work up close and personal, including a drawing she did of a severed hand shortly after I moved in with her that scared the crap out of me. She innocently asked for ice, and when I opened the freezer, there it was. It looked so realistic and was angled to appear three dimensional, covered in frostbite and frozen blood.

I was so shocked that I didn't hear Cali come up behind me until she yelled, "Boo!"

I screamed and slammed the freezer shut as I ducked down for cover. Cali's laughter and Milo licking my face to soothe me clued me in that I had been played. It was intended as a harmless prank but definitely made my heart pound.

Cali even kept the hand, and we used it to prank Mickey a couple of months or so later. Only that time, Mickey walked into our apartment while Cali and I were mid-argument over what to do about it.

It was a little less harmless the second time around—Mickey held it against us for over a week.

I turn the corner with Milo, and we make our way back toward our rental. On the way back, I think again about Cali's dream and the clear message we've been given.

Stealing *The Book* could go wrong in so many ways. But I've seen what Cali is capable of creating, and if we're able to pull this off, then no one will know someone made a switch until the next time it's removed from the display case.

When I get back to the apartment, Matt and Cali are ready to go, so I take a quick shower and get dressed in jeans and a ribbed long-sleeved, dark green shirt. I grab my bag and jacket and tell Milo to be good before locking the door behind me.

The two of them are waiting for me downstairs in the lobby of the building. Matt has a backpack over one shoulder. I look at it with minor confusion, and he explains that it has Cali's art supplies.

Matt walks a few feet in front of Cali and me as we retrace our path from yesterday. I link my arm with hers and shorten my stride to match. She is, after all, four inches shorter than me.

"Remember the hand you drew, and we scared Mickey with?" I ask her.

"Of course, it was some of my best work."

"You think you could do a drawing like that of *The Book*?"

"I could, but anything other than the correct angle to the paper, and it would look completely wrong. It'd be more convincing as clay. I could really match the texture and appearance of age and everything."

"How long do you think that will take?"

"I'm honestly not sure," she says. "Maybe a week or two?"

"Was there clay or anything at the store where we got your sketchbook and colored pencils from?"

"No, that wasn't really an art store. It was more like how in a drugstore back home, there is a section with school supplies that happens to have colored pencils. You don't go there for that stuff in particular, but you get it just to have some.

"But don't worry, Roz. We're in *Rome*. There must be dozens of stores that have what I need."

Walking into the building, Cali takes her bag from Matt and peels off to go back to the room housing *The Book*. Matt goes to the computer lab and sets up at the one English-language computer.

Before meeting Matt in the lab, I go to the large front desk and enquire about joining the library. The young man sitting there looks up as I approach. He offers a wide, friendly smile as he says, "*Buongiorno, signorina.*"

"*Buongiorno,*" I say. "*Scusami. Parli inglese?*"

"*Si.* Yes. How may I help you?"

"Thank you, sorry about the language barrier. Um, my friends and I inquired yesterday about joining the library, and we were told to speak to the head librarian?"

"Ah, of course. *Mi chiamo Philippe*, I am the head librarian. Do you live here in Rome, *signorina*?"

"Um, no. But we'll be staying here for a while, I think."

"Wonderful and welcome! For membership, I will need your name and uh—*come si dice, i indirizzo*—uh, location? No, no, um, place?"

"Do you mean where I'm staying? Address?" I ask, trying to be helpful yet not offend him.

"*Sì. Scusa signorina, grazie*. Address."

He hands me a membership form, and I ask for two more. He hands them to me and says, "Of course. *Ancòra due*."

Philippe helps me fill out the information, translating for me when I run into trouble. As I'm handing the form back to him, he says for me to keep it and use it as a guide for my friends.

I put the paper into my bag and say, "*Grazie, ciao!*"

"*Prego!*" he calls after me.

As I walk into the lab, Matt flags me down from the computer he's sitting at. I walk over and drape my bag across the chair at the station closest to him. I take off my jacket and put it over my bag, making sure it, and the very important contents within, are out of sight. Matt turns in his chair to talk to me.

"Check this out," Matt says in a typical library whisper. "I figured that if Darius created a portal from his world to ours, it might've created some sort of physical trace, right?"

"Good assumption," I nod.

"So I've been looking to see if there were any occurrences at the time that could've been interpreted as a natural disaster like an earthquake or fire, or something, but was actually the arrival…" He looks around to make sure no one's listening before whispering even quieter, "…of a certain someone.

"I haven't found anything yet," he says. "But I have a good feeling about it."

I can't help but smile at him but don't say anything.

"What?" he asks with a smile of his own.

"Nothing," I say. "Well, not nothing. You're just really cute."

"I'm not cute. I am rugged and manly and handsome."

"I'm not arguing with that. You also picked up your whole life to come with me on this absurdly unbelievable adventure. And, you're just really cute."

I lean down and give him a quick kiss. Matt's hand comes up immediately to hold my cheek as he kisses me back.

"I'll, uh," he stops and clears his throat before speaking again. "I'll keep looking."

I nod and go back to the table that I reserved with my bag and jacket. I can feel Matt's eyes on me while I situate myself, but I don't look at him. It's hard enough ignoring *The Book* pulling me toward it to add in denying my attraction. I let out a slow, deep breath, organize the papers in front of me, and get to work.

• 2 9 •

Cali

As Roslyn picks up the forms for library membership, Cali sets her bag down at a table inside the gallery where *The Book* is on display. She takes out her sketchbook and her tin of Faber-Castell colored pencils. Leaving both items on the table, Cali moves over to the display case keeping her possessions within her line of sight. Making sure the flash is off, she uses the camera app on her phone to snap pictures of each of the books contained inside.

The image of the open book with the colorful, intricate drawings comes out perfect. Cali takes a step to the side to take a picture of the stacked books. She shifts backward and gets the same stack at a different angle. They are older and in rough condition but will offer her a challenge to get the detail just right. When Cali moves again to stand in front of *The Book*, she goes up on her toes to take a few photos from directly above.

Checking her phone after each picture, Cali brings her heels down and bends slightly to get shots through the case's front and sides. Satisfied that she has *The Book* from every angle, she goes back to her table and sits down. After selecting her drawing playlist on her phone, she puts in her earbuds and starts sketching the images she took. Once she's done with a light outline, Cali uses the pencils to start expertly blending and shading to create depth.

The twenty-two-year-old gets lost in her art. It's the thing that has always been her solace. Of course, over the years, she used her skill to impress girls she's had a crush on, especially in college, but it's primarily been like a reset button for her.

With her headphones in, Cali doesn't realize how much time has passed or hear that someone has come up behind her. The person peeks over her shoulder to see the piece Cali is working on. They move around the table and slowly slide into the chair opposite the auburn-haired woman. They observe Cali noting the slight crease in her brow, the tip of her tongue just barely poking out of the side of her mouth.

Rather than startle her and possibly mar the drawing Cali is working on, the person waits until she reaches for another pencil. When Cali feels another hand already on top of the tin, she jerks her hand away and looks up.

"Jesus! Scare the crap out of me, why don't you?" Cali pauses her playlist and removes the buds from her ears.

"Sorry," her friend says with a chuckle. "You were really in the zone, and I didn't want to mess up your mojo."

"Mojo?" Cali asks, quirking an eyebrow.

"It's a technical term," Roslyn says straight-faced. "So, how's it coming?"

"I think pretty good." Cali opens the pictures she took of *The Book*. Half of them are purposely blurry or have a glare from the case, and the others are perfectly clear.

"This is great," Roslyn says, flipping through the photos. "When I tried to take pictures of it in Portland, everything came out blurry. But I was trying to get the inside, not the outside."

She hands the phone back to her friend and quietly asks, "Can you work with these?"

"Yup," Cali says. "The only thing I need now is an accurate measurement so that the size matches. But that's just a matter of using a scaling app.

"I'll show Carmela the pictures of the other books and my drawings and then the blurry ones of our *Book*. Tell her I just couldn't get the right angle, but maybe she knows a way I could see it in person or something."

Roslyn lets out a big exhale, "Okay. Matt is waiting in the computer lab for you to email him the pictures so he can print them out," she says.

Cali takes her phone back and taps away. "Done."

"Alright. Ready to go?"

"What do you mean, go? We just got here."

"It's almost four o'clock. We've been here almost the entire day, kid."

"Really? No wonder I'm so hungry."

"You're always hungry."

"I take offense to that," Cali fires back.

"Do you really?"

Cali thinks for a moment. "Actually, no. That was just a knee-jerk reaction."

The two of them stand, and Roslyn helps Cali pack up her things. Before they meet up with Matt, Roslyn gives her the library membership form and has her fill it out but tells her to leave the name blank. She's become a bit cautious of them using their real names since their flight arrived in Rome. They exit the gallery and head to the main lobby. Cali walks over to her best friend, and he dutifully takes her heavy backpack handing her the printouts as he does.

"Where is Roslyn?" he asks.

"What am I chopped liver?" Matt rolls his eyes at his friend. "She went to hand in the forms to the head librarian," Cali says, looking down at her phone. "There's an art supply store not far from here that I can get everything I need."

Roslyn comes back with three temporary passes and hands one to each of them. There is a strip on tape across the center that their names are written on.

"Guy Reeves?" Matt asks. He tries to peek at Cali's and asks, "Who'd you get?"

"Tracey Billmock." She tosses her friend a confused glance before they both turn to the witch.

Roslyn shrugs. "There are enough lists with your real names on them, wasn't going to add another."

****

The three of them enter the apartment lugging Cali's art supplies. Milo greets them at the door, happily wagging his tail, but quickly moves to the side to let them in.

In addition to Cali's backpack, Matt is carrying two canvas bags with twenty pounds of clay in each. Roslyn follows with two canvas bags of her own, but hers contain drop cloths and tarps, paints, and glue.

Cali brings up the rear with one canvas bag from the art store with paintbrushes, X-acto blades, heavy-duty cardboard, and texturing tools. The other bag she is carrying has their dinner.

The trio takes out their food and sits down at the table in the kitchen to eat. Cali keeps watching the time, taking the difference into account, for when she can call Mickey again. It's Wednesday, which is her girlfriend's early day, so Cali only has to wait another couple of hours until Mickey is on her lunch break in Portland.

So when the phone rings just after they finish eating at 6:30 P.M. their time in Rome, all three are startled and immediately on edge.

Cali grabs the phone before it can ring a second time and answers the call on speaker.

"Hello?" she asks in an audibly distressed voice, automatically putting the call on speakerphone.

"Hi, baby," Mickey says over the phone. "Both my eight o'clock and nine-thirty canceled, so I thought it'd be a good time to call."

The tension in Cali's body visibly untangles as she hears her girl-friend's soothing voice. She takes the call off of speaker and gets up from the table. She tells Matt to leave her food alone and not clean up—she's not finished yet—before going into the bedroom and closes the door behind her.

"I'm so glad you're okay," Cali says.

"Why wouldn't I be?"

"I don't know," she quickly answers. "I'm just worried, I guess. I miss you so much."

"I miss you, too," Mickey coos. "I actually had this amazingly hot dream about you last night. When I woke up I reached for you, and it made me miss you even more when you weren't there."

"I can't wait until I'm with you again."

"Do you know when that could be?" Mickey asks, hopefully.

"Soon, I think. We're coming up with a plan." She details the dream she had and how they are preparing to steal the real *Book*.

"I know how talented you are, and if anyone can pull this off, it's you, baby. So after that, then you'll be home?"

"God, I hope so. Moose and I are not meant to live together. But tell me more about your dream," Cali says, reclining in the bed and making herself comfortable.

"It was really hot."

KERRI MCLOONE

"You said that, but tell me more," Cali says, feeling the constant underlying longing for Mickey intensify. "Don't leave anything out."

"Well, do you remember the shower sex we had a couple of weeks ago?"

Cali feels a simultaneous surge in her arousal as well as guilt. That was their last night together before Cali had to leave her girlfriend literally and physically in the dark. "Yes," she says, her voice cracking slightly.

"It started like that. I could even feel the cold tile behind my back. But it was like there were four of you. You were kissing me, but your tongue was also hitting all the right spots on my body. All at the same time."

Cali gulps as she pictures the image. She remembers their night in the shower vividly since it was the last time she was able to actually touch Mickey. Hearing the older woman talk about that time together now and the dream she recently had, makes Cali's body burn for the brunette. She sucks in a ragged breath. "Damn, baby."

"It gets better," Mickey responds in a sultry voice. "We got out of the shower, and somehow, you were able to carry me to the bed without stopping the movement of your tongue all over me. The first time you used your hand, I came so hard that I could feel it in my eyes."

She continues describing the dream until neither woman can take it anymore, and they coach each other over the phone to simultaneous strong climaxes.

They help bring each other down from their peaks before reluctantly ending the call so Mickey can get ready to start her day. Before Cali hangs up, she makes sure she's given explicit permission enabling the group's plan to proceed. She tosses the phone onto the bed next to her and sighs physically satisfied, but left emotionally wanting.

• 3 0 •

"ROSLYN"

It's midday on Thursday here in Rome. The Central Library in Portland exploded nine days ago, but it feels somehow both longer and shorter than that.

Last night I used Cali's tablet to check on the news in the states. The investigation into the cause of the explosion, and my alias's subsequent death, is still an ongoing major headline for most Portland news sites, but national coverage has quieted some.

I couldn't help but think how terrifying it must be for my family to see and read these stories. They obviously know that Alexa Pearce was one of the identities they armed me with for my quest to find *The Book*.

The first spell I ever cast is the one that's even now keeping them out of Darius's grasp. I convinced myself that they know I'm still alive because *they* are still alive and turned off the tablet deciding to ignore any more news about my "death" until it becomes something that absolutely cannot be ignored.

I woke up this morning with a new resolve. Matt and I left Cali at the apartment for her to begin working on the replica. With our new temporary passes, we walked in full of confidence—libraries are familiar turf for us.

After working through the morning on the computers, Matt and I sit outside near the library's entrance, eating our lunch of fresh mozzarella and prosciutto paninis with roasted red peppers. I'm enjoying the warm late-April weather and the bright azure Italian sky. I can feel my arms prickle in the direct sunlight.

Around each bite, I'm telling him what I've translated from *The Book*. "It was pretty strange to read the part about the actual curse this morning," I say to him.

"But you knew about it, right?"

"Well, yeah, I knew about it," I answer after I swallow a bite of my sandwich. "But it's one thing to be told a story as a kid versus seeing it copied down from a twelve hundred-year-old book."

Matt takes a drink of sparkling water and clears his throat. "What exactly does it say?" he asks.

"Without saying exactly what spell they used, or how they went about cursing him, it explains what happened." I take out my notebook from my bag and flip through the loose sheets I tore from a pad back in Portland. I smooth the page out in front of me and begin to read.

" 'The power of our good magic does not have the strength to defeat the evil that currently dwells within our realm, yet one day it shall. The demon has not been vanquished, nor has he conquered us.'

" 'We have united our magic in confining the spread of evil born from the demon. For only the strongest of our lineage will have the power to bring Darius to an end. A child born from an unending magical line at the sun's highest point on the day of the spring solstice will grow to be our guardian.'

" 'Should the evil conquer this child, his full strength shall be released and expand with the taking of hers. It is foretold that she will be the one to save us. She will have the power to heal us all.' "

Matt gets up from where he is sitting across from me and gently takes the page from my hands. He reads it again silently, mouthing the words as he does.

"But your birthday is in June."

Oh, right. Shit. I bite my lip and say, 'Umm, well no. Alexa Pearce's birthday was in June. My actual birthday is March twenty-first."

"Oh," he says quietly.

"Yeah..." I say. "I'm sorry it's just—"

"No, it's okay. I understand," Matt clears his throat loudly. "So you're like the fulfillment of a prophecy," he says, slightly changing the subject.

"I guess so," I shrug.

"That's pretty cool," he says. "My girlfriend is a badass!"

My stomach somersaults as I hear that word. I chuckle and can feel my cheeks start to burn at how happy this guy makes me. But then I stop and think to myself, *I* am *a badass.*

"And don't you forget it," I say, taking the paper from him. I put it back into my notebook and pop the last bite of my sandwich into my mouth. I feel Matt's eyes on me as I chew.

"What?" I ask with my mouthful.

He looks down at his sandwich. The mood has changed just that quickly. "I'm just wondering what your real name is."

I swallow hard, but it does nothing to clear the lump that has suddenly formed in my throat. I stay quiet.

"I guess I'm hoping that you can trust me enough to tell me."

"Matt, it's not that I don't trust you. If I didn't, I wouldn't have told you anything about me at all."

"Then what is it?"

I start and stop a few times before I tilt my head back and close my eyes. I take a deep breath before I answer, "It's complicated."

"Complicated," he repeats sullenly. "What does that even mean?"

"It means it's complicated. I don't know what parts of me are attached to it."

He gives me a confused and frustrated look.

"What I mean is that I haven't said my real name out loud for the past five years. I haven't even thought it. I've taken on these false identities and convinced myself that there are no powers attached to those names, so then there are no powers attached to me. It was the only way I could figure out how to stay hidden without any extra help.

"And now, even though I have help, I don't know if thinking of or acknowledging myself as who I really am will make it impossible to keep my powers quiet or if it'll do nothing at all."

I sigh and say, "I can't take that chance, and for now, continuing to think of myself as just Roslyn James, an ordinary girl with nothing else attached to that is what I have to do."

Matt finishes his sandwich silently, thinking. He balls up the wax paper the sandwiches came in, walks over to the trash can, and tosses it in. When he sits next to me again, he takes my hand and brings it up to his lips to kiss it.

"You're anything but ordinary," he says. "But I understand. And I'm sorry. I forget that you're not doing any of this because you feel like it. Everything you do has a reason behind it."

"Thank you, babe." I pull on his shirt to bring his body to mine. Our foreheads touch, and I breathe him in. He smells so good, and I'm blanketed by a sense of safety. I give him a simple kiss on the lips and pull away.

"We should get back to work," I say. "See how much more we can both get done today."

He helps me up, and we hold hands as we walk back toward the glass doors of the library. I feel Matt's eyes on me again, so I look at him. He's smiling this time and his light brown eyes sparkle.

"So you won't tell me your name. And I accept that," he adds quickly. "But that doesn't mean I can't take a guess at it, right?"

I quirk an eyebrow and say, "No, I don't see why you couldn't."

"Good." He grins at me mischievously and, in that moment, looks strikingly like Cali. "Is your name Gardenia?"

"No," I say.

"Petunia? Daisy?"

"No."

"Any member of the flower variety?"

"No," I laugh.

"Umm, Thea?"

"No, sir."

"Yvette?"

I silently, slowly shake my head.

"Oh my god, it's not Calamari, is it?"

"Yes," I say sarcastically as the glass doors to the library slide open for us. "You got me, Matt."

He wraps a strong arm around my shoulders as we walk and pulls me to his side. He whispers into my hair, "I knew I would."

• 3 1 •

When we walk into the apartment later that day, we're greeted by Milo and Cali in very excited states.

"Oh, good, you're home!" Cali says. She takes my bag and tosses it on the couch, then drags me by the arm into the kitchen. "Look!"

She points at two cardboard rectangles with four outer walls, each about *The Book*'s shape and height, though slightly smaller. The table is covered in one of the tarps we bought yesterday with a drop cloth spread out underneath. Scrap pieces of the light brown cardboard are shoved over to one side. Next to a ruler are smaller triangular pieces of cardboard in a small stack. The X-acto knife is next to an open bottle of glue that is filling the kitchen with a strong odor.

"Looks good, kid," I say. "What are you going to do with these?"

I reach out my hand just to point at the triangles, but Cali grabs my hand.

"Don't touch!!" she shouts. "It hasn't dried yet." I put my hands up in surrender and back away.

"Geez, Squirrel," Matt says, startled.

"I'm sorry, it's just that I have them set up perfectly, and I don't want it to move or anything."

"It's okay. Explain to me what I'm looking at here." I gently pull out one of the chairs, careful not to bump the table, and gingerly sit down.

"What we have here, my friends, is the hollow base that we will begin constructing our clay on top of."

"What are there two for?" Matt asks.

"Oh, I figured it might be a good idea to have a backup just in case."

Just in case of what? I can't help thinking. But instead of going down that rabbit hole, I ask, "So, what's the next step?"

"I have to glue the top piece of cardboard on, and then, I'm going to cover the boxes with about a centimeter of clay to start sculpting. Then when the clay dries, I just have to paint it and let that dry. Then we switch it one, two, three, and we're done."

"One thing at a time, please," I say. I'm starting to get a headache from the fumes, so I go over to the stove to turn on the exhaust fan and crack some windows. I open the fridge and take out a bottle of wine we got at the market the other day. I take down three glasses from the cabinet and motion for Cali and Matt to follow me as I go to the living room.

I sit down on the floor with my legs tucked under the coffee table, and Milo immediately sits down next to me. I gesture toward the couch for Cali and Matt to sit down facing me.

"You're not the only one who had a productive day, Cal." I pull the cork from the bottle and pour each of us a glass. As I hand them across the table, I say, "I translated more of the pages I copied, and they proved quite interesting."

KERRI MCLOONE

"Other than the curse, you mean?" Matt asks before taking a long sip of the wine.

"What curse?" Cali asks.

"The one that's prevented Darius from ending the world so far. And the prophecy of my girl Calamari over here, too, Squirrel!"

"Calamari?" Cali asks, looking highly confused. Matt jerks his head in my direction.

"Don't ask," I say.

I quickly read her the same thing I read Matt earlier while we were eating lunch today. Cali has a similar reaction to her friend when she finds out when my real birthday is. Other than a mumble about her understanding her "kid" nickname a little more, she takes it in stride.

"But this," I say, turning the paper around so both Cali and Matt can see, "is what I really want to tell you."

"What is it?" my short friend asks me.

"For the sake of being cautious, don't read anything out loud, but this is the spell my grandfather gave me five years ago to hide my family from Darius."

"Really?!" Cali grabs the paper and reads it to herself. Matt swipes it from her and reads it himself.

"Are you serious?" he asks.

"Yeah, but that's not all." I gently take the paperback and put it on the table, flattening the wrinkles. "It's only partly here. There are only three lines, but there should be four. See?"

I point to each line. Their eyes follow every move of my hand.

"That's nuts. Where is the rest of it?"

"I don't know, but I think it has something to do with your dream, Cal, and why you had it. I think there *is* hidden text in *The* Book. I think it's there to protect it from being read by the wrong person, and your dream tells us how to see it."

"What's this next part?" Matt asks. He's picked up the paper again and is reading the next thing I translated today.

"That's the other thing that's interesting," I say. "I've never seen this before, but based on the similarity to the one above it, I'm guessing this is another spell."

"Another one?" Cali takes the page from Matt.

"Yes, and here's a third," I put the next page down on the table and point to the words on it. "And a fourth."

"Spells for what, though?" my friend asks me.

"I honestly have no idea. Except for the Extensios spell, which is in its own section, none of them look complete enough to even be able to tell. But this fifth one, though, is really interesting. It looks like a how-to for enchanting an animal to guide and protect you." I cock my head toward Milo as I say it.

"So you mean Dog Man wasn't born with magic?"

"Nope. We adopted him on my seventeenth birthday from a shelter. I didn't know he was magical until Darius attacked the following year. But look, the spell is very similar to the Extensios spell."

I show them the paper, and Matt shakes his head.

"This is crazy," he says. "Imagine not only putting a major evil threat on hold but then planning out all of these spells and having to wait hundreds of years for them to be used. I can't imagine the energy and the foresight your ancestors and family needed to plan all of this out."

"Yeah, Roz. The prophecy doesn't name you specifically, but they always knew you'd be the one."

It's silent between the three of us as we all consider that. A chill run downs my spine, and as it all sinks in. I shiver a little then tell them, "But there's even more. This page looks more like a recipe than a spell."

"Recipe. You mean like a potion or something?" Cali asks. "Awesome!"

"All of this makes so much sense," Matt says. "I mean, we all agreed that *The Book* couldn't just contain stuff about Extensios and Darius. But to see it for real? And let me guess, that's not complete either."

I shake my head, no.

"Okay, so *all* of this is pointing to one thing," Cali says. Matt and I look at her quizzically. "I was totally right."

"Yes, Cal. You were right," I laugh.

"Well, you weren't the only one who found something today."

We both look at Matt as he takes folded pages out of his back pants pocket. He smooths them out, and I see they are computer printouts of multiple websites.

"You found something?" I ask him.

"I'll tell you what I didn't find," he says. "Anything about a natural disaster or an event in Europe twelve hundred years ago that I could pinpoint as the arrival of Darius. My first thought was maybe the volcanic eruption in Pompeii, but that happened about seven-hundred years before Darius showed up.

"So, I expanded my search and checked African history, Asia, Australia, and the Americas. I found something interesting in Native American folklore. There is a story about a great shaking of the ground from multiple tribes, and from what I can see, it's from about the right time."

He hands some papers to me and some to Cali. "I printed out everything I found, but the tribes are spread all across the middle of

North America. So I'm running into the same issue. I can't pinpoint if the stories are coming from earthquakes, if they are part of cultural teachings, or if it was Darius."

"But that's still progress!" I say encouragingly. "It feels like we're on the right track."

"We're getting close," Cali agrees. "And the closer we get to finishing this, the closer we are to going home."

At the word home, Milo sits up from where he had laid down half under the coffee table. His black head flicks between the three of us.

"Soon, buddy," I say, ruffling the fur around his neck under his lime green collar. I rotate it around his neck and gently hold the red crystal. I rub my thumb over it slowly and say more to myself than anyone else, "Soon."

• 3 2 •

Cali and I are sitting at the kitchen table. Earlier, we had eaten dinner in the living room off of the coffee table, so we didn't disturb the drying cardboard bases. She's using the triangles she had cut out before to reinforce the corners of the rectangles.

Milo is lying underneath the table in between us. His snout is resting on my barefoot. Matt is washing the dishes from dinner. When he's finished with the last plate, he puts it next to the other plates and utensils on a dishtowel unfolded on the counter to dry.

"I'm going to do a load of wash. You guys have anything?" he asks.

"Yeah," I say. "My dirty clothes are in the hamper in our bathroom." I force myself not to think about how my boyfriend is about to wash my dirty underwear. Boundaries have been reduced out of recent necessity.

"Same for me, but in my bathroom," Cali says as she gently glues another triangle into a cardboard corner. "Thanks, Moose."

"Yeah, thanks, babe!" I call after him as he leaves.

"I took Dog Man for a W-A-L-K before," Cali says, trying to keep Milo from springing up, ready to go for one. He thumps his tail twice from below to let us know he heard her, but he's comfy right where he is at the moment.

"I bet he loved that," I say.

Cali hums her agreement as she gets up and changes seats. She starts measuring bigger pieces of cardboard, making small marks every few centimeters in pencil. She uses the metric ruler to connect the dots with a light line. I expect her to pick up the X-acto blade and cut the cardboard, but she measures again, making sure it's precise. Cali retraces her light pencil line, darkening it, then she picks up the blade in her left hand and slowly begins to cut the cardboard.

"On our outing, we passed a workout place. And I was thinking that we should all take a class or two to keep us in shape."

"I've actually been thinking the same thing," I respond honestly with a nod. "Can't hurt to refresh our muscles."

"I was thinking in terms of next time we go up against that bastard."

"What do you mean?"

Cali stops what she's doing to look at me as she answers. "I don't know if Moose and me will just have to use our Extensios power, or if we'll actually have to defend ourselves hand to hand against his Victus. I mean, if there are more potions in *The Book*, I assume they could be useful, but I don't want to just depend on that, you know?"

"Yeah, I know," I say quietly.

"I want to kick some butt, Roz. I want those losers to weep when a tiny little girl majorly kicks their demonic asses!"

"Hell yeah, Squirrel!" Matt calls from across the apartment.

"I'm with ya, Cal." I hold out my fist, and Cali bumps it with her blade-free right one. "Did you go in to check it out? Are there classes we can take or a trainer?"

"Well, I couldn't go in since I had Dog Man with me, but I can go back tomorrow."

I bite my lip as I think. I know Cali is completely capable of taking care of and protecting herself, but I have an immediate hesitation about her going anywhere without Milo. I feel the same way about Matt or myself going somewhere alone.

"Where was this place?" I ask her.

"Just a few blocks up and over," she answers. Her head is bent, and her tongue is just barely poking out of the corner of her mouth as she finishes with the blade. She measures the piece checking that she's cut clean lines.

Across the apartment, the dial on the washing machine clicks as Matt sets the cycle and water starts to fill. After another moment, the door thunks closed. My boyfriend comes back into the living room with headphones in. He's changed into basketball shorts and moves the couch over slightly. When he hikes the shorts high up on his thighs, I get a glimpse of the bottom half of the long scar on his leg from when he threw himself in front of a sharp piece of metal aimed at me in the library basement.

I catch myself staring at his muscular body as it moves from one yoga pose to the next. I get an image in my head of ways I could give him a workout that would have both of us breathless and spent. This must be what Cali feels like whenever she sees Mickey working out, I think.

I swallow hard and force myself to return my attention to what Cali is doing. I meet her eyes, and from her expression, it's clear she's caught me staring at him too. I'm thankful that my mocha skin tone mostly camouflages the deep blush I feel covering my face and neck at being caught. I adjust my glasses on my nose and rest my head on my hand, angled to block my view of Matt and prevent any further blatant ogling of him.

She gets up again and bends over the replica. She uses the ruler to measure the height. Cali sits back down in the chair she just vacated and begins marking the rest of the piece in front of her. She traces out her markings into what looks like four strips, two a bit shorter than the others.

I don't say anything as I watch my friend carefully cut out the strips. Cali gets up once again and sits down in the seat in front of the half-made cardboard frames. She takes the two longest strips and puts them inside one base. She positions them evenly, ultimately dividing the interior into thirds.

Happy with their placement, she marks the exterior cardboard with pencil before taking them out again. She applies glue to both ends and along the bottom of one. Cali carefully reinserts it into the baselining it up perfectly with the pencil marks. She holds it in place and starts talking again.

"You're sitting there so quietly that I feel like I'm on display here or something."

"I'm trying not to distract you," I say in a loud whisper.

Cali exhales a short laugh and whispers back, "Oh, good."

"What are you doing?" I ask her.

"I'm reinforcing the inside of the cardboard base before I glue the top on so that it doesn't buckle under the weight of the clay."

Cali glues in the next long strip as I hear Matt plop on the couch to watch TV. While she's holding it in place, I decide to talk to her about being careful when she's alone.

"So, listen," I start. She looks up at me while keeping her hands completely motionless on the wet piece. "I was thinking that since you're going to be here alone for a while, that I should teach you some of Milo's commands."

"How come?"

"Protection, mainly. I think both you and Matt should know some."

I wiggle my toes under the table, so Milo lifts his head. I push back my chair and duck my head down to talk to my dog. "Hey, bud. Can you go get Matt for me?"

My dog dutifully gets up and goes over to the couch. Cali and I watch as he lifts his upper body to put his front paws on the cushions. He tilts his head to the side at the same time I hear a snore come from Matt.

How do guys fall asleep so easily? I ask myself. Milo's ears twitch as the snoring continues. My dog starts to whine softly, gradually building up to a faint bark.

When that doesn't wake Matt, he barks again, slightly louder. Milo looks at me when there is still no change. I nod, and Milo barks twice at full volume. That does the trick, and Matt snaps awake sitting up quickly.

"What! What!" he shouts. Milo licks his face and comes back to me, sitting next to my leg.

"Can you come in here? I want to teach you and Cal some of Milo's commands for protection and stuff."

"Okay," Matt yawns as he gets up. He looks at the table and the things covering it and decides to sit at one of the stools at the counter.

"Well," I say, standing and patting my thigh, so Milo comes to me. "I know we all feel pretty safe here, but we still need to be careful. So Cali, since you'll be home working and you do it with headphones on, and Matt you've been out on walks with him, I think you guys should know about how he can protect you.

"Remember, he can understand everything you say, but he has four commands that he will follow to the letter.

"The first is casual. Tell him that, and he'll look like he's on a regular walk, trotting along, but he'll really be on high alert, scanning everyone you come across for a threat. If he senses anything, he'll growl and physically put himself between you and them. But even without the command, if he senses something hinky, he'll step in."

"I remember," Cali says quietly. She mindlessly rubs her arms as we all remember how the same two Victus that Darius brought with him to the library bumped into her on the street in Portland.

She was on her way to meet Matt and me at the library for lunch and had Milo with her. Cali said he was trying to block her from them and was straining on his leash, just waiting to get the go-ahead. The two Victus didn't let go of Cali until Mickey intercepted them and said she was going to call the police if they didn't leave.

"The next one is side," I say, continuing as I watch Milo, who's gone over to Cali to comfort her for the moment. "And wherever he is, he'll immediately come over to you. Like this: Milo, side."

Without hesitation, Milo comes over to me and places himself at my left knee.

"Milo, side," Matt says. Instantly again, Milo gets up and goes over to Matt's left knee. Matt ruffles the hair around his collar and says, "Good boy!"

"The next two should really only be used if you feel like you are in absolute danger, or like if someone won't back off. I'm not going to say them as a command, like Milo, side." Milo gets up from his spot next to Matt and comes back to me. He flops his head back to look up at me, making his ears flip straight back. I hold my fist out, and he touches his nose to it.

"The other two commands will tell him to attack. Set and seek, in that order, and that'll tell," I point downwards, "to go after whoever is front of you. And I mean *go after*."

"So how does he indicate, or whatever?" Matt asks.

"If he senses something, he'll press into you and growl. Then he'll either put himself in front of you or stay glued to your side. He doesn't just growl for the hell of it, so if he does, pay attention.

"Set?" Cali asks. "Isn't that the command you gave him at the laundromat when Tyler was being a real douche?"

I nod. "So, if he presses himself into your leg while you're working with your headphones on Cal, there's something up. Same thing for you on a walk with him, Matt. And just because you can't see anything doesn't mean there is nothing there. You guys need to trust him over anything else, including your own senses."

I move from where I'm standing further into the kitchen and get out a crunchy bone-shaped cookie for Milo. His last command was 'side,' so he follows me step for step. I hand it down to him and say, "Good boy, bud."

He trots into the living room to enjoy his treat. I sit back in my chair and say, "So we all on the same page? Casual, side, set, seek. Trust Milo when he signals anything and use the commands."

They nod at me in agreement. Cali goes back to work on the bases just as the washer cycle buzzes. Matt and I stand to hang our wet clothes and give Cali some space to finish what she's doing tonight in peace.

● 3 3 ●

TYLER

About the same time as Matt and Roslyn return from the library over fifty-five-hundred miles away, Tyler is following Mickey as Darius instructed on the other side of the world.

He's spent the majority of the morning positioned at a table in the front window of a cafe directly across the street from Mickey's Kick Boxing and Training Studio. He watched Mickey arrive at 9 A.M. in the pouring rain and saw her teach one class at ten and another at eleven. When she meets a client at noon and goes in the back where the machines and free weights are, he waits another ten minutes until he thinks the session is in full swing before he leaves the cafe.

As he crosses the street dodging puddles and cars, he puts his hand in his pocket and feels the one-inch by one-inch thin plastic square safely stored there. It's one of a set of GPS chips he'd purchased online.

Making sure no one sees him, Tyler enters the studio and slinks his way to Mickey's office. He scans the entire room, but her purse is nowhere in sight. Her phone, however, is on her desk near the computer.

Tyler picks up her phone and removes the case. It's a large, extended battery case. He falters for a moment, unsure of whether the battery will interfere with the GPS signal or not.

Deciding he just has to risk it for now, he peels the backing off, exposing the adhesive. He tucks the film into his pocket then sticks the chip to the back of her phone. He replaces the cover and puts the phone back exactly where Mickey left it.

He's about to leave her office when he decides to check one more thing. He pushes the button on her phone, and the screen turns on. He recognizes the background as a drawing of what looks like the Hawthorne Bridge done from Waterfront Park. He pushes the button again but is prompted for the passcode.

Not knowing her code, he mouths, "*Fuck*" as he presses the power button to darken the screen. Tyler goes to the office door and looks around the jam carefully to scan for anyone who might spot him.

Before leaving, he checks that he didn't leave anything behind and sees something he'll have to deal with immediately. While he stood at Mickey's desk, putting a GPS tracker on her phone, his jacket and shoes dripped water all over the floor.

"Fuck," he says out loud.

Leaving the small puddles like this would be a dead giveaway that someone had been in here. He has no choice but to go deeper into the studio to the men's locker room and get something to wipe them with. He's been a member for the last few months and knows exactly where to go. Keeping his head down, he darts into the men's room and grabs the industrial-sized roll of brown paper towel from its holder next to the sink.

First, he wipes down his jacket so that it doesn't drip again. Then he wraps the paper around his arm multiple times, tears it, and puts it on the floor. He steps on it to dry his shoes.

Tyler takes the whole roll into Mickey's office and wipes down everywhere he sees water. He's down on the floor, behind her desk and out of sight, when he hears a woman's voice in the doorway.

"Great session today, Aaron. I'll see you next week."

Tyler holds his breath. His mind is already coming up with a dozen ways to explain his presence to Mickey. He knows none of them will fly and can't help but brace himself for the figurative, but most likely literal, ass-kicking he's about to receive.

"Thanks, Mel," a male voice responds. "Listen, is uh, is Mickey seeing anyone right now?"

"Yeah," the women's voice responds wistfully. Tyler realizes it's Melanie, one of the trainers. "She's taken."

"Oh, okay," Aaron says. "I'll see you next week then."

Tyler exhales slowly and counts to fifty in his head. He finishes drying the water on the floor and takes all of the paper with him. He brings everything back into the bathroom, throwing out the used paper towels and replacing the roll to its holder.

For appearance's sake, he goes to his locker and unlocks it with his combination. The only thing in there is a sweat-stained gym towel. He tucks it into his back pocket, so it hangs down behind him.

He leaves the locker room and strolls over to the main door. Tyler stands by the bulletin board where the schedule of classes is listed. Pointing to a random date on the board, Tyler takes out his phone and pretends to check his calendar. Instead, he launches the app to check the GPS chip.

It's transmitting clearly with a strong signal. He leaves the studio and steps out onto the sidewalk. Rather than go back across the street through the rain, he ducks into the wide doorway of the business next door.

Satisfied with what he's accomplished today, Tyler puts his hood up to ward off the chilly, damp air, and reclines his back against the building's brick wall. He switches between the apps on his phone, resuming an alien invaders game.

He's gotten lost in the game and hasn't realized that more and more people are walking by him and entering the studio. A loud voice saying they can't wait for class today makes him check back into reality.

The time on his phone says 12:55 P.M. He steps out of the doorway to get a look through the windows and see if Mickey is teaching the class or one of her employees. He quickly darts back into the doorway when instead, he sees the trainer herself coming out of her studio.

"Jack, I'm going to Marty's," Tyler hears her call out to her employee.

He carefully peeks around from his hiding spot and sees her holding open the glass door of her studio with her foot. She's putting on her black leather jacket and undoing the Velcro strap keeping her red umbrella in a collapsed position. "If you or Mel want me to bring anything back, just text it to me. I'll be back for my two o'clock."

"Okay, thanks!" Tyler hears a voice answer from within the building.

He turns, so his face is hidden from Mickey as she passes by him, waits for five beats, and steps out of the doorway to follow her. Tyler keeps his head down, eyes on the GPS app on his phone, following the blinking purple dot coming from the chip attached to Mickey's phone.

Glancing up every so often to make sure he's not too close or too far from the red umbrella, Tyler follows her all the way to Marty's Deli. He stops at the storefront before Marty's and pretends to make a phone call. Keeping his hood up, he goes into the deli and heads straight to the drink coolers, maintaining enough space between him and Mickey that she doesn't notice him.

"—tomato, provolone, and honey mustard."

Tyler discreetly glances around his hood and sees Mickey giving her order to Marty himself.

"You got it, Mick." Marty brings the paper he wrote the sandwich order on back to the kitchen. He reappears from a door next to Tyler and walks the counter's length to embrace Mickey in a hug.

"How ya doin'?" he asks softly. He directs her over to one of the tables and sits with her. Without waiting for her to answer, he continues, "I just still can't believe everything. I mean, Lexi was in here only a few days ago, it seems. Unbelievable, unbelievable."

Marty clears his throat and blinks rapidly; his eyes shine. Mickey reaches out and takes one of his hands in both of hers.

"I know, I'm still struggling with it myself. I'm sorry I haven't come in sooner," she says.

"That's alright, hon, don't worry about that."

Tyler sits down at one of the other empty tables with his back to the pair. The way he's positioned, he can see them in the reflection of the sliding glass door of the cooler. With his hood still up and head bent, he mindlessly swipes at his phone screen, eavesdropping on the conversation.

"I just, I see something about it every time I turn on the news. The whole area is blocked off still, so I've had to change my route into the city. I don't even know if I'd be able to drive past it anyway," he adds quietly. Mickey pats his hand, letting the older man talk.

"You know, there's been no talk of a funeral or memorial service. And it's strange, I haven't seen Matt or Cali since then either."

Tyler slightly turns in his chair, listening more carefully.

"I thought I'd be able to see them. Ya know, Moose is crazy about that Lexi. Or was, I guess.

"Have you seen them?" he asks her.

"Um, well," Mickey stutters. "I uh, I hadn't really seen any of them. Not since Cali and I broke up."

"What?!" Marty practically yells. "I just saw you all just a few days before the library! What happened!"

"It's a long story, Marty," Mickey says. Tyler sees her take her hands back and drop them into her lap. "A lot happened after you last saw us, and it became too much."

"Oh, dear. I'm so sorry. I don't want to pry or anything, but do you think you two'll work it out?"

"I'm not sure, Marty. I haven't spoken to her."

Mickey runs her hand over her head and then slides her fingers down through her ponytail. Tyler opens the notes app on his phone and types in the gist of their conversation.

"Order for Mickey," one of the cooks says, putting a paper bag on the counter near the register. Tyler watches as Mickey pulls out her phone, glancing at it briefly before she talks to Marty again.

"I gotta go back to work. I have a client coming in soon. I'm sorry, Marty."

"No, no, of course. I understand. If you need anything, you just let me know, Mick."

"Thank you."

He gets up and goes over to the register. "No charge," he says.

"Oh, no, that's okay, Marty," Mickey says, taking out her wallet from a pocket in her jacket.

"I insist. This one is on me. You come back and see me again soon."

"I will, thanks," she says, taking the bag. As she's pushing open the glass door to leave, Marty calls out to her and stops her.

"Maybe you should give her a call. I think things will work out for you and Squirrel."

Mickey doesn't say anything but nods as she leaves. Tyler puts his phone to his ear and fakes a conversation for a few minutes before getting up and ordering his own lunch.

As he waits for his food, he watches the purple dot move as Mickey retraces her steps back to the studio. He eats slowly, checking the GPS signal every couple of minutes or so. When he's finished eating, Tyler leisurely walks back to the cafe and parks himself in the same seat he had this morning.

He waits there for the rest of the day, going through his entire supply of edibles and ordering multiple black coffees until the next time Mickey leaves the studio.

The rain had stopped earlier, but Tyler leaves his hood up as he walks parallel to Mickey on the other side of the street. With his phone as his guide, he carefully follows her as she walks home. He stays in the shadows as she enters a building on SW Morrison Street.

Tyler leaves his hiding spot and darts across to the door. He opens the outer door and looks through the locked inner door. Above the elevator in the lobby, the digital display shows it stopped on the fifth floor.

The buzzer panel on the wall lists three apartments on each floor. Tyler runs a finger down the panel until he reaches the listings for the fifth floor. In a plastic covered slot, the name for apartment 5M is written in as Combes, Je. He moves his finger down one more line to apartment 5N—Westin, Mi.

Tyler flicks the plastic and takes out his phone. He adds the building address and apartment number to the entry in his notes app underneath Mickey's conversation with Marty.

Tyler pockets his phone and catches a cab back to his apartment on SW Jefferson. He tosses his phone on his coffee table, leaving the GPS app open. Tyler spends the rest of his Thursday night on his couch, getting high, trying to quell the lingering anxiety of whether or not today was enough to keep him alive a little while longer.

Before he falls asleep, through slitted, bloodshot eyes, Tyler sets an alarm for the next morning so he can get up and follow her all over again.

• 3 4 •

"ROSLYN"

Matt and I are walking back from the National Central Library on an unseasonably chilly afternoon for the start of May. Over the hours we've spent inside working, the partly cloudy sky filled in and became a dark gray.

The air feels damp, and rain is threatening to fall. A cool breeze comes by and cuts right through my thin, rust-colored jacket. I shiver a bit and rub my arms to ward off the chill. Matt puts his left arm around my shoulders without a second thought and pulls me into his body for warmth.

"So about that dinner," he starts.

"Dinner tonight?" I ask obliviously. "I was thinking some steak and an arugula salad. It should be in the fridge."

He chuckles and presses his mouth to my ear, "I meant me taking you to dinner at a fancy restaurant."

We're on a walkway in the Piazza dell'Indipendenza, almost halfway between the library and our apartment, when he stops walking and pulls me further to him, wrapping both arms around my waist.

"There's a nice restaurant not too far from the apartment, and I would love to take you there."

I put one of my hands on his shoulder as the other snakes around his neck to play with his hair. I smile up at him and hum my agreement. I lightly brush my lips against his and ask, "Then what?"

His grip on me tightens ever so slightly. Matt swallows and licks his lips. "Then maybe we'd go back to the apartment and go up to the little patio on the roof and have some wine, sit under a blanket together, enjoy each other's company."

"I like the sound of that." My voice trembles a little as I speak, showing both my excitement and nerves about it.

I'm not completely inexperienced when it comes to sex, but it wouldn't be a stretch to say that I'm a bit out of practice.

I was a late bloomer, so prior to Matt, I've had only two other boyfriends in my life: one in eleventh grade and one senior year of high school. My first boyfriend was more like a really close friendship than anything because we both knew and understood that he was just using me as a cover to keep his strictly conservative family from finding out he's gay.

My last boyfriend, I lost my virginity to. We got together the summer before senior year, and we didn't wait very long before we had sex. We were both seventeen at the time, and things were hot and heavy and stayed that way. We dated straight through the holidays and even past Valentine's Day. Actually, we technically never broke up because my eighteenth birthday is when all hell broke loose—literally.

Once I was on my own, sex was nowhere near the top of my list of things to do. There were a couple of times when I just really needed a release—an itch I couldn't quite satisfy for myself—so I would go to whichever bar was closest to meet someone. A one night, physical liberation.

But until I landed in Portland and met Matt, I was never in one place long enough to formulate anything close to resembling a real relationship with someone. Nor was that a priority before I found *The Book.*

Now in his arms, I can't help but picture the ending I hope our night will have. My chest tightens as my excitement rises, but my uneasiness increases with it also.

I bite my lip, and Matt can see the uncertainty written all over my face. He kisses me in the middle of my forehead. His lips linger for a moment before he removes them. He replaces the contact by touching his own forehead to mine.

"What's wrong?" he asks sweetly.

"I'm nervous," I whisper. I close my eyes and take in a deep breath. "It's been a very long time since I've felt like this about anyone. It's probably more true that I've never felt like this about someone ever. And I, well, I don't want you to be unsatisfied, or disappointed, or anything."

"Unsatisfied? In what way?"

I move my head back and look him right in the eyes. "Sexually," I say frankly.

"I don't think that's possible," Matt says, grinning, his smile tugged over to just one side of his mouth. He unwraps me from his arms and leads me over to a bench a few feet away. As we sit down, I take my bag from my shoulder and put it in my lap. I nervously adjust my glasses before dropping my hands to grip my bag. Matt reaches out and takes both of my hands in his.

"Roslyn, Alexa, Royal, Calamari, whoever you are, I love you. So much so that I feel a physical emptiness when we're apart. And I find you extremely attractive. Your mind, your voice, your laughter, your body, your strength, your everything.

"But nothing has to happen, sexually or otherwise, until we both agree we're ready. Even if it's in the middle of something and you're uncomfortable, then we stop. It's like you said at the hotel in Amsterdam, respect is our base. We build everything from there."

He lifts my hands to his mouth and kisses the tops of each of them. I take in a long breath to calm my heart and stop its whirlwind rhythm.

"I want you in every way imaginable, but nothing happens until you're ready. However long it takes, it takes. And I'd wait for you forever."

I lean in and kiss him. Not deeply, but firmly. 'That was quite a line," I say when I pull back.

"It's not a line when it's true."

Matt leans in and kisses me again. His hand lets go of one of mine to caress my cheek. Just as I tilt my head to the side to get better access to his mouth, I feel the first drop of rain land on my jaw.

"Uh oh," I'm able to say before a torrential downpour starts. Matt and I are somewhat sheltered under the canopy of branches from the trees around us, but neither of us stays very dry.

"Do you think we should make a run for it?" I ask. Our apartment is still about eight blocks away, well over one thousand feet. And let me just say it's a pain to run in glasses as it is, but add any type of precipitation, and it's worse. Between the beads of water blinding me and the constant slippage down my wet nose, it's safer to just walk and get drenched than run and risk crashing into something I can't see coming.

"Not especially," Matt answers. "But I don't want to sit here getting wet either."

"I say we go for it." I stand up and put the strap on my bag across my body. Then to make sure nothing falls out, like my notebook with all of my translations, I cradle it like a football. Matt stands up with me and bounces on his toes. "Ready?"

"No," he says, still bouncing. "But go!"

He takes off to his right out of the Piazza and down the sidewalks of Viale Enrico de Nicola. He has long strides, and I'm left chasing him, but I'm faster and quickly catch up. I turn on some speed and blow past Matt. I pass a few restaurants and multiple hotels, and quickly I'm at Via Napoli. I make a right, and after a few more turns, I'm at our apartment building.

I enter the lobby and take deep breaths to control my breathing. My clothes are drenched, and my shoes squish with every step. Matt is nowhere in sight, meaning I won by a landslide and want him to know it. I lean against the elevator door, bend one knee so that my foot is propped up by my lower thigh, and cross my arms to wait. I'm trying to think of something witty I can say when I see him open the door to the building.

"Took you long enough," I blurt. I bite the inside of my cheek as I think, *I was hoping for something wittier than that, "Roslyn."*

Matt smirks at me and shakes his head quickly, making water fly off of his hair and launch everywhere. "Like everything I do, I wanted to take my time and do it right."

"Well, then," I say with one eyebrow raised. "If that's true, then I guess I have a lot to look forward to."

Just like that, the air around us becomes charged. His expression darkens. He takes two long steps forward, and our bodies crash together. Our mouths find one another, and immediately I open mine to allow his tongue in. When he pulls it back, mine follows, and I lick the roof of his mouth.

He presses me into the elevator door behind me and continues to kiss me fiercely. My excitement is quickly rising, and I tingle even more as I feel the door start to vibrate, the elevator inside beginning to move.

Knowing we're about to be interrupted, I take his face in both of my hands and slow him down. I kiss him languidly for a few more seconds. He releases me, and we move to the side right before the elevator dings and the doors open.

We let the single occupant exit before we step in. Matt hits the button marked with a four, and the doors close. I shudder as a chill runs through my body from my wet clothes and shoes. As the elevator rises, I look over at my boyfriend and watch as he runs a hand through his soaked hair.

I think about our upcoming date and imagine the ending I'm hoping the night will have. A warmth spreads through my body, and suddenly I'm not so cold anymore.

• 3 5 •

I unlock the door to our apartment, and things are relatively quiet. Milo pads over to me and presses his head between my knees. There is a squishing sound as an air bubble is moved in my rain-soaked jeans by his head. I scratch his ears and ask him where Cali is. My dog turns around and goes through the living room to the kitchen. I take off my drenched shoes and soggy socks before I follow him.

Cali is hunched over one of the replicas. She finished the second cardboard base and covered one in gray clay yesterday. On the table, the other base is now covered also. She has the printed pictures she took of *The Book* propped up in front of her, and she is glancing back and forth between the two.

She has her earbuds in, and before I even fully make it into the kitchen, I can hear the music pouring out of them, which means she doesn't hear me. Cali is holding one of the modeling tools in her left hand and running it along the side of the clay.

As she uses it, she again checks one of the printed pictures but also the other model to make sure the two match. I don't know what the tool is called, but it looks like a chopstick and is tapered to a dull point, or like a worn-down pencil but without the carbon center. The lines it's making look just like the uneven edges of the pages in *The Book*.

Cal's wearing an oversized long-sleeved shirt with the sleeves pushed up and shorts. She's covered all over with smears of wet clay—from patches on the top of her thighs to a streak down one side of her jaw. Her hands are coated with a loose clay and water mixture that's rubbing off on everything she touches.

I tell Milo to brush against her gently. She doesn't even jump when she feels him but does look down at him. His distraction allows me to announce mine and Matt's presence, so I take it. I reach over and tap her phone to pause her playlist.

"I knew you were there," she says as she uses the back of her wrist to knock her earbuds out.

"Did not," I fire back.

"Did so! Milo was lying next to me all day, and when he got up a minute ago, I looked to see why. I saw you guys come in."

"Well, I didn't want to "scare the crap out of you" like I did at the library when you were drawing."

"Much appreciated." She puts the chopstick looking tool down. I see her wipe off a strip of clay from the tapered edge. She takes a step back from the table, comparing the two clay covered bases.

"What do you think?" she asks.

"Wow, Squirrel," Matt says, coming into the kitchen. He has a towel from the bathroom in his hands, drying his hair but is still in his wet clothes. He's barefoot like me, having taken off his shoes and socks at the door. "I'm choosing to ignore how dirty everything is for the moment."

"Wise choice, because it won't be clean anytime soon, Moose."

"But I think it looks exactly like the pages in the real thing. And the two of them are like exact copies of each other. How did you do that?"

"It wasn't even that hard," Cali says, beaming. "The page ends are uneven and different lengths, and so thick to begin with, that it just took a few swipes the length of the clay. I think it's pretty close.

"Just a little more of the page edges here, and then more texturing and detail around the rest of it."

I pick up the picture she took of *The Book* that she's using as a guide. Careful not to touch the clay copies, I hold the page up and scrutinize the two.

"Pretty close?" I say. "They're literally the same. Damn kid, that's really amazing."

"Oh, come on," Cali says bashfully. Then adds after a beat, "Well, yeah, it is."

Matt moves further into the kitchen and picks up a jar of dark chocolate covered almonds from the counter. He pops a few into his mouth before offering the jar to Cali and me. I decline, but Cali opens her mouth. Her hands are covered in damp clay, so Matt drops one in for her.

"What do you do now?" he asks around a mouthful. "Any way that we can help?"

"I think I've got the general shape, but I have to finish texturing the rest of it. Add in the details. This is air-dry clay, so it isn't going to dry that quickly when the weather is this damp. But that also means I have some wiggle room in case I need to change something."

"Can't you put it in the oven on low to help dry it?" I ask.

Her eyes widen, and she shakes her head no. "Absolutely not. This stuff is way flammable. Even on low, it could burst into flames and take the whole kitchen out with it."

"Okay, did not know that," I say. "But glad I do now."

Cali opens her mouth wide again. Matt grins and drops in two more chocolate almonds.

"And Moose, I appreciate the offer, but you know what I'm going to say. Maybe you should explain to our friend here what happened in fourth grade and why you're not allowed to touch."

The smile falls off his face. "That wasn't my fault, and you know it."

It's Cali's turn to frown. "I'm *pretty* sure it was."

"How was it my fault? Your sculpture fell off the table."

I look down at Milo seated by my leg, and he looks just as confused as I feel about the sudden shift in their moods. "What are you two talking about?"

When they turn to me and direct their unexplained fury at a new target, I'm suddenly sorry I even opened my mouth. I put my hands up in surrender and push my chair back, removing myself from the danger zone.

"She's going to say I knocked her sculpture off the table in art class, and it fell flat on the floor and got smashed," Matt says as he throws another almond in his mouth. His jaw clenches tightly from the force of his chewing.

"You did knock it down!" Cali shouts. "It was a really good sculpture too, Roz. Of a squirrel holding a nut no less! And your boyfriend challenged me to an arm-wrestling match and made the thing fall. It hadn't even dried yet, so the poor thing looked like it had crashed against a glass door or something. It was completely smashed in and ruined!"

I snort as the image forms in my head. Cali crosses her arms and glares at me. "It's not funny, Roz."

"You're right; the situation was not funny. I'm just picturing what that would look like, and..." I'm stopped by Cali's cold look. I clear my throat as I say, "Sorry."

"Well, I didn't have enough time to fix it, so I not only got a bad grade on it, but that's what was presented in the school's art show. I had to stand there next to it and explain to all the parents, and teachers, and everybody what it was."

"I didn't knock it off!" Matt yells, defending himself. This is clearly an argument they've had before. "And *you* challenged me!"

"What?! I did not!"

I think to myself that that's something Cali would do when Matt says, "You absolutely did, Squirrel! And you lost and got upset, and when you stood up, the table got bumped, and that's how the thing fell."

"No! That is not—" Cali's eyes widen as she stops short. She must be having a flashback because the next thing she says is, "Oh my god. Son of a bitch, you're right."

Matt huffs in annoyance and spins away to open the fridge. He takes out the raw steak wrapped in butcher paper and throws it on the counter. He ducks his head down and reaches in again. I hear bottles clinking and things moving around. When Matt reappears, he has the container of arugula, balsamic vinegar, a bottle of mustard, and a jar of minced garlic to make a marinade. He puts all of it on the counter and slams the door closed.

He takes a large bowl down from the cabinet. Without measuring, he pours the vinegar and some mustard in, seasons it with salt and pepper, and a large scoop of garlic. He starts whisking it as he pours olive oil in. He shallowly scores the meat in a criss-cross manner before putting it into the bowl.

Cali stares at him. It looks like she's about to say something but doesn't. When he starts rinsing the arugula, she goes back to working on the replica. For a brief moment, it seems like their squabble has ended as quickly as it began.

I'm about to ask Cali how she thinks we could get Carmela on board with us for the next part of our plan when Matt whirls around from the sink and jumps back into it with her.

"And since you're so keen on bringing up ancient history, why don't you share what you did to me as retaliation? Hmmm?"

"Oh, no, no," Cali says, instantly timid. "I don't come off good in that story at all."

"What'd you do?" I ask. Cali sucks her bottom lip into her mouth and shakes her head no.

"Fine, I'll tell," Matt says. "*Your* friend pushed me off the slide at recess."

"She pushed you off the slide," I repeat.

"Yup! Not down, off. I broke my arm when I hit the ground. I had to wear a cast for two months!"

"Cali!"

"Well, he ruined my squirrel, Roz!" Cali says, defending herself. Matt spins to face her, and she holds up her soupy, gray hands. "Okay, okay. At the time, I thought you had ruined my squirrel, and I was really upset. Now I know I was wrong.

"And I apologized for the push multiple times. It was not cool. I'm still very sorry about it." They're both quiet as they size each other up. Cali's hands are still up, and she slowly moves them apart until her arms are spread out for a hug. She bends her fingers to her palms a few times and says, "Come on, Moose. Let's call it a truce, yeah?"

Matt raises one eyebrow and stands firm.

"Come on, Moose," Cali whines. "Bygones I absolutely concede that, as you have said all these years, that I am the one who ruined my poor little squirrel."

Cali takes a tiny step forward. Her arms are still outstretched, and I see three drops of murky clay water drip from her wrist.

"Can you forgive me and accept my apology about the slide? Come on, man. We can leave this all behind us once and for all."

I can see Matt's resistance start to crumble, but he holds firm even as a smile threatens to form on his face. Cali dramatically makes her lip quiver as if she's about to cry. Matt's will cracks, and he laughs at his friend.He is about to reach out and hug her when his scowl returns in full force.

"Is that my shirt?!"

• 3 6 •

Cali looks down quickly before she darts out of the kitchen with Matt directly on her heels. She circles the couch as he chases after her—Milo barks at them, ready to join in with their game.

I loop a finger through his collar and keep him in place. "Nope. Not our fight, big guy. This has to play out."

I turn in my chair and lean against the backrest taking in the spectacle in front of me. I've seen them argue, I've even seen them wrestle, but this fight is different. It's not playful; it's all the tension that has been looming since we first landed in Europe spiked way past a boiling point.

Cali and Matt are slowly circling the coffee table now. Every time he lunges for her, she jerks the opposite way just out of his reach.

"Moose! Come on, man!" Cali squeals. One sleeve slides down from her elbow, and she pushes it back up, getting even more clay on it. "It's not like it's one of the new shirts you just got. It's just an old one from home, from college! I'll just get you another one."

"No, it's not, Squirrel!" he counters. "That's the shirt from our senior year in high school. It's not like I can just go to a store at home and get another one."

"It is?" Cali stops long enough to look down at the shirt she's wearing. "Well, would you look at that?"

With her distracted, Matt leaps through the air and tackles her. Cali lets out an "Oof" as she's taken to the ground. She's trying to push him off, but Matt is bigger and takes each of her wrists in his hands.

"Now, say you're sorry for everything, my arm *and* my shirt, or I'll make you give yourself a wet-willy."

"No way! I'm not sorry now. And you're about to feel the full force of my wrath!"

"Your wrath?" he asks. Matt moves his arms to make Cali slap herself lightly multiple times. Each time her hand comes away, it leaves a gray splat behind on her face. "What wrath would that be?"

"Moose! Stop it! Stop! I give, I give!"

"Say it. Say you're sorry."

"You're sorry," Cali parrots with a smug smile. Then since she can't cover it with either hand because Matt is holding both, she sneezes right in his face.

"You didn't," he says in disbelief. He lets go of one of her wrists to wipe his face, and that's all the space Cali needs.

She wipes her hand on her—well, his—shirt, sticks a finger in her mouth, then puts the same finger in Matt's ear. Matt shrieks and lets go of her other wrist. Cali wiggles out from underneath him and pops up, shifting her weight to the balls of her feet, ready for Matt's next attack.

I watch as my boyfriend wipes his ear with the damp shirt he's wearing. He stands up, shaking his head vigorously. I can't help but sympathize with the intensely icky sensation he must have right now. Growing up with two older brothers, I know exactly how he feels all too well.

Matt's face is getting red; I can tell that if I don't step in now, I'm going to have to explain to Mickey that it wasn't a demon who murdered her girlfriend, but Cali's own best friend. I retract my finger from Milo's collar and stand up.

"Alright, that's enough."

When they don't immediately relax and let the fight end, I clap my hands loudly three times and say, "Hey! I said that's enough."

"She started it," Matt grumbles, still wiping his ear.

"Well, I'm ending it." I immediately hear my father's voice in my head and get a major case of deja vu.

Milo has positioned himself between the two of them. When Matt moves to lunge at Cali again, Milo stops him with a loud bark. When Cali laughs at her friend being fended off by the dog, Milo spins around and barks at her in the same way.

I cross my arms and wait until they both look at me. Cali looks like she's about to be scolded, and Matt hasn't let go of any of his anger yet.

"Matt," I say, addressing him first. 'We're both still drenched from the rain. Why don't you go shower and change into dry clothes?"

He huffs and storms from the living room toward our shared bedroom. Cali relaxes as she watches him go. We both flinch as he slams the door. When her eyes finally meet mine, she immediately tears them away from my gaze.

"Cal, I know you like to get a rise out of him, and most of the time, it's funny. But what just happened? It was different, that was—"

"I know," she cuts me off. "Too much."

Since I can't think of anything else, I say, "Yeah."

She comes back into the kitchen and checks on the clay. She picks up the same tapered tool and goes back to work. I go to the fridge and take out a new bottle of white wine chilling on its side for her and sparkling mineral water for me. I grab the corkscrew and two glasses from the cabinet to pour each of us a hefty amount of our drinks.

I resume the same chair as before and slide the glass over to her. I leave it far enough away, though, so that it won't bump or spill on anything. She reaches over and lifts the glass. Cali brings it to her lips but doesn't take a drink.

"You okay?" I ask, taking a sip from my glass. It's the dumbest question to ask because she obviously isn't, but I can't think of anything else to say.

Cali puts the drink back down on the table and sighs. She shakes her head no and goes back to work, texturing the clay covering the cardboard base. She draws the tool along the side again, creating the edge of another page.

I try to wait her out. I know she'll talk to me when ready. After several minutes of silence, though, I get impatient.

"Cal," I say softly.

She sighs and puts the tool down. She's about to run a hand over her hair but thinks twice and wipes both on her shorts. She looks like she's about to start talking, but instead picks up another tool and begins working the clay where the spine of *The Book* will be.

Again I wait.

"It's just," she finally starts. "I'm jealous."

I blink in surprise. I don't know what I was expecting, exactly, but I'm surprised none the less.

"Jealous? Of what?"

"Of him. Moose." Using a triangular ended tool, she cuts a shallow line into the clay with a sharp, straight edge. It looks like the natural fold that a cover would create from being opened and closed.

"All I had to do to get him to come to the library was say, 'Lex needs our help.' That's it. That's all I had to say.

"I didn't have to explain; he actually didn't even ask anything other than what could he do. I told him to pack a bag with a few changes of clothes and meet us late that night.

"It took him all of two seconds to decide to drop everything and help, because he loves you. He really, really loves you."

Her eyes flick between the pictures and both replicas as she begins texturing the side of the clay. Her hands move swiftly and deftly across the clay, gradually working the surface to make it look like the stretched leather that covers the spine of *The Book*.

"And I don't know if it's possible for anyone to," she continues. "But if they can, then he loves you just as much as I love Mickey. And seeing him with you, and how he looks at you or reaches for you, just reminds me over and over that the person I look at that way, that I reach out for, is thousands of miles away.

"It makes me jealous. Angry. And when I see you two try to hide it, or not be obvious with each other—which, by the way, you suck at —it makes me feel guilty on top of it."

I don't know what to say. I thought we were respectful of her feelings, but now I realize we just might've made things worse by acting secretive about it.

"Cali, I'm so sorry," I say. "I know how much you love Mickey, and I know how hard this must be for you to be away from her. I thought we were doing the right thing by keeping it kind of hidden."

I take my glasses off and clean the frames with the edge of my soggy sweater sleeve. I finish my wine before putting my glasses back on.

"I don't know what to say," I speak truthfully. "How long have you felt like this?"

Cali bites the inside of her cheek before she says, "Since you went to the currency exchange at the airport in Amsterdam."

"Really? Why didn't you say something to me before?"

"I didn't know how to," she says quietly. "I didn't think I could just be like, 'Hey! Keep it in your pants!'"

"Well, yeah! Just maybe with a little tact." She half-smiles at me. "Have you said anything to Matt about it?"

I already know the answer, and Cali confirms it when she shakes her head no.

"I thought I'd pick a fight with him instead," she says drily.

"Hmm. And how'd that work out for you?"

The joke works as intended, and the tension in Cali's shoulders finally drops a little. Her hands continue moving across the clay, and she laughs quietly.

"I know it wasn't the best idea, but I won this round, didn't I?" she says offhandedly with a shrug. She looks up at me, her mouth shaped by a smug smile.

"Give him the idea to pour water on me to wake me up tomorrow morning or something. Let him have a little revenge. He'll feel better."

Unscrewing the lid from the bottle once more, I refill my glass. My friend has barely touched hers, but I top off her drink anyway. I get up from my chair and come around the table to stand next to her.

Cali is just about finished with the detail work, which is honestly quite remarkable in how perfect the clay replicas look. As long as we aren't caught making the switch, I don't think anyone at the library would know the difference.

When she finally puts down the tool and takes a step back from the table, I give her the hug I've been waiting to.

"No, Roz, I'm all dirty," she says, trying to pull back.

"I don't care." I pull her in and hug her tightly. Cali is a cuddly person by nature, so it takes her less than a second before she's clinging to me. Our four-inch height difference allows her to nuzzle her forehead into my neck.

"Cal," I say softly without letting her go. "I spent the first eleven months of knowing you and living with you lying to you. It was really hard. There were things I wanted to tell you but thought I couldn't, that I thought maybe you wouldn't be able to handle. But I did tell you. And it felt like a giant boulder was lifted off of me."

I see a neon sign start to flash HYPOCRITE in my head as I remind myself of the giant secret I am keeping from her right now. I pull the plug to shut it down so I can focus back on the moment in front of me.

"You know that I trust you. I've literally put my life in your hands. So, I hope you know that there is nothing you could say that I wouldn't hear and nothing you need to keep from me because of how I might react to it. No matter what it is, please don't underestimate me the way I underestimated you."

Cali is quiet for a long time. She doesn't relax her grip on me, so I keep mine just as tight. Finally, she moves back, and we disentangle from each other. She lifts her chin and stares into my eyes. Even though there are still secrets between us, the ones *I'm* still keeping, I do feel like a new level of trust and understanding has been reached between us.

"Okay," she says. Cali nods once and returns to her project on the table, constantly checking that every detail matches.

The steak that has been marinating on the counter is ready to be cooked, so I turn my attention to fixing dinner for the three of us.

"Roz," Cali says behind me. I turn toward my friend and see her open her mouth to speak again. I'm pretty sure of what she's about to say, so I beat her to it and smirk as I say it first.

"I gotchu, kid."

• 3 7 •

DARIUS

Early in the morning of a New Orleans' Sunday, the demon's eyes slowly open. He's lying on a bed in a nicely furnished but modest hotel room. The walls are bright white plaster with dark wood molding the same color as the floorboards. A padded wooden armchair is angled in the corner next to a wall of windows.

Outside, the sun is just starting to rise, gauze curtains drawn over the window allow soft gray light to fill the room. The bottoms billow gently from the air conditioner that rattles as it cools the room.

Lifting his head gingerly, Darius sees that against the wall opposite his bed is a burgundy couch bookended by faux candle sconces attached to the plaster. The demon sees Viribus's significant size stretched across the sofa. The backs of his knees are draped over the armrest, and his large feet are dangling barely an inch above the floor.

The demon's head is pounding and heavy from the Victus transformation. In all his time on this earth, he has never done two conversions at once. And now he knows why. Both men willingly joined him, making the demon's recovery easier than when he forced the transition of his last Victus, Damon.

He knows that the trance he falls into post-transition has restored barely enough strength to do the next two men, but he's unwilling to slow down. His desire to increase his ranks before his next face-off with the witch outweighs his body's signals that it is still dangerously depleted.

"Viribus." The demon's usually smooth and commanding voice comes out a whisper. He licks his lips and swallows. A coppery taste lingers in and around his mouth. The demon ignores it, not having the energy to think about it.

"Viribus," he tries again, louder this time.

The snores coming from the Victus soldier continue without interruption. Darius looks for something to throw at the man. His eyes land on the TV remote on the nightstand to the left of his bed. He reaches out with his scarred hand and throws the long plastic rectangle.

Viribus stirs as the remote rebounds against the wall and lands on the floor but does not wake.

Angry at the lack of response, Darius summons all the strength he can muster and whips his right arm out, first to the left, then again to the right. His telekinesis power breaks the front leg on each side of the couch, causing it to sink forward on an angle. Viribus is rolled off of the cushions; the impact his face makes with the floor is finally a big enough jolt to wake the man.

He groans and slowly sits up. Darius watches the oaf rub his face and yawn. Shaking his head, the demon lays it back on the pillow and stares up at the ceiling.

"Get up, you mountainous idiot."

"Wha—?" Viribus looks around sleepily.

"Now!" Darius shouts.

"Oh! Sorry, boss." Viribus scurries over to the bed, half crawling, half leaping. "What do you need?"

"Call Blue and tell him that in two hours, I want him here with the next two men ready to go."

"Yes, boss," Viribus replies obediently. "Do you need... anything else?"

"I'm strong enough," the demon says tightly. To prove his point, he sits up in bed. He ignores how difficult the movement is and how it makes the room spin, silencing the signals his body is begging him to heed.

"How long?" he asks.

Viribus hesitates to answer right away. Only after Darius glares at him with a clenched jaw does he finally say, "Three and a half days."

"What?!" Darius shouts in shock. "It should have only been two! Why didn't you do what I told you and give me food to quicken things?"

"I did, boss," Viribus says meekly, refusing to make eye contact with the ancient evil. "You woke up to eat and said to do it again today before you passed out again."

The giant gets up and moves across the room to a microwave-refrigerator combination tucked into a corner next to an open mahogany armoire housing the television. He pulls the fridge door open to reveal multiple bulky items wrapped in brown butcher paper. Viribus reaches in to grab one.

The demon grumbles to himself, infuriated by his lack of energy. He won't admit, to himself or anyone else, that he has yet to recover entirely from the injuries he sustained at the hand of that infuriating witch. The more he tries to push himself, the longer it will take for him to regain full strength.

"Give it here," Darius says impatiently with his arm extended. Viribus quickly hands him the package. The demon rips the paper open and violently bites a hunk of the raw beef tenderloin off. He barely chews it before swallowing and taking another greedy bite.

"Call Blue," he orders again, with bright red blood dripping from the corner of his mouth. "I want those men here in an hour."

"You said two."

"Well, now I said one!" he shouts. "Don't question me, you god-damn troglodyte. I want this all done as quickly as possible. I am tired of waiting on that bitch! I want this whole thing to be goddamn over with, do you fucking understand me?!"

"Yes, boss," Viribus says quietly.

"We're upping the speed here, Viribus," Darius continues. "Go back to wherever you got this and buy out everything they have. You will give me one of these every four hours. I want to be awake from each transition after no more than thirty-six hours. You force it down my throat if you have to. Got it?"

The behemoth nods.

"Good. Now get the fuck out of here."

"Yes, boss. I'm on it."

Viribus backs away from the demon, leaving him to continue tearing into the slab of bovine. Through the door, Darius hears the deep baritone voice make the call to Blue to get the day going.

After finishing the meat and sucking every last drop of blood off of the paper, Darius relaxes back onto the bed. His body rests again as his mind gleefully plays through every horrific thing he's planning to do to the girl once he catches her.

****

Blue and Viribus are standing outside the closed bathroom door waiting for the demon. Two parolees are sitting awkwardly on the same couch that Darius had broken the legs of to wake up his sol-dier. They are waiting silently; neither man looks at the other.

The doorknob to the bathroom turns, and Darius emerges. He's washed the blood from around his face and neck. His jet black hair is wet, droplets of water fall onto the dark gray button-down shirt he's changed into.

The demon moves to stand at the foot of the bed facing the two men on the couch. The convicts remain silent as they wait for whatever is about to happen. Darius points to the open floor space in front of him.

"Kneel," he instructs.

The men obediently slide from the couch to the floor. Darius rolls up the cuffs of his shirt, exposing his tattooed forearms. The marks on his left arm look as though they've been scorched into his skin against the background of the red scars.

He looks toward Blue and Viribus, who are still standing near the bathroom. "You have your instructions," the demon says to them. They each offer a clipped nod yet do not move further into the room.

Darius closes his eyes and takes a deep breath. He lets it out slowly, then says in Latin, "*Ut malediceret tibi me virtus mea.*"

My power I curse to thee.

Because the two men in front of him are willingly joining his ranks, the spell is slightly altered from the one he used during Damon's forced conversion.

The fingertips on both of the demon's hands turn black. He says the spell again, "*Ut malediceret tibi me virtus mea.*"

As if he's dipping his arms into an invisible vat of ink, the black starts to creep up his fingers and over his palms. His tattoos begin to grow, connecting into solid black as the color continues the climb up his arms.

Darius recites the Latin words a third time, and every visible inch of his forearms is completely black. He reaches out but does not touch the men yet. As his hand hovers, he closes his eyes and says the next line of the spell.

"Corporalis motus animi." Physical movement of the mind.

The same dark, inky color that covers his hands creeps up following the tracks of the veins in his neck until it reaches his eyes. Darius opens his eyes, and they glow a bright red yet are simultaneously as black as his arms.

He reaches out and touches both men, one hand on each head. The black seeps from his hands into the men's blood vessels and spreads throughout their bodies from their heads downwards. Whereas this caused Damon excruciating pain across his body as he fought the transition, the men in front of Darius only feel mild discomfort.

Darius quietly chants, *"Ego ut malediceret tibi." I curse to thee.* His hands stay firmly planted on the men's heads until the black pools in their eyes matching his own. The demon releases the men as the black fades from their irises.

His knees buckle, but the demon catches himself to maintain authority in front of his new recruits. He gently sets himself down on the bed. The skin on his arms and hands has returned to normal; the black swirls returned to their regular shape and size.

Viribus steps forward and tells the men to get up. They obey the colossal man and stand. Both are slightly unsteady but quickly regain their senses. Blue herds them out into the hall and watches over them as he waits for Viribus to join him.

"You good, boss?" Viribus asks quietly.

"I'm fine," Darius snaps. "I just need to rest. Keep an eye on them, Viribus. You and Blue get them situated. They do anything stupid—it won't be only their heads that roll."

The demon lays back onto the bed fighting off the uncontrollable fatigue that ripples through his limbs and torso, his mind clouding as unconsciousness beckons.

"Before you leave here, give me another cut of meat from that fridge. And remember, I want the next two here in thirty-six hours from now. Thirty-six hours, Viribus. And not a fucking second more."

• 3 8 •

Cali

She's slow to wake up this morning, as her dreams continuously lull her back to sleep. She can feel Milo's body pressed up against her back. The warmth he's radiating makes it that much harder to keep her eyes open. The high-pitched squeak from the doorknob as it turns severs the haze and wakes her.

"Psst, Milo!" a voice whispers. "Come here."

As Milo hops down and the bed shakes, Cali smiles to herself. She's been waiting for Matt's payback since Saturday night. She had made amends and washed his shirt, but when the only thing that happened yesterday was the silent treatment, she knew it would most likely come today.

She stays completely still even when she hears some water slosh out of whatever bowl or pot he's using. Matt softly curses as it splats onto his feet. It's quiet in the room until the bed moves again as he bumps into it.

"Damnit!" he hisses.

Cali debates moving out of the way, maybe even bolting up and scaring him. But she decides to let him have this win, still feeling the guilt about getting into it with him on Saturday. The bed dips, and she assumes that it's Matt situating himself above her.

She squeezes her eyes shut, preparing herself to be doused. But no amount of anticipation could have prepared her for what hit her.

The water is *freezing*. Matt must have let the water run for a while and then put in at least three trays' worth of ice cubes. Some even bounce off of her forehead as the water pours onto her.

Cali lets out a piercing scream as she scrambles to get out of the bed. She's wrapped so tightly into the sheets that she only manages to fall off the side of the bed in a heap. A thud sounds as Matt jumps off the bed with her.

As she struggles to free herself from her covers, Matt continues to dump the water on her slowly. Cali screams again, thrashing to get out from under the ice-cold stream pouring onto her.

"Okay, okay!!" she shouts. "I give. You win, Moose. You win! Stop!"

"What is going on in here?!" Roslyn shouts as she rushes into the room. She sees Matt standing over a helpless Cali stuck inside a now soaking wet comforter and top sheet.

"Nothing to worry about, babe," Matt says over his shoulder.

"Oh, okay. Carry on."

"No, don't go! Help me!"

"Mmm, nah. Seems like everything is under control here. But I have a tiny headache, so can you keep it down, please? 'K, thanks."

Roslyn waves to the two friends and closes the door behind her. Cali shakes her head to clear the water from her eyes. She looks up just in time to see Matt tilt the enormous stockpot to dump the rest of the water inside.

"Jesus, enough! No!" She squirms as the water torturously trickles onto her. The covers are getting heavier as they absorb the cold water making it even harder for her to get out of the way.

"Come on, Moose!" she gargles as the water fills her mouth.

"Okay, that's enough," Matt says. He puts the pot on the bed and helps Cali untangle herself. She's out of breath from trying to escape, and once she's finally freed, she sits up and wipes soaking wet hair from her face.

"We good now?" she asks.

"Almost," Matt says. He quickly picks up the pot again and, in one gush, dumps the rest onto Cali's head. "Now, we're good."

He smiles sweetly at her and bows before exiting the room. Cali huffs and crawls across the floor, using the foot of the bed to help her stand. She leaves her bedroom and goes to the kitchen, where she finds Roslyn and Matt each hunched over a bowl of cereal at the peninsula counter, her clay undisturbed on the table under damp cloths. Milo's head is ducked into his bowl, enjoying his breakfast like he's in on the joke.

"Well, since I'm already soaking wet, I think I'll just take a shower now." Matt and Roslyn don't look up, just nod as they each spoon another bite of cereal into their mouths.

"Right," Cali continues. "So we calling a truce, Moose? You know, the war is over, and the kingdom has been restored to order?"

Matt looks up at his friend and narrows his eyes as he chews, considering her offer. Cali waits for his response, which doesn't come until Roslyn jabs his side with her elbow.

"Alright, truce," he says. He holds out his hand, and he and Cali smack hands twice, pound their fists, then snap their fingers.

"You guys have been friends for too long," Roslyn mumbles around a mouthful of cereal. Before she can scoop up more of her breakfast, she winces and rubs her temple with her free hand.

"You okay?" Cali asks her friend.

"Yeah, just a headache is all."

Cali frowns and comes around the table to put her hand on Roslyn's forehead. "Hmm." She leans down and presses her lips to her forehead, then touches her cheeks and the back of her neck. "You're really warm; you might be coming down with something."

"Am not," the witch protests. "I haven't been sick in over a year! Plus, we don't have time for me to get sick."

Matt reaches over and touches his girlfriend's head. "You're definitely running warm. Maybe you should stay here today and—"

"No!" Roslyn cuts him off. "We're going back to the room with *The Book* today."

"I know, babe, but you need to take care of yourself. I can go."

Roslyn pops out of her chair to object again. Cali sees her eyes swim in her head, and she slumps back into her chair. Before she even lands in the seat, Milo is at her side, whining as he presses into her leg.

"Okay," she says, rubbing her temple again with one hand, the other resting on Milo's head. "Maybe I should stay home."

She gets up, slower this time, and goes to pick up her bowl. "I got it," Matt says. Roslyn eases her way into the living room and lays down on the couch. Milo moves with her and sits down, facing her.

Cali and Matt share a look before they both start moving. Cali heads back toward her bedroom while Matt places both bowls in the sink. She rifles through the medicine cabinet in her bathroom for the pain reliever they bought once they got to Rome.

They meet in the living room—Matt, with a glass of orange juice, Cali, with the medicine. Roslyn's eyes are closed, and her breathing is even. Milo hasn't moved from his spot, and Cali can tell he doesn't plan to.

"Should we wake her?" Matt asks.

"Yes," Cali says without hesitation. She sits down on the edge of the couch and rubs Roslyn's shoulder lightly. "Roz, honey, come on, wake up just for a second."

Roslyn barely opens her eyes, and Cali offers her the medicine and the glass of orange juice. "Drink the whole th ng."

Cali watches her friend do as told before easily falling back to sleep. She pets Milo and motions for Matt to follow her into the kitchen.

"I think you should go to the library soon, spend the morning there and come back around lunchtime. I'm going to keep working on these," she gestures to the table. "But, this afternoon, I was going to go and talk to Carmela again. I don't want to leave her here alone if she's sick."

"Okay," Matt agrees as he angles himself to be able to see Roslyn on the couch. He looks back at his friend, and they nod before going separate ways again.

Cali goes into her bedroom and peels off the pajamas that are clinging to her small frame from the cold dousing Matt greeted her with this morning. Foregoing a shower, she gets dressed.

Cali picks up the comforter and top sheet and hangs them in her bathroom to dry, turning it into a makeshift fort. She throws a couple of towels on the floor to mop up the excess water and checks to make sure the mattress is dry.

After agreeing he'll be back by one this afternoon, Matt leaves for the library to continue researching the poss ble location of Darius's portal. As Cali gets herself situated to work on the clay to make it look as close to the real leather as possible she periodically peaks behind her to check on Roslyn asleep on the couch. Milo hasn't moved from his spot keeping watch.

Cali puts in one earbud so she can hear if Roslyn needs anything and gets to work. She finishes manipulating the clay on both until they perfectly match the rounded leather spine of the real thing.

Once satisfied with the binding, Cali moves on to the inscription on the front.

Cali learned a long time ago that the best way to forge writing is to look at it upside down and consider it a design rather than handwriting. She turns the printed pictures and tries it by hand with a pen on plain paper. She repeats the upside-down markings until it comes from her hand smoothly. Confident that she's got the rhythm of it down, Cali circles the table to face the replica from the opposite direction, and with her right hand steadying her left, carefully traces the inscription.

She straightens up and steps back to admire her work. Flicking her eyes back and forth between the photos and the clay, Cali nods and says to herself, "I'd buy that."

Repeating the process on the second carbon copy, Cali takes a break before finishing the texturing of the top. While eating some sliced fruit, she checks Roslyn's forehead, and it's cool to the touch. Milo watches her every move as she gets closer to and then moves away from her friend.

Cali cranks up her music and locks in on what she has left to do. Using a straight, needle-like tool, she gets to work on the texture of the stretched leather *The Book* is made of. Similar to the cracked earth of a dry lakebed, she gingerly copies a square-inch at a time before going back over to make the indentions slightly more defined.

Inch by inch, she moves over the clay, the likeness taking shape in shockingly precise detail. When the top of the first duplicate is done, she stretches her back, cracks her neck, and jumps right into work on the second. She's finished half of the top by the time Matt returns from the library.

He darts through the apartment with excitement and is out of breath as if he ran back to the apartment. He holds up printed pages that are crinkled and marked up. It's clear Matt has read through what's on them multiple times.

"I think I found where the portal is."

• 3 9 •

"ROSLYN"

I wake to someone softly rubbing my shoulder. My headache has gotten marginally better, but I still feel run down and weak. My eyes feel so heavy I can barely open them.

"Come on, honey," I hear a voice. For the briefest of moments, I'm a teenager again, and I hear my mother's voice trying to wake me in the morning before school.

As my mind clears, assisted by someone rubbing my back, the first thing I can tell is that the sounds and smells of where I am are different than home. As the voice cuts through more clearly, it changes to Cali, and a sour mixture of sadness and disappointment makes me sag further into the couch.

I am at my most vulnerable when I don't feel well. At these times, especially, I ache for my mother's comfort, but I force myself to reject the instinct to seek her out to heal my ailment. I shake off the emotions and silently remind myself of what's at stake.

I repeat one of my mantras until I'm strong enough to open my eyes and return to reality. *She's safe because she doesn't know where you are. It's okay. She's safe, everyone's safe.*

"Roz, we have to tell you something. Are you up?" Cali coaxes again. I force myself to open my eyes fully and sit up.

My eyes spin with the room as I'm hit with a dizzy spell. I rub both of my temples before nodding and answering her, "Well, I'm conscious, but I don't know how awake I am."

I see Cali's small smirk as she hands me another glass of orange juice and some more pain relievers. I wash the pills down and drain the glass; I'm still thirsty and am about to ask for some water when my best friend swaps the glasses and hands me a large glass of cold water.

I smile my thanks before I drink every drop. She uses the back of her hand to check my forehead and makes a mostly satisfied face.

"Okay," I sigh. "That's a little better."

"You need to hear this," Cali repeats.

Both of my Extensios are looking at me with eager faces. "Okay," I say. "I'm all ears."

"I think I found the portal," Matt says. Six words that clear the fog in my head and make my heart rate spike.

"What?" I ask, already excited. "How? Where?"

"Well, remember how I was finding multiple Native American stories about a great shaking?"

I nod.

"I looked into it more, and the stories all come from tribes that lived in the southwest."

He starts laying out sheets of paper on the coffee table as he talks, "The Hualapai, the Navajo, the Havasupai, even the Hopi, and the Zuni.

"I'm paraphrasing, of course, but each has similar stories about a violent shaking of the earth that made a great open space wider and deeper. Most have details about rocks crumbling, boulders rolling down the sides, and red smoke billowing from the depths of the earth when a group of beings came up over the edge. They could move things without touching them, caused death and pain at every village they came across, and the leader could conjure fire that would fly from its hands.

"There are even pictures from paintings found on the walls of caverns depicting the whole thing," Matt puts the last piece of paper down, and there are multiple images of the paintings. Each one shows a general portrayal of beings emerging from a large break in the earth's surface.

"Sounds like the Grand Canyon," Cali says in an offhand manner.

As soon as the words leave her mouth, it's like a lightning bolt strikes my head. "Holy shit, it's the Grand Canyon."

"I was kidding Roz," Cali says. "The Grand Canyon was formed by water that gradually carved the stones. Plus, it was formed way before Darius got here. Like, millions of years before."

"I know that, Cal," I say. "But that doesn't mean I'm not right. I've read that there are certain points around the world where the earth's magnetic field changes, like, gets stronger or weaker, and I think the Grand Canyon is one of those places.

"And a change in the magnetic field could explain how Darius was able to create a connection between his home and earth. It would've been like a lighthouse signaling a ship to shore in the middle of the night."

I take one of the pieces of paper and turn it over. "Can you draw an outline of the world map for me?"

Cali takes the pen from the Sudoku book under the coffee table. Since she's left-handed, she starts with Asia and works her way west. When she's done, she rotates the page to me and hands me the pen.

"Okay, this is approximately where we are," I put an X on the boot of Italy sticking out into the Mediterranean. Next, I put a mark on where I believe Portland to be and say, "And this is where we all came from.

"A big part of the story I was told as a child is that when Darius got here from his homeworld, he came armed with the knowledge that to remake earth in his image, he had to destroy any and all of the good magic that already occupied it.

"Basing that in truth, in order for the Native American stories to have been passed down through generations, that means that some of the people in the villages survived after he attacked. But if Darius was only out for total destruction, why wouldn't he just kill them all?"

They both stare at me, blankly. "Because he wasn't just randomly killing. He was hunting."

With my headache forgotten and my energy restored by finally having something of a solid lead, I forge ahead, filling in all the gaps of the story about Darius's arrival and his ultimate goal. I circle the general area of the Grand Canyon and continue.

"If the portal is here, then the most likely course for him was to go west up into Alaska and over the Bering Strait into Russia and across until my ancestors' curse stopped him.

"There are magical beings all over the world, but this is where he was finally taken down." I draw two vertical lines down the middle of the paper. Inside them are the continents of Africa and Europe—two continents that contain all of the countries of my roots.

"This is amazing. We've narrowed down the search from the entire planet to, like, two-thousand square miles."

"It gets better," Cali says proudly. "When Moose got back, I was almost done with the texturing detail of the second model. I made him wait until I finished to wake you."

Cali gets up and motions for me to follow her. As I stand, the room whirls again, and I have to grab the arm of the couch to steady myself. I feel Matt's hand at the small of my back, and I relax backward into his touch for the briefest moment. I straighten up and move to where Cali is standing in the kitchen.

"Once they're dry, all that's left to do is paint them," she says.

As I come around the table to face the clay replicas head-on, my heart starts to pound, and a chill runs up my spine. Both reactions could be from whatever bug is wearing me down, but I know it's more supernatural than that.

"Oh my god," I whisper.

The copies so perfectly match the original that I'm having the same physical reaction as the first time I saw *The Book* in Portland. The hair on my arms stands on end, and my skin starts to tingle. I feel drawn to touch the clay just like I was to touch the leather all the way back in CCR3.

I reach my hand out, but Cali catches my arm. "Don't. It's not dry enough yet."

"These are incredible. Look," I say, pointing to the goosebumps on my arms. "I feel like I'm looking at the real thing.

"If I'm having such a strong reaction and they aren't even painted yet, then no one is going to know the difference once we make the swap.

I exhale heavily and say sincerely, "Bravo, kid."

Cali beams at the compliment and says, "Well, speaking of swaps, now that Moose has returned, it's time for me to shower and get all prettied up to put that particular part of our plan in motion."

She backpedals to her bedroom to get ready. I sit down in the chair closest to the clay and scour every inch of them. In the corner of my eye, I catch Matt staring at me.

"Yes, Mr. Moorely?" I ask playfully.

"Nothing, you're just really cute."

"I am not cute," I say, parroting his own words from the computer lab. "I am strong and intelligent, and beautiful."

"Mmm, you're all of that and much, much more." He leans over and gives me a quick peck on the lips. As he gets up, he asks me what I want for lunch.

"Just some toast or something plain like it."

"Coming right up, babe."

Thankfully with little time and no charred messes like the other day at breakfast, Matt puts a plate of perfectly toasted Italian bread in front of me. He hands me a knife and places the butter dish down on the table, then sets about making himself a sandwich with bruschetta and sharp provolone. We eat in comfortable silence.

When we're finished, Matt says he's going to take Milo for a nice long walk. I go into the bedroom we're sharing and lay down under the covers. Now that the excitement from figuring out where the portal most likely is and seeing the clay copies has dissipated, I'm feeling weary and worn out again. I fall back asleep faster than I thought I would.

When I wake up again, I feel Matt's body pressed against my back; his arm wrapped protectively across my waist. Milo is curled in a ball on top of the covers near my feet. I smile briefly before the comfort of their combined warmth lulls me back to my dreams.

• 4 0 •

The next time I wake up, there is pale light coming through the bedroom's single narrow window. I can't tell if it's early morning or early evening. The pressure of Milo's weight on my feet is gone, and Matt's snores are loud next to me.

Morning, I decide.

I take inventory of how I'm feeling. My headache is reduced to just a dull throb, but even without having moved yet, I have more energy than I've had in any of the last few days. My inability to sleep for more than a couple of hours at a time, plus the stress of traveling in general, and having the fate of an extra two lives relying on my capacity to keep them in one piece, must have finally caught up to me and wiped me out.

But even as my eyes clear from the sticky heaviness of sleep, I feel a sense of dread and fear replacing the rundown feeling I've been carrying around for the two weeks.

God, I think. *How has it only been two weeks?*

I focus on it to figure out exactly what I'm feeling. With a sudden jolt, it fully forms into one of inevitable tragedy.

It encompasses and paralyzes me entirely as it seeps into my very being. I can feel it in every fiber of my soul—something that I can't stop is coming. It's something unwelcome, destructive, devastating. And while different than my fight against that demon, it's not unalike, maybe not even wholly separate.

I'm frozen by the feeling, and I briefly consider bailing on Matt and Cali. Leave them here with a note of apology, use my powers to steal *The Book,* transport with Milo to somewhere hidden, and go it alone. Remove the danger I've put them in.

I scold myself for being so careless with other people's lives and the reckless choice of bringing them with me in the first place.

Having help from two extra people should have made things easier, not more troublesome. And I need to be honest with myself that it absolutely has. I have to stop fighting the need to be in complete control just because that's how I've done it for the past five years. They've proven it's okay to share the responsibility.

Without Cali's artistic skills, it's impossible to know how long it would have taken me to formulate a plan to get *The Book* out of the library. If she weren't with me, Emel's dream that gave her the idea to make the swap would never have happened because it would put me in direct danger. Without Matt, I'd be balancing all of that, trying to translate the thing on my own, and searching for the portal's location.

Not to mention that, save for Milo, I would be completely alone again. In a country where I only know the bare basics of its language. On my own, exactly like when I was eighteen, all the way back at square one.

I don't know if I could do that again.

Yes, you could, my brain counters, finally sparking to life. *You can do anything because it's what you have to do.*

Inevitable tragedy? Well, then you do everything imaginable to make sure the chances of that are as low as possible. You are the one thing standing between this world and the reign of anguish Darius would certainly force upon it.

With my mental pep talk hitting the nail on the head, the overwhelming dread is quieted from a booming roar to a nagging whisper. I swing my legs over the side of the bed and let the momentum pull me up into a sitting position. I give myself a beat to make sure the room doesn't spin like it did yesterday.

In the bathroom, I look at my reflection in the mirror. My thick, curly hair is all over the place, making me look more like Medusa than myself. I run the water in the sink until it's warm and cup my hands under the flow. I bend down, bringing my hands to my face letting the water wake me up.

I rub from my forehead to my chin before I look at myself again. As the water drips from my jaw to the sink, I scrutinize what I see. The under-eye circles that were stark even against my dark-caramel skin have faded. My eyes are bright, my expression one of determination.

I stare for a moment before I repeat the same words I told myself when I first found the listing for *The Book* at the Central Library in Portland, "Time to work."

I pat my face dry with a towel before I leave the bathroom for the kitchen. I haven't eaten much the last twenty-four hours, and my stomach is grumbling its displeasure. I open the fridge and immediately see a package of sliced pancetta. I grab that, some jam, and two eggs. I think for a minute and add a couple of croissants from the bag on the counter to my pile of food.

As I warm up a frying pan on the stove, I stack three slices of the pancetta and cut it into cubes. When the pan is hot enough, I put in the pancetta, making sure to spread it out, so each square gets sufficiently crispy. When cooked to just the right side of burnt, I put the Italian bacon on a paper towel to drain and crack my eggs right into the leftover grease. I let the eggs fry for a few minutes before I flip them over.

While the eggs finish—no runny yolks for me—I cut one of my croissants in half and generously apply the jam to both pieces. I leave the other whole; I haven't decided if I want jam on it or not yet. I plate my eggs and pancetta, put the croissant on the rim, then pour myself a tall glass of orange juice before I sit down at the counter to enjoy my breakfast.

As I'm chewing, my gaze is repeatedly drawn to the clay replicas drying on the table. I have to remind myself that neither is actually the real thing and stop myself from reaching out to touch them.

I hear a doorknob squeak as it turns somewhere in the apartment. I stop mid-chew, unsure of what door is opening until I hear the tapping of Milo's nails on the floor meaning Cali's awake.

My dog comes right over to me and presses his head against my thigh. I wipe my hands on a napkin before I ruffle his fur and scratch behind his ears. I know I've got the right spot when he angles his head toward me and pushes into my hand.

"Something smells amazing in here," Cali says, yawning as she walks in wearing pajama boxers hidden by an oversized t-shirt with two squirrels printed on it, one in light red the other in light blue. Where the two images overlap, the color changes to dark gray.

She goes right over to the coffee maker before doing anything else. She fumbles with it until it beeps to life.

"You want some?" I ask, motioning to my plate. Cali comes over and takes my fork from my hand. Before she can stab any food, I slide my plate out of her reach. "What are you doing!"

"You asked if I want some," she says, confused.

"I meant I'd make some for you. This is mine." I put my plate back, pull my fork out of her hand, and continue eating. She raises one eyebrow at me then shrugs.

"Okay, but how come you didn't just make a bunch at once?"

"It's better to order," I say as if it's the most obvious thing in the world.

"Alright then," she says through a yawn. "I'll have my pancetta crunchy and my eggs over medium."

She takes a mug down from a cabinet turning back to the coffee maker. The aromas in the kitchen right now are wonderful—fresh coffee brewing and crispy bacon. I imagine it'll draw Matt from bed soon.

"I take it you're feeling better," she says as she sips.

"I am." *Aside from waking up drowning in dread,* I silently add. "I think it was just one of those 24-hour things. I needed a day to recharge."

She comes over and uses the hand not holding her hot mug to touch my forehead. "You're cool. That's good. You were in bed when I got back yesterday, so I didn't get to tell you what happened with Carmela."

"You can tell me now," I say as I get up to put my plate in the sink.

Cali gives me space by plopping down in my recently vacated seat. I turn the stove back on as I cube more pancetta exactly as I did before.

"So," she begins. "The whole walk there, I was going over in my head what I was going to say to this girl. I actually walked right past the library because I was so nervous."

"You? Nervous talking to a girl?"

"Well, not nearly as nervous as when I first talked to Mickey, just more so than I normally would be. There's like, a lot, riding on this, Roz."

I motion with my silicone spatula for her to continue. "She was just getting up from her desk when I walked in. I pretended to look around but watched to see if she recognized or remembered me."

"I take it she did," I comment.

"Of course," Cali says, gesturing to her own body. "Wouldn't you?"

I don't respond but look at her with an increculous expression.

"Anyway," Cali says after waiting me out to see who would crack first. "She approached me, and I realized I couldn't just outright ask her for a favor, I have to butter her up first. So I asked her to go for coffee.

"She showed me a little cafe that has possibly the most incredible espresso I've ever had. Her English is lightyears better than my Italian, so it's pretty easy to communicate. She was very responsive— kept putting her hand on my thigh, touching her neck, would grab my hand when she laughed.

"She remembered giving me the list of books and asked if I found what I was looking for. That was my opening, so I took it. I told her I did and then explained that I'm an artist, and I'm working on my ability to recreate textures with pencils. So I showed her the picture on my phone of the drawing I did at the library."

As Cali talks, I remove the pancetta and crack her eggs into the pan. I fill Milo's food and water bowls while the eggs cook. Cali knows I'm listening, so she keeps talking.

"I showed her the blurry photos explaining that it's exactly the kind of detail and texture I'm looking for but that I just couldn't get a clear shot of it. And, Roz, she *offered* that she knew the head librarian there and said they are friends.

"I played it totally cool and said something like, 'If I could get a look at it out of the case, that would be amazing, but right now, I'm more interested in getting to know you.' Good, right?"

"Smooth," I drawl in agreement.

"She said that today is her day off, so I asked her if I could get a local's tour of Rome."

"Let me guess," I say. "She said yes."

Cali just nods with a satisfied smirk. "But I need to stall seeing *The Book* in person until the replicas are completely finished. So I'm thinking that while I'm finishing them and with Carmela, you and Moose should stakeout the library."

"Stakeout? Like we're planning a heist? I suddenly feel like we're in *Ocean's 8*."

"More like *The Italian Job*," Cali says with a smirk.

"Touché."

"And we kind of are," she adds. "When you sift through all the layers of what's going on right now, at the bottom of it, we're planning to rob the National Central Library of Rome."

I pause as the weight of that settles on my shoulders on top of everything else already stacked there. Cali must realize the change in me because she quickly says, "It's going to work, Roz."

I shake my head quickly to come back to the moment. "So, what do Matt and I do while you're with Carmela?"

"You keep going to the library, but instead of going to the computer lab, go to the room where *The Book* is on display and set up for the day there. One of you should stay there and pretend to be working on something, and the other can walk around the room looking for a book or something.

"Use my phone and take a video in the slo-mo mode with the front-facing camera so we can see what the security camera set up is. It'll just look like you're looking down at your phone as you're walking."

"You must have really thought this through," I say as I place her breakfast in front of her. "But why slo-mo?"

"Because then you or Moose can walk normal, not draw attention to yourselves, and the video will still be slow enough that we can see everything."

"Oh, that's good, kid. Real good," I say, holding my orange juice up. Cali clinks her coffee mug to my glass and smiles as she eats her eggs.

• 4 1 •

Cali and I continue talking, figuring out the best way to make the switch, real for fake, until Matt comes into the kitchen. He's wearing basketball shorts and a t-shirt that matches Cali's, but with two moose on it instead.

The first thing he does is come and check my temperature the same way Cali did. *Sometimes they are so similar,* I think. He nods, silently satisfied that whatever bug I had has left my system, and pours himself a cup of coffee.

"Breakfast?" I ask.

"Say yes," Cali says with her mouthful. "Woman is on a roll."

"Okay, yes," Matt says sleepily.

I turn on the stove one more time and cut up the last three slices of pancetta. "Eggs?"

"Scrambled," he says through a yawn.

"You're not getting sick now, are you?" Cali asks, leaning away from the counter.

"No, I don't think so. I just didn't sleep very well last night."

"How come?"

"Honestly, I don't know." He takes his coffee over to the kitchen table, and from a safe distance, stares at the replicas. "I think I'm worried."

"About what?" I ask as I crack two eggs into a bowl and whisk them with a fork.

"About all of this," he gestures toward the clay. "I mean, how are we even going to make the switch, first without anyone seeing and then without anyone realizing? What if there's a tag or a chip attached that sets off an alarm if removed from the case?

"What if Carmela doesn't leave you alone with it? You can't just say to her, 'Hey, don't look for a second, I just have to steal this real quick.'

"And then there are probably cameras. What about security, librarians, other staff? After we steal the thing, do we continue going there or just stay here hiding out?"

He sits down next to Cali at the counter and pinches the bridge of his nose. Cali hands him the last half of her croissant with jelly as a peace offering. He takes it and pops the whole thing in his mouth.

"Moose, you're overthinking this way too much," she says. "We have to slow down and take it one thing at a time. There are too many moving parts to half-ass any of it."

"She's right," I say, placing a plate in front of him. He's still chewing the croissant, so he smiles his thanks at me. "We were actually just talking about this."

"Indeed, we were. About the cameras and finding out the spacing of them and how many et cetera, et cetera."

"No 'et cetera.' Explain," Matt says as he starts shoveling his breakfast into his mouth.

Cali and I give him a rundown of the plan we came up with while he was still asleep. Matt swallows and looks back and forth between Cali and me. "Huh, that's pretty smart," he says.

"Don't sound so surprised, Moose. Must we go through this again? I am way smarter than you."

"Yeah, yeah," he says, waving her off to finish eating. He gets up for more coffee but gives me a kiss on the cheek first. "Breakfast was really good."

I can't help but smile until I look at Cali again. She rolls her eyes so dramatically that it must physically hurt her eyeballs. I let my face fall to neutral and shake my head at her once. She smirks at me in response and gets up to put her plate in the sink.

I open a cabinet and take down the container with Milo's treats in it. His tags jingle as he bolts up from his prone position, ready for a treat. I take out one crunchy bone cookie and put the container back. I can feel Milo on my heels as I walk out of the kitchen to the living room. I give him the bone as I sit down on the couch.

"Cal, if we're going to go full spy movie on this, do you think you can draw the layout of the library?"

"Sure," Cali says, coming into the living room with her topped off mug and Matt right behind her.

She puts her coffee down and goes to her room. When she comes back, she has a drawing pad and a tin of colored pencils. I pop into my bedroom to grab my notebook with the copied pages in it. I put it on the coffee table directly above where Milo has settled down next to me.

"This obviously won't be to scale, but here's a rough estimation."

Cali draws the room where *The Book* is on display, the computer lab, the front entrance, and all connecting hallways.

"So we're going to be here," I point to the exhibition room. "And we have to find all of the cameras from there to both the computer lab and the exit. We'll start that today."

"What time are you meeting Carmela?" Matt asks. The two of them must have talked about her date last night while I was asleep.

"I told her I would meet her at the Palazzo Colonna at noon. As soon as I told her I was an artist, she said I absolutely had to go there, and it gave me another opening with her, so I took it."

"Okay, so maybe now we should decide how we're going to switch the replica for the real thing."

"Bathroom?" Matt offers.

Cali and I grimace and look at each other. "That's not really a normal thing girls do," Cali says. "It's not like, 'Oh, I have to go to the bathroom, let me just bring this really old, big book with me.' I mean, I at least don't do that. Roz?"

"I'm more of a tabloid kind of girl," I say drily. "But, getting Carmela out of the room would obviously be helpful. We'd only need a few seconds."

"A few seconds for what though?" Matt asks. "We've got our in; Carmela has already offered a chance to look at *The Book* outside of the case. But we still don't have any idea how to do this."

We sit quietly as we think of what the best way to do it would be. Cali opens her mouth as if she's got it but deflates without saying anything. Like Matt and I, she's got nothing.

Milo sits up, and his head bumps my notebook that has all the copied pages from *The Book*. It teeters but doesn't fall off the edge. He lifts a black paw and purposely knocks it down. It opens when it hits the floor and the loose pages inside scatter everywhere.

Milo looks at each of us with his mouth open, spotted-tongue out, panting—knowing exactly what he just did. We stay silent until it clicks in my brain.

"Oh my god," I say.

"What?" they both ask in sync.

"Look at how the pages fell everywhere. If we're all bending down to scoop up sheets of paper, we could use that as a distraction to switch the real for the fake. We'd be able to do it without having Carmela leave."

They sit there, absorbing what I said and probably running the scenario through their heads. Cali smiles first, with Matt following close behind.

"Dog Man, you are a certified genius," Cali says as she stands to pick the pages up.

"If I haven't said it before, I'll say it now," Matt says. "I love this dog."

• 4 2 •

DARIUS

A voice calls out but sounds very far away. It fades before he can even determine what it said. The demon isn't dreaming but is immersed in the hollow blackness that allows his body to recharge. He's been in the coma-like meditative state more times in the last thirty days than he has in the prior three hundred years.

The voice comes through again, closer but just barely discernible. "Boss.... Boss, can you hear me?"

The demon doesn't respond to the sound His body only reacts once it smells the meat. Another piece of the red, thick tenderloin that his Victus has been supplying him with. The repetitive strain on his body means he needs to replenish it continually.

There's a pressure on his shoulder, and the bed he's laying on is jostled. The pressure increases with another jostle. The force intensifies, shaking Darius back into consciousness. He growls, ready to lash out, his awareness slower to respond than the rest of him.

"Boss, it's me," Viribus says, easily subduing the demon with his massive hand. "Here, eat."

The soldier hands over the fresh-cut of raw meat and Darius instantly devours it. Savagely tearing off large chunks, barely chewing before swallowing and taking the next bite.

"More," he says roughly, once he's consumed the entire thing. Another cut of cold flesh lands in his hands. The ancient man inhales the second piece just as quickly as the first.

After the last hunk slides down his throat, he finally opens his eyes. He blinks slowly and gingerly sits up. He can already feel his body absorbing the food aiding in the slow return of his energy.

"Better," he says quietly. He glances in Viribus's direction. The behemoth is standing, quietly waiting with a damp towel for the demon to give him a sign he's ready for the next transformations.

"Have Blue come in first before the next two men," Darius orders while wiping the blood from his face and hands.

"Yes, boss."

Viribus leaves quickly to retrieve the parole officer. They stand at the foot of the bed Darius is sitting on. He stands before speaking to make sure everything he says comes from the point of authority.

"I want us to go back to Portland after the next two transitions and do the last *six* there." He looks at Blue, indicating that the man's request to formally join his ranks has been granted. The short man swells with pride and takes in a deep breath.

"Viribus, get in touch with that dirty runt and tell him we'll be back within the week, and I expect him to have something for me when we get there. And make a large batch of transport potions while you're at it; three each should do it.

"Blue, now is the time I expect you to prove your worth and your use. My men need to be able to travel freely without fear of consequences. There will be no second chances for anyone who attracts attention or gets pinched. And if that happens, your head will be the first to roll. Understand?"

"Yes, sir. There is a form I can fill out and bury in each of their files," Blue replies. "If anyone gets suspicious as to why they haven't shown for check-in, the forms will be more than enough."

"You do that," the demon placates the man. The Victus and parole officer turn to go. Darius stops them by clearing his throat. "One last thing."

"Boss?" Viribus asks, waiting for instruction.

"I want every single man in here now. I have something they each need to hear, and I only want to say it once."

The men agree in unison and leave the demon alone in the room.

Darius moves to the window and looks at the bright blue sky. He thinks how much better it will look as the blended swirls of amber, gray, and black from his homeworld.

He spends another brief minute at the window before going into the bathroom. He checks his appearance in the mirror as he runs water to wash off the remaining blood from around his mouth. He rolls up his sleeves and cups his hands underneath the flow of the faucet.

Darius knows from centuries of experience that he gets the best response from his Victus when they both fear *and* respect him. A bloody, disheveled mess doesn't demand the same obedience as well-groomed and in command.

When his face is clean, he runs his wet hands through his black hair. The stark contrast between them is still jarring to him—an ever-present reminder of his failure to kill the little witch, of being stuck waiting on this decrepit planet.

A swirl of anger surges in his throat. He's ready to break the mirror with his fist when the door of the hotel room clicks open. The demon decides to let the anger simmer and use it to drive home the point he's about to make.

Darius exits the bathroom and sees all thirteen men crammed into his moderate hotel room.

"If your transition is complete, stand over there," he says, gesturing to the space between the window and bed. Four of the men move to take their places. "Blue, Viribus, you as well."

The room's been divided, with six on one side, seven on the other. Darius turns his back on his soldiers and faces the men awaiting their turn.

"Spread out across this wall," he orders, pointing at the wall that separates the bathroom from the bedroom. The men obediently respond.

Darius uses his telekinesis power to shift the bed closer to those behind him and walks an imaginary line pausing at each human man and staring at them. Darius stops at the last man, the only one to look away, the same man who stood in the conference room ready to leave until Blue convinced him to stay.

"Collin Kings," Darius says.

"Yes, sir?" the man asks nervously.

"You want to be here?"

"Yes, sir," he says with more conviction.

"Well, now, I don't know about that. When I gave your associates the chance to walk out in the parole office, they stayed seated. You were the only one who stood to go." The demon tilts his head in curiosity. "Why?"

"No, no, sir. I stood, yes, but I was only unsure for a moment. I want to be here, sir."

"I'm not convinced, Mr. Kings."

"Sir?" Collin begins to tremble slightly.

"No, I believe you to be unreliable, untrustworthy. That's not something I can tolerate. Nor do I believe you'll follow my orders to the letter as I expect."

The man now starts to sweat as he promises his loyalty. "I will, sir. I will. Anything you need me to do, I will do it in a second."

Darius steps back and bends his elbow to raise his left hand. With a snap of the demon's fingers, Collin Kings becomes pinned to the wall behind him. He begins to beg the demon, but his words cut off as red fingers tighten into a fist crushing the man's airway.

"Let this serve as a lesson—no, a demonstration—of what will happen should any of you doubt my decisions, question my orders, or waiver in your commitment to me," Darius says to the rest of the men in the room. "Do you understand?"

While holding Collin steady, he connects his eyes to each of the men in the room. He starts with Viribus. He receives an immediate nod and moves his gaze to Blue. The short man repeats the action. The new Victus soldiers mimic what their predecessors have done. The six left waiting for their turn also accept the demon's hard line.

The pale hand that rests at the demon's side begins to glow. Darius raises it to shoulder height and cocks his arm. Collin's face is a dark purple, the life almost gone from him. Darius relaxes his grip enough so the man can suck in deep breaths, but not so much that he can move away from his impending punishment.

"Everyone to the other side of the room," he orders. He pauses until the men move, then says, "Watch and let this be a glimpse into the fate each of you will suffer if you disobey me."

"Please," Collin manages to choke out. "Please, don't!"

His hand brightens to a blinding light, and a ball of fire appears in his palm with a hiss. With an indifferent toss, the fire leaps from Darius's hand through the air and lands square on the human's chest.

There is no time to react or even scream before flames cover every inch of his body. The scorching inferno melts his flesh, reducing it to ash before it can even fall from his bones. Within seconds there is nothing left of the man but a smoldering pile of embers and a swath of charred paint on the wall. The room is silent as each man absorbs what they've just seen.

"The next two awaiting transitions will stay. The rest of you, out."

The room comes to life again with the rustling sounds of men moving. The officer nods at the demon once as he corrals eight bodies from the room. Darius turns to his senior Victus, "Viribus, we're almost done here for the day. As soon as I'm settled after this, I believe you have a phone call to make."

"Yes, boss."

He motions for the two men to position themselves in front of him, "Kneel."

• 4 3 •

TYLER

He couldn't sleep at all last night. He'd almost ignored the phone call yesterday when the caller ID came up as BLOCKED. He had been sitting on his couch, getting stoned and watching a home renovation show, ready to let the call dump to voicemail when his eyes landed on that black cigarette still sitting in his ashtray.

Remembering who that belonged to, he grabbed for his phone, almost knocking it from the couch, and answered it.

"Hello?" his voice was timid and shaky.

"Tyler," the voice on the other side said. He instantly knew who it was. He remembered the deep baritone of the giant who tagged along with the freak that almost killed him.

"Yeah?"

"The boss wants you to know that we'll be coming your way soon."

"We? Who's we?

"You fucking know who, you little twat. We're coming Friday, and we'll have another twelve guys with us. No, eleven. One got out of line."

"Eleven guys? You don't think you're all staying in my apartment, do you?"

"No, you dumb fuck. I feel like Julius right now."

"Who's Julius?" Tyler asked.

"Just shut up, will ya? Jesus. There will be thirteen of us total, but if I remember correctly, and I know that I do, upstairs is also available."

"Oh, yeah. I guess it is. But thirteen? Is that necessary?"

"Are you questioning me right now? Do you even understand how close we are to just getting rid of you? We'll be there Friday. The boss expects you to have a report of what the fuck you've been doing. And if I were you, I wouldn't disappoint."

Tyler shudders, remembering the threat. Replaying the conversation all night led him to where he is now—on his way to Mickey's Kick Boxing and Training Studio. He'd been monitoring from his house, following her every move with the GPS chip attached to her phone case.

But the monster's threat, delivered through his immense lackey, is making Tyler put in a little hustle today. He's out of his apartment early, blending in with the crowds on their way to work this Wednesday morning.

He has the GPS app open, but the purple dot shows that Mickey hasn't left home yet. When Tyler gets to the studio, he veers across the street to the coffee shop. An early-May heatwave has allowed the shop to set up an outside dining area. Tyler sits at a table mostly blocked with a large potted fern that keeps him hidden but gives him a relatively clear line of sight to the studio across the street.

He drops his gym bag at his feet and kicks it underneath the table. Tyler leans over, putting his elbows on his knees, pulling a ball cap down over his eyes to hide his face more from anyone who may look. The dot on his phone is just starting to make its way closer to him. He stares at it as if his life depends on it because, as he learned last night, it does.

Within half an hour, Mickey arrives at the studio. He watches through the large front windows as she goes in and says hello to everyone she passes.

Leaving his hat on and his empty cup on the table, Tyler gets up and darts across the street, heading straight for the men's locker room once inside. As he passes it, he peers inside Mickey's office and sees her sitting at her computer.

Hoping nothing happens in the short time it takes him to change, Tyler enters the locker room and puts on the workout clothes he had packed in his bag. When he exits the locker room, he turns back toward Mickey's office and immediately bumps into someone.

"Watch it," he says before he registers who he collided with.

"Tyler," Mickey says flatly.

"Oh, hey, Mick."

"What are you doing here so early?"

"I, uh, I was coming to your office to see if you had an open session today?"

The brunette narrows her eyes at the man, making him gulp to tamp down his nerves. After a pause, she says, "I don't. You can check with Jack or Mel, but I don't think they have anything open either."

"Uh, okay, I'll check with them. Thanks, Mick."

"Don't call me that, Tyler," she says over her shoulder. "We're not friends."

He glares at the back of her head as she walks toward the equipment room at the back of the building, clenching his jaw and

scratching the patchy stubble that covers his cheek. He follows after her into the large open space. As Tyler looks for an available
machine, he also takes inventory of where Mickey is and who she's
with.

She's working with a middle-aged woman doing a plyometrics
warm-up. Tyler finds an empty treadmill in the perfect spot. He gets
on and starts a slow jog while keeping one eye on the trainer. When
he quickly gets winded, he slows the machine to a crawl. Every
time she moves, his eyes follow her and her client.

Glancing around the room, he sees three printed schedules taped
to the wall near the equipment room entrance. He stops his machines and hops off. Tyler leaves his phone and headphones on the
treadmill to mark it as reserved and trots over to check the weekly
schedules. They're in alphabetical order, so Mickey's schedule is
the last one.

Both Jack's and Mel's schedules have open slots, but Mickey's is
full. The only time slot that does not have a client's initials or a class
is noon. Instead, ADMIN/PERSONAL is written in marker across all
seven days.

Tyler goes back to his treadmill and checks his phone. The time
says 9:27. He plugs his headphones into the jack on the treadmill
and turns on the TV. He sets the treadmill to one of its lowest
speeds, content to stroll in place, watch, and wait the next couple of
hours to find out just what the "personal" on Mickey's schedule actually means.

****

Tyler follows at a safe distance while Mickey walks with her second
client toward her office at the end of their session.

"You did great today, Toni."

"Thanks, Mick," the woman responds with a laugh. "You're really
kicking my ass, though."

"Hey, the better you do, the harder it gets."

Tyler bends at the water fountain for a long drink as the women finish talking and say their goodbyes. Mickey goes into her office and mostly closes the door, leaving it open only a few inches. He considers changing for a brief moment, but when he hears Mickey's cell phone ring, he stays rooted to the spot.

He scoots as close to the door of her office as he can, then relaxes against the wall with his phone out, so it appears that he's just waiting for someone. Right as she answers the call, he opens the notes app on his phone and gets ready to get as much of the conversation as he can.

"Hello?" Tyler hears her let out a sigh. "Baby, it's so good to hear your voice. How are you? What are you guys doing over there?"

Baby? Tyler mouths. He remembers her saying that she and Cali broke up. There is a pause as the other person on the phone talks.

"Slow down," Mickey says. "Are you serious?... Are you sure about this, Cali?"

Tyler's heart rate quickens as he thinks, *She lied.*

"Babe, listen to me. I've been thinking, and all of this is getting way out of hand. If that goes wrong even in the slightest, it could be really bad. Are you and, what's her name now again?...Right, are you and Roz prepared for that?"

Tyler quickly types Roz into his phone with multiple question marks. His thumbs fly across his screen as he tries to type Mickey's side of the conversation.

"Are two days enough to figure out where they all are?... Okay, just please be careful. I mean, should I get some cash together in case I have to get on a plane and bail you guys out?...

"Really? She can do that?... Yeah, I'm here. I'm just trying to wrap my head around all of this still... So then, if that's the case, why not just have her do that and avoid all this in the first place? How is this all going to even work?

"Wait, you're seeing her again?... Why can't Roz flirt with one of the guys there to get you what you need?" Tyler hears the woman laugh at whatever response Cali offers.

"I know, I do. I trust you. It's just difficult being so far away and still not entirely understanding everything going on there... After that, then what?... Okay, but what about me? When ca—"

Mickey's office phone rings and blocks out the rest of what the trainer says. Tyler hears the male trainer, Jack, answer it in the equipment room. It's quickly followed by a beep in the brunette's office and Jack's distorted voice saying, "Mick, Carl is on line three for you."

Another beep, "Okay, thanks, Jack. I'll be right with him.

"Cal, I have to go. I'm done at six today, can I call you then?... Right, I keep forgetting how big the time difference is. Okay, tomorrow then... I love you too, baby, so much, and I can't wait to see you again... Okay, bye."

Tyler hears the thud of her cell phone as it lands on the desk, followed by a heavy sigh. The office is silent for a beat before Tyler hears the click of her receiver picking up, and, "Carl! My favorite equipment salesman. What have you got for me today?"

Tyler saves the note on his phone, making sure that all of the details from Mickey's call with Cali are still there, and pockets his phone. He ducks into the men's locker room to retrieve his bag and bounces out of the studio back to the street.

His steps are light the entire walk back to his apartment. He whistles as he trots up the stairs to his door. Carelessly tossing his bag into a corner, he plops onto his couch. Tyler hums as he rolls himself a joint, thinking that overhearing that phone call might've just saved his life.

• 4 4 •

"ROSLYN"

Since my 24-hour bug, the last two days have been pretty identical to each other. Cali has spent most of each day with Carmela while Matt and I have been at the library.

Being this close but not being able to touch something I've spent so much time and energy searching for has been way more difficult than I expected. I am so drawn to it; the pull is significantly more powerful than it was in Portland. Each time I walk into the room, my skin tingles, and my hands twitch, ready to reach for it and pick it up.

Now that we have the portal's likely location narrowed down along with Cali's dream about how we should be able to read The Book effortlessly, there isn't much left to do at the library except figure out the camera locations. But, in the room that houses *The Book*, we can't find a single one. And that worries me.

Earlier today, I made my way throughout the room, recording everything as I moved. It reminded me of looking for cameras in the basement back in Portland. I examined the exhibits multiple times and lapped the room twice. Still found nothing.

Now sitting in the living room back at our apartment, we're watching all of the videos we've taken. We make the screen as bright as possible to make sure we don't miss any detail.

"I don't see any cameras in the room," I say.

"Me neither," Cali says, touching the screen to pause the video. "I can't decide if that's good or bad."

"Both," Matt chimes in. "If there are no cameras inside the room, then that's good, and it won't be too hard to make the switch. But it could also mean the cameras are hidden or camouflaged, meaning we'd get caught right away. It's kind of hard to believe that there wouldn't be some sort of security, especially with all of the stuff on display in there."

Cali picks up her tablet, leaves the phone where it is, and starts searching the web for information about the National Central Library exhibits. She taps through multiple pages, scanning the information.

"There's nothing here about security measures. But Carmela said she knows the head librarian. So maybe they can help us some more, without knowing too much."

"What do you mean?" I ask her.

"Well, we're not going to be able to just take *The Book* from the room. So to use Milo's genius distraction of the papers falling, we'd *all* have to be in the room."

"I don't think I understand," Matt says.

"Say there are hidden cameras," she says. "If the head librarian is in the room with us, or at the very least knows that we'll be there, they can turn the system off so that it doesn't go off when we move *The Book*.

"With the system off, when either you guys drop all the papers and everyone stops to help, that's when I would make the switch."

"Yeah, about that," I quickly say. "No screw-ups. We'll only have seconds to get it right, so we need to practice it."

"Are the replicas ready to be painted?" Matt asks.

"They're really close. One more night to make sure they've completely dried, and I can paint them tomorrow."

"There has to be something around here that we can use as a stand-in to practice," I say.

We all simultaneously stand and begin to search the apartment. Milo jumps onto the couch in our stead. Cali goes into her bedroom, Matt begins searching the living room, and I go straight to the kitchen looking for a cookbook or two. I lock in the cabinets beneath the sink, nothing. I pull open every drawer I see without any luck. The next place I check turns out to be the last; in a cabinet above the sink are three cookbooks. None of them are that big, but together the three of them about make up the size of *The Book*.

"Okay, Milo," I say, walking back into the living room. "We're going to play a game."

Milo barks and hops off of the couch. I tell him to sit down in the doorway of the kitchen and wait. He does but stomps his front paws, excited by whatever game he's about to play. Cali comes out of her bedroom with a wide messenger bag that's plenty big to hold either the replica or the real thing.

"I forgot I packed this," she says. "Had it shoved way down in my bag. They're the same color, so I just thought it was the bottom. I couldn't find anything to use as a stand-in, though."

"I found these cookbooks that will work as one, but we need something else to practice the swap."

"How about reams of paper?" Matt asks, holding up one unopened package and one half empty.

"Where were those?" Cali asks.

"Behind the TV," Matt shrugs.

The three of us stand behind the couch, in a clear sightline to Milo in the kitchen. Cali puts the bag over her shoulder, the full ream of paper inside it, and holds the cookbooks to her chest. I divide up the sheets of paper and give Matt half.

"Okay, buddy," I say to my dog. "We're going to drop these papers, and while we all get down to pick them up, Cali is going to do something. If you can see what Cali does behind Matt and me, I want you to bark twice, okay?"

Milo barks twice to confirm he understands the game.

"Good boy! Ready?" I ask my friends. They nod, and I say, "Drop."

Matt and I drop the papers that spread out across the apartment as soon as they hit the floor. We drop as a group. Matt and I try to block Cali as much as possible while we pick up the papers. I've barely grabbed a handful when I hear Milo bark twice.

"Damnit," Cali grumbles. "Good job, Dog Man. Let's go again, people."

Matt and I finish gathering up the papers, and we all stand as a group. We go through the whole motion again. The second time, Milo barks after five seconds, which was only enough time for Cali to get the cookbooks into the bag, but not the ream out.

"Good boy, Milo," I say to him. "Again."

We drop the papers over and over. Milo barks every time. On the eighth time, Cali has the ream of paper halfway out when Milo barks.

"Alright," Matt says. "Let's try it differently. What if, instead of side by side, you and I are facing each other? We can fake bumping into each other and drop the papers. It might hide her more behind us."

I check with Cali, and she shrugs, "We haven't gotten it yet, so it can't make us worse."

"Okay." I face Matt with Cali behind me. "Go."

Matt and I take a step toward each other and lightly bump. We drop the papers and all bend down. Matt and I pick up the papers, and we all stand up again. Milo is still sitting quietly in the kitchen doorway, wagging his tail. I turn around to Cali and see her holding the ream of paper, a triumphant smile across her face.

"Shut up. Did that just actually work?"

"Let's do it again. Remember Milo, when you see Cali doing something other than picking up papers, you bark, okay?"

Two quick barks, and we start over. Matt and I fake the bump and drop the papers. Again, we stand without any noise from my dog.

"Unbelievable," I say. "If it's only us and Carmela or even if someone else is in the room too, and they bend down with us, they'll be at Milo's eye line and not be able to see anything."

"Can we do it a few more times?" Cali asks. "I want to make sure this isn't a fluke or something."

We do it again and again. With Matt and I facing each other, Milo never barks. When we switch back to the original way to try one more time, Milo barks immediately.

"Dog Man! You are so good at this game!" Cali squeals when it's clear that we're done for the night. "I think we should all go for a long walk to congratulate our top dog."

Milo doesn't have to be told twice and bolts to the door of the apartment. We all follow after him, and I hook him into his harness as Matt and Cali gather the keys and our coats.

Feeling lighter than any of us have in days with our plan firmly in place, we happily leave the building and head down Via Napoli before turning right onto Via Nazionale. Not even a block later, we pass a book store that I make a mental note to try and come back to. The four of us go left on Via Torino and quickly come across a really nice restaurant.

I instantly think that it would be a perfect place for my dinner date with Matt and subtly glance at him. I'm not surprised to find his eyes already on me, but it still makes my heart jump.

"This would be a nice place for dinner," Matt says. Cali hums in agreement.

"Maybe you should ask Carmela, Squirrel, and the four of us can go together."

"Yeah?" she asks.

"Yeah, we can butter her up as a group. You know?"

"Definitely," I add. "I've asked a lot of you; I keep asking a lot from you. And I think you've surpassed everything I asked for, so it's about time we joined in, so all you have to do is focus on that winning Cali charm."

"And it makes sense for her to meet us properly," Matt adds. "Then it won't be such a surprise when we're with you the day we perform our... deed."

"Okay, I get what you're saying and weird way to put it, Moose, but thanks."

● 4 5 ●

In a flash, it seems, we're back at the restaurant waiting for our table to be ready. We're a foursome again, but this time we've left Milo behind.

Cali spent the morning painting both of the replicas while Matt and I went back to the library to double-check our findings security-wise. Once there was nothing more she could do for the day but let the paint dry, she went to *Biblioteca Hertziana* and asked Carmela to dinner for tonight.

She said the Italian woman immediately and flirtatiously agreed. Cali quickly told her it was a double date with the friends she's traveling with.

"That briskly put her libido back in its holster," Cali joked.

After telling Carmela where to meet us tonight, Cali went shopping for an outfit for the night. She also got each of us a new pair of shoes and picked up some extra things for Matt. Peeking through the window last night, the men who were dining were wearing coats and ties, and Matt hadn't thought he would need either, so he had failed to pack them.

Cali and I had gotten dressed in her room while Matt got ready in ours. She told me she would do my hair again like the night we went to Kris's Tavern—the same night Matt and I kissed for the first time.

While Cali finished her makeup in the bathroom, I pulled on the deep blue dress I had bought a few days after arriving in Rome. I pulled the zipper up my back as far as I could reach, but it got stuck in that limbo just above my bra but still too low to grab over my shoulder.

Cali came out dressed in a sleeveless, linen, wide-leg jumpsuit with a tailored waist and a top that looks like a faux vest. The light olive color aided by her heavier than usual eye shadow and mascara makes her green eyes pop.

I let out a low whistle and turned around so Cali could zip me up the rest of the way. We put on the new, strappy heels she had gotten us earlier and left her bedroom with only a few minutes to spare. Matt was standing in the living room next to the couch. He was bent over, giving Milo a big belly rub, and didn't turn to look at us right away.

"Are you guys rea—" he trailed off.

"Wow," he and I both said at the same time.

Cali had gotten him a deep blue suit that matched my dress exactly. The fit was so perfect; it looked like it had been made specifically for him. With a bright, crisp white shirt, a thin black tie, and black dress shoes, the man in front of me was possibly the sexiest creature I had ever seen in my life.

Cali cleared her throat, told us to keep it in our pants for a little longer, and reminded us that she looks just as hot as we do. With the sexual tension defused and put on pause for the moment, the three of us left the apartment and walked to our meeting spot.

We met Carmela outside of a hotel on Via Delle Quattro Fontane. It was not incredibly far from our apartment, or so far that our feet would start to hurt in our new heels, but just far enough, she would be more likely to think we're guests at the hotel rather than that we have our own digs.

We got to the hotel less than a minute before Cali spotted Carmela walking toward us. She had a long black trench coat on, so it wasn't until we got to Ristorante Rosa that she revealed a blood-red, form-fitting dress underneath. Neither excessive nor over-stated, just classic and elegant.

The four of us are shown to our table, handed menus and a wine list. The waiter stays at the table while we each glance through the extensive list of wines. I say I would like a glass of Pinot Grigio. When the rest of the group says they would like that, we change our order to a bottle.

It gets quiet as we settle in our seats and decide what we're going to eat. I scan the menu looking for my favorite dish, the one thing I would get anywhere but especially in Italy: *Linguine con le Vongole*—linguini with a white clam sauce.

I lower my menu slightly to take a discreet glance at each of my companions. Carmela looks relaxed, comfortable next to Cali. My Extensios, on the other hand, have furrowed brows, probably trying to translate each dish's name in their heads poorly.

The waiter comes back with a chilled bottle and pops the cork in front of us. He offers me a glass with a small amount poured in for my approval. I mimic what I've seen others do—I sniff, swirl, and slurp. I have no idea what I'm supposed to pinpoint that makes it good or not; wine is wine to me. I just nod, and after topping off my glass, the other three are also filled.

The waiter hands off the empty bottle to a colleague and asks in Italian if we are ready to order. I can tell by both Cali and Matt's faces that they aren't, and I politely ask for a few more minutes and another bottle of wine.

I had prepared something in Italian to say to Carmela, and once the waiter takes his leave I decide to use it. *"Mi dispiace che non conosciamo la lingua migliore. Va bene se parliamo in Inglese?"*

That's the translator equivalent of: I'm sorry that we don't know the language better. Is it okay if we talk in English?

"Nessun problema. Is no problem," she answers.

"In that case," Cali says. "Can you help me figure out which one says fish?" Carmela chuckles slightly and leans over to point out the dishes to Cali. They talk quietly for a moment as Cali chooses her meal. "Thank you. And, I think Moose could use some help too?"

"Moose?" she asks. "I don't understand why this name."

"Uh, it's a nickname from when we were very young. I'm Moose, and she's Squirrel," Matt explains.

"And you, you are animal too?" Carmela asks me with a soft laugh.

"No, no. I only met these two a few years ago, so I don't get a fun name like that, just Roslyn. Or, Roz, as Cali calls me."

"Roslyn, it means pretty rose, beautiful," Carmela says. "Cali also means most beautiful in Greek. And you, Matt, means gift." She holds her glass and offers a toast. "So I say, to the beautiful gift of new friends. *Saluti!*"

We all join her toast and clink our raised wine glasses together. It's only as I'm bringing the crystal to my lips for a drink that it truly hits me how blatantly we are using this woman. She hopefully won't ever know the real reason why we need her and will just chalk it up to the stereotypical rude American when Cali deserts her.

I quickly dart my eyes to either side of me to gauge Matt and Cali's response to the toast. Both of them have drained half their wine and are staring down at the table. *Shit.*

"Have I said something wrong?" Carmela asks.

"No, not at all," I answer quickly. "I think you just caught us off guard with your wonderful toast. I am very grateful for your new friendship as well."

"Squirrel and I have been friends for so long," Matt adds swiftly. "We aren't used to being addressed so eloquently. It's refreshing.

"Squirrel," he says, focusing his attention on Cali. "I would like for you to toast the gift of my friendship every day."

"Yeah, no," Cali says without pause. "Not unless I get toasted in return. Only fair."

"Of course," he says and raises his glass, clears his throat. "To my friend, you are beautiful, intelligent, strong, fiercely talented, and without a doubt, *the* most annoying person ever."

"Oh, Moose, you're too kind. But do let me offer one of my own. You, sir, are loyal and kind. You certainly are not the brightest bulb on the Christmas tree, but you always give it the old college try."

They clink their glasses with mock grandiosity and finish the last drops. It was a ridiculously corny save on their part, but the moment's awkwardness seems to have passed.

The waiter returns and takes our dinner orders. Carmela also orders the linguini with white clam sauce. Cali orders swordfish over risotto with a parsley anchovy sauce. Matt decides on rigatoni bolognese and a glass of Chianti for his meal. Before returning to the kitchen, the waiter refills our wine glasses.

Cali keeps all of us laughing—similar to last month at the bar when our foursome included Mickey—with stories of her and Matt as kids. This time it's mostly an elaborate prank they played on Matt's younger brother Josh. They traumatized him by convincing him they were werewolves, scaring the poor kid half to death.

When our food comes, I turn the conversation toward Carmela. I ask where she grew up, how long she's lived in Rome and worked at *Biblioteca Hertziana*. Cali uses that as a segue to ask about getting access to *The Book*.

"I don't think it will be a problem," Carmela responds. "Philippe and I are good friends, so I'm sure he won't mind turning off the security for you to see it."

"All the books inside the case were really beautiful with their intricate illustrations," Matt says. "I can only imagine what's in the last one. It seems really old."

"*Sì*! It is!" Carmela says excitedly. "I looked it up after Cali and I spoke about it, and it is over one thousand years old! And in such good condition, too, is quite remarkable."

"It's not the only remarkable thing," Cali coos in the direction of the librarian, making her blush.

With little resistance, Carmela guarantees us that she'll talk to Philippe the next day and work out with him when we will be able to see *The Book*.

The conversation never dulls, even as our meal winds down to a natural close. It's warmer out than when dinner started, but late, so the three of us offer to walk Carmela home. She protests, saying it isn't too far, but we insist.

I'm sure she is hoping for just Cali to walk with her, but she doesn't know that we aren't willing to let any of us walk the streets alone at night. It isn't a matter of the neighborhood being unsafe, just of us being supernaturally cautious to remain vigilant to any searching eyes.

We pass *Biblioteca Hertziana* on our way to Carmela's apartment. She lives near the Piazza del Popolo right off of Via dell' Oca. At her door, Cali gives her a hug and a kiss on each cheek before saying, "*Buona notte.*"

Matt and I wave at her and say our own goodbyes, and the three of us head back to our apartment. The majority of the walk is spent with Matt trying to guess my real name again. Without needing an invitation, Cali immediately jumps in, the two of them each trying to top the other with more and more outlandish speculations.

"Is your name Norma Jean?" Cali asks.

"No. Nor is it Marilyn Monroe, unfortunately."

"What about Ophelia?" Matt posits.

"Nope."

"Valencia? Darby? Hadley?" Cali spitfires.

"Not even a little bit."

"Michelin?"

"I take offense to that," I say, throwing one of Cali's lines back at her.

"Honey?" Matt jumps in. "Basil? Ginger? Saffron? Paprika?"

I don't even dignify that with anything more than a roll of my eyes.

"Alright, last guess," he says, making all of us stop on the sidewalk. "Xena?"

"I may technically be a warrior princess, but I am not named for her."

Matt huffs in frustration but quickly wraps his arm around my shoulders. "Alright, you've won again. But don't think I'm going to stop trying."

We walk in a comfortable silence the rest of the way. We're about to get on the elevator when Cali shrieks.

"I've got it!" Cali says, stepping in front of me to block the way. "It's Mavis. I'm right, right?"

I frown sympathetically. "Sorry, kid. I do know someone with that name, though. But that doesn't count."

"I don't like this game," Cali grumbles. She crosses her arms over her chest, steps into the waiting lift silently.

After unlocking the door and saying hello to Milo, the first thing I do is check his bowls. I give him some fresh water and another half scoop of food even though he already ate what I gave him. He goes right over to scarf it down.

Cali must've gone straight to her room to change because she's in yoga pants and a tight thermal long sleeve shirt when she comes back. I see her start to lace up her sneakers, but before I can ask where she's going, I get my answer.

"Come on, Dog Man, how about a run?" she asks with Milo's harness in hand. Milo bolts over to where she's standing. She squats down, ready to strap him in, but his paws can't get traction on the wooden floor to stop, so Milo barrels right into her. She lands flat on her face on the floor with Milo on her back.

"Oh my god!" I gasp, trotting over in my heels. "Are you okay? Cal?"

She doesn't answer me, and my first thought is that she's hurt. Milo doesn't appear too big, but he's got a lot of muscle underneath his long fur and chunk. I quickly undo the buckles of my shoes and kick them off. I crouch down next to her and gently touch her back. Cali rolls over, and I finally see she's laughing so hard that she can't breathe.

"Cali!" I scold. "You scared me! I thought you were really hurt."

"Oh man, that was hilarious! You couldn't see it from where you were standing, but his eyes got wide when he knew he wasn't gonna stop, and you could see the 'oh, shit' look on his face!"

Cali sits up and hugs Milo tightly. She's still laughing, so he starts licking all over her face. "It's all good, pup. No blood, no foul, right?"

She stands to clip his leash on and puts the keys in her pocket. She says she'll be gone for twenty minutes tops. Enough to tire both of them a bit and for Milo to get his business done.

I hear something clinking behind me and see Matt coming out of the kitchen with another bottle of wine and two clean glasses. He's taken off his jacket and is barefoot but is still wearing those perfect pants and the bright white shirt and tie. I turn back to Cali, and she winks.

"Just keep it down," she says quietly.

I scoff. "Do you know how many times you and Mickey woke me up when you were right across the hall? At least these bedrooms are further apart."

"True, but still, that's like my brother over there. So for my sanity and my stomach just..." She pinches her thumb and index finger together, leaving only an inch of space between them. "Okay?"

"No promises," I say.

"Gross," she mumbles as she and Milo take the stairs down.

• 4 6 •

Within seconds of closing the door behind her, I feel Matt loosely wrap his arms around my stomach and his chest press against my back. He kisses my hair, moves it off of my shoulder, kisses my neck. I tilt my head to the side slightly to give him better access. The glasses and wine bottle clink again as he hugs me tighter.

"What do you say we drink this on the roof?" he asks.

"Okay," I say. I untangle myself to leave Cali a short note while Matt opens the door. I make sure it fully closes behind us and lead the way up the stairs. I open the roof access door and test the handle. It moves freely, so I don't think we'll have to worry about getting back in but place the stone in the doorjamb just in case.

Matt walks over to the half-wall and places the bottle on the makeshift railing that the top forms. He pulls the cork and pours each of us a glass. We stand quietly next to each other, just enjoying the company.

I turn slightly to look at his profile. It strikes me that everything I could ever think of or want for a partner I can find in Matt. He's kind, loyal, decent. He's protective but not possessive. He holds the doors open for me and holds my hand; he doesn't belittle me; he listens to me. He respects me. He's a good man. He's my man.

I love him.

"Hey," I say. He swings his head to face me, and I cup his cheek in my hand. I kiss him softly. I can taste the wine he drank tonight, and I lick my lips when we part. "I love you."

His whole face brightens, and he quickly wraps me in a tight hug. "You do?" he whispers in my ear.

"I really do," I whisper back.

"I love you, too."

"I know, baby," I say. He squeezes me again before letting me go. He brings my hand to his mouth and kisses my open palm. We take our wine glasses and bring them over to the bench. He sits down first, and I curl into his side.

We stay there quietly, enjoying the feel of each other being so close. We sip our wine, and he points out the few stars we can see. Some of the neighborhood's Friday night sounds drift up to us— groups of people laughing as they walk the street, a TV set turned up loud in the building opposite ours, a driver presses on their horn somewhere nearby.

The fingertips of his left-hand ghost up and down my left arm. I put my glass down near the leg of the bench, take his and do the same. I turn to him and put both of my hands on his face and pull him toward me. I connect our lips gently. He wraps his strong arms around me, responding to my kiss instantly.

I don't know how long we sit there softly kissing like that. Time tends to not matter whenever he encompasses me. A chilly breeze suddenly gusts across the roof, making me shiver; my body breaks out in goosebumps.

"It's getting late; maybe we should go back in," I say. I reluctantly untangle myself from his grip and stand. He nods up at me and picks up the glasses before he stands. I turn toward the door. I'm two steps away when I hear the glasses shatter on the floor. I spin around in alarm.

"Roslyn," I hear Matt say huskily when I face him. I'm swept backward until my body connects with the door behind me. He stares into my eyes. His pupils are blown wide, making the green flecks in his light brown eyes all but disappear.

"I want you so badly. I *ache* for you," he says hungrily. "To touch you, to be with you."

The sudden change in his tone catches me off guard and leaves me breathless. I pull him against me, so our bodies are touching completely. I can smell the wine on his breath and want nothing more at that moment than to taste it on his lips again.

So I do. It's exactly as if the dream I had over a month ago is finally coming true.

I kiss him hard. My breath comes back, but it's ragged. My back is flush against the door, and Matt is pressing his entire body into mine. I can *feel* how much he wants me. I push my tongue into his mouth, manipulate his with my own.

One of his hands is on the side of my neck, his thumb on my jaw. My hands are tucked into his belt, trying to pull him even closer to me. My heartbeat is rising. My breath is coming faster.

I pull his bottom lip into my mouth. He sucks in a breath when I untuck his shirt and move my hands under it. I play with the tuft of hair just beneath his belly button. I drag my nails down his tight abs and move my hands back to his belt and unbuckle it.

His lips move from my mouth to my cheek, to my jaw, neck, and mouth again. I pop the button on his pants. His scent surrounds me —Old Spice deodorant, laundry detergent, and peppermint.

He licks the roof of my mouth. The hand on my jaw trails down to my collar bone, passes it, and gently massages my left breast. His thumb whispers over my nipple, and through the cloth sends a jolt of arousal directly through my body.

His other hand slides down my right thigh. When he trails his hand back to my hip, he pulls my dress up with it exposing my skin. He moves his hand across my hip bone around to my ass and grabs. I moan at the contact; my hips buck toward him on their own. I feel my arousal drastically increase with every deft touch of his mouth and hands on me.

He bites my lip and slips his hand down again to my knee, pulls it up to his hip. I hook my ankle behind him, move one hand from his pants to grab his tie, and pull him impossibly closer to me. His lips still on my mouth, he gasps again as I reach under the elastic band of his boxers to grab—

"Wait, wait," he says, stopping me.

"What?" I ask, breathless. "Are you okay?"

He slowly lets go of my knee, bringing my leg back down. He slightly shakes his head, barely moving it side to side. He chuckles and kisses me again.

"I am more than okay. I've been dreaming of this moment for longer than you know. But I never imagined it happening outside with a possible audience."

"Mmm. Then let's go downstairs. Because I am definitely not finished with you yet."

Matt nods breathlessly and steps away. I whip around and throw the access door open. The two of us rush down the stairs as quietly as possible and skid to a stop on our floor. The apartment door is held open by the deadbolt, meaning that Cali has returned from taking Milo out.

I open the door of the apartment and peak around the wood. The living room is empty. Matt and I enter the apartment and look around. The note we left for Cal is still where I left it, but she crossed out what I had written and wrote her own response.

" 'Dog Man and I are in for the night,' " I read out loud. " 'PS - I have headphones on.' And then she drew a winking face."

Matt takes the paper from my hand and crumples it up. He tosses it over his shoulder, takes me in his arms, and gives me a scorching kiss that sends my heart rate back into overdrive. We pick up right where we left off up on the roof. I push into him, silently directing him to backpedal toward our bedroom.

As soon as we clear the doorway, I kick it closed. In one motion, I spin around to lock the door and whirl back toward the man I love. I push him back further until the backs of his knees hit the bed then, less than gently, shove him onto it.

As he sits up, I straddle his lap and capture his mouth again with mine. He runs his hands up my spine; one stops between my shoulders, the other continues up to the back of my neck. I relax into his touch, finally letting go of all reservations I've had. I get out of my head, deciding to just live in this moment.

"Zipper," I say in the brief moment I remove my lips from his.

Matt doesn't waste a second. The hand between my shoulders grips the top of my zipper and slowly pulls it down. It stops just below the band of my lace underwear. I remove my arms from around his neck, and he pulls my dress forward and down, exposing my matching bra.

I take my arms out of the sleeves, and the next thing I know, Matt has lifted me up and flipped us around. My back lands on the bed, and Matt's body tenderly comes down on top of me. He ghosts my lips before he leans up to pull my dress the rest of the way off.

Matt stops to take in my body. I use the moment to my advantage and sit up to rid him of his shirt. "No, wait. Let me just look at you," he says. "God, you're beautiful."

I feel my body heat rise as I recline back into the bed. It's not a blush of embarrassment but of my desire surging. I count to ten slowly in my head and then inch my way back up to sitting. I pull the thin end of his tie through the knot and throw it somewhere behind me.

"I'll apologize to Cali tomorrow," I say. He tilts his head in minor confusion before I rip his shirt apart, sending buttons scattering across the room. In the next second, I yank his open shirt down off of his shoulders and immediately kiss each of his exposed abs. He pulls his shirt the rest of the way off and tosses it in the same random direction as his tie.

He cups my jaw and pulls my face back to his. His lips attack mine as he lays us back down on the bed. I can feel how aroused he is through his pants as he presses me into the mattress. When I lick his bottom lip, he opens his mouth to me. The same moment I stick my tongue into his mouth, I slide my hand into his boxers, gripping his erection for the first time tonight.

He moans at the contact, and it suddenly becomes my favorite sound. I want to hear him make that noise again and again.

I start stroking him, and he throws his head back in pleasure. Without releasing my grip, I expand the space between us by pushing him to the side so he lands on his back, and now I'm the one in charge. His arms encircle me, his fingers dance across my skin, somehow unclasping my bra in the process. I scoot back to hover on his legs and remove my hand from around him.

"Please tell me you have condoms," I say as I pull his pants down and off, leaving him in only his boxer briefs.

"I do," he says, panting. "In my bag."

"Good," I say. I drag his underwear down and take the lead completely. I crawl up his body and kiss him hard. I move my mouth to his ear and suck the lobe into my mouth. I bite down slightly before I drag my mouth down his neck to his chest. I follow the valley between his pecks and six-pack down with my tongue.

"Oh my god," he gasps as I lick his shaft from bottom to tip. I taste his salty pre-cum on my tongue. When I wrap my mouth around him, he moans again. He is so hard already and so big that I can't take him fully into my mouth right away.

I start to bob my head up and down, easily finding a rhythm. Each time down, I take a little more of him in. I grip the base in one hand and the rest of him in the other. I make sure to flatten my tongue to drag it along the thick vein underneath as I bring my head up and release him from my mouth.

Matt's hands gather up my thick hair gripping it tightly. I look up at him as I take as much of him as I can into my mouth again. Our eyes lock until I start stroking him, too, then his eyes roll into the back of his head in pleasure. I go back to the bobbing rhythm in addition to stroking him. I let out a moan knowing the vibrations will travel throughout his body.

"Oh my god," he says again. He tugs on my hair firmly with one hand as the other hand glides down to my freed breasts. I continue sucking and stroking him, gradually increasing my speed. I finally let him fall from my mouth and kiss my way up his body.

I keep stroking him with my right hand as I kiss him on the mouth, letting him get a taste of himself on my tongue. Angling myself so my weight is propped on my left arm, I stop rubbing him. I take his hand with my right and bring it to my drenched underwear and say, "This is how badly I want you right now."

He practically growls at me as he flips me onto my back. Matt is somehow able to take off my soaked bottoms without his lips ever leaving mine. Quicker than I know what's happening, he flips us again, so I'm back on top. He's moved mid-flip, and my knees are now on either side of his head. He puts his hands on my hips and pulls me down to his waiting mouth.

I cry out in pleasure the first instant I feel his tongue flick and then suck on my clit. He pulls me down harder and pulses his tongue in and out of me. My hips begin to move on their own, and I grind on his face. He replaces his tongue with two fingers and returns to sucking.

His fingers thrust in and out of me in a steady motion. He curls his fingers inside, making sure to hit the bundle of sensitive nerves every time.

"More," I say. "I need more." Matt doubles down on his efforts, quickens his pace. I can feel my body start to break out in a slight sweat as my arousal continues to grow. I want all of him inside of me. "Please."

I lift myself off of him and stay upright, kneeling on the bed. He gets up and comes around to face me. His chin is glistening with my juices, and it is sexy as hell when he puts the two fingers that were just inside me into his mouth and sucks them clean. I let out a low, guttural moan urging him on.

Matt gnashes our lips together for too brief a moment before he spins away to search his bag for the condoms. He finds them, opens one wrapper, and puts it on. He comes to the bed and kisses me again. I push him onto his back and straddle him. I position myself and lean forward to kiss him as I slowly sink down on top of him.

It's been a while since I've been with someone, so I gasp as I'm stretched. I don't feel an ounce of pain, only incredible, deep satisfaction as I'm filled. I lift myself until only the tip is inside and glide back down. I am so wet that there is no need for a slow start to get used to the feeling.

I lift again, and as I come down, Matt presses his hips up to go deeper. It's exactly what I want, so I tell him.

"Just like that, baby."

We build a tempo together and match each other thrust for thrust. We're both breathing hard; our bodies shine with sweat. I can see as his face scrunches and his eyes close that he's close, so I take his hand, lick his thumb, and press it to my clit. Matt takes over and immediately knows what I want him to do. I quicken my pace as he rubs his thumb where I need it most.

He thrusts harder up into me as I crash down on him. I can feel my orgasm building; my walls begin to clench around him. My toes curl into themselves, and seconds later, I shout my release. Matt follows, and his abs tighten as his shoulders lift from the mattress. I ride out my orgasm until the waves of ecstasy decrease to a simmering pulse. I collapse boneless onto his heaving chest and try to catch my own breath.

"That... was... incredible," he says, sucking in breaths. He kisses me again. I am so spent from my long-awaited release I can only sloppily return it.

"It was. You are amazing," I tell him.

He pulls tissues from a box on the floor, and after we both clean up, he falls back onto the bed. I use all of my remaining energy to get up and use the bathroom quickly.

Matt grabs the top sheet from its bunched up heap on the floor to cover the both of us when I lay down next to him. I'm completely wiped out and can feel my body being drawn toward sleep. I close my eyes just as I feel Matt maneuver us, so I'm laying half on his chest.

"I love you," he quietly says as he kisses my tousled hair.

Before I can say it back, my zapped energy and the rhythmic motion of his breathing combine to lull me into the best night's sleep I've had in the past five years.

• 4 7 •

DARIUS

His eyes feel gummy as he opens them. His tongue has a coppery film on it, most likely from the raw meat he instructed Viribus to shove down his throat. His body feels heavy, as though he's physically tied down. The demon growls at the amount of energy it takes for him to roll to his side.

The cuts of beef he consumes while in his meditative state are becoming less effective in replenishing his strength. Even though the men aren't fighting the change, doing double transitions at once is dangerously draining. But what other choice has he left himself?

He sits up using his arms to push himself upright. The zing of pain that shoots down to the fingertips of his left hand reminds him again of the fact that he's barely running on fumes. "*Bitch,*" he hisses, shifting his weight quickly off of his arm.

Darius blinks rapidly to clear his vision. When it does, he sees the slight discoloration on the wall from the destruction of Collin Kings' body. The demon sweeps his eyes across the rest of the room and finds it empty of anyone but himself.

A yellow sticky note is on the small table next to the bed. He peels it off of the wood and skims it. It's from Blue telling the demon that he and Viribus are gathering the men and are ready for the next location.

"Humans," Darius grumbles, letting the note disintegrate to cinders in his palm. Just as the cinders flutter to the floor, the door opens, and Viribus peeks his head in.

"Good to see you up, boss," he says as he strides in.

"Yes, it's quite the miracle," the demon says drily. "Everything in order?"

"Yes, sir," Viribus replies. It was a statement, not a question, and the Victus knows it. He bends to open the small fridge. As he turns to hand the demon another section of beef tenderloin, he continues. "The guys are ready, one bag each with just the essentials, and Blue has buried the correct forms deep in each of their files. He doesn't expect any issues, but he made copies of each in case."

"Potions?"

"Black and bottled. Everyone is waiting on your order."

"Waiting where?"

"Room down the hall."

The demon briefly nods, then sinks his teeth into the fresh cold flesh. He wipes his hands on his shirt as he slowly stands. Keeping his back to his soldier, the demon pauses as the room swims in his vision. After taking a steadying breath, he turns and begins to unbutton his shirt.

Darius removes and uses it to wipe any residual juices left from the uncooked steak. Darius sees Viribus trying not to look at the scars the witch gave him out of the corner of his eye.

In addition to his left arm healing an angry hue of red, darker snaking tendrils of maroon are splayed across the skin where his shoulder connects to his lean torso. A slash of crimson colors his right side just below his ribs. If that strike had hit a few inches to the left, the fight would've been over before it even started.

Not looking to stand around and be gawked at, he snaps his fingers at the Victus, breaking him from his reverie. The giant tosses him a dress shirt in a drycleaners' bag. Heading to the bathroom, Darius rips open the package and shakes out the clean, midnight-black shirt.

Quickly rinsing his pale face once more and running his damp hands through his hair, Darius dons his pristine shirt and exits the bathroom. Viribus is standing at the door to the room with the remaining tenderloins in his mammoth hands.

"Ready when you are, boss."

The demon turns to his lieutenant, and with a nod, the two leave the room. Viribus leads the way to the second room. Darius can hear the men talking and laughing before they reach the room, but as soon as Viribus puts the card in the electronic lock, the click of the mechanism silences them all.

"Gentlemen," Darius says, stepping through the door his soldier holds open for him. "There are four of you left, and once we arrive at our destination, your transitions will be taken care of. It's going to be cramped where we're going, so if you have an issue with one another, you better fucking figure it out because any bitching will be met by a swift fate."

He's been gesturing as he talked, and he ends his speech with a flaming orb that pops into each hand. It's done so casually that even Blue's eyes widen along with the other ten men in the room. Darius claps his hands together, extinguishing the flames—a favorite trick of his—and turns around to face Viribus.

"Ready."

Darius uncaps his vial and downs the contents. Viribus follows, prompting Blue and the parolees also to drink. Darius instructs the men to grip each other by the shoulder then says Tyler's address in Portland.

In a lone excruciating second, the group of thirteen is moved the twenty-one-hundred miles to Oregon and appears directly in front of

Tyler's door. Darius uses his telekinesis to swing the apartment door open and steps in.

The scent of weed immediately hits his sensitive nostrils. Tyler is slouched into a corner of his couch, watching the cooking competition playing on his TV, completely unaware of anyone being in his home. Darius shakes his head as he steps further into the apartment. Viribus looks ready to pick Tyler up and shake him, but the demon stops him by holding up his hand.

Instead, he calmly steps around the couch and sits down on the coffee table directly in Tyler's line of sight.

"Holy fuck! How did you get in here?!" he squeals like a startled pig.

"Do you want to explain why you're here and not following the girl, or should I just kill you now and get it over with?"

"Why I'm not what?"

Viribus blocks the TV with his body and claps his large hands loudly three times as he yells, "Look alive, dip shit!"

Darius holds up his hand again, silencing the giant. "I asked why aren't you doing what you've been told to do?"

"I have! I mean, I am!" Darius narrows his eyes as he inhales deeply. When he breaths out, his chest rumbles like a growl. "I am, I swear! Look, look! I put a tracker on her, and I follow wherever she goes with my phone."

Tyler shoves his hand into the pocket of his stained jeans and pulls out his phone. He taps the screen a few times and hands it over to Darius. The screen shows a map with a blinking purple dot.

"She's at her studio and has been all morning." He double clicks the home button on his phone and pulls up his notes app. As he scrolls through it, he says, "I've been checking it every few hours, and if her dot changes, I put it on the list."

Darius scrolls up to the very top and reads everything Tyler has written down. His eyes widen slightly before a vile sneer graces his face. "What is this? Is that from two days ago Wednesday?"

The demon hands the phone back to the stoner and points to what he means. Tyler reads what he had typed and looks up excitedly.

"Yeah, two days ago. I went to the studio and asked her if she could train me. She said that her schedule was filled and told me to ask one of the other trainers. When I was check ng the schedule, I saw that she had time that day to see me, but it was marked off as personal."

"Get to the fucking point," Darius snaps.

"I, um, I watched her all morning, and when she left the training room, I followed her to her office. She didn't close the door all the way, and I heard her phone ring. It was Cali. She lied to you. They didn't break up."

The rumble in the demon's chest returns, and this time it's clearly audible as a growl. Tyler's face pales slightly as he hesitantly speaks again.

"T-t-there's more. When she was talking to Cali, she kept asking, 'Is that a good idea,' and about someone named Roz, and she asked if she should get some money together in case she has to get on a plane and bail them out."

"Blue!" Darius calls over his shoulder.

The short man shuffles up to the demon. "Yes, sir?"

"Get me everything you can about the girlfr end."

"Yes, sir." The parole officer takes out his phone and immediately starts tapping through his contacts. He walks into the kitchen of the apartment for some semblance of privacy.

"Tyler," Darius says quietly. He watches the man swallow hard, fear blatantly apparent. "You did well."

Tyler exhales heavily and visibly relaxes. Darius claps him on the back hard.

"You did well. Now I have a new job for you," Darius says as he stands. "I don't trust you with my cash, so you and Viribus are going to go together and get enough food to feed everyone. Understand?"

Tyler nods quickly and swallows again. Darius waves him away as Blue joins them, having finished his phone call.

"I put it out there, should get something back soon," he says.

Darius grunts his acknowledgment. "Here's what's going to happen now. Viribus, you and I will go up to the witch's apartment and use it for the transitions. Blue, send up the next two men in twenty minutes, then watch them and the rest until Viribus returns with that idiot.

"And have that moron continue to keep tabs on the girl. I expect daily reports from both of you about her movements. Blue, go and talk to her yourself, see if you get something more out of her.

"Sunday afternoon, I want to be up and doing the last pair. Then Wednesday morning, it'll be your turn to join the ranks, Mr. Blusseau.

"And once I'm back from that, I think it'll be the perfect time to pay one more visit to Ms. Westin. Perhaps I'll find a way to persuade her to tell the truth this time."

PART THREE

• 4 8 •

Cali

Little whimpers and paws gently kicking her in the back wake Cali Saturday morning from a dreamless sleep. She slowly scoots to the side of the bed hoping that Milo won't stir. She yelps, startled by her bare feet landing on the cold floor.

Cali searches the floor looking for the socks she kicked off last night in her sleep, finding one snagged on the bed frame and the other flat on the floor. After sliding her feet into the cotton and throwing on one of Mickey's sweatshirts that miraculously still smells like her girlfriend, Cali opens her bedroom door and heads to the kitchen in a desperate search of caffeine.

She sets up the coffee maker and sits at the table as it brews. Cali dips her head further into the pullover, her nose searching for every reminder it can find of the brunette nearly six thousand miles away. Propping her head on her left hand, she gets lost in memories of the woman she loves. As the smell of the coffee overpowers the scent of Mickey, Cali slowly comes back to reality.

She rubs her green eyes and gets up to pour a cup. Making it just the way she likes, Cali brings the cup back to the table. As she sips, she stares at the clay replicas. The two are practically finished; all that's left to do are the tiny details that will let it pass a double-take.

Cali is concentrating on her creations and doesn't realize that Milo has woken up. She yelps for the second time this morning when he lays his chin on her thigh. A splat of coffee lands on the floor next to the dog, he sniffs it once but turns his nose away.

"You are getting really good at stealth mode. You don't like coffee either, do you, Dog Man?" she asks.

"He likes to be just like his momma," Roslyn says, striding into the kitchen. Milo whips around and sticks his head between her knees, tail slashing through the air. She sighs deeply and bends over to scratch his ears. Her long hair spreads out like a curtain hiding them both.

"How's my good boy? How's the best, best boy? Oh, he's my best boy!" she coos to the black dog. Roslyn bends over further and kisses him all over the top of his head. The attention makes Milo's tail swish even faster. When she stands up, Cali is looking at her, barely stifling a laugh.

"I'm sorry I had to see that," Cali says, unable to keep her laugh at bay.

"He loves it, don't you pup?" Roslyn holds her hand out for Milo, who obediently jumps up to smack it with one of his paws.

"Jesus, it's cold this morning!" Roslyn goes to the fridge and takes out the milk to make hot chocolate. She sets a saucepan on the stove to heat up, then opens a few cabinets until she finds what she's looking for. Roslyn reaches in for the can of Miscela d'Oro cocoa mix and places it next to an empty mug.

Leaving the milk to simmer, Roslyn turns back toward the table to find Cali staring at her. "What?"

"So?" Cali drawls. "How was last night."

Roslyn smiles warmly and peeks around the kitchen doorway in the direction of her bedroom door. Seeing it's closed, she hops back into the kitchen, taking the seat next to her friend.

"Un-fucking-believable."

Cali smiles at her, waiting for the spark of jealously to fill her chest like it has whenever it comes to Matt and Roslyn lately. She's surprised but grateful when it doesn't come. "Please don't go into too much detail 'cause I plan on keeping this coffee down, but really?"

"Oh my god, yes," her friend gushes. "I was worried, actually, because it's been so long since I've been with someone. But when the moment finally came, I felt open and secure, and all of my anxiety was quieted. I was just, like, in the moment with him. It was everything I wanted it to be."

"I'm happy for you guys," Cali says honestly. "I'm also happy I packed my headphones. I didn't hear a thing. Can't say the same thing for Dog Man, though, poor guy."

Roslyn lightly slaps Cali on the arm, laughing. She gets up to pour her hot milk into a mug and stirs in the mix. Bringing her cup back to the table, the two women sit in comfortable silence, enjoying their drinks.

Milo breaks the quiet by nudging his bowl with his nose, requesting his breakfast. Roslyn gets up again to feed him and asks, "What's on tap for today?"

"I've got some detailing to do on these," Cali gestures to the dried clay. "There's some laundry that needs to be done, and we could use some more groceries. Maybe practice the switch again and take Milo for a nice walk at some point?

"Oh, and then decide when we're, like, actually going to do this."

"How about as soon as Carmela can arrange it?" Matt asks, walking into the kitchen. He's wearing basketball shorts and a sweatshirt, and there is a crease across his cheek from his pillow. He bends over to give Roslyn a sweet, lingering kiss. "Good morning, baby."

"Good morning," Roslyn murmurs in response.

"Look who finally decided to grace us with his presence," Cali teases.

"I was up late last night," Matt shrugs.

"So I heard," Cali winks at him.

"Cali!" Roslyn protests.

"Anyway," Matt says, drawing the word out, but not before wiggling his eyebrows at his friend. "I really think we should get in there and get out of here as soon as we can."

"I'm with ya, Moose. I'll text Carmela and see if we can meet for coffee today or something. I think if I'm going to ask her to be an accessory to theft, at the very least, it should be in person."

"Seems like the courteous thing to do," Roslyn says, taking a sip of her hot chocolate. "Do you want us to come with? I can bring Milo; let him use some of his puppy eyes on her."

Hearing his name, Milo picks his head up from his nearly empty bowl. He stops licking his jowls long enough to come over to the table and sit in front of Cali. He ducks his head and looks up at her with just his eyes, tail slowly wagging. The freckled woman visibly melts into herself at how cute he looks.

"That's so mean," Cali laughs. "No one can say no to this face!"

There isn't much in the ways of food in their apartment, so the three agree to shower and get ready to spend their Saturday out and about. Cali is the last to shower, using the time to paint some details on the clay. It will be dry by the time they get back, and she'll be able to layer on more, adding to the subtlety that will help the duplicate pass even the toughest of scrutiny.

After they've all dressed, Matt puts in a load of laundry, Cali makes a grocery list on her phone, and Roslyn hooks Milo into his harness. She packs his collapsible bowl and a squeaky tennis ball into her bag, double-checking she has baggies to pick up after him while they're out.

Carmela writes Cali back practically as soon as her thumb hits send. They agree to meet at the same coffee place they had gone to before. When the three of them show up, Carmela is already there. All three Americans register the barely masked disappointment that the Italian will have to share Cali again, but her face lights up as soon as her eyes land on Milo.

"*Che bel cane!*" What a beautiful dog.

The group joins Carmela at her table and chat easily. However, when Cali brings up getting access to *The Book* and Carmela says she will ask Philippe, she sees a change in her friend. It's as if Roslyn has come to some kind of realization that's shaken her. She immediately begins to choke on her Pellegrino and spills most of it down her shirt. Matt reaches over to rub her back and asks if she's okay.

"Yeah, yeah, I'm fine. Just went down the wrong pipe." She wipes her mouth with some napkins and says, "Excuse me, I'm going to clean up."

She hands off Milo's leash and gets up, quickly striding into the coffee shop, bumping into a few people as she passes them. Cali frowns, watching her friend leave. She stands after a few moments and tells Carmela and Matt that she's going to check on her.

Cali opens the door to the ladies' room and sees Roslyn with her back to her standing at the sink, dabbing her shirt with paper towels. Cali can see in the mirror that her friend's face is scrunched in frustration. Both stalls are thankfully empty, and the women are alone in the bathroom.

"Cal, we have a problem."

"It's just sparkling water. It's okay."

"No, not this."

"Oh. Then what do you mean?" Cali asks nervously. Her first thought is that Roz saw someone or something that made her nervous. The shorter woman's mind starts to race with the possible scenarios they might be about to face.

"I can't believe I didn't think of it sooner. It was so stupid of me!" Roslyn keeps scrubbing away at her shirt, making the paper towel tear from the friction.

"What? What's going on?"

She stops wiping and crumples the towel in her hand. Keeping her back to Cali, she talks to the girl's reflection next to her own. "Do you remember the name on your library card? You know, the *fake* name on your library card?"

"Yeah, so?"

"Well, if I'm not mistaken, the Philippe that Carmela keeps referring to is the same Philippe that gave me the forms I filled out for your library card with the fake name on it."

"So?"

"So, we told Carmela your and Matt's real names." She throws the damp towel balled in her hands into the sink and drops her chin to her chest. "Don't you think it's possible that when she introduces us to him that he might remember that I'm the American girl who asked for three forms for library membership? And don't you think it might be confusing to him if the other two Americans are introduced with different names than the ones on their forms?"

"Well, fuck," Cali says. The two of them stand quietly for the slowest minute either of them has ever experienced, each of them trying to find a plausible way out of this. Cali finally lands on optimism. "Look, what if all this worry is just for nothing, Roz? I mean, he probably won't even remember us."

"I don't know," Roslyn sighs, turning around to lean against the stone sink. "I just don't know, Cal. There aren't many people of my skin tone in Rome, so I don't know if he'll remember me. I don't know if he'll have to take down our information in case something gets wrecked. I don't know if he'll have us sign a form or whatever because the security measures will be turned off. I don't know if we're worrying about nothing, and he doesn't care who we are. But this could be a complete disaster."

Cali watches the mocha-skinned girl take off her glasses and pinch the bridge of her nose. She looks defeated. The artist sighs and steps in to hug her taller friend.

"Roz, it's okay. I gotchu." Roslyn chuckles in her friend's embrace, the response Cali was hoping for. "Look, on the small chance that this guy remembers you, we can just come up with an explanation about the names—tell him we lost a bet or something—if he doesn't, then there's nothing to worry about."

"Okay, yeah," Roslyn says, beginning to calm down. "There's nothing to worry about until there's something to worry about, right?"

"Exactly," Cali soothes. She brushes Roslyn's hair off her shoulders with her fingers before stepping away from her friend. She takes Roslyn by the hand and pulls her toward the door. "Come on, let's go back."

When the two finish winding through the crowd, they see Carmela putting her phone into her purse, hanging off the back of her chair.

"Perfect timing," Matt beams at his friends. "Carmela just got off the phone with Philippe."

"*Si,*" the Italian says. "He does not work tomorrow since it is Sunday and is off the next day, but my friend would be happy to give you access on Tuesday morning. Does that work for you?"

• 4 9 •

"ROSLYN"

Matt and I sit at a table in the gallery with a stack of paper in front of us. We plan to spend the day sifting through all of the pages. We're easily making it look like we're studying what's printed on them because we actually are.

I continuously feel the intense pull of *The Book* in all the cells of my body. I catch myself staring at it and have to use every ounce of restraint not to break the glass protecting it and just bolt.

We're researching the Native American tribes around the Grand Canyon, scientific papers about ways the magnetic field around and within it change, and possible routes Darius might have used as he crossed the world.

Now that we have a general idea of where the portal is, I want us to pinpoint it as much as possible. I want to learn everything I can about the Native American tribes that called that area home, their tales and legends, and use that information to figure out where it was that Darius first landed.

As I'm making some notes in one of the pages' margins, Matt stands up for a stroll. He and I had agreed this morning that once we sat in the gallery, every half hour or so, one of us would get up to stretch our legs and take a short walk throughout it and the surrounding hallways.

Cali hasn't been back to the library for the past twelve days, devoting all that time to making the clay replicas look as realistic as possible. She's counting on us to show her how to get from the gallery to the main entrance smoothly. If Matt and I know the layout of this building as seamlessly as we did the Central Library back in Portland, then being able to make an easy exit is one less thing we'll have to worry about on Tuesday.

I look up from one of the many pages I printed on the Hualapai tribe in time to see my boyfriend walk the last five steps to our table. He's wearing a plain, gray t-shirt and jeans, but I have never seen a more attractive man in my life. *He looks good in everything,* I think. *And in nothing.*

That thought led my brain back to our night a few days ago—and each night since then—which leads to remembering how good every time has felt.

I physically shake my head to wipe the slate clean and take a deep, steadying breath. I'll have plenty of time to revisit his body once *The Book* is safely in my possession. Until then, I have to take on the mindset of a professional athlete: No sex before the big game.

Out of the corner of my eye, I can see Matt looking at me. I meet his gaze head-on and know I have a fraction of a second to exercise whatever's left of my willpower not already occupied by my proximity to my magical guidebook. I clear my throat and look back down at the stack of pages in front of me.

Matt scoots his chair closer to mine, leans into me, and brushes his lips against the side of my neck just below my ear. A place we've both recently come to learn is my biggest weakness.

"Now, that's just not fair," I say, gripping the pen in my right hand tighter—the plastic creaks under the pressure.

"What do you mean?" he asks teasingly.

He doesn't stop the tantalizing contact, making it harder for me to maintain my resolve. I clench my jaw and lean away from him, trying to distance myself from his skilled lips. "Stop it. We *can't*."

"I saw what looked like a closet on my way back in here," he whispers against the skin of my neck, closing the distance once more. "Maybe we can pop in there."

"Mmm," I respond. "And when someone opens the door and catches us and asks us not to return to the library, what then?" He groans and finally relents the torturous pleasure. "Thank you, baby. Now, back to work."

Before I know it, it's my turn to walk the perimeter. I take enough papers with me that they form a stiff enough writing surface. I shorten my stride as I count my paces and turns from the gallery's doorway until I reach the main entrance, noting each movement. I step outside the building and bask in the sunlight for a full one-hundred seconds. I count again on the way back to the gallery and make sure they match.

I slide back into my seat next to Matt. The two of us quietly continue sorting through our papers for another few hours. It is monotonous work, but it's important to be as informed as possible. I take off my glasses and rub my eyes hard.

Matt stands up from the table. He stretches his arms over his head, making his shirt ride up a little. It reveals the delicious V-cut the muscles around his hips create. Before he can leave the table, I hold out the page I wrote my turns and steps on.

"Can you take this with you and check my counting?"

"Sure, baby," he says with a smile crowded over to one side of his face. He gently takes the sheet from me.

I decide as I watch him walk away that if his count matches up with mine, we'll call it a day. We've put in enough time here, and my willpower is zapped from having been surrounded by the strong distractions of *The Book* and Matt all day.

Plus, I want to get back to the apartment with enough time for Cali to memorize the turns and steps and for the three of us to practice switching the real for fake a bunch of times before we all go to sleep.

Within five minutes, Matt returns. He puts the page down and leans over my shoulder, pointing to it as he speaks

"I counted, and taking into account Squirrel's shorter strides, I think you're right on the money."

"Good." I start to collect all of my sheets of paper, stack them, and tap them into a tight form. Before Matt can sit, I stand stretching my arms up, "Are you ready to go?"

He nods in agreement. Matt takes my stack of papers and piles it on top of his own. Checking that we haven't left anything behind, we exit the gallery and head straight to the main entrance, no stutter to our step, no having to double-check our path.

When we get back to the apartment, I can hear Milo's tags clinking together as he does what I can easily assume is a happy dance on the other side of the door. When Matt unlocks the door and steps in first, I see my dog jump up for a quick greeting before he sidesteps to get to me.

"Hey buddy," I say, kneeling to his level. "Were you good today? I'm sure you were."

"You're home! Come see what I did! I've just had another genius idea!"

"I can't wait to hear this," Matt says, placing the stack of paper on the coffee table. He goes into our shared bedroom, coming back out quickly, having changed into basketball shorts.

"Good enthusiasm, Moose! I applaud you," Cali says, choosing to ignore the obvious sarcasm as we walk into the kitchen. "While, yes, I have made a flawless replica—two actually—I have also created a fake cover that can slide right over *The Book* to conceal it for an extra safe getaway. Boom!"

She holds a hand up to me for a high five. I'm beaten to the punch by Milo, who never misses a chance to get involved.

"Let's go over the plan one more time, shall we? We meet Carmela at the library tomorrow. I bring my sketchbook, take some pictures, then start a rough sketch. You guys bump, drop papers, switch. Then I ask Carmela out to lunch. I complain my bag is too heavy and ask my chivalrous friend, Moose, to bring it home for me. I have a quick meal with someone whose kindness we've taken significant advantage of, and then when I get back, we crack that shit open!"

"Hell yeah, Squirrel!" They high five before Matt mentions starting dinner and heads to the fridge with Milo on his heels.

I can feel Cali's eyes on me as I'm looking at the clay. She comes over to me and puts her hands on my shoulders. "I feel really good about this, Roz; it's all going to work tomorrow. It's going to work, and we're gonna get to go home."

• 5 0 •

By no stretch of the imagination could I ever be called a "morning person." I've never even been a mid-morning person. But today, Tuesday morning in the heart of Rome, Italy, I'm awake before the sun can peek over the rooftops of our neighborhood.

As the bedroom gets lighter and brighter, my adrenaline rises with it. When my foot starts shaking the bed from the speed of its tapping, I know it's time to get up. I sit up carefully to make sure I don't disturb Matt.

The three of us went to bed last night as prepared as possible, but as I stand in the kitchen unsure of what I want to eat, I run through the plan a few more times in my head. I hear Milo scratch from behind the door of Cali's bedroom. I let him out, and he beelines to the front door. He whines loudly, making it clear he's got to go.

"Okay, buddy," I say. I pop back into my room, peel off my pajamas, and throw on jeans and a sweatshirt. Milo is spinning circles at the front door and comes over to nudge me as I'm bending over to jot a note. "Okay, okay. Here we go."

I snap his harness on quickly, slide my feet into my sneakers, and we're out the door. After Milo relieves himself on the first exterior surface we come across, we keep going. Heading up our block, we make a left on Via Nazionale in the opposite direction of the National Central Library. It's quiet and warm even this early in the morning, hinting at the hot day ahead. Within minutes of leaving, I'm pushing the sleeves of my sweatshirt up past my elbows. Milo starts to pant in the rising humidity.

I suddenly have the fear that the moisture in the air could affect the clay in some way. Before I can stop it from taking over, the feeling starts to snowball. If the clay isn't believable, then that means we'll be found out and thrown in jail immediately, and I'll have to use my powers to get us out of there, and then I'll have to use them again to steal *The Book* a second time, and—

Milo's loud barks release me from the tendrils of my own fabricated peril. I look down to see him staring straight up at me. As our eyes make contact, he plops down on his rump. My dog tilts his head slightly and whines at me in what I can only interpret as a sympathetic way.

"You can sense my panic right now, can't you?" I ask as I squat down to his level. In response, he shuffles his black paws and inches closer to me, his mouth open as he continues panting. "Are you trying to tell me to cut and run?" He grumbles and closes his mouth.

"So then, are you saying that today's going to work out terribly, and I should prepare a jailbreak?" He covers his face with a paw, making me laugh. "Are you trying to tell me that everything is going to be okay? That we can do this?"

I must finally guess the right message because Milo stomps his front paws, opening his mouth to begin panting again, the clusters of spots on his tongue showing. I hold out my hand for him to give me a low five. He smacks it with his paw then bumps his nose against my closed first. He barks at me two more times as I stand and say, "You are a good dog."

We make a left onto Via Milano, then make our third left in a row onto Via Palermo. We follow that to Via Venezia, a short block, for our fourth left. That brings us back to Via Nazionale, which we make a right on and follow back to our apartment.

Since I'm already a sticky mess from the muggy day and am still resonating with a tense hum of adrenaline, I challenge Milo to a race up the four flights of stairs. I know I need to go into today with my nerves at the right level—can't be too anxious, nor too calm— and if we were at the library this very moment, I would probably blow the whole thing.

"Okay, here are the rules: we race to our place, first one to touch the door wins. And absolutely no cheating. Deal?" Milo barks making his floppy ears bounce. "Ready? Go!"

We take off at the exact same moment, and for a second, I think it's going to be close, but the weeks of not regularly exercising begin to show their consequences as Milo easily lengthens his lead. He gets upstairs a full six seconds ahead of me and is just standing near the door, not actually touching it. He waits until I'm on the landing to let his curled tail relax down; the edge of it brushes the door claiming his victory.

"You little shit," I say affectionately. I bend down to give him six kisses right between his eyes. One for every second, he had to wait for me.

I open the door, unhook Milo from his harness, and head to the kitchen to feed him. Cali is at the table, still in her pajamas. She's gently sliding one of the clay replicas into her bag. I watch her place the fake cover she made over it before putting her sketchbook in beside it.

"Good thing I used the cardboard and didn't make this sucker too heavy," Cali says, placing the strap over her shoulder to lift the bag from the table. "Even hollow, it weighs a ton."

She laughs tightly, the height of her own nerves apparent. Milo brushes up against her leg. I watch her strained expression lessen as she reaches down to pet him. He's silently reassuring her as he did for me on our walk.

"Don't worry, kid. We've thought it through; it'll be fine," the slight quiver to my voice undermines the vote of confidence meant by my words. "What time did Carmela say to get there again?"

"Just before noon. She said Philippe would put up a sign saying the gallery will be closed around that time."

"Okay, so then, breakfast?"

****

After more waiting than I was hoping to do—more than enough time to add some other outlandish imaginary outcomes to today—we finally leave the apartment to head to the library. When Matt suggested getting to the library before Carmela to wait for her there, neither Cali nor I disagreed.

I had warned them about the heat of the morning, but Cali, Matt, and I—respectively dressed in capris and a billowy tank, shorts and a t-shirt, and jean shorts with a ribbed tank—are all shining with sweat after minutes outside. Matt puts down Cali's bag when we get to the library. It leaves a wet stripe in the cotton that covers his shoulder. The top page from the stack we printed yesterday is damp from being clutched to my chest for the duration of our walk here.

"Fuck, it's hot," Cali says, wiping her forehead. "I'll text Carmela that we'll wait for her inside 'cause this is ridiculous out here."

The moment the door slides open, we're blasted with the artificially cool air from the climate-controlled environment. The three of us let out long, content sighs. I quickly get goosebumps as the sweat on my skin evaporates.

Cali tells us that Carmela replied that she's walking up the path and will be here in a few moments. By the time she's done telling us that, I see the beautiful Italian woman entering the building.

"*Ciao, bello vederti,*" she says. Matt and I echo her greeting with our own as she kisses Cali on each cheek. "I will tell Philippe we are here and meet you at the gallery. *Sì?*"

"Perfect," Cali says with a flirty smile. "Come on, Moose. That bag won't lift itself."

Matt rolls his eyes as he follows her further into the library. Every step I take after them places more distance between myself and the safety of an exit. It makes my adrenaline start to creep back up to that dangerous level—one that can easily generate a costly mistake.

I count my breaths for the remainder of my steps as I catch up to Matt and Cali, waiting outside of the gallery. I silently remind myself that I am a powerful and formidable woman, and a witch to boot, and anything we run into, I am more than capable of sorting out. Magically or not.

It does the trick so that when I come to a stop in front of my best friend and boyfriend, Cali gives me a look, soundlessly asking what's gotten into me. All I offer as a response is a quiet, "We're ready."

Warm laughter echoing through the hallway announces the approach of the two Italian librarians. Carmela introduces Philippe when they reach the three of us. Thankfully I see no hint of recognition in Philippe's eyes and hope that means he has forgotten the American girl who asked for three membership cards. In halting English, he explains what has been done for us.

"There is a security chip in the pages of the item Carmela has requested access to. The sensors are turned off, so when the item is lifted from the case, the alarms will not be triggered. But if you remove it, be sure to replace it when finished. Carmela knows how it works. I must return to my desk, but I am here to provide any further assistance you may need."

"*Grazie Philippe*," Carmela says. "*Verrò a prenderti quando avremo finito.*" He nods and turns to walk away. She watches him turn the corner. "Shall we?"

The four of us enter the gallery. It is eerily quiet as if the air has been sucked from the room, taking all sound with it. As I walk further in, I start to hear a thumping sound. When the jingle of Carmela's keys cuts through, I realize that the thumping is my own heartbeat and the silence was from the pull of *The Book* blocking everything else out.

I inhale deeply as the case is unlocked. When it opens, Carmela turns to Cali and asks something I don't catch. My vision is locked on the ancient volume, the manual to figuring out exactly what I can do and how to do it. I see my friend take out her phone and snap some pictures.

When Carmela reaches in and lifts it from its glass housing, a fierce stab of possessive jealousy flashes through me. *Mine,* is the only thought that my mind produces. Carmela brings *The Book* over to the first table so Cali can continue taking pictures. She must've said something to Matt because he opens her bag to hand over her sketchbook and pencils. The Italian returns to close and lock the case before going back to Cali's side.

I can't tear my eyes from it. I watch every minuscule movement it makes as Cali rotates it for her rough drawing. When she opens it, she gently flips through the pages. I again see the impressive drawings inside, the perfect Latin words.

I catch Cali removing the security chip. It looks like a smaller version of a hotel key card. She palms it as she continues flipping through. After reaching the end, Cali turns back to a particularly beautiful image. She reaches forward with her phone to take another picture of it. She frowns, and I immediately suspect the photo came out blurry, just as it did in Portland.

As she sits, she says, "I think that's it. Is it okay if I start a rough sketch of this before we put it back?"

"Of course," Carmela answers, taking the seat next to my friend. I grimace at her placement, thinking it might hinder us when Cali has to make the switch. Matt stands across the table from them, quietly watching and waiting for his cue. I silently begin to fan out the pages I'm holding so that they will scatter easier when dropped.

"You and Roz are going to hang here for a little and do some more work, right?" Cali asks Matt.

He nods. "Yeah, we were going to head over to the computer lab for a little."

"In that case, do you want to go grab a bite to eat after this?" Cali asks Carmela. The woman's face lights up at the chance to be alone with Cali, and she nods eagerly. "Awesome. Do you mind hanging onto my bag then, Moose?"

"Sure thing, Squirrel," he responds.

That's the first of two cues we agreed to beforehand. Matt moves around the table to stand behind both women looking over Cali's shoulder at the drawing. She finishes the beginnings of her sketch and closes *The Book*. She leaves her sketchbook and pencils on the table, stands, gathers *The Book* up, and turns back toward the case.

Carmela steps around us to unlock the glass case again. With her back turned to us, we strike. Matt bumps me for the sake of authenticity. I gasp and drop all of my pages. They balloon out across the floor beautifully.

The librarian spins around at the commotion leaving the key to the case hanging in its lock. "Oh, no!"

"Oh my god! Roz, I am so sorry!" he says.

"It's okay," I huff in frustration. "Can you guys just help me pick them all up?"

The four of us bend to the ground and begin to gather the pages. Carmela is a few paces away, the same spot Milo occupied while we practiced. I force myself not to look at Cali but to watch Carmela. She has her back to us as she grabs the sheets around her.

"This is going to take forever. Let me put this back so I can help too."

It's the second cue. It means Cali did it. She switched them. My heart rate thunders in my ears, but I don't dare look up. I stay in my crouch, picking up the pages around me one at a time. I hear Cali turn the key in the lock of the case and the clink of the keys as she puts them down on top of the glass.

We scoop up the rest of the pages quickly; they've served their original purpose and do not need to be tidy anymore. Sighing, I stand with my stack and tap it on the table to straighten it. Carmela, Matt, and Cali each offer me a stack of their own.

"Here are your keys," Cali says behind us, handing them back to Carmela.

"I think that's all of them," Matt says. He has the good sense to look sheepish. "I'm really sorry, baby."

"It's fine, I guess." I say it with mock irritation before I mumble, "Just need to watch what you're doing."

"I said I was sorry," Matt snaps at me.

"Well, it wouldn't have even happened if you were more careful," I fire back.

"Guys, come on," Cali says, trying to placate us as she packs up her supplies. "It's fine now. We got them all, right, Roz?"

"I think so," I sigh in annoyance. "I'll just sort through them in the computer lab and make sure."

"I am sure we got them all, Roslyn," Carmela offers, trying to soothe the situation.

"See? It's all good." Cali tries to put her arm around my shoulders. I shrug her off as Matt and I continue arguing back and forth about the papers. Behind me, she turns to the librarian and says, "Uh, why don't you and I go get some food now and let them figure this out. Moose, my bag if you please."

"Yeah, yeah. I got it," he says quickly over my shoulder before jumping right back into our faux fight. "You know, you always do this. Everything is always my fault."

"Well, it is your fault when *you* bump *me* and scatter hundreds of pages I spent a ton of time researching and sorting!"

We don't let up on each other until I hear the quiet thump of the door closing behind Cali and Carmela. We simultaneously go quiet, and my eyes widen before my face splits with a smile so big I'm pretty sure all of my teeth are showing. I launch myself at Matt and squeeze him tightly.

"Oh my fucking god!" I squeal as quietly as I can.

"Should we double-check?" he whispers into my curly hair.

"We don't need to," I answer in a muted tone. "I can *feel* it. It's in the bag. Literally."

• 5 1 •

I keep a tight grip on Matt, so I don't rush from the library and sprint back to our apartment. I force myself to go at a normal pace. I hold his hand and maintain a leisurely stroll from the moment we leave the gallery to the second we reach our building. However, as soon as Matt and I make it through the door, I yank the bag from his shoulder.

I carry it to the coffee table and gently set it down. Taking a deep breath, I open the bag. The first thing I do is remove the fake cover. When I see the spine of *The Book*—the real one—nestled safely inside, a feeling of pure power begins to build in my chest just by my unimpeded proximity to it. In Portland, I had to touch the twin to feel this intense strength, but here I can feel it just by being close to it.

I reach in to take out *The Book*, but I stop myself before my hand connects. I remember the intense, invincible feeling I had the first time I touched it, and I take five steadying breaths. I remind myself that power is neither good nor evil—it is the intention of the being using it, which swings the magic's character.

I've ignored Milo since I walked in, but I pay attention to him now. He is sitting in between the couch and the coffee table directly beside my left knee. He's staring at the bag as intently as I imagine I just was. Using his presence to ground me in who I am and what I was made for, I place my left hand on the back of his neck and use my right to reach for *The Book* in Cali's bag.

The moment my fingertips make contact with the old leather cover, they grow warm. When my whole hand grasps the spine, the feeling spreads up to my shoulder. I lift the heavy tome from the bag and place it in my lap. My skin is alive, quivering at the connection I feel from its power to the very depth of my soul.

I can't take my eyes off of it, this manual for how to access every inch of my abilities. My gaze unblinkingly scrutinizes the cover, tracing the words there over and over until my vision blurs from dryness. It's not until I hear the rumble of Milo growling that I glance away from *The Book*.

What I see is more shocking to me than having this magical text finally in my possession: Milo is growling and baring his teeth. At Matt.

My dog is in full protection mode. His ears are pricked at attention with only the very tips flopped over, the hair on the back of his neck is standing on end, and his eyes take in every movement of the man in front of us.

Milo knows what this is, I think.

I lay my left hand back on his neck, softly massaging his fur to calm him. I coo at him, telling him it's okay while my eyes silently tell Matt to freeze.

"Milo, it's alright," I say softly. "You're a good boy, it's okay. Matt isn't going to take this away from me, he's allowed to come near."

I watch my dog's jowls slowly come down to cover his bright teeth, but his readiness to protect and the tension in his body hasn't released yet. Matt shifts his weight, causing Milo to growl once more.

"It's okay, buddy," I try again. I lean down and place my left cheek on top of Milo's head. I hook my arm around to pet the fur on his chest as I speak to him softly. "We've been on this road a long time, haven't we? But we're close to the end. And Matt and Cali are helping us to get there, Milo. We couldn't have done it without them. Now that I've got what we've been looking for, I won't let anyone take it away from me. Not ever."

I don't push him. I let Milo relax on his own time. He has to not only trust what I say but believe that Matt will not betray us in any way. When the tension finally ebbs from him, I hug him tighter and tell him again he's such a good dog. I pepper the top of his head with a dozen kisses before I let him go.

I nod to Matt, who takes a tentative step to come sit next to me. Milo stays quiet at his movements. Matt offers his palm for my dog to sniff. Milo inspects it thoroughly before licking it in acceptance.

I sigh in relief. I use the ring finger of my right hand and run it along the words on the top cover, just barely touching it. I want so badly to open it and pour over everything inside, but I owe it to Cali to wait for her. All of this was possible because of her, so I will wait until she gets back. The three of us will open it together.

Matt reaches out also. Milo shifts closer to me and lets out a soft bark, almost like a warning to Matt that he's watching closely. He runs his finger down the edges of the uneven pages.

"Don't you want to open it?" he asks.

"Of course," I answer instantly. "But we'll wait for Cali to come back, and then the three of us will do it together."

"Okay." He wraps an arm around me and strokes my hair.

I don't know how long we sit like that before I hear an insistent knock on the door—Milo sprints across the apartment barking, immediately on guard. I shush him as I tiptoe up to him.

"It's me! Let me in!" Cali suddenly says through the door. I undo the latch and yank her into the apartment. "Jesus, woman! Where's the fire?"

"What do you mean, 'where's the fire?' How did you leave things with Carmela? Were you followed?"

"Whoa, whoa! Roz, relax. One, Carmela is on her way home. Two, no one followed me because there is no reason to follow me. We pulled off a seamless switch, girl. And three I told Carmela I'll call her."

Cali goes into the kitchen to pour herself a well-earned glass of red wine. I glance quickly at *The Book* on the coffee table as I follow her. She downs the whole glass before she continues.

"What Carmela doesn't know is that there's about to be a "family emergency" that requires us to fly back to America as soon as possible. Clean break, no worries."

"The next time I have no worries will be when Darius is dead, and we're all safely home where we belong."

"Okay, Squirrel is here now," Matt says impatiently.

"I am," she says. "What are we waiting for? Let's open this bitch!"

I bounce on my toes a few times before darting into the living room. I plop onto the couch, ready to finally open it, and realize I'm alone. I look back toward the kitchen and see Milo blocking both Cali and Matt from coming over to me.

"What's up with Dog Man?" Cali asks.

"He knows what that is," Matt says. "He's been in full protection mode since before she even took it out of the bag. He even growled at me and showed me his teeth. She had to talk him down."

Cali's eyes widen as her jaw drops. "Really?!"

I hold up my hand to silence both of them. I stand and come up right behind my dog. I straddle him before I bend at the hips to put my chin on the top of his head. I stroke under his chin with one hand while the other hugs him.

"We talked about this, buddy, remember? You know Cali and Matt don't mean either of us harm. They are on our side, pup. They're with us. You don't need to protect me from them, Milo. It's okay."

I don't stretch upright until I can feel his tail wagging again. I cover his head with more kisses as he lets Matt go by. Cali waits with her hand up for a high five, so I get out of the way to give them room.

For a minute, I think he won't grant her the truce, but eventually, he jumps up to smack her hand. I watch her squat with her hand out still, which he hits again for a low five. Then they both spin in a circle, and Cali holds her fist out for a bump, which Milo grants. Then they fling their heads back and howl in unison.

"Where the hell did that come from?" I ask, shocked.

"We've spent a lot of quality time together these last couple of weeks," Cali says with a shrug. I chuckle and pinch the bridge of my nose under my glasses, completely unsurprised that my best friend has made up a secret handshake with my dog. Matt is anxiously waiting for us on the couch with an eager expression I imagine matches my own.

"Don't we have to wait until it's dark, though?" Cali asks. "I mean, that's how I dreamt it."

"Let's just at least try it now and see what happens," Matt offers.

I nod and set myself up in the spot Milo occupied earlier, on the floor in between the coffee table and couch. Matt and Cali bookend me on the couch and look over my shoulder as I finally open the original, sole remaining copy of *The Book*.

At first glance, it looks exactly the same as the one in the Portland library. As I turn the page, something catches my eye. Above a lengthy paragraph in Latin is my date of birth written in flourishing calligraphy: 21 March 1998. I turn through the next five pages checking for other changes but can't readily see any. We could take the time to wait for the sun to go down completely, but I don't have the patience for that. Not now, not after all this time.

"Grab every candle you can find," I say as I jump up from my seat on the floor. I run around the apartment and close every blind I see, throw every curtain across every exposed pane of glass. Before I sit back down, I make sure the stack of printed papers is nearby so I can write down everything I see on the backs. Cali and Matt come back with three candlesticks and a box of matches.

"If I were renting my place out to strangers, I would minimize the fire risk as much as possible, too," Matt says with a slight shrug.

I scoff, not believing the three sticks will produce enough light.

"Look, why don't we run down to a market real quick and just buy a bunch of candles? It won't take very long. Milo can stand guard over *The Book* until we get back."

"Moose is right, Roz. Put Dog Man in charge, and let's go real quick."

"No," I answer tightly. "Now that it's in my sight, I am not leaving this apartment without it. And it would be foolish to do that this quickly after what we did to get it. The two of you can go. I'll stay here with Milo. I'll try and hang blankets or sheets over the windows to make it even darker in here while you're gone."

My tone clearly does not invite an argument, and the two of them pick up on it. With assurances that they will be back quite literally as soon as possible, they leave. I waste zero time beginning exactly what I said I would do—I make it as dark as I possibly can. I take the extra blankets Cali and I each packed and hang them over the windows in the kitchen since they are the primary source of daylight into the apartment.

I close each of the bedroom doors, which further adds to the dim. Taking the top sheet from one of the extra sets stashed away by the owner, I drape it across one of the door frames, but I don't see any change. However, when the sheet accidentally falls from my grasp and pools on the floor, that does help. Instead of dirtying two clean sheets, I fold the sheet and replace it with a dirty towel from our laundry at the crack between the door and floorboards.

After I put another towel by the other bedroom door, I can't take it anymore and decide to test my blackout skills. The candles don't have holders, so I position them in between the fingers of my left hand, tucked in by the webbing. I move to the light switch, strike a match, light the wicks, and cut the power.

I return to the coffee table, and careful not to light my hair or *The Book* on fire, lean down, bringing my left hand as close as I dare to the paper. At first, I don't see much of anything. But as I tip the candles, angling them closer, I see bright gold lettering begin to appear. The swooping Latin fades as the gold brightens. It's as if they are materializing out of nothing right in front of me, exactly how Cali described it in her dream.

A gasp, relieved sigh, and choked sob combine into a strange sound that escapes me as I see that the gold lettering is in block printed, easily legible English. I turn back to the page that had my date of birth, and my breathing all but stops. The words here are the same languid, easy stroke as in the letter that initially told me what to do when I had to flee on my eighteenth birthday.

" 'My darling girl,' " I read aloud.

My eyes fill with tears preventing me from reading any further. I tip my head back to keep the drops in place. I freeze, letting myself silently feel all of the emotions swirling within me from just those three words. I don't know how long I stay like that, but it's the position Cali and Matt find me in when they return.

I haven't even realized that the ones I'm holding have been dripping hot wax onto my knuckles until Matt turns the lights back on, and I see it for myself.

• 5 2 •

"Hey, it's okay," Cali says gently. "We're here."

She blows out the candles in my hand before gently taking them away from me. I think she can see on my face the substantial emotion I'm barely keeping control of. She rubs my back lightly, making a wide circle with each stroke. Matt crouches down across from me, the table separating us.

"I'm sorry. I couldn't take waiting anymore, so I tried to see if anything would show up with just these candles." My voice trembles as I speak. "And it worked a little bit, but I had to get real close."

I point to the date on the page still open in front of me, the gold lettering once again concealed by the artificial light filling the room. "This is my birthday, my real one, and it wasn't in the other *Book*. When I held the candle up to the words underneath, they lit up in gold, and I saw that 'My darling girl' was written there. It's what my mom calls me, and it's in her handwriting."

Neither Cali nor Matt know what to say. I've never shown this much vulnerability to him, and Cali has maybe only seen me like this once or twice before. She keeps rubbing my back silently. Even Milo is struggling to make me feel better. He nudges my hand so that it settles on top of his head.

I sniffle, trying to keep the internal waves of emotion calm and not let them come pouring out. I chuckle glumly. "I don't know what I thought it would say, but I guess I wasn't ready for it to be written by her specifically."

My friends let me quietly work myself back to base level. Offering their support without having to say anything. I sniffle again and look first at Matt then at Cali. She silently and deliberately checks my face for how I'm feeling. She's usually so energetic that I easily forget there is a depth and stillness to her sometimes that can be the most comforting thing in the world. I nod to her that I'm okay.

She starts to unpack the candles they bought, her best friend following her lead. The majority of them are white, with a few pale greens and blues thrown in. They vary in size, though, everything from votives to candlesticks with bases, to pillars of different heights.

They position as many of the candles as can fit on and around the coffee table. I ask them to start lighting as I get up to search for my red notebook. I originally wanted to use the stack of paper I printed at the library, but it occurs to me that it makes more sense to transcribe it into the notebook that has the other translations already inside it. It's exactly where I left it, so I quickly bring it back to the table.

"Ground rules," I say, retaking my previous spot in. "No reading anything out loud, English or Latin. You guys are my Extensios, so you have powers, and even though we're not sure if you can cast spells, we're not nearly prepared to find out now.

"I want to write down everything that we see, and we can pour over it tomorrow during the day. But, before we start, Cal, we should make sure nothing happens to the other copy. We could need it at some point."

"It's good in the kitchen a few more days. We can pack it away later. I want to see what's inside this first."

She turns off the lights. It's still daylight out, but the blankets in the kitchen and towels under the bedroom doors are helping to make it nice and dark inside. With the amount of candlelight amplified by the sheer number of candles, the gold lettering easily comes to life on the page.

I turn past the note from my mother, not ready to face it again yet. I gently flatten the spine and scan what the next page says. Like the copy back in Portland, this is a brief history of who Darius is and who I am. I wait for a cue from Matt and Cali before moving on. When they both tap their index fingers on the table, I turn the page.

It's about Extensios and Victus. So we scan the page to make sure there isn't anything new and skip to the next. The first thing I see on the left side is the spell I used to hide my family from Darius five years ago. And, unlike when it came up in the translations from Latin, this time, it's complete.

I'm about to explain again what the spell does, but there is a blurb of sorts beneath it, which does it for me. It's my mother's handwriting again. It's like she's giving me the CliffsNotes so I can quickly understand everything.

The right side of each of the next five pages have new spells I've never seen before. I poise a pen above the notebook, ready to write down everything I see. There are paragraphs beneath each of the rhymes. The first spell is how to reverse a forced Victus transformation.

I hope this doesn't come in handy, but I'm glad to have it, I think.

Second is a chant to call on all of my magical ancestors for a one-time amplification of my projection power. While the gold lettering is still showing the English translation, it also has the missing Latin half.

Next is a reversal of my mind-reading power, a way to send messages telepathically to other supernatural beings. The fourth spell grants my Extensios use of my transport power and increases the strength of their telekinesis.

The last spell is not only clearly a powerful one but is also down-right terrifying. It's an alteration to the part of my projection power that lets me heal people. But instead of healing someone, it allows me to drain the life of someone else and channel it through my body to use in assisting my restorative power for another person.

I can't imagine a situation where I would have to use this spell. Even worse, though, I hope there is never a situation that I *want* to say the words.

"That's fucking scary," Matt says, pointing to the spell we all just read.

"You can say that again. Plus, it's creepy as hell," Cali agrees. She shivers before quickly turning to the next page.

Again, I easily recognize my mother's handwriting. Only this time, it looks more like the old cookbook she pulls out for every birthday and holiday to follow the margin notes written on every recipe she's ever tried. These are clearly potions.

What each potion does is plainly stated before the list of ingredients and instructions. I see five distinct and separate recipes on five different pages—one each for replicating my fire-throwing power, a stun that temporarily paralyzes someone, and a protective shield that deflects three attacks per dosage. The fourth potion can reproduce my transport power, and the last is the completed recipe to enchant an animal guide.

My hand has long since cramped at the speed and amount I'm writing down, and at this point, I can barely even read my own writing. Between the spells, potions, and illustrations dispersed throughout, we've quickly reached the last page. I put the pen down and just stare. Whereas the back cover of the twin in Portland had the clue that led us to Rome, this is blank.

I flip back to the front and read what my mother wrote to me. I mouth the words as I read them but don't make a sound: *Our darling girl, we believe in you. You have all of our strength behind you, and no matter what, we are always with you.*

I lean back against the couch and exhale heavily to process everything that's happened today. It has been a long day, and the sun hasn't even fully set yet. I stand up and turn the lights back on, hiding the gold lettering once more.

"Do you think we have enough time to get some of the things we'll need for the potions?" Matt asks, blowing out the candles.

"I honestly wouldn't even know where to go for any of it," I sigh.

"Google to the rescue," Cali says. She takes out her phone and types in some of the ingredients. "It looks like there's an herbalist not too far from here. Actually seems more like an apothecary, so it'll probably have everything we'd need."

I flip back through the pages in the notebook. "It seems like some of them can take up to eight days to finish brewing. We should start making them now, right?"

"Yeah, we're not talking instant pancakes here," Cali says, taking the notebook from my hands. "I don't want to take this with me, so I'm just going to write down what we need on one of these computer pages. Moose, you'll come with me again?"

"Yeah, of course."

As I watch them prepare to leave me again, my anxiety perks to life, and I tell them to be as careful as possible.

"Make it fast, please." It could very easily sound demanding, but my tone is simply pleading.

When the door closes behind them, I point to *The Book* and tell Milo to watch it for me. He situates himself as a blockade between the front door and the coffee table. Everything I've seen of brewing potions involves large capacity pots, and I'm afraid our humble international rental won't be able to make that accommodation.

Rather than searching for one big vat to brew batches in one at a time, I take out every stock pot the kitchen has hiding within its cabinets. I wind up with two that are about five quarts and one big one that must be ten.

Once I heft them up onto the cooktop and rummage through the cabinets for the right lids, I have nothing to do but wait. I start to pace the entire length of the apartment. I walk without watching where I'm going; my eyes can't help but stray to *The Book* to make sure it's still there. Milo stays riveted to his spot, taking his command seriously.

At the end of my spin that will take me back in the direction of the kitchen, I scoop up my notebook and bring it with me. I can't just stand around waiting, so I hunt through every cabinet to see if there is anything we already have.

After looking through every package, box, jar, and bottle, it seems the only thing we have that will work are a couple of sprigs of fresh rosemary and purified water.

"What the hell is a "stomach full" of water?" I pose to the empty room after looking at the first potion recipe, frustrated that it isn't answered by my mother in her notes. Milo barks at me three times in response. I angle my body backward to peer around the doorway to see him. "Do you know?"

He barks three times again. "You do know. Okay, three. Three what? Cups?"

Milo doesn't respond. "Hmm, pints?" Still nothing. "Okay, stop me when I get to it. "Cups? Pints? Quarts? Gallons?" My dog stares at me without response.

"Oh, for fuck's sake. We're in Europe. It's liters, isn't it?" His enthusiastic yips act as a bell, indicating I've guessed correctly. I straighten my back upright so I no longer can see him at his post. "Okay, liters, it is. Now what in here can help me measure liters?"

I look for the measuring cup we've used for breakfast a couple of times and, of course, cannot find it now that I've moved everything around. Potions have to be exact, so I rummage through everything I've moved until I find it.

I'm in the middle of filling the second pot when I hear the grind of a key sliding into the locked front door. Matt and Cali walk in, again with full bags. Milo is still performing his watch command, so I tell him he's all done. He chooses to stay where he is.

"You should have seen the looks we got asking for some of this stuff," Matt says. He puts his bags down on the floor of the kitchen and kisses me on the cheek. His eyes widen as he takes in the mess I've made, having pulled out almost every item in the kitchen.

"Don't worry about it; we can clean it up in a minute," I say quickly to calm his increasing anxiety.

"We did get everything on the list, though," Cali throws in. "So thankfully we won't have to go back there. It was just a tad odd."

"Okay," I sigh in relief. "We are in for the night. We have *The Book,* we have ingredients to get cracking on these potions, we have enough food for a few days, and we have Milo on guard duty. We're set, kids."

Cali pops up onto her toes and hooks an arm around my neck. The other reaches up to Matt and yanks him down to her level. She pulls us into her, so our three foreheads touch.

"Darius doesn't know what the fuck he's in for now," she says with determination. "Let's get to work, bitches."

• 5 3 •

DARIUS

A week after *The Book* found its way out of the library in Rome, a beam of bright light streaming in the window of the witch's living room wakes the demon from the last of his transitions. It's been eleven days since the demon came to Portland and his ranks are now full. All of the parolees, as well as Blue, have been turned into Victus.

He gave Viribus strict instruction to let him recover an extra two days after the last transition to recharge fully. On this mid-May Saturday morning, he feels the best he has since he faced the witch four weeks ago.

He rolls to the side of the mattress pulled from the roommate's room. Two of his soldiers had cleared out the blown apart couch and laid the bed down for him. As he stands, the tension releasing from his joints makes unnatural popping sounds. He's put his body through more in the last twenty-eight days than he's ever done before on this planet.

Padding over to the fridge, Darius opens it to look for the raw meat he expects to be there. He grabs the brown butcher paper upon seeing it, tears it open, and sinks his teeth into the cold flesh. On the counter directly next to the fridge are six bottles of his whiskey of choice. The demon uncaps the first bottle, downing half of it in one gulp. The alcohol burns, warming his cold-blooded body as it chases the meat down his throat.

Viribus opens the apartment's front door just as Darius is finishing both the loin and the bottle.

"Good to see you up, boss," he says, squeezing his girth through the frame.

The demon tosses the empty bottle into the sink, paying no attention as it shatters. "Report," he demands.

"We've gotten nothing back on Blue's search for Cali Jacobs," the deep voice responds. "Seems like we aren't the only ones looking for her, and Blue doesn't have a high enough clearance to join the ongoing investigation. He's getting flack for being way outside his jurisdiction, too.

"I shadowed the woman a couple of times, brought that weasel with me too. We've been able to keep close tabs on her with the GPS chip he put on her phone case. Blue went in to talk with her in person, but she stonewalled him like she did you."

The demon nods. "Well, we'll have to find a way to loosen her tongue. What use does Tyler have left to us?" The Victus soldier stands quiet with zero change to his expression. "As I suspected. Send him up."

Without a sound, Viribus turns to leave. He bows his head to avoid hitting it on the doorjamb. Shortly after the thundering steps down the stairs cease, a soft shuffling can be heard coming up.

The demon eyes the straggly, odorous man as he comes into the apartment. He's wearing the same clothes, or another version just as dirty, as the last time they were face to face, a week and a half ago.

"You wanted to see me?" the human asks.

"That's right," Darius says, opening the next bottle of whiskey. "I want you to know that you've been of use to me. I have another job for you. Go and find out her schedule for the next three days and bring it back to me right away. Understand?"

"Yes, sir."

"Dismissed." He silently watches the scrawny, unkempt, lemon-of-a-human leave the apartment. Darius stands in the same spot, un-thinking and motionless save for periodic sips of the amber liquid until Tyler returns.

He takes the piece of paper the mortal hands him and puts it down without a glance at it. "Normally, I get great joy out of what I'm about to do, but this time, I don't. And I want you to know it's not because I regret it or that I've become fond of you in any way.

"It's simply that you are not *worth* the effort it would take to feel any-thing over," Darius says in a bored way. "You've exhausted what menial use you had, and I have no need to keep pets around that are of no benefit to me."

Tyler sees the man's hand begin to glow and understands whats's about to happen. He spins around to dart back to the door and es-cape. Before he can even reach it, Darius's arm has shot straight out and launched a scorching ball at his back. The fiery orb hits Tyler directly between his shoulder blades, engulfing his entire body in less than a second.

Ash scatters to the hardwood angled toward the door. The momen-tum from Tyler's attempt to flee prevents the formation of a peaked pile. Darius finishes his second bottle of whiskey and tosses it into the sink, the glass shattering like the first. He picks up the schedule from the counter and makes his way from the kitchen to the door. Walking without emotion through the cinders that were, moments ago, a man, the demon exits the witch's place to grab his second in command from the apartment below.

"Viribus," he calls out for his lieutenant while descending the stairs. The giant meets him as he reaches the bottom step. "I'll be ad-dressing the men, and then you and I are leaving."

The Victus silently agrees, stepping out of the demon's way. Darius enters the apartment and, with a wave of his hand, switches off the

TV. A groan sounds from the group who were watching a bikini contest, but when they see who interrupted them, their jeers promptly stop.

"Boys, I have a few things I would like to address. First, I will need someone to go upstairs and sweep up the little mess that Tyler left behind. Next, Viribus and I will be out for the remainder of the day, and we'll be returning with a guest. Let me make this exceedingly clear right now: *hands off.* If any of you goes near our visitor without explicit instruction or permission from me, you won't exactly be joining Tyler, but you'll be wishing you were. Lastly, Blue is in charge until I return. Am I clear?"

The room remains quiet as the new Victus soldiers obediently acquiesce. Darius pauses long enough to make sure no one thinks to question him. Satisfied that the batch of blockheads intends to follow his directions, he runs his red hand through his slick black hair and swiftly leaves. The shaking of the staircase signals that Viribus is right on his heels tagging along.

They pull up in front of Mickey's studio in a luxury SUV and park halfway down the street. Far enough from the entrance to not be noticed, but close enough that they can see the comings and goings.

From the backseat, Darius watches the time displayed on the car's touchscreen tick slowly by. Gripping the paper Tyler gave him, he waits until the trainer's last class begins to trickle out. He leans forward to tap Viribus on the shoulder, the noiseless communication telling him to move the car closer.

The demon gets out of the vehicle and, making sure to keep his scarred hand out of sight, enters the gym alone. Easily spotting the tall and gorgeous woman, Darius makes a beeline right to her. Mickey sees him coming and makes a point of drawing out the conversation she's having with a client. When it's clear that they've gotten what they need, she finally turns to Darius with a forced smile.

"Mr. Sanger. What can I do for you this time?"

"I'm sorry to bother you again, miss, but I won't take up too much of your time," Darius replies smoothly. "I believe a colleague of mine came by to ask you some questions a few days ago."

"He did," she says, crossing her arms. "And I told him the same thing I told you. I don't have any information about Alexa's family or why she was there that night. And if you still haven't been able to reach Cali, I don't know how to help you because, like I said, we broke up."

Darius silently checks out the room, glancing into the mirrors that cover an entire wall. He remains quiet until the last person leaves. When the two of them are finally alone in the front room, he drops his act and says, "I don't believe you."

"Excuse me?" she asks, aiming for an indignant tone, but the demon can tell she's rattled.

"In fact, I know you've been in touch with Ms. Jacobs. I also know you know where she and "Alexa"—as you call her—have gone. And, I know you know why they've gone there."

Mickey moves away from him, angling back toward her office as she says, "I don't know what you're talking about."

"Oh, yes, you do," he growls. "I also know you're calling her by a different name, that you know what powers she possesses, and that by revealing all this, you've figured out who *I* am." He hears Viribus come into the studio to block the door.

"The only thing I don't know is where she is, and that is what you're going to tell me."

For her part, the brunette raises her chin and looks him straight in the eyes. "No, I'm not."

"Pity. And this could've been over so quickly too."

In movements quicker than Mickey can register or defend against, Darius telekinetically delivers an uppercut to Mickey's chin without touching her. The powerful supernatural blow knocks the trainer off of her feet. She hits the floor out cold.

Darius heads to her office to search for the woman's phone to get a line on the witch and her friends. He easily finds it on her desk. When he returns to the front, Viribus has the unconscious woman thrown over his shoulder, waiting for his boss. The demon nods to him, and the men exit.

"How rude of me, assumptions being what they are and all, I forgot to formally introduce myself," he says to the non-responsive woman. "I am Darius, and I assure you, the pleasure is all mine."

****

"Hey, wake up," Darius says, trying to rouse Mickey. He snaps his fingers but gets no response. The demon has no patience to wait, so he flicks the air with his middle finger. Mickey's head jerks to the side, causing her to groan.

"That's it. Come on, let's go."

She wakes further and tries to rub the bruise on her jaw with her right hand. When it stops short from the rope tied around it, her eyes snap open, and she panics. Mickey tugs at the rope as hard as she can, which only tightens it further, making it cut into her skin. She kicks her legs, swiping wildly at her captor.

"Stop," Darius commands. "You're not going anywhere. And you shouldn't want to. As far as I can tell, you should be quite comfortable here."

The demon gestures to the room he's holding her in. Mickey looks around and sees she's been tied to the radiator in Cali's bedroom. Rather than calm her, it makes her panic even more. She fights her ties harder and doesn't stop until blood begins to smear on her wrists from where the rope has cut even deeper into her skin.

"By all means, keep struggling. I have only one question, and if you answer truthfully, then you'll be free to go." The words cause Mickey to still her movements. She won't look at him but stays quiet, waiting for him to ask. "Where *is* she?"

"I don't know," Mickey says through gritted teeth.

"Yes, you do!" The loud sound of his palm connecting with her bare cheek rings in the enclosed room. The blow lands, swinging her head violently to the side. He jabs a finger in her face as he says, "Yes, you fucking do."

"I can't tell you because I don't know! I haven't spoken to Cali in weeks, and Alexa is dead!"

"Weeks?" Darius chuckles cruelly. "You spoke to her just the other day, Michaela. She and *Roz* were about to do something? You wanted to know if you'd have to get on a plane and bail them out."

Mickey's eyes widen, and her head whips back to face the demon in disbelief. She holds his gaze, looking him dead in the eyes. After a long silent moment, she sets her jaw and says, "I'm not telling you anything."

"You'll tell me, you know you will. The question is, how long is it going to take, and how much can you take before you do?"

"You can't hold me here, you fucking piece of shit!" Mickey yells. "Help! Somebody help!!"

Darius lets her yell. He waits her out, looking at his nails in a bored fashion. When she falls silent, he asks, "Are you done? I think you're done. Now, where the fuck is she?"

Mickey stares at him with hatred in her eyes. He rears back and slaps her again. At the very least, he's expecting her to whimper from the repeated blows, but this time she doesn't make a sound. His tolerance for the situation has completely evaporated, so the demon decides to up the ante. He holds up his scarred hand.

"You see this? Your little bitch friend did it. She burned me, and you know what? I could tell you about how much it hurt. But I'd rather show you."

The tip of his index finger brightly glows as he touches the already raw skin of her right arm just above her restraints. He uses his other hand to magically hold her still. The sound of sizzling flesh is quickly drowned out by the trainer's shrieks of pain.

Darius releases her and steps away. Mickey cradles her tied arm to her body as best she can, gasping in pain. Tears are streaming down her face, dripping from her chin onto her workout clothes, still sweaty from her last class.

"Now, do you have something to tell me?"

"Yeah," Mickey hisses. "Fuck you."

Darius's features morph with anger as his finger heats up again. He touches it to her skin an inch above the last burn. He holds her in place, ignoring her screams.

Over the next seven hours, Darius is relentless as he torments Mickey to give up the witch's location. He revives her with smelling salts three separate times after she passes out from the pain. Her exposed skin is covered in its entirety with nasty burns, but still, she reveals nothing.

"I must say, I'm impressed by your resilience," Darius says, rolling up the sleeves of his shirt. He has to hold her face still as her eyes swim, unable to focus through the torment. "Better than most men I've done the same to.

The demon reaches a hand into her shirt. It reappears, holding a piece of platinum jewelry. He thumbs the ring she's wearing on a necklace, making it spin on the chain.

"You know, you're much too beautiful to kill. I'd rather keep you to play with, but you have something I need and have left me no other choice. Let's see how it feels to go through your heart and force your lover Cali to bring the witch to me."

He places his hand on the top of her head, closes his eyes, and takes a deep breath.

"*Per vim, virtutem meam te esse maledicam.*"

By force, my power I curse to thee.

• 5 4 •

Cali

Around noon on Wednesday, the potions have all finished brewing, and the last two batches are cooling. There were five potion recipes within *The Book*, but they don't need the transports potion since Roslyn can do that for them, and Milo is already Milo.

The firepower replicator has been brewed and bottled, reducing to a thick liquid that will explode on impact. The protection and stun potions have also thickened and are almost completely cooled.

They've spent the last week going only to the market for food and to a work out class a couple of blocks over. They've spent the rest of the time studying *The Book*. Roslyn loaded the spells into her translator app to learn the correct pronunciations. She listened with Cali's headphones so that none were inadvertently cast.

As they are clearing the table for lunch, Cali tells the other two that she had a dream about Mickey last night, that she misses her, and she's anxious to talk to her before work today. Matt encourages her to call her girlfriend as soon as the time difference lines up.

The three sit down to have open-faced sandwiches and salad. Milo hovers close by, waiting for someone to share. Before Cali even begins eating, she starts to rub her chest.

"You okay, Cal?"

"Yeah, I think so," she answers. "Just a little heartburn, I guess."

Two bites into their meal and the auburn-haired girl gasps clutching her chest again. She stands up so forcefully from the table that her chair topples over and slides across the tile floor.

"Cali!" Roslyn cries in alarm. "What's wrong?!"

She and Matt stand from their seats to come over and check on their shorter friend. Before they even reach her, Cali lets out an ear-splitting shriek. She falls to the floor writhing in pain. Milo starts barking incessantly but keeps his distance from the girl. Roslyn can't tell if she's breathing or not, but her skin is turning dark red and has erased her abundant freckles.

The witch goes down on her knees and hovers over her friend. When Cali stops thrashing, she lifts the smaller woman into her arms. Milo stops barking and begins circling the two of them huddled on the floor, whimpering and sniffing as he moves. Matt stands nearby pale-faced and unsure of what to do, one hand gripping his hair the other pulling on the collar of his t-shirt.

"Cali?! Cali, can you hear me? Talk to me, what's going on?"

Cali's response is a slight choking noise. Her body begins to tremble in Roslyn's arms. She stops shaking but begins to breathe rapidly, on the verge of hyperventilating. She says something, but Roslyn doesn't catch it.

"What? Say that again," Roslyn says, ducking her ear close to Cali's mouth.

"It burns," Cali hisses faintly.

"What burns?" Roslyn asks. She notices that all of Cali's visible skin is still dark red. Her eyes are clenched shut so tightly that the crow's feet around them turn stark white against her blotchy skin.

"Ev... everything."

Suddenly Cali's body goes violently rigid in her friend's arms, and her eyes shoot open. They are completely black, no green iris, no white sclera. Milo rushes in and lays his head on her shoulder, Roslyn makes no sound, but Matt gasps and falls to the floor next to the two women.

"Cali!!" he yells as he reaches for her hand and holds it tight. His face is panic-stricken. "Should I call a doctor or something?"

"No, no, we can't!" Roslyn shouts. "Milo can sense if she's okay and what's going on."

Just as quickly as her body tightens, it abruptly relaxes. Her eyes are still open. They slowly clear of the black, leaving only bloodshot green to stare back at Roslyn. Her gaze is unfocused, searching for something that can't be seen.

A moment before her eyes roll back into her head and she passes out, Cali whispers one word. "*Mickey.*"

Her body goes limp in Roslyn's arms, frightening her friends all over again. For the moment, she doesn't feel Matt let go of her hand or the light taps on her cheeks that try to rouse her, nor does she hear them calling out her name. She isn't tickled by the quick breaths of Milo sniffing her face and neck as he checks her.

She's slow to come around, but when she finally does, she's met by two sets of petrified eyes scanning every inch of her. A big wet tongue swipes across her cheek. She groans and weakly tries to swipe it away.

"Cali," Roslyn calls softly. "Can you hear me?"

She groans again. "What happened?"

"We were hoping you could tell us, Squirrel." Matt is right next to her but hasn't touched her since he let go of her hand.

"I don't know. I felt this burning in my chest, and it started to spread all over me. It was like being filled with lava or something."

She tries to sit up, but Roslyn presses her down, keeping her prone on the floor. "You said Mickey's name right before you passed out."

"I did?" Her eyes have been hooded, faraway, but now they snap open wide, filled with tears. She whimpers in pain again. "Oh, my god, I saw her, Roz! She's in trouble."

"What do you mean?" Roslyn asks, alarmed. "Tell me exactly what you saw."

Cali is crying too hard to be able to say anything. Roslyn adjusts her grip so Cali can wrap her arms around her neck. She cradles her friend, gently rocking them both back and forth.

Matt gently places his hand on her knee, squeezing lightly. Roslyn stops rocking when Cali removes one arm to reach down and grip her long-time friend's hand. Milo wedges himself against Cali's back. He pushes in tight, the warmth and pressure of his body weight, helping Cali calm down enough to catch some of her breath.

"I saw her in my bedroom back in Portland," Cali says before breaking down in sobs again.

"It's okay, sweetie," Roslyn coos as she tucks her head in close to her friend. "Just breathe and tell me everything you remember."

Cali lets go of Matt to rub her hair away from her eyes and takes in a deep, shuddering breath. Around hiccups, she says, "I can see it so clearly in my head right now. She was tied to the radiator and had burns on her arms and neck."

Cali begins to cry again. At this moment, she looks so small, curled in on herself surrounded by her friends. Her body shakes so hard from her tears, Roslyn tightens her hold, trying desperately to comfort her. "Hey, we're here, kid. We've got you."

"She was screaming in pain," Cali says in a voice thick with tears. "And it looked like someone had traced every vein with a dark black marker."

Roslyn's grip on her friend, which has been so strong and steady up to this point, loosens almost imperceptibly. But in the comfort of others, Cali has regained enough of herself to notice it. She peels herself away and sits up to face the witch. "What? What is it?"

Unable to answer the puffy, desperate eyes that are suddenly super focused on her own, Roslyn looks away and doesn't see her friend's face contort in agony again.

"No," Cali pleads, tears filling her eyes once more. "Tell me it's not him. Tell me!" Roslyn stays silent. A look of guilt on her face the only response Cali gets.

She forcefully pushes Roslyn away and jumps to her feet. She ignores Milo's barks at her rough act. Cali paces the kitchen pulling on her hair, trying to fully understand what's happened to Mickey.

She wheels around on her friend and thrusts an accusatory finger at her spot, still on the floor. "You swore! You told me that she would be okay! You said as long as she stayed away from our apartment that she'd be fine. You lied to me!"

"I did not lie to you, Cali," Roslyn says carefully, slowly standing to face her friend. "I honestly believed that Mickey would be okay."

"How did this happen then?!" Cali furiously demands. Her face momentarily pales before it reddens from a new rush of anger. "The fire inspector. She said he was pale with black hair, had tattoos. I didn't catch it at the time because I was so relieved that she was okay, but it was *him,* wasn't it."

Roslyn doesn't answer audibly. Cali clenches her jaw and launches herself at the taller woman. Her arm is cocked back, ready to take a swing, but Matt catches her. He pulls her back, keeping space between them.

"You fucking liar!" Cali screams. "How *dare* you let me believe she was safe when Darius has obviously known who she is and how to find her for weeks now!! That's my *family*, Lex, Roz—whoever the fuck you are!"

"I'm sorry," Roslyn says softly. "But I couldn't tell you. We had just found *The Book*. It could've ruined everything."

"It did ruin everything!! Don't you even understand that?"

"I'm so sorry," Roslyn says again. "Please let me explain."

"Explain? Explain what? How you've lied to me, used me, and all this time knew that Mickey was on that demon's radar?"

"Cali, please. Mickey is family to me, too. You know that."

"Do I?!"

"Yes! Just like you and Matt are! If I had told you that I suspected the fire inspector was actually Darius, you would have demanded we go back and get her."

"You're goddamn right I would've!"

"And rightfully so. But how would it have helped us? It couldn't have! Mickey said he left, she watched him go. So at that moment, she was okay, and we still had work to do. Going back could have exposed all of us. That I didn't die in the blast, that the three of us fled the country, that Mickey knew all along. t could've put us in the middle of a spotlight that none of us were prepared for.

"I made the decision not to tell you my suspicions. I made the decision that we had to get *The Book* first, and then we would go back for her. But Mickey never saw him again. She never said anything else about it, so I thought she was okay and that we were in the clear."

"That still doesn't give you the right not to fucking tell me, Roslyn!"

"I know, and I am very, very sorry for that. I should have told you. I'm sorry, Cali."

"I don't believe you," Cali says. Her anger and betrayal are evident. "You don't know what this has been like for me to be away from her.

"Darius was wrong when he said that you care more about your friends than you did your brother," she says with a hateful glare.

"You only care about yourself."

• 5 5 •

"ROSLYN"

My head snaps back as if I've been struck by more than just her words. My eyes water from the sting. For a second, I can't believe she just said that to me.

But then again, I can. I've been deceitful toward her, cowardly in my blatant misdirection. I've kept things from her that I had no right to, and every time it was so that *I* could get what I wanted out of the situation.

"Whoa, hey. Come on, you know that's not true," Matt says, attempting to mediate things, although it does nothing to make me feel better.

"Cali," I begin. "I do care about you, and you know I care about Mickey, too. Yes, I lied to you. But it was to keep you safe."

Cali rolls her eyes at me, ready to launch another attack. I hold up my hand to quiet her. "Please let me finish.'

She stays silent, granting me a courtesy I don't think I would've been able to if the roles were reversed.

"All I want—the *only* thing I want—is to keep everyone alive and protected. And if lying to you helped me do that, then I lied. I never wanted Mickey to get caught up in this. And now that she has, I accept that it's completely my fault. But please, this is the absolute last thing I wanted, you have to know this is the last thing I wanted. Please."

Cali won't answer me. She's staring me down, but I refuse to look away or blink. I can see that she's still angry, and I don't blame her for it. I try it again.

"Cal, you're my best friend, the best I have ever had. And I am sorry that I lied to you that I've kept things from you. But can't you understand where I'm coming from?"

"How can I?" Cali asks, crossing her arms over her chest. "You have no idea what it's like to leave the person you love the most in the world behind and then find out they've been in danger the entire time."

It's a slap in the face again. However, I'm the one who feels betrayed this time. It's as if she's never listened to anything I've said about who I am and why I've always been so guarded.

"I don't know what it's like to leave loved ones behind? *I* don't know what that's like?! I can't believe you just said that. I haven't seen my family in over five years. I haven't even been able to *think* about my family for more than a second at a time because it could jeopardize their safety!

"Do you know why Darius tried to taunt me with my brother in the library?" Cali shakes her head. She's listening, but I haven't won her back.

"It's because the last I saw, my oldest brother stood up to fight immediately, to protect me. And all I did was run. Darius killed Tripp. That's how he chose to tell me. That he killed a part of me and that you guys would be next."

Her expression changes. Matt takes a step away from her toward me. I hold up my hand again. "Stop. I didn't tell you that for sympathy. I'm just trying to make you understand why I'm doing what I'm doing. I left everything I ever knew when I was eighteen. I had to leave where I grew up, my *home,* and run.   don't know what's left of it, or even if the rest of my family is safe.

"I tell myself they are, but I don't know for sure."

Milo brushes up against my leg, silently offering support. He's the only one who's been with me the entire way. I reach down and ruffle the fur around his collar, grateful for the support.

"Look," I sigh. "Every time you've asked me about my past, I've ducked the question. But there is a very good reason for it. There is a good reason for everything I do."

"I'm sure you think there is, but at the end of the day, why should I believe you? I mean, you haven't even told me your real name yet."

"And I'm not going to tell you. Not just now,' I say. It's not the right time to let the rest of my secrets go.

"Seriously?" Cali asks incredulously.

"I think I can answer this," Matt says, playing the peacekeeper role. He turns to face Cali. "I asked her why she wouldn't tell me—us—what her name is, and her answer really makes sense. She's had to be guarded for a long time, Squirrel. She's had to hide who she truly is with no safety net; any slip could jeopardize not just her but literally the entire world. She said that claiming her name again could unleash a part of her that she won't be able to hide again. So she can't tell us who she really is until she's ready to be that person and take on all of the responsibility that goes with it, for good."

Cali pauses for a minute as she considers Matt's explanation. She takes a deep breath before she finally says, "Okay. That I understand. But it still didn't give you the right to keep me in the dark about the danger that was so close to Mickey. That was entirely unfair."

"Fair?" I snort. "How is any of this fair? To any of us?"

I pause and let everything settle for a moment. "I am sorry, kid. I understand that you're mad and hurt. And f you never forgive me,

I'll understand that too. But that from now on, if I can't tell you everything, then I promise I will tell you as much as I can. Okay?"

The briefest of nods is all I get in agreement. It's a start, and the entirety of our friendship is precariously balanced on a steep edge, but I'll take it.

"Okay," I sigh. "So, do you have any questions for me?"

"Yes," Cali says immediately. "I know you must have some plan already working in your head, and I want to know what it is."

"You're right," I nod. "I do have a plan, but I'm not sure you're going to like it."

"Why won't I like it?" Cali asks, her temper rising again.

"Because I want to stay here and wait."

"What?!" Cali leaves the kitchen heading to her bedroom.

"Cal, please! Hear me out," I plead as I follow her. I go into the room and see her tossing her bag on her bed. Before I can stop her, she starts pulling out her clothes and making a pile next to the bag. "Cali, please."

"No! How can you expect me to wait here? I told you that I saw Mickey, my soulmate, the person who I missed my anniversary with and left there to come with you, is hurt and tied to a radiator. And I remember you swore to me before that demon radar be damned, if she was in trouble, you would use your powers to go back and get her.

"So now that she's past trouble and in full-on danger, you want to break that promise? You want to wait, and you expect me to stick around here with you?"

"Yes, Cali, I do."

"Well, why the fuck would I, Roslyn?!"

"Because it's a trap!!" I shout at her.

"Look," I take a breath to try and calm my emotions. She's not going to hear anything I say if I just keep yelling "Soulmates are real. Certain people in this universe are made to find each other, and that bond is unbreakable.

"So you're right—you and Mickey are soulmates. Your love for each other is on a higher level than anyone around you. And Darius has used that against us.

"He did a forced transition, the only thing that could explain your severe physical reaction to Mickey's situation. He did it to draw you back to her. So she's going to be guarded with more security than the Queen of England.

"If we go back now, without a plan and with emotions running high, you can be sure that the other Victus will be waiting for us. Going back, blind to anything but saving Mickey, will do nothing more than get us all killed."

I move further into the room and stand between her and the bed to stop her from packing. I put my hands on her shoulders, but she immediately rips them off. She doesn't push me or try to get around me, so I lift my hands in surrender. I leave them up as I speak to her again.

"When I swore I would go back and save Mickey if she was ever in danger, I meant it. You know I did. But I want us to be careful and smart in how we do it. We *need* to be."

I don't want it to, but my voice breaks as I plead with her to trust me. I'm on the brink of letting five years of emotion crash down, but I bite the inside of my cheek hard and stay as stoic as possible. There will be time to open the dam later.

"Cal, right now you have no reason to trust me, but I am asking you to. I am begging you to trust that I have a plan, and I will get Mickey out. If I have to trade places with her myself, I will. I promise right now on my life that I won't let you down. Please."

Cali owes me nothing at this moment, and she knows it. It's written all over her face. She has every right to leave and never waste another second on me. But maybe there is a force at play here stronger than either of us because something makes her stay. Her expression loses some of its edge, but her justified anger is still hot under the surface.

I stand before her, unsure of what I should do. I don't know if I should reach out to hug her or if I should leave her alone for a few minutes to unpack. I choose to stand and wait for her cue.

She doesn't offer me a hug but does hold out her fist for a bump, which I quickly pound. I'm aware that Milo and Matt have watched our entire interaction by Milo's nails tapping across the floor as he comes in for a bump too.

No one has ever been able to resist Milo, and Cali falling victim to his cuteness is exactly what I'm hoping for. I see her smile for the first time since she collapsed onto the kitchen floor. It seems like that was days but could only be an hour ago at the most.

"Alright, so tell me your plan. And don't leave a single thing out."

• 5 6 •

I take a deep breath and begin, "I have a couple of ideas. But both of them include us hanging tight for a bit. We can't rush into anything; we have to think everything through and from every angle.

"The first plan involves us waiting just long enough to make it seem to Darius that we know what he's done and are still running, that we're abandoning Mickey.

"That gives us a chance to really prepare for anything we might face. You guys can practice your powers again, or we can try the spells. Now that we have *The Book*, I guess it doesn't matter if we leave a magical trace. It might even work in our favor."

Cali doesn't look impressed with my idea, so I quickly move one to my next idea.

"Plan two involves the other replica. In a day or so, we call Mickey's phone and demand to speak first to her and then to Darius only. We get him on the phone and make a one for one trade—Mickey for *The Book*.

"He doesn't know you made a fake one. So he'll still be thinking that I'm desperate to keep it, that it's the only way I'll be able to beat

KERRI MCLOONE

him. We set a time on our terms only. When he sees it, he should think I'm either desperate or stupid, probably both, to give it up.

"But, from now on, we decide as a group." I exhale sharply, "Thoughts?"

"I think that we should do the second plan," Cali says without hesitation. "It has the least amount of risk to Mickey. She is my only priority right now. He's been looking for you and for *The Book* for a really long time. Now we have it, and he has something we want. It's quid pro quo."

"But he's a demon, Squirrel. You can't trust him, or that he won't find a way to double-cross us."

"Of course, he will. So we prepare for that and double-cross him first, Moose."

"How, though?"

"I don't know! But we obviously can't leave a single thing to chance. Not when it comes to Mickey. Anything else happens to her, and I'm done, I'm out."

She looks at me as she says it, and I believe her completely, so I quickly say, "She's right. We don't know who Darius has in his grip, so if we call Mickey's phone now, it could give them a chance to trace the call and figure out where we are. We can't give them that extra leg up."

"Break this down for me," Matt says. "How much longer do we stay here?"

"I think another day or so, just until the time difference works in our favor. Whether that's here in this apartment or just in Rome in general, I don't know. But, we need to keep our heads. He's no doubt going to try and get us to respond emotionally, irrationally."

"If leaving a magical trace isn't as dangerous as it was before we got *The Book,* then I say we stay right here," Cali says. "Moose and I can practice the Extensios power, and if it leaves a breadcrumb,

• 352 •

so be it. We don't even know if he can trace us like he can you. We don't fucking know anything."

She mumbles the last part under her breath. Our temporary truce is on shaky ground; I need to give her something concrete to hold on to. Like where we will go to get Mickey back. I'm trying to think of a neutral location when it suddenly hits me.

"Mount Tabor Park," I say.

"What?" they both ask at the same time.

"That's where we should go to get her back. It's a mostly neutral location, so Darius won't feel vulnerable. But we sort of know it, at least what the layout is, and can use that to our advantage."

"Okay, so, what do we do now?" Matt asks.

"Now we make sure everything is in order so we can just get up and go when the time comes. The firepower is done, but the stun and protection potions need to be bottled. There should be more than enough for at least six little bottles of each."

A delicate, painfully awkward silence falls amongst the three of us. We leave Cali's bedroom and head back to the kitchen. Matt walks in between her and me, Milo is glued to my side. The stainless steel pots have cooled plenty and can be easily handled.

I find a turkey baster and use that to transfer the liquid to the bottles Matt and Cali picked up at the apothecary. Each is a little smaller than an airplane liquor bottle; one squeeze of the bulb fills each to the brim.

After I fill each one with the purple liquid, pass them on to Matt, who screws the tops back on. I rinse the baster thoroughly before Matt and I repeat the process with the green-colored protection potion.

He's handed off each bottle to Cali, who's separated them into three groups with two of each. I see it and think, *she doesn't need to do that*. The boosts that the potions give are technically already in my arsenal. I just have to access them.

"You can do two groups of three," I say carefully. "The potions are for you guys."

Cali pauses momentarily before she silently rearranges the bottles on the counter.

"Umm," Matt tries. "There is a little of each one left. Can we play with it?"

"What?"

"Like, can I drink it? I want to see how it works."

"Well, you only drink the protection one. The other two you throw at someone else."

"Okay, so let me drink the green one and then have you throw something at me."

"First hand me the rest of the bottles," I say. "There are only a few left, and I want to fill them for Mickey. The moment we have her, we make her drink it and keep her out of the way."

Cali has been rotating the small, different colored bottles as if playing a shell game, but her head snaps up at the mention of Mickey. "Good," is all she says.

Matt hands me the last three bottles. He bounces on his toes as I fill each one. When I've finally finished and hand him the last one, he's grinning like a kid on Christmas morning.

"Now?" he asks.

"I guess." I hand him the turkey baster. He pinches the bulb, suctions a good amount, and immediately puts it in his mouth. He frowns as he swallows. I can't help but smirk at his expression as I ask, "Good?"

"It definitely wasn't made for taste. I can tell you that."

"How do you feel?" Cali asks. Her green eyes are beginning to twinkle slightly. I can see the mischief building in her mind.

"Tingly and warm," he says. Matt sees the look on her face, and his own morphs into one of competition. "Gimme your best shot, Squirrel."

Cali looks around the kitchen for something to throw at him. I'm hoping she'll find something innocuous so that if there is a lag time between drinking and working, it won't hurt him too much. She takes the wooden spoon out of the utensil holder, and I get an instant flashback of being told to quit doing something as a kid and not listening until my mother pulled out her own wooden spoon.

Cali steps back to give herself more space. She cocks her left arm back and lets the spoon fly. It rotates as it flies straight for Matt's head. To his credit, Matt doesn't flinch. The spoon is about six inches away from him when his body lights up with a bright green glow making the spoon drop to the floor without ever touching him. "Awesome!" Matt and Cali say together.

Immediately she starts looking for something else to throw at him. I look around too, and the first thing I see is an orange. I toss it to Cali. She leaves the kitchen, beckoning Matt to follow her.

They stand at opposite ends of the living room. Cali throws again, adding some strength and speed to it, but the same thing happens. It stops half a foot away from Matt and falls to the floor harmlessly. Milo, ever helpful, gently picks up the orange and brings it back to Cali. She goes through the same motion and gets the same result.

When Milo hands it off to her again, I think, *That's three. This time it should connect.*

Cali must remember that also because she doesn't throw as hard. As expected, the orange smacks Matt right above his belly button.

The two of them look down at the orange on the floor and back up at themselves twice. Cali's face finally shines with a real smile as she says, "My turn!"

• 5 7 •

After both of them had each taken two swigs of the protection potion and launched various objects back and forth, it was clear Cali's mood had bounced back some. Still, I knew that one more mistake on my part could mean the absolute end of our friendship.

With her contempt for me quiet at the moment, I suggest again about taking one last kickboxing class. It sobers the moment, but both agree with me. We branch off from the living room to go to our bedrooms and change.

I'm about to take off my shirt when I feel Matt's arms wrap around me from behind. He kisses me on the back of my neck and says, "I understand why you kept things hidden, why you still are, but I'm here for you when you are ready to tell me everything. And even though Squirrel is upset right now, I know deep down she gets it too."

I relax backward into him and nod my head. He squeezes me gently before loosening his grip. The two of us finish changing in comfortable silence. When I step out of the room, Cali is sitting on the couch, looking at her tablet.

"The next class starts in half an hour,' she says without looking up. "It's a beginner level class of Krav Maga. A little different than the others we've taken there."

I nod. I whistle for Milo to come over, and, as usual, he responds quickly. "Okay, bud, you're in charge while we're out. Your primary responsibility will be *The Book*. Potions we can make again, so don't worry about them. Sign here if you agree to the terms of this contract."

I hold out my fist for his response. He bumps it offering his consent to the conditions. I check his bowls before I put my sneakers on at the front door. Matt and Cali join me outside in the hallway, and Cal hands me the keys after she locks the door. I half expect her to throw them at me, so I let out a quiet sigh when she doesn't.

When we get there, we realize that it's going to be difficult keeping up without knowing the language that well. We end up spending most of the class just following what we see everyone else doing, which is enough to have all three of us sweating and gasping within minutes.

Once the class is officially over and I have a moment to think again, I realize that I'm so exhausted I could collapse right here and take a nap on the floor. My knuckles are raw from punching the pads, my legs are jelly from sprinting, but I don't really care. At the same time, I'm feeling satisfied and confident. I feel like I could take on anybody and cause some serious damage.

I put my hands on my knees to catch my breath a little more before we make the walk back to the apartment. I take my glasses off and shake some of the sweat from them. There isn't a dry patch on my shirt I can use to wipe them, so I just put them back on my face wet.

"Ready?" Matt asks when I stand upright.

"Yes," I nod. "Is there enough food at the apartment for dinner, or should we pick something up?"

"I'm too tired to do much of anything, so we might as well pick something up," Cali says. It's more than she's said to me in hours, so I gladly take it.

We pass a pizzeria on our way back. Without needing to consult one another, as a group, we instantly decide it's what we want. As we're waiting for our order to be ready to go, Cali comes over to me and hooks her arm into my elbow. It's a soft touch, but the familiarity of it brings tears to my eyes.

"I am really sorry," I say quietly, risking this new truce but needing to say it anyway. "I honestly thought that I was doing it for the sake of all of us. But it was selfish and dangerous."

Cali sighs deeply. "I get it. I'm still not happy about it, and I haven't forgiven you, but I worked through some of my aggression while I was punching the mat you were holding. We're not good, but we're okay. I meant what I said, though. If anything else happens to Mickey, I'm out, but for now, we're okay."

I bow my head slightly, fully accepting her terms. It's better than what I'd be able to say if the situation was flipped.

We walk back to the apartment linked together in easy silence. Matt strides just in front of us, holding the food.

I listen at the door before I put my key in. It's quiet; there's no movement on the other side of the door. There's still no sound as I unlock the door. It isn't until I call out for Milo and tell him it's okay, does his black head peek around from the corner of my bedroom doorway.

"Good job, buddy," I praise him squatting down for him to come to me. He flops onto his back and gets a trifecta of belly rubs from all of us. Milo must sense the tension has been lifted slightly and relieved of his watch duty, he playfully tries to lick all of our faces while laying flat on the floor.

We eat an early dinner by Italy standards crowded around the coffee table in the living room. I sit on the floor, facing Matt and Cali on the couch. Milo sits next to me patiently waiting for the piece of my crust he knows I always save him when I eat pizza.

The conversation is light; the three of us are even able to joke with one another a bit. But in the back of my mind, I'm considering our next move now more than ever. We have everything we should need to get Mickey back and then some.

"Guys," I say. "Do you think we should stay here tonight, or should we go somewhere else?"

My serious tone rapidly changes the playful air. Cali swallows her bite of pizza and quietly thinks before she responds.

"You said that Darius needs time to recover from a transition. Like a day or two, right?"

"Yes."

"Well, I think we only need to stay here one more night and leave tomorrow morning since he probably can't track you while he recovers. And I think you should transport us home."

I inhale deeply. "I wasn't planning on using my power to get us back. But you could be right; if he has to recover, it may mess up his ability to track me."

"We have what we needed to get, Roslyn," Matt says. "We have *The Book;* we made potions. There's really no reason to stay except to shower and rest."

"Plus, even if he *can* track you while recovering, we've still got the upper hand," Cali adds. "We can defend ourselves against him and whatever imbeciles he brings with him."

They look at me expectantly. I can't argue with their logic. They're vocalizing everything I'm already thinking. We have no reason to stay.

"You're right. We should clean up, pack, and figure out when and where and how to go." I tell them I'm still hesitant about using my transport power.

"*Fuck*, Darius. If he can find us, let him. We can take him," Cali says confidently.

I look back and forth between my best friend and my boyfriend. They stare back at me, determined and ready. As I look at them, I feel a mixture of gratitude and conviction. *We've fucking got this,* I think to myself.

I slap my palm on the table in agreement. Cali says she'll shower first and that Matt and I should start to clean things up. We've cleared the empty pizza box and thrown all the other garbage away by the time she's done.

I shower quickly and start to pack as soon as I'm dressed. I put my shoulder bag on the sheets next to my canvas laundry bag. *The Book* is tucked away inside of it, but I just want it close for the moment.

I have on light wash stretch jeans and a white long sleeve shirt, with my rust jacket and hiking boots. Comfortable and practical. I roughly towel dry my thick hair before throwing it up into a messy bun. I gather the rest of my clothes and shoes from the drawers and closet and stuff them inside the bag as tightly as I can. The only item I fold carefully is the expensive blue dress I wore on our double date.

Once my things are packed, I gather up all of Milo's. In the kitchen, I grab the potions to put in my shoulder bag with *The Book*. I spin in place, scanning the kitchen for anything I've missed. When I come up with nothing, I do the same in the living room.

Satisfied I haven't left anything, I bring Milo's things into my bedroom and stow them in my bags. I sit on the bed leaning back against my laundry bag, waiting for Matt to finish with his shower.

The next thing I know, Matt is rubbing my shoulder urgently, saying, "Babe, wake up."

"What? What is it?" I ask, disoriented. I must've dozed off.

"I was just thinking," he says, standing next to the bed. "Darius must have someone who can search for us; how else was he even able to find Mickey, right?"

"Yeah..." I respond. I'm still drowsy and don't exactly know what he's talking about.

"The only way he'd find Mickey is if he knows who Cali is. And if he knows who Cali is, then he knows who she was to Alexa Pearce. And since we used our real passports to come here, th—"

"Then he might already know where we are and how long we've been here," I finish for him as my eyes shoot fully open. I'm wide awake as I scramble off the bed to get Cali. I burst into her room; she's standing next to her bed, folding her clothes.

"We need to leave. Now."

• 5 8 •

Cali

When Roslyn whirls around with Milo hot on her trail, Cali begins to shove her clothes into her bag. She foregoes the neat, Tetris-like stacking opting for speed over efficiency. Whatever doesn't fit, she throws into the duffle bag, zipping each forcefully enough that the zippers almost break off.

She tosses the closed bags out of the room, narrowly missing Roslyn as she does. Before following her things into the living room, Cali glances around the room to make sure she's left nothing important behind. She briefly thinks about her toiletries in the bathroom but decides she'll write a note to the owner apologizing for leaving them.

Cali picks up her bag and drags the duffle over to the front door where Matt and Roslyn have already dropped their own. When she turns around, she sees them ping-ponging around the apartment. She calls Milo over, squatting down as she does. He pads over to her then stands still obediently so she can put on his harness.

Both of them wait there patiently for the other two. Cali takes out her phone to look for the closest dog-friendly hotel in case they need it. She doesn't know if they will be leaving just the apartment or Rome altogether, but her vote is obviously for them to go home to Portland right away. Her friends finally join her at the door, Matt holding two garbage bags. It seems like he emptied all of the trash and the fridge so nothing would spoil for the owner to come back to.

"Ready?" Roslyn asks. Cali and Matt nod. He bends to lift his bag and the duffle. They open the door and exit with Roslyn bringing up the rear. She closes the door, firmly locking it. Thankfully the elevator takes seconds to arrive. The group crowds in; it's a tight fit now that they are all carrying their baggage.

In the lobby, Roslyn returns the apartment keys to the correct lockbox on the wall next to the door. When she turns back to face the other two, Cali takes her chance.

"I looked up the closest hotel if we need it, but I think we should go home."

"If we go back to Portland right now, where do we go?" Roslyn asks. "We can't go to any place that would put anyone else on Darius's radar. So that rules out Matt's place, Mickey's studio or apartment, our own apartment, or even Marty's deli."

"The park," Cali says quickly. "I mean, we're gonna go there anyway, and isn't that why we went there after the library blew up *because* it wouldn't expose anyone else to Darius?"

"She's right," Matt says. "We've got more than enough supplies in the duffle bag to get us through a night outside. We can camp out, and we'll be close enough to get Mickey."

"I know," Roslyn says, rubbing her forehead "But I—"

"You what?" Cali snaps immediately angry. "You need another reason not to listen to me? To us? This makes the most sense, Roz. We have to go home."

"I know that!" Roslyn shoots back before she takes a deep breath to steady herself. "What I was going to say is that it's night here, but it's broad daylight in Portland right now. We can't just pop up in the middle of the park in front of who knows how many people. I don't have enough control of my power to transport us to a specific spot covered by woods.

"We'd have a lot of explaining to do about how three people and a dog just appeared out of thin air. Especially when one of them," she points to her own chest, "is supposed to be dead."

"So then we stay here until it's dark enough at home to provide us camouflage to transport," Cali says. It's not a question or suggestion; it's the plan they will be doing.

"Which is what I was going to say," Roslyn agrees. "It's time to go home."

They know that they can't sit in the lobby for the next nine or ten hours, so they decide as a group to go to the hotel Cali looked up. The three of them walk over to the hotel on Via Delle Quattro Fontane as quickly as they can. Milo stays glued to Roslyn's side, forming a physical barrier between the bag on her arm housing *The Book* and every person they pass.

As they arrive at the hotel, Matt and Cali hang back with the bags while Roslyn goes to check in with Milo, watchful of everyone nearby the two of them as she does. She pays with cash, counting out the Euros on the counter.

The clerk hands her a key card and directs her toward the elevator. Roslyn cocks her head to the side, quickly signaling for Matt and Cali to follow. She meets them at the bank of three chrome elevators.

"Sixth floor," she says, handing the key to Cali.

They load into the steel cube and press the corresponding button. As the doors close, Milo plops himself down right in front of them. If the elevator stops between the lobby and six with someone wanting to get on, they'll have to go through him first.

The group has no problem getting to their double room safely. They drop their bags near the door except for Roslyn. She gently puts her bag down on the table closest to the first bed.

"Let's repack our stuff," Matt says.

"Why?" Cali asks.

"I think we should divide up the stuff in the duffle bag amongst our own bags, maybe keep one or two changes of clothes, but put the rest in the duffle."

"Because?"

"So that if we are only able to take the bag on our back when we get Mickey, we don't leave all of our supplies behind."

Cali sighs, "Well if nothing else, it's something to do while we wait."

Matt lifts all of the bags onto one of the beds. They each begin un-packing their things, making stacks as they go. Once the clothes are divided, and they've chosen what to keep with them, they put what's left on the other bed.

After repacking what they've kept aside, Matt dumps out the entire-ty of the duffle on the now empty bed. Cali and Roslyn take their blankets back and put them with each of their clothes. They divide the items in the duffle bag as evenly as possible, making sure each of them has a little bit of everything.

They especially take care to make sure they each have an empty water bottle with a built-in filter, some glow sticks, bandaids, and chapstick. They split the remainder of the package of baby wipes into thirds and put them in the resealable plastic bags. The rest of what's left, they randomly spread out, concerned more with not making any single bag too heavy.

Cali and Roslyn empty out their shoulder bags onto the bed also. They place *The Book* from Roslyn's bag next to its replica that was in Cali's. Roslyn shivers before letting out a sharp exhale.

"It's still so unbelievable," she says to her friend. "First of all that we actually got *The Book*, and secondly, that the copy is so goddamn exact it tricks my senses into thinking it's the real one."

"Good," Cali says firmly. "That means that Darius won't be able to tell the difference either."

They put only the clay replica back into Roslyn's bag. Cali keeps the printed pages about the Grand Canyon and the Native American myths about the demon in her bag. She puts her potion bottles into the front pocket of her sweater. She's about to put the most important item into her shoulder bag when she stops.

"Do you think I should put *The Book* at the bottom of my backpack instead?" Cali asks. "I don't know if it could get damaged just in my bag. I could wrap it in my blanket."

Roslyn nods her head quickly at the suggestion. "Protect it as much as possible. There aren't any more copies, that's it." As Cali unloads her backpack again to make room for *The Book*, Roslyn hands the rest of the potions to Matt.

"Keep those near," she says as their hands touch.

He sticks one of each in his hoodie and puts the rest into the pockets of his pants. He zips closed his own duffle bag that's been packed with precision and uses the strap to wear it across his back. He tightens the nylon until the bag is tight against his skin. Matt bounces a few times on his feet to check the weight distribution. Satisfied, he takes it off, turns to face the opposite bed, and begins to pack the rest of the clothes into the larger duffle.

Cali follows his example. She puts her shoulder bag across her torso, strap on her right shoulder, bag on her left hip. She puts her backpack on over it, securing the shoulder bag in place. She also tightens her straps, so the backpack stays in place and doesn't bounce around as she moves.

Roslyn makes sure that Milo's things are safely nestled in her canvas laundry bag. There's no way for her to cinch it tighter, so she can only make sure the drawstring is securely tied.

Now that there is nothing left to do but wait, the group cuddles up on one of the queen-sized beds. Cali sets the alarm on her phone for 11 P.M. Portland time. Before they know it, the length and stress of the day catches up to them, and all four of them are fast asleep.

After what seems like just half an hour, Cali hears soft chimes and a buzzing sound next to the bed. She reaches over to lift her phone and check the time. It's seven in the morning in Rome. It's time for them to go.

Cali rouses her friends just this side of rough. She's anxious to get home, to get back to Mickey. Matt and Roslyn wake up slowly, but once they see the morning's sunlight coming through the window, they snap awake fully alert.

Milo is dancing around them, indicating he has to relieve himself, but Roslyn shakes her head at him. "Sorry, bud, we don't have time. You have to wait until we get to the park."

The three load up their bags, checking pockets for potions as they do. Once they've secured their packs, they face each other in a circle. Roslyn calls Milo over, and he sits down in between her feet. Matt and Cali put a hand out to hold each of Roslyn's shoulders. She reaches down to hang onto Milo's collar then looks at each of her friends in the eyes.

"Ready?" she asks. They nod back at her. Roslyn closes her eyes and takes three deep breaths. She's concentrating on the power she wants to use, visualizing their destination with as much detail as she can. After a momentary pause, she finally says, "Mount Tabor Park, Portland, Oregon."

• 5 9 •

DARIUS

Shortly after eleven o'clock, the demon's eyes snap open and flash white even in his comatose state. He's been resting less than twenty hours after his forced transition of the trainer and has only marginally recovered from the effort. He can barely see, but the call of the witch's power pulls his body upright.

She's near, he thinks.

Through his haze, he hears a phone ringing. He sways from exhaustion, barely able to keep himself vertical, and is about to fall over onto his back when he feels the massive paw of Viribus supporting him.

"Boss," he says. The baritone voice sounds miles away to Darius. The giant's hand gently shakes him until the unfocused black eyes come to attention. He's holding out a purple rectangle for the demon to take. "It's her."

Darius clumsily reaches for the phone in its bulky charging case. He growls an order to bring him food and the last Victus he made, but to leave the girl where she is. The lieutenant doesn't quite understand the order but leaves the room to obey it regardless.

He looks at the screen of the phone displaying the call is already connected. The demon vigorously shakes his head, attempting to steady his jumbled mind. He clears his throat before lifting the phone to his ear, unwilling to sound as weak as he currently feels.

"You've returned, I see," he says, not wasting time on pleasantries.

"I have," comes her curt response. "Let her go, Darius."

"Now, why would I go and do that when having her in the first place has achieved precisely what I wanted?"

"Because I have something you want."

"Other than your bleeding heart in my hand as it pumps its last beat, I doubt you have anything I want."

"*The Book.*"

The demon is quiet as he tries to figure out if she's trying to trick him or not. He knows he saw the witch dive into flames and rubble, searching for it. "Nice try, you little bitch. A clever ruse a lesser demon would fall for. But I saw it destroyed by my own power."

"You saw a copy destroyed. I have the real one."

Darius stays quiet, thinking through what it would mean to have The Book in his possession finally. She would be entirely exposed, with no guidance or protection. He would finally have the upper hand.

"So, shall we make a trade?" she asks.

"Well, then," he says calmly. "You know where I am. Feel free to stop by."

"Yeah, I don't think so. You'll be coming to me."

"Will I?"

"Yes, you will. And if you harm another hair on Mickey's head from now until she's back safely with me, the only way you'll see *The Book* is when I'm shoving your face in it as I decapitate you."

"Don't threaten me, child," Darius growls.

"And don't test me," she fires back. "You know where I am. Come and get me."

The witch disconnects the call abruptly. Before his simmering anger at being told what to do can boil over, Viribus returns with a large cut of steak and the newest Victus soldier. Darius grabs the meat and devours it savagely. All the while, he never takes his eyes off of Blue.

When he swallows the last bite, he doesn't even bother to wipe the blood from his face before he speaks. "Blue, you've done well refilling my ranks, and have been of great help to me. But it's come time for you to help me even further."

"Anything you need, boss," the petite parole officer says.

Darius reaches a hand out for assistance. Viribus easily lifts him to a standing position. He pats Blue on the shoulder three times.

"*Quid tibi meus erit. Animae vestrae, amissis viribus meis addere.*" What's yours becomes mine. Your life, your being, your strength adds to mine lost.

The giant Victus tilts his head when he hears his name said, but it's clear the demon is talking directly to Blue. All eyes in the room widen as Darius's arm moves from Blue's shoulder to the center of his chest. Blue gasps as the demon's hand thrusts through his skin and closes around his heart.

Blue trembles as his body ages rapidly. To Viribus, it looks as though a time-lapse video taken over decades has been sped up to play in seconds. Blue's hair turns stark white, his skin wrinkles and becomes sallow. He grabs the demon's arm to yank it from his body but can't grip it firmly enough with the bony, arthritic nubs that have replaced once strong hands.

His knees sag and his back bows, his energy and muscles drained like an old tap. His eyes cloud over both bloodshot and jaundiced. The parole officer collapses to the floor, Darius's hand never leaving his chest until he's absorbed every ounce of Blue's life force.

"*Damno lucrum est.*" Your loss is my gain.

Blue closes his eyes as his body becomes still. Darius removes his hand. He stands up and turns away from the dead, frail body on the floor to face his Victus. Viribus looks terrified and nauseated. He stands motionless unsure of what to do but unable to look away from what's left of the man lying on the floor.

When he finally looks at his boss, the demon looks younger and stronger than he's seen him since his battle with the witch a month ago. His dark eyes shine with energy. His black hair is smooth and glossy. Even the visible scarring on his left hand seems to have faded some.

"It's a pity I'm down a Victus now, but it had to be done," the demon says casually. "You go get the men ready to go. I want everyone loaded in the cars in twenty minutes. I'm going to wash up and then have another little chat with our friend."

Viribus gulps and nods, acquiescing to the order. Now that the demon has revealed another of his abilities to him, the immense man has no plans of winding up on the wrong end of it. He turns to leave but is stopped by Darius, calling out to him one more time.

"Dispose of this, will you?" he asks, gesturing to the crumpled, curled body on the floor.

Darius doesn't wait for Viribus's response. He heads to the bathroom and runs the cold water. He splashes it on his face to wash away the remnants of his steak. After he dries his face, he marvels at himself in the mirror. He hasn't used that spell in centuries. Right now, he feels fresh, spirited, powerful.

He also knows he's started a ticking clock. It's an artificial fix, and once his body uses up the added energy boost from Blue, he'll be even weaker than before. It should provide him just enough time to kill the witch, take her powers, and then rest after the portal to his home is forever unobstructed.

From the bathroom, he goes into the bedroom to untie the brunette. She's sitting up but has her head resting back against the radiator with her eyes closed. Her breathing is slow and uneven, but she's sleeping.

Darius kneels down in front of her and gently cups her cheek with his left hand. Mickey wakes slightly, pushing into the comforting touch.

"Cali?" she says groggily. When she opens her eyes to see black ones looking back instead of the green she expects, Mickey scrambles out of his touch as far as possible. The radiator blocks her movement, and she bangs her shoulder blade hard against the metal.

"You've served your purpose," Darius says. "It's time to go, but first, you will tell me about a place called Mount Tabor Park." Mickey steels her jaw and refuses to answer. Darius sighs impatiently. "Come now. You've seen what happens when you don't talk."

"Why Mount Tabor?"

"Because it's where the witch and your lover currently are." Mickey's expression doesn't change. She thinks he's trying to trick her into revealing something. "You don't believe me? That's alright. See for yourself."

He holds up her phone to show her the call log. She sees the call from Cali's phone, displaying a length of fifteen minutes. Her eyes brighten, hoping it's real. But she's learned this is an evil being in front of her and will never trust his word.

"Call her back and prove it first," she says defiantly.

Darius narrows his eyes at being told what to do by some lowly mortal. He obliges simply to get the woman moving. It's an easy trade to make, her for *The Book*, but only if he can actually get her there.

"*Humans,*" he grumbles as he taps the screen to place the call. He puts the phone on speaker.

"What?" the witch's voice gruffly answers on the third ring.

"It seems as though your friend believes I'm trying to trick her and is reluctant to leave."

"Mick?" she asks quickly. "You there?"

"Lex? Is that really you?"

"It's me. We're all here, Mick. All of us. Moose and Milo and Squirrel."

"She's there?" Mickey's voice breaks as she asks.

"I'm here," another voice says. "I'm here, baby."

"Oh, my god. Cali, I'm so sorry. I tried. I tried to—" Mickey breaks down into tears, hearing her girlfriend's voice.

"It's okay, we're here now. You're gonna be okay."

"Satisfied?" Darius asks. He hangs up the call as he uses his telekinesis to untie the ropes keeping Mickey in place. "Now, get the fuck up."

• 6 0 •

"ROSLYN"

The three of us stand in a circle for a minute, breathing the fresh, familiar Oregon air for the first time in a month. I study my friends and see from their body language that returning home has instantly made them relaxed and ready.

We drag our bags into a thick grouping of trees on the east side of Reservoir Five across from two paved roads right at the start of an incline in Mount Tabor Park. I keep my shoulder bag with the clay replica on but leave my canvas laundry bag on the ground with the two duffles. It creates a nice pile with Cali's backpack, which holds *The Book,* on the very bottom.

I unlatch Milo and slide Cali's phone into the back pocket of my jeans before I give him his side command. He tucks himself against my left knee and won't leave until I release him.

It's a gorgeous night. The sky is clear and littered with stars, and the moon is full. Now that my eyes have adjusted completely, I have no trouble seeing anything. Even Milo, with his black fur, is clearly visible.

"Guys," I say to Matt and Cali. I wait for them to look up at me before I motion for them to follow me back toward the water. "We're not in the basement this time. We don't have those giant glass cubes to provide cover from Darius and whoever he brings with him. We need to practice, to be prepared to fight this time, physically.

"But, you've also got potions now, so make sure you use them. As soon as Darius comes, the first hint I get of him, drink the protection potion. When you use the other two, first throw the stun potion—the purple one—that'll freeze whoever is close to it when it goes off. There are only so many potions, so be strategic. If a few Victus freeze, first move them close together with your Extensios power and then throw the fire potion."

They are quietly nodding, absorbing what I'm saying. I look around to see if there is anything we can practice our powers on when Cali's phone begins to ring in my pocket. I take it out and see it's Mickey's number calling. I know it's not really her, so I don't waste time with pleasantries.

"What?" I say brusquely.

"It seems as though your friend believes I'm trying to trick her and is reluctant to leave," the demon's irritatingly silky voice sounds over the phone's speaker.

My heart rate picks up. "Mick?" I ask anxiously. "You there?"

"Lex? Is that really you?" She sounds weak, tired, hurt. I grit my teeth in anger at Darius for stooping to this level, but at myself too for allowing him to get close enough to her in the first place. I reassure her as best I can that we're all here.

Cali takes over to talk to Mickey until Darius abruptly ends the call. I look at my friend's face as it morphs first to shock and desperation, then to anger and resolve. She's pissed again. I can't help the small flicker of relief that it's only partially directed at me this time.

"That motherfucker is going down," she snarls.

"You're goddamn right," Matt agrees, putting his arm around her.

"We need to practice," I say again. "It won't just be deflecting whatever they send at us this time. We're going to have to go on the attack. Look around for any fallen trees, big rocks, or logs. Anything large that you can perfect moving from one spot to another. We are going to have to stand our ground and work together."

"How many Victus is he bringing with him?" Matt asks.

"I don't know," I answer. "He underestimated us and only brought two last time. I don't think he'll make that mistake again."

"Can't you spy? Like you did in the library?" Cali asks. "I want to know what we're up against, and I want to make sure Mickey isn't in trouble while they're on the way."

Darius already knows where we are. There is no harm in me using my powers to check on him to get a better read on what we're in for.

"I'll try," I respond. "Maybe if I focus on Mickey, he won't figure out I'm looking and block me."

I sit down on the ground with Milo still by my side. I hold onto his collar to anchor myself the same way as when I snooped on Darius before. I look up at Cali and tell her, "Sixty seconds, just like the last time."

She taps away at the screen of her phone. When she nods at me, I nod back and close my eyes. I picture in my mind who and what I want to see. I crystalize the image of Mickey and allow myself to project a link to her. The picture of her in my head slowly replaces itself with a live look at my friend.

She's on the stairs of my building. Darius has her by the arm and is practically dragging her with him. The angry burns on her arms and neck are blistered, her wrists are raw and bloody from where she was tied. But her face is set; she's brave and determined.

I feel a fire start to burn in my chest at her appearance. My anger threatens to sever the connection, so I control it for later when I come face to face with the monster that did this to her. The image in my brain pans as I follow Mickey.

I see a group of people waiting in the lobby, all looking up to watch Darius take the last few steps down with his grip still firmly on Mickey's arm.

"The cars are ready, boss." The sound comes from the largest man I have ever seen.

"Good," I hear the demon answer. "Ladies first."

An evil chuckle ripples through the group as Darius parades Mickey through them. She keeps her head up and her gaze straight ahead. I watch the men turn to follow their leader outside to two oversized SUVs.

I can hear Cali saying my name to get my attention, so I quickly count the men with Darius before I'm pulled back to reality. My eyes open when I've only reached nine. I inhale heavily as I realize that we're outnumbered by at least three to one.

"What'd you see?" Matt asks anxiously. "How many?"

"I couldn't get a full count, but he has at least nine men, and one of them is, like, the Mount Everest of people," I say. I can see them both immediately deflate, most likely doing the same math I just did.

"Guys, we've got this," I tell them with more confidence than I feel. Their doubt is plain as day on their faces as they look at me.

"We are fast, we're strong, and now we're on home turf. We keep the water to their backs and the trees to ours. The three of us know how to move seamlessly around each other. We've done it every day for a month. We'll use that to our advantage."

I pause, letting what I've said sink in. I'm thinking about what I can say next to bolster their faith in themselves some more when Cali speaks.

"You're right," she says. "You're the most powerful force of good on the planet, and Moose and I ain't too shabby ourselves. That piece of shit has the love of my life, and I'll be damned if I waste an ounce of my energy being scared of him rather than focusing on getting her back."

"Can we use the Extensios powers to break the potion bottles?" Matt asks suddenly.

"I don't know," I honestly reply. "Why?"

"Because if we can, then we could place the firepower potions like mines, and then when Darius or his Victus get close, we break them."

"How are we going to test it, though?" I ask. "I don't want to waste one of the fire potions on the chance that the bottle just breaks and doesn't actually explode."

"We have to use one," Matt says. "We'll use one of mine. If it works, then we can set the rest. If not, then we think of something else."

I really don't like the idea of leaving either one of them less protected. Especially when there are at least ten men with powers of their own on the way here, Matt and Cali need every advantage they can get.

"Okay," I say. "But I don't think we should use all of them. If we test it with one and it works, then I think we should only leave two hidden. That way, when they go off and the Victus start to move, you guys can use the stun potion and save the last fire potions for when they're all clumped in a group."

Matt jogs five paces away, just to the other side of the dirt path that circles the reservoir, and carefully puts the vial down. Once Matt comes back to us, I stand back and let them decide who will try to blow it up.

Cali wins the rock, paper, scissors match without any gloating. *Unusual for her. She must be really focused,* I think, as she calmly steps up to the plate. I watch her set her feet firmly and concentrate on the bottle. I want to coach her to think about the liquid inside, blowing the glass apart, but before I can say anything, she jerks her arm forward.

Nothing happens.

"Okay," she says, rolling her neck out and shaking her hands loose. "Take two."

She stares intently at where Matt put the vial. If it doesn't work this time, I'm going to suggest we scrap the idea.

When Cali whips her arm out again, I hear the distinct *clink* of the glass breaking right before a roaring boom sounds. I'm momentarily blinded by a giant cloud of fire that briefly appears before it's replaced by smoke spiraling up into the air.

I'm speechless, but Matt sums it up for all of us, "Fuck yeah!"

"Alright, that was insane. Moose, go quick, and set the other two."

"Where?" he asks.

I think for a moment as I scan our surroundings. Darius is coming from my old apartment, which means his most likely entrance will be from Salmon Street directly northwest of where we're currently standing. He'll likely come up Reservoir Loop then use the dirt path to come around to me. If we stand in the small clearing across the paved access road, Darius should come to a natural stopping point in between two large pine trees.

"Between these trees," I say. I quickly explain why there and Matt trots over to place down the two fire potions, each about five feet from the tree closest to it.

I tell Matt and Cali to find something they can use to practice their telekinesis on while I check on my own. I'm going to have to be able to summon my active powers instantly. I focus on a large branch of the nearest tree. I lift my right hand to chest level, then quickly bend my elbow and jerk my shoulder back, mimicking a pulling motion. The treetop sways and the branch shakes but it doesn't rip free.

I narrow my eyes in frustration. Reaching my hand out again, I imagine that my fingers can feel the rough bark. I close my hand into a fist and yank my arm backward. This time the limb is forced cleanly off by my telekinesis power.

Using any of my abilities is still so new to me that I can't help the immense satisfaction I feel at being able to control them. My whole body sings as if my powers are circulating through my veins right along with my blood. I steer the branch through the air until it hovers above my head.

I keep my arm raised but close my eyes, trusting my powers to keep it aloft and me safe underneath. When I open my eyes, I cast an image in my mind of the branch turning stark white as if covered in snow. I smile as my projection power causes the green and brown above me to instantly morph.

Next, I check on my firepower. I remember what I felt in the library when I last faced Darius. Hatred turned into a burning in my chest that then traveled to my hand, where it appeared in tangible form. It doesn't take much to build up enough usable anger at the demon.

"Sorry, branch," I say before I launch the ball into the air. It catches in seconds.

I'm considering for a moment detaching another branch to work on pressuring myself into doing my transport power when something freezes me in place.

The hairs on the back of my neck stand up straight. My magically heightened senses are kicking in. I can tell Darius is very close. Milo feels it too. He presses into me as his chest begins to rumble.

"Hey!" I hiss at Matt and Cali. They stop short, the dead log they were practicing with falling to its side. Milo growls again, even louder than before. "Drink your protection potion. It's time."

• 6 1 •

"Get behind me," I say. "Stay focused and be ready to trigger the potions on my signal."

Milo stays by my side. The rumbling in his chest gets more intense as he continues to growl. He's facing the direction I correctly assumed Darius would come from. I place my left hand on the back of his neck just as I see movement in the distance.

"I see him," I tell my dog quietly.

The demon is sauntering toward us as if he doesn't have a care in the world. When he's finally able to see me clearly, he looks back at his group of Victus, then sneers at me and my two Extensios.

Five men flank the demon on each side, a mixture of heights, weights, and ethnicities, but every one of them is staring at us with pure hatred. I don't know where Darius found these men, but none of them are giving off any hint of being forced into this. It seems like they all came willingly.

When they are about two hundred feet away, I finally find the face I've been searching for. Mickey is at the back of the group. She's walking next to the giant that called the demon boss at the apartment building. Every few feet, he shoves Mickey forward closer to the group of men.

Behind me, Cali gasps when she gets a glimpse of Mickey's wounds. Even from this distance, it's clear that she's hurt badly. For a second, I feel my friend's eyes boring a hole into the back of my head before they're focused back on the demon.

Darius slows his stroll and comes to a stop directly between the two hidden vials. His sneer never changes as he puts his hands on his hips. The twelve men plus Mickey face us in total silence. He makes a show of looking to his right at Cali, swinging his gaze to the left to take in Matt, before bringing his eyes back to me. His sneer broadens further into a full, cocky smile.

"Well, well," he says in a sing-song. "I may not have paid much attention to evolving theorems over the centuries, but even I can do this math. You're outnumbered, little girl."

He adds a malicious chuckle, which is quickly copied by his gang of cronies. They spread out on either side of Darius, getting closer to the potions with each step. The behemoth pushes Mickey again until she's standing next to the demon. He keeps a paw on her shoulder to hold her in place.

"I believe we had a deal," Darius says evenly. "You'll see, I've kept up my end."

Until now, none of us have said a word. I need Matt and Cali to keep their focus on their powers and the potions. I silently reach into my shoulder bag and withdraw the replica of *The Book*. Darius can't help the slight widening of his eyes as he gets a glimpse of it. I make a real show of holding it tight to my chest as if I can't bear to part with it.

"Let Mickey go, and you can have it," I call out. I use telekinesis to let the dried clay hang in the air in front of me. I allow my hands to drop to my sides slowly but magically hold tight to keep the duplicate floating. Darius nods to his Victus, who removes his large hand from Mickey's shoulder.

The moment she's released, Mickey takes off at a run directly for us. I send the clay copy slowly through the air as I watch her get closer. My friend is feet away from safety when Darius's arm shoots out to jab the air. Mickey's head snaps back as if punched in the face, and she drops to the ground unconscious.

I'm stunned for a moment, but Cali's scream of "You son of a bitch!" brings me back to action. I force the replica through the air fast. Darius can't react in time, and it slams into his chest as hard as I can make it. He doubles over and drops to one knee; it looks like he got the wind knocked out of him. Before his Victus have a chance to retaliate, I yell, "Now!"

Matt and Cali hurl their arms straight out. The vials respond immediately to the command. The potions break the glass, exploding outward. The trap works and five of the Victus are engulfed quickly in flames. With one shot, his ranks have been cut almost in half.

The rest of the men instinctively cower to escape the blast. I don't waste any time watching the bodies burn. Instead, I focus my attention on Mickey lying on the ground. I rush over to lift her off the ground and bring her to safety. Milo sticks to my side the whole time. I can't expend the extra energy to lift Mickey physically, so I use my power to carry her through the air to the other side of the paved road. I gently rest her underneath a tall tree.

I turn back to help my friends. Darius is just getting back to his feet with a ball of fire in his hand. He pulls back to throw it. Before he can launch it, I knock it out of his hand with my power and send it into another Victus. *That's six,* I count in my head.

I'm running in the direction of the fight when I'm suddenly swept off of my feet and flung through the air. I'm thrown backward into the limbs of the same tree I just put Mickey underneath. The sharp edges and rough bark easily cut through my clothes, leaving bloody scrapes across my entire body.

The branches give way with my weight, and I fall to the ground. I put my left arm out to catch myself and land awkwardly on it. I feel searing pain coupled with a loud popping sound and immediately know my shoulder is dislocated. My head hits the ground hard as my arm crumples underneath me.

The left lens of my glasses has a large crack running through it from my impact with the ground. I don't know who threw me, but I can't lay here waiting to find out. My skull throbs where it hit the grass; I can already feel a welt forming on the side of my forehead. I shake my head to clear the clouds that threaten to roll in as I cradle my left arm with my right and scurry back to my feet.

I frantically search for Milo but don't have to look long before I feel him at my side again. He's completely unharmed—he must've been too low for the telekinetic swipe that took me out. I force my hand into the pocket of my jeans to try and hold my arm in place so my right hand is free to use my powers. Even the slightest movement causes agonizing pain to shoot out from my shoulder. I grit my teeth against the pain and force myself to move.

I take off again toward my friends. I see Cali throw the purple stun potion at a Victus. It hits its mark, freezing the man in place. Right as she's about to move him toward another frozen Victus, she's struck squarely in the chest with a fireball. Her body glows green as the protection potion stops the flames from reaching her. But the force is enough to knock her off of her feet. She lands hard on her back and glows green again as the potion kicks in once more.

"Shit, that's three," I hear her say as I come to her side. She reaches into her pocket to pull out the next green vile. Her hand comes out wet, covered in liquid. She looks up at me with fear in her eyes. "I must've landed on it."

"I've got you covered," I tell her. I turn in time to redirect the next fire attack at one of the frozen Victus. There are now only three left, plus the giant and Darius.

"Moose!" I call out. He doesn't take his attention away from the one on two battle he's having but calls out to acknowledge me. "Squirrel needs a green bottle."

He tells me it's in his sweatshirt pocket. He's too far away for me to leave her uncovered, so I have no choice but to use my power to retrieve it. I can't close my eyes to the fight around me and get snuck up on, so I have to force my brain to concentrate on all that's going on around me while I imagine reaching into his shirt and feeling my hand close around the vial. When I chance a brief look down at my hand, the bottle's been projected to me, safely tucked inside my palm.

From her spot on the ground, Cali has thrown her other two freeze potions as hard as she can. Both miss their target but get close enough to make the Victus dive out of the way.

I hand the green vial to Cali then take off toward Darius and his giant bodyguard. Darius launches an orb of flames at me, but I redirect it to the huge man beside him He's able to easily deflect it back to me at the same time Darius hurls another.

The only way I can explain what happens next is that I've magically caught the two globes. I put my right hand up in front of me, and both balls instantly stop moving. I merge them into one massive sphere and use my one good arm to force it back to them.

It's too large for me to keep control of, so when Darius and the Victus easily duck beneath it, the fireball doesn't stop moving until it hits a tall pine tree at the edge of the reservoir. The entire thing bursts apart into fragments that rain down across the water.

While the two men are distracted by the explosion, I take the chance to attack. I swoop my arm in an underhand arc, lifting both of them thirty feet into the air. I let them hang there helplessly before releasing them, letting gravity slam them to the ground.

As Darius falls, he manages to throw another fiery orb at me. I crouch low to let the ball pass by. It dislodges my left hand from my pocket, and I cry out as pain shoots down my arm. The sphere keeps going until it reaches the slightly elevated Loop Drive behind me. It blows a crater into the pavement sending chunks of asphalt and dirt in all directions.

I hear the thud and a groan as Darius and his Victus hit the ground. Both the demon and the giant get up quickly. I pull my arm back to launch a fireball of my own, in full attack mode now. The twist of my torso dislodges my left hand again from my pocket. The stabbing pain from the shift of my dislocated shoulder causes my throw to go slightly off course.

Instead of hitting Darius head-on, I hit his left arm. It's the same arm that was severely burned last month in the library basement. He's knocked to the ground and dragged along the grass by the impact.

Fuck! I think. *Six inches to the right again, and this whole thing could've been over.* He screams as he slides, causing the two Victus that Matt and Cali have been facing to look behind them.

My boyfriend takes the chance to launch his purple-colored stun potion, but the giant Victus has regained his senses. Before the vials hit their mark, the soldier sends them back in the direction they came. I see the potions strike Matt and Cali. Both are thrown backward off their feet as their protection potions work again.

When they land, their legs buckle underneath them, and their momentum makes them tumble end over end. Cali glows green twice more before her body stills, but Matt hasn't since the first strike of the bottle. My friend quickly gets back to her feet to return to the battle, but my boyfriend stays motionless on the ground.

My entire attention focuses on Matt. He doesn't roll over in pain, doesn't cough to try and catch his breath. I wait for him to move. He *has* to move. With every second that goes by without a response from him, my already thundering heart slams harder in my chest.

"Roz, watch out!" I hear Cali call out to me. I turn away from Matt just in time to see the enormous Victus throwing a thick branch at me like a javelin. I let my fear about Matt morph into anger at the monster who hurt him.

I hold up my right hand to stop the tree limb from reaching me. With a guttural yell of pure anger and hatred, I rotate it around in the air and send it back toward the Victus that was frozen by the stun potion.

The same moment the wood pierces the spot between the man's collarbone and neck, I spin around and launch two quick fireballs at the two Victus soldiers that were just facing off with Matt and Cali. They are engulfed in flames before either can move out of the way.

The frozen Victus is choking on blood as it pours into his lungs. I throw another ball of flames at him to end his suffering.

I'm ready to face off with the only opponent currently standing, the titan warrior when I'm stopped cold in my tracks by a loud animalistic roar.

• 6 2 •

DARIUS

With an anguished scream, he pulls his battered body into a sitting position. Darius takes inventory of what damage the fireball did. His scarred arm is no longer there. It's severed from his body. Thick black blood pours from the gaping wound.

"Enough!" he shouts, pulling himself to his feet. Viribus stops immediately to listen to the demon. The witch and her friend are stunned to inaction.

"Enough!" he repeats. The demon staggers forward on unsteady feet. Darius looks around, wondering how she was able to best him once more and reduce his forces to just the goliath. He can feel himself getting weaker as he loses more blood. The strength he stole from Blue is quickly waning with the severity of his injuries. "I demand you surrender to me, you pathetic, inadequate, waste of life!"

"Are you fucking kidding me?" the shorter Extensios asks with uncontrolled anger. "You'll have to kill us before we give in to you, you limp-dicked Hades reject."

The witch smirks at her friend's gall, but Darius can tell she's still engaged, ready to continue the fight. He sees her twitch right before she makes her move. When she launches the fireball, he's ready. He sends it right back in the direction of the other girl.

The Extensios directs the ball off to the side with quickness, where it engulfs another small tree along the shoreline. His eyes follow the light, so he doesn't see the witch pull back to shoot again until the burning sphere is already on its way.

He turns back in time to deflect it directly back at her. She stops it in midair, the ball suspended between them.

"Get behind me, Cal," she says to the other girl. The human obeys, running over to the witch. Darius can't hear what she says next, but the girl quickly turns away and runs into the trees behind the witch. The mutt that's always at the bitch's side follows the girl into the forest.

"Brave, are you?" he taunts. "You think you can face my strongest Victus and me on your own?"

Darius tries to push the ball of fire closer to her, but the witch holds her ground. He can see her left arm hanging limp at her side, matching injuries that force them to hold their powers steady or be in danger of being swallowed by flames.

Viribus is standing to the side, waiting. The demon shouts at the incompetent man, "You dumb fucking oaf, do something!"

"What do I do?" the deep baritone voice responds.

"You go after the others, you goddamn fool.'

"I wouldn't do that if I were you," the witch warns.

"You do as I say, Viribus. Get moving and kill them, you imbecile!"

The witch speaks again, "Don't listen to him, Viribus. If you go after my friends, they will kill you. It'll be three against one, and we have something you don't."

"Oh, please do tell," Darius mocks. "What could you possibly have that would make either of us listen to you?"

The witch smiles at him and begins to laugh. His eyes practically jump out of his head at the blatant disrespect. To his further dismay, the fireball moves through the air closer to him.

"Look what's at your feet, Darius," she says. "Call me crazy, but I don't think a book that's over a thousand years old would break apart like that. Do you?"

He chances a quick look at the ground. The item she threw at him is lying in pieces at his feet. He looks back up to make sure the fireball hasn't moved; it's holding steady. Another glance down, and he sees that the pieces are mostly bright gray, almost white.

"Stone?" he asks in disbelief. The witch doesn't answer.

As Darius stares at her with open ferocity, she begins to glow. First, an amber color, then it brightens to white as if a spotlight is focused on her. The demon doesn't know what she is doing, but he refuses to back away.

He glances up quickly, not quite registering what he sees exactly, then returns his gaze to her. Darius watches the witch move her right hand away. He thinks this is his chance and tries to send the flaming orb straight to her heart. It doesn't budge. When he looks up to try again with his full attention, he sees where the light is coming from.

The fireball has grown to ten times its original size and continues to spread out even further as he stares. The demon inherently knows that if the moment comes where it reaches his skin, he's done for. All he can do right now is stop trying to push it back to the witch and instead throw it off to the side somewhere.

A thick clump of trees directly back and to his left looks like a promising place to dispose of this fiery mess. He's gathering his strength to move the last obstacle to taking her down when the witch surprises him again.

With her smile still in place, she closes her eyes as the fire starts to close in on itself. Although shrinking in size, the intensity of its light doesn't dim. The demon drops his hold on the ball, opting instead to get ready to defend himself, unsure of what she's about to do next.

The witch's smile disappears from her face a millisecond before everything goes dark.

• 6 3 •

"ROSLYN"

"Stone?" Darius asks.

I don't respond to him.

I'm focusing on calling as much of my magic up to the surface as I can, releasing the tight hold I've kept on it. I need him distracted for my plan to work. I smile at Darius, confusing him.

I imagine the ball above us growing larger and brighter. I picture it as a tiny sun hovering feet above the ground. I don't need to look up to know it's working. Darius's face becomes clearer to me as if someone is turning up a dimmer switch.

His eyes can't help but be drawn to it, just like I hoped they would, but they come back to me too quickly. I focus all of my energy on keeping it stable in the air. I feel so much control over it that I chance releasing my grip. The ball holds steady.

Darius thrusts his arm forward, trying to push the ball back toward me, but I have complete command over the suspended inferno. The lack of response to his power causes him to look up again. The bright light holds his gaze this time. *Perfect,* I think.

I close my eyes, absorbing the energy from the glowing ball back into myself. I don't know how I'm doing it; I'm working solely on instinct. I feel my whole body charge with raw strength. I keep my eyes closed but can feel that while the light hasn't dimmed, the ball has begun to shrink in on itself.

The smile drops from my face a split second before the ball completely disappears, plunging everything into darkness. I open my eyes. Since I never looked up, my pupils are still dilated, and I can see everything in front of me clearly.

I draw my right arm across my body up to my left shoulder. With a quick thrash outward to the right, I release all of the power I had siphoned in the demon's direction.

It sends out a shockwave that bends the trunks of the closest trees until they break. Darius is spun through the air in a tight spiral off to my right. His Victus is flung forcefully high into the air. He flies high out of sight, well above the tree Mickey is safely under.

There is a sickening crunch, coupled with a tortured scream of pain in a treetop that blocked Darius's trajectory. A series of snaps and groans sound as he breaks through the branches falling to the ground.

That's how it feels, you fucker.

I decide not to worry about the big guy for now. Cali's armed with the last fire potion, and she has Milo with her to warn if the Victus starts moving in their direction. I grit my teeth as I reposition my left arm so my hand can be tucked into my pocket again, then walk slowly in the direction Darius was hurled.

I keep my guard up, ready to defend or attack at any movement. I hear panting and whimpering as I get closer to the dense, dark area I last saw the demon.

It's harder to see with the tall trees creating an inky blackness that blocks out the moonlight.

My right hand begins to tingle as I prepare to conjure a ball of fire, ready to let it fly and end this battle once and for all. I walk as quietly as I can through the brush and come upon where I last heard the demon moan in pain.

But he's not there.

• 6 4 •

DARIUS

The burning ball of light disappears. The darkness temporarily blinds Darius; his eyes cannot adjust quickly enough to ward off the witch's next attack.

A percussive blow hits him square in the chest, launching him off of his feet. The demon spins through the air with no way to steer himself nor see where he is going. He comes to an abrupt stop when a tall pine unbroken by the shock wave gets in the way of his arc.

The force of his collision with the trunk causes the top half of the tree to split in half with a booming crack. He shrieks as his already torn body absorbs another blow. For a brief second, Darius slowly bounces up and down on a shaking branch. He hears it begin to creak as it gives way underneath him.

The branch breaks clean off the tree and drops like a rock with Darius on it. It seems like he hits every possible protuberance the pine has to offer as he descends. Every jostle to his body elicits another involuntary moan until, with a dull thud, he lands on the hard ground.

He sits still, breathing hard, every inch of him screaming with pain. As he takes inventory of himself, a light breeze picks up, blowing in his face. His sensitive nose picks up something in the air.

Blood, he thinks. But it's not the chalky, methane and creosote mixture that comes from his own. It's coppery, human.

The girl is coming for him. Darius has to move, or it's all over. He's suffered too many injuries to stay in one place. He needs to find a place where he'll have the upper hand, can take her on by surprise.

As he stands, his right knee buckles, completely unstable. For the first time in over a thousand years, the demon feels real fear. Immediately it morphs into anger at how he's been reduced to such an indignity.

Darius wills his body up and drags himself further back into the trees just as he hears the witch's footfalls come through the brush. He knows that even the slightest glint from a fireball will give away his position, so he waits, letting her get closer.

He limps further away, coming out to a clearing where the closest of the paved roads cuts through the greenery. His unsteady gait scrapes the road as he moves, the noise deafening in the quiet of the night. He stops short, instinctively knowing he just gave his position away.

He shoves his hand into his pocket and pulls out his only remaining defense. Darius turns back toward the direction he came and waits.

• 6 5 •

"ROSLYN"

A grating sound further back in the trees alerts me that the demon is on the move. With an internal roar, I crash through the rest of the trees in pursuit.

He's standing on the pavement, waiting for me. Thick, black blood trickles slowly from the jagged wound where his arm used to be. His pale face is blackened in spots with dirt. His right knee bends at an unnatural angle, and he's barely putting any weight on it.

My white t-shirt is stained red from my blood and black from defending against fireballs. My jacket is torn, barely held together by threads. My glasses are broken. My friend and my boyfriend are unconscious. I am exhausted and want this fight to be over.

I hesitated to kill him last time in the library, and he got away. I won't let that happen again. I don't waste time telling him he's lost, that all of his Victus are gone. I pull my arm back and let a scorching ball of fire pop to life in my hand.

I hurl the ball as hard as I can at him. I focus on it with my telekinesis power to make sure it hits its mark.

With the loudest, angriest yell I've ever heard in my life, Darius raises his remaining hand and swats the ball out of the air down to the ground between us.

It ruptures the pavement, leaving a gaping hole behind. I'm so focused that I don't even feel a one-foot wide section of asphalt graze the side of my thigh with enough force that it slashes open my flesh like wet newspaper.

I let out a yell of my own as I rear back and launch another ball at the demon. He deflects it once again down into the ground. It lands in the same place sending up dirt that showers down on both of us. I grit my teeth and quickly launch a third sphere.

The demon again deflects, but it's shallow. The flames land closer to him, and he's knocked over by the fire shooting outward from its place of impact. The blaze covers his left leg. Without his left arm to smother them, the fire is left to burn. I watch him roll around to try and put it out without success.

"Fuck!" I hear him scream. "Fuck, fuck!"

He drops something from his right hand to use it to extinguish the flames. From his position on the ground, he launches a fireball at me. It lands short, sending up another sprinkling of dirt. It makes me flinch enough that Darius picks up what he dropped.

Even in the dim light and with the distance between us, I can still tell it's a potion bottle filled with a dark liquid. He drinks the entirety of its contents then tosses the bottle to the side. I've seen him do this before and know what is about to happen.

"No!" I scream.

"*Conpedibus!*" he shouts at the same time.

I rush forward with fire in my hand and let the ball fly. I immediately know that it won't make it there in time. Darius disappears with a loud bang right as the ball sails past where he just was. It connects with a small pine that is quickly incinerated.

As the boom fades from my ears, I hear something to my right and behind me. It's Milo barking, which can only mean something is wrong. I take off, half running, half limping, to where I hear my dog.

I see Milo guarding Mickey's still unconscious body while Cali tries to ward off attacks from the large Victus. She's barely hanging on; his size seems to be amplifying the strength of his power. Matt is sitting up against the trunk of the tree next to Mickey. I had told Cali to get and move him like I did with Mickey. Even from here, I can tell he's barely alert, still shaking off the substantial hit from before.

"Hey!" I yell, trying to distract the giant. He doesn't turn away from my friends, but I hear him let out a deep baritone laugh at Cali's feeble efforts at fending him off.

I pick up my pace and try to use my physical momentum to increase my telekinesis effect as I wave my arm through the air to try and knock the Victus away. He stumbles as his head whips to the side but quickly regains his footing.

Only then does he actually turn to face me. He takes a few steps backward, getting closer to Matt and Mickey. I try to keep his attention on me while Cali goes to her girlfriend's side and pulls her closer to Matt further under the tree and its safety.

She swings out to her left, running over the paved road closer to the reservoir to flank the Victus. He sees her, and with a forceful wave of his hand, catapults her away. She's thrown into the air out over the water. She's up too high and falling too fast; it'll be like hitting cement.

I make the decision to slow her down for a soft landing on the water. She lands feet first with a splash but comes up quickly and begins to swim back toward shore.

"Milo!" I call out. "Go get Squirrel!" My dog takes off in a flash, galloping down to the water's edge. He jumps in without hesitation and begins to swim out to Cali.

With no one else left standing but the Victus and myself, I turn my full attention to him. I take three steps toward him, and he backs up one. We square up. I move forward again, and he backs up in turn.

He's too close, I think. *He's too close to Matt and Mickey.*

I have to draw him away from them. Any attack I make could hit them instead. I back up, hoping to lure him away, but he must know what I'm trying to do. The Victus sneers at me and takes another step backward.

I start to panic. I have to get him away from them. I desperately try to come up with something that could neutralize the threat.

The Victus and I hear splashing as Cali and Milo walk from the shallows of the reservoir to the shore at the same time. He's distracted by the sound. I see his eyes dart to the side to take them in. It's a split second, but I think, *This is my chance.*

While his concentration is momentarily not on me, I do the only thing I can think of. I lift him into the air like I did to him and Darius earlier in the night. He yells, surprised to be suddenly lifted even higher in the air than last time.

I can't drop him this time. He's proven he'll just get back up again. I have to end this now. My left arm is still useless at my side, so I have to summon everything that's left in the depths of my strength to hold him in place with my mind.

I pin his arms to his side to stop any countermeasure. He struggles against my hold as he sees my hand turn amber, my firepower beginning to pool there. The Victus thrashes back and forth, trying to fall from my grip. I don't let him. I channel all of my remaining energy, anger, frustration, and extreme fatigue into taking this guy down.

"Darius is gone," I call up to him. "He abandoned you here. Just stop fighting, and I'll let you go."

"I serve him to my last breath! I will never stop!" the Victus yells down to me.

I feel the heat fill my hand as the ball materializes. I remind myself that this is not a man hanging in my grasp. This is someone who willingly chose to side with evil, with a demon that wants to destroy this planet and remake it in his own delusion. On top of that, this creature has been actively trying to kill me for the last two hours.

I narrow my eyes, draw my arm back to throw, and let the ball fly. The Victus stops struggling as he watches the ball come at him. I expect him to try and release his arms to deflect the ball, but what he does, I could have never imagined.

The Victus gets one arm free, catches the fireball, and holds it to his chest. I'm stunned enough that I lose my grip on him. As he plummets to the ground, he winks at me before he pushes the flames into his body right before he hits the ground.

The explosion happens within feet of where Matt and Mickey are. Neither of them can get out of the way, and both absorb the devastating shock wave. I gasp and run as fast as my broken body will take me to them.

Mickey has started to bleed from her nose, and she's slumped over completely limp and unmoving. Blood from a gash on her head begins to pool around her and slowly grow. It's getting too big to mean anything good, and she's barely breathing.

Matt was right below the impact and took the worst of it. His stomach is slashed open from the blast, bleeding heavily. He looks at me with wide, terrified eyes. His breathing is shallow, and blood is trickling out of the corner of his mouth.

"Oh my god. No, no, no, no, no, no," I say, falling to my knees. I press his stomach, trying to keep some of the blood from pouring out. "Just hang on, you're gonna be okay.

"Cali!" I scream over my shoulder. "CALI!"

It seems like she just appears out of thin air at my side. She's stunned into silence. Her hands hover above Mickey as she hesitates, unsure of what to do. She looks at me, trembling with fear.

"What do we do?" I don't answer her. "Roz? What do we do?!"

"Get *The Book*," I tell her. "There has to be something in there."

I look at her, both of us silent. The words hang in the air between us. There *has* to be something there.

• 6 6 •

Cali

"CALI!" Roslyn screams.

The water soaks her clothes, making them stick to every inch of her body. Drops fly from her auburn hair as it whips behind her while she runs full speed toward her girlfriend and two best friends. Even though she saw the Victus blow up, she still can't believe her eyes when she finally reaches Mickey's side.

There is blood everywhere—her head, her nose, her ears. A circle grows beneath her. Matt has blood trickling from his mouth. He's holding his stomach, trying in vain to keep his blood inside the large gash. Roslyn has her right hand on him, desperately hoping to stem the flow. Cali notices for the first time that the witch's arm is hanging limply to the side.

"What do we do?" she asks, panicked. Her friend doesn't answer her, so she tries again. "Roz? What do we do?!"

After what seems like an eternity, a response finally comes. "Get *The Book.* There has to be something in there."

They look at each other silently for a beat before Cali gets up and bolts into the trees where they left all of the bags. The night is at its darkest now, right before the sun begins to show, and the stars have faded away. Cali can barely see where she's going, she just runs to where she remembers.

At full speed, she trips over a fallen branch that was hidden by the darkness. She lands on something soft rather than the cold, hard ground. It's the duffle bag. She throws it to the side and heaves her backpack out from under Roslyn's laundry bag.

Cali darts back to the group as fast as her tired legs will take her. She slides to a stop next to Mickey and throws the bag to the ground. Without wasting time on unpacking it, she rips it open and dumps out the contents. *The Book* lands on the top of the pile. She immediately opens it and starts flipping through the thick pages.

"I don't know what I'm looking for," she cries desperately.

"Try to find a spell or something," Roslyn replies. The fear in her voice is blatantly apparent.

"It's too dark to see anything clearly. And it's all in Latin."

"Okay, okay," Roslyn pants. "Alright, uh, come over here and put your hands on his stomach."

Cali obeys and scuttles over to her best friend. Matt groans in pain as she presses on his wound with both hands to stem the bleeding. Roslyn materializes a ball of fire and lets it float above them, illuminating the scene and the hidden writing. The three of them finally get a good look at the damage to Matt's body.

His stomach hasn't just been cut. There is a gaping slash from one hip diagonally to his ribs. Under his and Cali's hands, it's clear that his organs have been damaged. Some are even poking out.

"Oh my god," he says flatly in shock.

"No, it's gonna be okay," Cali sobs. "We're gonna fix you. You'll be okay, Moose."

"No, it's not," he answers hoarsely. He looks at his best friend, the person he's turned to for everything since they were little kids, then looks to his side at the love of her life lying unconscious next to him. Tears begin to trickle down the sides of his face. He turns his attention to Roslyn and says, "You have to use the spell."

"No," Roslyn answers immediately.

"What spell?" Cali asks.

"The spell that will drain one person to give to another," he says weakly.

"No!" Roslyn yells. "There'll be something in here." She furiously scans *The Book* for an answer. Her blood covered hands leave a trail on every page. When she comes to the end without finding a remedy, she starts over. After the third pass through, she freezes.

"Did you find anything?" Cali asks through her tears. Roslyn sadly shakes her head no.

"Why can't you heal them both?"

"Their injuries are too much. We'd lose them both before I could heal one."

"So, that's it?!"

"The spell," Matt says again, his voice almost a whisper.

"No, no, we don't need to use the spell. We'll find another way to fix you!"

"Cali," Matt says sadly. He shakes his head slightly, making a line of blood drip down his cheek toward his ear. It dilutes as it lines up with the tracks his tears have made. He starts to tremble in pain. "Look at me, I-look at Mickey. You're gonna I-lose us both if she d-doesn't."

Cali's eyes furiously search everywhere around her, as if she's looking for something that will have another plan written on it. Matt squeezes her hand and tugs on it. She looks into his eyes. He opens his mouth to speak again. Blood has stained his teeth red and filled in the small lines between them.

"Just hang on, Moose!" Cali pleads. "Please! We'll find a way to fix you both."

"Roz, baby. Please, b-before it's too late. You have—" he starts.

"No!" Cali cuts him off. "You fight, you hear me? You fucking fight this!"

"You have to save Mickey," he says around heavy breaths. "You love her."

"But, I love you, too," Cali quickly replies as sobs wrack her small body.

"It's okay, C-Cali, it's okay. This is my choice. It doesn't even h-hurt anymore, okay?"

"You can't leave me! You're my family! Please don't leave me, I don't know what to do without you."

"Yes, you do," Matt coos. "I love you, Squirrel. It's okay, you got this. And I… I gotchu."

His skin becomes waxy as his body loses more of what's left of his blood. He weakly pulls one hand up to hold out for Cali to take. Tears are pouring down her face, but she knows what he wants. She grabs his hand around the thumb, then releases and quickly cups the rest of their fingers together—one last dap between friends.

"Ros—" Matt says weakly. "Roslyn."

From her spot on the ground, she shifts her weight over so that she's crouching between them. Cali watches her stroke his cheek with her good hand. Her eyes are shinning, filled to the brim with tears.

"I'm here, baby," she says.

He reaches up to cup her cheek with his blood-covered hand. "You know h-how much you mean to me, how m-much I care for you. Nothing has made me h-happier in my entire life than being lucky enough to love you. T-Take care of my Squirrel for me, okay?"

Roslyn nods and lowers her face to his. She holds his face to her own, kissing him slowly on the lips. When their lips part, she moves her face to the side and whispers something in his ear.

Matt's breathing becomes more labored as he's unable to take in a full breath. Every exhale causes pinkish bubbles to form at the corner of his mouth. Roslyn looks at Mickey and uses her telekinesis to gently lift the brunette in the air. She gracefully places her down as close as she can to him.

Roslyn uses her right arm to lift her dislocated one and place her hand in the center of Matt's chest, then puts her right on Mickey's chest that scarcely rises and falls with her shallow breath. The witch inhales deeply before exhaling shakily.

With a choked voice, she looks at Matt and begins the spell. "*Quid agis tuus erit illorum. Animae vestrae, amissa sua virtute addit.*"

Her hands glow with a soft, white light. It branches out across Matt's body before returning to her hand. As Matt closes his eyes, the light travels up Roslyn's left arm, flows through her chest, and comes down her right to Mickey. Matt's breath is sporadic. He takes two more inhales then his body stills.

"*Damno lucrum est,*" Roslyn finishes the spell.

Matt's body goes dark, no longer illuminated. The light spreads across Mickey's as it had previously to him. It absorbs into her skin and disappears. Roslyn lifts her hand away and sits back heavily onto the ground.

The pool of blood from her head, which had continued to grow even after Roslyn moved her, gets smaller as her body takes it back in. Her eyes shoot open as she takes a deep inhale, gasping for air. She looks around, breathing heavily until her eyes land on Cali, kneeling right next to her.

"Cali? Oh, baby, is it really you?" she asks.

"It's me," Cali says through a sob before kissing her girlfriend desperately. She strokes the brunette hair, stares at the bright blue eyes. Cali places her forehead against Mickey's. When strong arms wrap around her and grip her tightly, she lets out a body-wracking wail.

Confused by her girlfriend's reaction, Mickey asks, "What is it?"

She turns her head to face Roslyn and sees Matt's lifeless body for the first time. "Oh my god. Oh no. Oh, Cali."

Mickey squeezes her tighter and lets the smaller woman cry. She's crying for the loss of her best friend, the relief of her love being back in her arms, and the night finally being over.

When she looks away from Mickey, she sees that Roslyn is sitting quietly next to Matt. Milo is lying down next to her with his head in her lap, whimpering at the emotions he feels around him. Her left arm is still painfully outstretched in the same place on his chest.

Cali reaches out for her friend. She squeezes Roslyn's shoulder. It takes a long moment for Roslyn to respond. When she turns her head to the shorter woman, she looks broken, like a part of her has been lost. Cali offers a sad nod. Silently thanking her for her sacrifice, but still consoling her over their shared loss.

EPILOGUE

Quickly after Mickey came back to us, it was clear that all of us needed healing in one way or another. She was unconscious most of the night and had endured so much before that, so I treated her first. The cuts and bruises around her wrsts disappeared entirely. Only two of the burns on her arm leave a scar just below the crux of her elbow.

When I finished, she hugged me hard. I winced at the pain in my arm but didn't say anything. She kissed me on the forehead before she released me.

I did Cali next. It was quiet between us, odd. I know I had promised to pay her back one day for everything she's done for me, but I never quite imagined the price tag would be so high. Thankfully for all of her being tossed around tonight, she wasn't hurt too badly, mostly some bumps and bruises.

When I released her, Cali moved over to Mickey and sat there, stroking her girlfriend's hair while she took inventory of how they both were feeling. Eventually, Cali stood and asked Mickey if she wanted to help her bring the rest of the bags back from the trees.

I told her to wait and turned to the page to reverse a forced Victus transformation. I told her honestly, "I don't know if this will hurt at all, but I think we need to do it so you can go back to normal."

The couple shared a look before the two of them agreed with me. Cali positioned herself to cradle Mickey from behind while I performed the spell. I put my hand on her forehead like I would make an Extensios and chanted the words three times.

"*Et nunc absolvo vos vires et male dicentibus vobis.*" I release you from the powers that curse you.

She whimpered in discomfort as the inky black curse from Darius was purged from her body. It left her and pooled in my hand. I tossed it up into the fiery orb, still hovering above us, bathing us in light and warmth. The black substance popped and hissed as it was destroyed.

When it was over, Mickey took a few relaxed deep breaths. After a moment, she and Cali got up and headed toward where our bags were stashed in the forest. The sudden quiet gave me a moment alone with Matt's body. Milo stayed nearby, but even he knew to give me some physical space.

I closed my eyes and used my projection power to heal myself finally. I had ignored my injuries until I knew for sure I wouldn't lose anyone else.

I sighed as my shoulder popped back into its socket. The cuts from the branches easily closed up; I doubt many will leave scars, maybe just the largest one or two. The gash on my leg took the longest to restore but had long since clotted and closed relatively easily.

Now pieced back together, I sit quietly next to what's left of the one I love. I take one of his hands in both of mine. It's still warm as I bring it to my lips and kiss the knuckles. I place his hand on his own chest and position the other on top of it. I let him go but can't make myself move from my spot yet. Every breath feels like glass shards are piercing my heart. I ache for him, though I am too hollow right now to even cry for the man I lost.

I know something has changed within me. With the last words I said to him, I felt something inside of me open. Something that I had held closed so tight for so long has finally opened.

I can hear Cali and Mickey; I can *feel* them near me before I even see them make their way back with our belongings. My senses are heightened.

Where do we go from here? I hear Cali's voice ask. It echos in my brain, as if she yelled it to me in a tunnel, but she hasn't said anything out loud. I'm reading her mind.

I realize how easily I said the spell in Latin, how quickly I healed our wounds. For the first time in my entire life, I'm accessing all of my powers without restraint.

It's an odd feeling to give myself permission to finally be my true self. It feels strange coupled with my current heartbreak. I've just lost a huge part of my life, a person I love more than anyone else. But I've never felt power this unimpeded before.

I don't have the capacity or the energy to process all of the mixed emotions I'm feeling and decide they need to just wait for now.

Before Mickey and Cali reach me, I sift through the dumped things from the backpack until I find Cali's blanket. I unfold it and gently drape it over Matt's body, covering him completely.

I move to the side and conjure a large fire for more light and warmth. The warm sun is still an hour away from rising, and now that I'm not fighting for my life, the chill of the night begins to seep in. Milo lays down next to me and, as always, is a comforting presence.

When the couple gets back, Cali begins to strip her wet clothes, searching for clean, dry ones. She opens the duffle and pulls out the first things of hers she sees on top.

After she dresses, she arranges the bags around the fire so that we each have something soft to lean against. She curls up next to Mickey. The two of them sit silently, relaxing into each other, taking solace in the ability to touch one another again.

I can't stop myself from glancing every few moments toward Matt, desperately hoping he'll pull the blanket off and come back to me. But not even I am powerful enough to bring someone back after they've died. The loss hits me all over again, and I quickly take off my broken glasses to pinch the bridge of my nose. I roughly wipe away the tears that gather in my eyes.

The minutes tick slowly by as the three of us sit in silence. Every so often, a breeze will pick up, but other than that, it's quiet in the park. I don't know how long it's been since anyone's spoken, but Cali is the first to break the stillness.

"Where do we go from here?" she asks. It's the thought that's been on her mind since she went to get the bags with Mickey, but I don't tell her just yet that I know that.

"Darius is hurt badly, worse than before," I say, looking down at my hands covered in Matt's dried blood. "I don't know where he went this time, but I know where I have to go."

"Where?" Mickey asks.

"I'm done hiding. Darius is not going to scare me into denying who I am. Not anymore. I'm going to the other magical creatures around the earth, my extended family members, and ask them to join my fight.

"Then," I swallow hard and say, "I'm going home to get my mom, my dad, my brother, and my grandfather and finish this thing once and for all."

Out of the corner of my eye, I see Mickey and Cali exchange a quick glance with a short nod to each other. "You know we're with you, we'll follow your lead. And we're ready when you are."

I nod in thanks but stay quiet. Last time my hesitation for bringing anyone with me was based on the chance they would be hurt. But once reassured they were on board, we left this very park and headed straight to our next destination in search of *The Book*.

Now I have *The Book*. But I've lost something just as important. What's holding me in place, my hesitation this time, is from a completely different force.

I hug my knees to my chest, dislodging Milo from my side. He repositions himself to sit up facing me. He inches closer until he's able to put his chin on the top of my left knee. I place my hand on his head, needing the contact. Milo whines softly, sensing my pain, trying to do what he can to ease it.

My eyes sting as I feel the full weight of the night's outcome again and realize that Matt isn't coming with me this time.

"I can't leave yet," I say thickly as I stare into the fire. "I can't leave him yet."

My friends get up and come to comfort me. Milo doesn't move an inch as they sandwich me tightly between them. My best friend puts her head down on my right shoulder and sighs heavily.

"I'm sorry, Cali," I say, my voice quivering with the words. "I'm so, so sorry."

"I know, honey," she says, reaching for my hand. She holds it tightly between both of hers. "I am too."

The sky continues to lighten, signaling that we'll have to leave soon. The three of us go on sitting huddled together until Cali says, "Can I ask you something?"

"Sure," I murmur.

"Will you tell me what you whispered to him before he died?"

"Cali," Mickey objects softly. "That's private."

"No, it's okay," I say, keeping my gaze on the flames. I take a deep breath before I continue, "I told him I love him. That I will never go another day in my life without loving him or thinking about him. I told him that Darius won't get away from me again, that I would make his life mean something.

"And then I told him my name."

She lifts her head from my shoulder and looks at me expectantly. It's ultimately the last secret I have left to tell her, the biggest one. When I tell her, there will be no turning back, no more hiding.

When I tell her my real name, for the first time in my fight with Darius, *he* will be the one running scared.

I'm finally ready to be who I was born to be, to fully take on the responsibility my ancestors have placed on my shoulders. I will not lose another thing to this demon.

I will own my name and my power and my place at the head of this war.

I turn my head to look her in the eyes. I can see all the puzzle pieces finally falling into place in her brain. It doesn't take magical abilities to figure out she already knows what I'm about to tell her, but as much for me as for her, I say it anyway.

"My name is Hope."

Acknowledgements

Thank you to the many people who provided love and support to this book. It seems so much sweeter the second time around.

Extra special thanks to:

Mom, while this book is dedicated to you, that doesn't even begin to scratch the surface of what it would take to repay all you have done for me. Any achievement of mine is yours. I would be less than half of who I am if I didn't have you.

My sisters—Meghan, Kaitlin, Jeanette, Lisa, Pamela—I am surrounded by strong women who lift me, who challenge me, who don't let me settle. Every day I reap the benefit of that.

To my nieces and nephews, all eight of you, I love being your aunt. I am proud and honored to be part of your lives. I also love having an excuse to play hide and seek as an adult.

Many thanks, especially to A, B, B, B, C, C, E, G, K, L, L, M, M, P, T. Every single one of you knows exactly why you are included and what you have done for me.

Thank you to my extended network of family, friends, and colleagues for your support and encouragement. However small or large your impact, I carry a piece of each of you with me always.

To Corie and Jax, your attitude and antics, past and present, have created a perfect model for all that is Milo.

Thank you to every single person who has deemed my books worthy of your time. My appreciation for you goes deeper than you could believe.

Last but never least, thank you to Joey. I could talk for hours about how much I love you, how much I love us and the life we're building together. You are undeniably the greatest thing that has ever happened to me. I hope I live one minute less than you, so I never have to go another without you.

ABOUT THE AUTHOR

Kerri McLoone is a lot of things: a musician, an artist, a student, a friend, a therapist, a lover, a fighter, a fur mom, and a writer, to name a few.

Kerri is described as someone who's had a long string of bad luck and experienced bizarre things that could only happen to her. But she is also someone who has learned how to keep herself going and take things in stride day by day.

She won the 2020 IndieReader Discovery Award for the Best New Adult category for her debut novel *My Name Is Not Alexa Pearce*, the first book in The Search For Hope Trilogy.

My Name Is Not Roslyn James is Kerri McLoone's second book.

How To Contact Kerri McLoone
Email:
KerriMcLooneBooks@gmail.com

Follow Kerri McLoone on social media:
facebook.com/KerriMcLooneBooks
instagram.com/_kmbooks_
twitter.com/_kmbooks_

www.ingramcontent.com/pod-product-compliance
Lightning Source LLC
Chambersburg PA
CBHW020927020726
47495CB00002B/378